ENCHANTED THRONE

BOOK 3

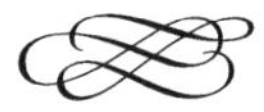

TRICIA WENTWORTH

Enchanted Throne
By Tricia Wentworth

This book is a work of fiction. The names, characters, places, and incidents are products of the writer's imagination or used fictitiously. Any resemblances to persons, living or dead, are entirely coincidental.

Published by Tricia Wentworth

Editing by The Book was Better Editing Services

Cover by Parker Book Design and Vila Design

Content Warning for violence, abuse, language, and mention of rape.

This one is for Schmidty.

When I am tasked with writing healthy friendships into stories, all I think of is you.

You are loyalty and kindness personified.
(Even if you cheer for those dang Buckeyes!)

Wylan

Brakken
Corsha

Agria
Dra Skor

CHAPTER 1

My hand reached across the sheets in search of him. A groggy fog enveloped me as warmly as the blankets did. It felt like I had only slept a few hours. The heavy curtains were pulled so the room was dark. I instinctively knew it must be morning. I inhaled deeply and smiled, though I was desperately tired. I thought of the previous hours, of his hands slowly trailing along my skin. Like a whispered promise, his touch had ignited a burn in both of us which was the sole reason we had been up until almost dawn. It had been *everything* and at the same time, never enough.

Feeling the buzz which was familiar to me by now, the buzz of his magic, I placed my hand on Krew's bare chest assuming he was having another dream which was causing his magic to flare.

As soon as I touched his skin, he jolted awake with a start.

I picked my head off the pillow as far as I possibly could this tired, mere inches.

A lazy smile graced his lips as his eyes found mine, but then it fell, his eyebrows reaching for one another immediately.

I gave my head a shake, remembering the rest of the night's

events. We had gotten married. And bonded. Not just bonded, we were evidently soul bonded. So though it was habit by this point, I wasn't even sure I could calm his magic anymore.

His magic which he had given me all but a drop of.

"Jorah."

The worry in his tone had me reaching for the covers and turning to sit up. "Hmm?"

Before I could form a full thought more, I was in his arms and we were moving.

"More sleep," I managed to mumble. I didn't know what he had planned, but I needed sleep first.

He sat us on the ledge of the tub and immediately twisted the knobs to turn on the water, placing my feet on the ground. We were taking a bath? I wasn't entirely opposed to that idea, I just wished I had more sleep first.

"Jorah, love," he said gently. Far too gently.

"What?" My eyes found his steel blue ones.

"Look at your skin."

I looked down at my hand. My right hand still held the cut from our bonding, though it was already almost gone this morning. Next to the pink cut, pale strands of magic were swirling in my palm and racing along my wrist. White strands? Was my magic white?

It hadn't been his magic that had woken me, it'd been *my own.*

I gasped and stood, taking a step back.

Krew grabbed the hand I was not looking at. "Jorah, listen to me. If it woke you up like that, you likely need to use your magic. Release just a little. It needs to be used and then we can go right back to bed."

"No. It was supposed to take days to settle." I shook my head, my eyes on him. "*Days.* Not hours. I'm not ready."

He cocked his head. "Yes, you are. It's going to be okay."

"I—" my eyes went back to him where he sat on the edge of the massive tub. "You're naked."

His eyebrows went up. "So are you. I believe we got that way together, love."

I looked down at myself realizing he was right and saw that my entire body now seemed to be lit up with my magic slithering and weaving along my veins. It almost felt like a faint pulse, I assumed matching with the beat of my own heart. All things considered, after the previous night, being naked and standing before Krew should be minor. I just hadn't expected to start day one of our marriage in quite this fashion. Powerfully naked.

"Will the magic to the water, Jorah. Envision turning it to steam and then let a little of it go to do exactly that."

My eyes trailed from his eyes down his body. That collarbone was still as distracting as ever, and as my eyes wandered lower, I knew the rest of him did not disappoint. This artwork before me of muscles and moodiness was now my husband. Prince Darkness, my soulmate. And I'd much rather go back to bed for multiple different reasons than figure out this business of my magic.

"Jorah."

My eyes snapped back up to his. "I'm sorry. I'm still not over the fact that you're naked."

A smile played with the corner of his mouth. "I gathered that. And you can ogle my naked body all you wish later, my wife. Right now, I just need you to release a little of that magic, okay?"

My eyes bounced between the rapidly filling tub and him. "Can you move, please? I can't think right with you just casually sitting there bossing me around while naked for my first time using my magic." My chest began heaving. The buzz was getting louder in my ears. Stronger. I bit out, "Not at all how I imagined this going."

He must have sensed I was about to lose it. He grabbed two towels from the towel rack and crossed the room. He wrapped one dangerously low on his hips and offered the other to me. Which I gladly took, tucking it around me.

I felt my hair move before his hand settled at the back of my neck, gently massaging with his fingers.

"Watch me." He closed his eyes while I turned to look at him, one of his hands still massaging the back of my neck, the other free. "I am going to think of wanting to use my magic to turn the water to steam." His blue magic flared in his veins, while still touching me, and he turned his palm outward. "Then I think of a small amount of magic flowing toward the water and release it." A strand of magic shot out of his hand and went toward the water, a small amount turning to steam as soon as the magic touched the water. He'd barely finished telling me what he was doing before his magic had already done it.

He turned to me. "Your turn."

I shook my head, feeling my panic growing. I was . . . not ready for this. I had figured the first time I'd need to use my magic was days from now. I would have more time to prepare. More time to figure out . . . *how.* I was nervous. No. It was more than nerves. When I had thought I was only getting a drop of magic, I had been nervous. Now I knew I held all but a drop of Krew's powers, I was terrified. Utterly terrified. And also hot. The magic was buzzing and almost burning beneath my skin.

"Jorah."

A tear slipped down my cheek. I managed to whisper, "I'm not ready. I don't know how."

He reached across to wipe it away. "I know. And this is my fault. Just try. Please. I promise you'll feel better once you try. I'm right here with you."

He moved his hand down to mine, turning it palm up and holding it between us. "Close your eyes."

I did.

"Think of turning the water in the tub to steam. Picture it in your mind. Like I just did. Then envision letting loose just a strand of magic toward the water, okay?"

I took a deep breath, feeling my palm get hotter and hotter by the second.

"Good. Now release it," Krew encouraged.

My breath caught. I didn't know how? Did I just will it?

"Jorah." Krew sounded more frantic. "Picture it in your head. Just like you've seen mine do dozens of times. Let it go. A small amount. Let it turn the water to steam."

Okay, magic. Just a little.

I gasped and opened my eyes as I felt something like a phantom touch skirt across my palm and down my pointer finger. Silver magic raced across the bathroom, landing in the water.

There was a loud hiss as the water began turning to steam. I was about to take a step forward to see how much water I had turned to steam when there was a cracking noise.

Not only was the tub completely dry, but it had split. Into two pieces.

Krew moved forward to quickly turn off the water still coming out of the faucet before it made a mess over everything.

I looked at my hand, which was now back to normal. I felt a bit better. Like I did after stretching my back after a long day at the bakery. Not as . . . tense. Yet I had apparently used far too much magic. I had broken a tub in half?

"I'm sorry," I heaved. "I tried to use only a little."

Krew came back and took me by the shoulders. "Don't be sorry. It wasn't your fault. Breathe, please. If you start to panic, so does your magic."

"No. So does *your* magic. All but the drop of it you gave to me," I argued.

He tipped his head toward his shoulder. "Well, yes. That. We can talk about that in a bit. Let's get you outside to try to use your magic one more time. Then we can talk about it all you want, all right?"

He was gone into the closet before I could say more.

We should have talked more about this last night, but it had been late. And the wolves had shown up. And Keir had stormed in. And then as soon as we'd made it back up to Krew's wing . . . well then *want* had superseded all needs.

Breathe, love.

I looked toward the closet confused. I was fairly certain he hadn't said that out loud. I hadn't heard it with my ears, yet I had somehow still heard it.

"Did you ju—" I rubbed a hand at my forehead. Was I dreaming?

He stuck his head back around the corner of the closet. Now wearing pants. Unfortunately.

"Sorry, likely should have waited for that too. Yes, I just spoke to you. Well, without actually speaking."

I was certain my jaw was on the ground somewhere. "How?"

None of this was making any sense. None at all. I was waking up the most powerful Enchanted in all of Wylan and all I had wanted was to go to bed married to Krew, with a mere drop of his magic to protect us both.

Tears of frustration burned my eyes. And then that dull buzzing was back.

Krew was there in front of me, again wrapping a hand around the back of my neck. "I know it's overwhelming. I get it. One step at a time, love. Take some deep breaths and let's get you outside. As soon as you've used a little more magic, you'll feel more relaxed."

I looked at my palm to see it swirling with magic again.

"Match your breathing to mine." He rested his forehead to mine and began taking deep breaths.

Not wanting to break anything else, I did as he requested,

though I kept my eyes on my palms. After three or four deep breaths, my magic was calm again.

Krew brushed a kiss to my forehead. "I love you. Let's get you dressed and get you outside."

"Won't someone find out?" I asked. "If I use magic in the forest? Isn't it morning?"

Krew gave his head a shake. "If my father is even awake yet, he is in his monthly meeting with parliament. If ever there was a day for him to be distracted, it is this one. But we will avoid the open meadow just to be sure."

I wasn't okay. None of this was okay, but I managed to slip my legs into the leggings he tossed at me. It was after I had my head through the hole of the shirt, I realized it was one of his and not mine.

I raised my eyebrows at him while he tossed me my coat.

"Forgive me. I do not know the inner workings of women's wear. I stood there like a fool for close to a minute and then decided that one of mine was just easier."

He'd also forgotten all undergarments, but now was not the time to point that out. Judging by his pace, we needed to hurry up and get outside before my magic flared again.

He handed me my snow boots and helped me slip into them. "Let's grab Owen, and then we'll be off."

He strode for the door, opening it.

Owen came in with a smirk on his face.

As soon as the door shut behind him, Owen put up a sound barrier. "Not expecting to see either of you for a while this morning, Your Graces."

Without hesitation, I blurted out, "I broke the tub."

Owen's eyes flew to Krew's. "I take it her magic is settling in already?"

Krew gave him a nod. "It appears so. She needs to use more of it. Maybe just once or twice more and then she will be able to relax. I woke to her skin crawling with it."

"Jorah," Owen said gently, turning to me. "It's going to be okay. We will help you. Just like we told you weeks ago, it usually takes about a week to get used to, and then it gets better."

"Yes, well I thought I was dealing with *a* drop of magic, not an abundance of it, so I wasn't really all that worried at the time."

Owen's attention switched to Krew's. "Speaking of, you should've told her, you ass. So she could've been better prepared."

"I realize this now," Krew said, hands in the air. "You both can have it out with me later. We need to get her outside. Now."

"Secret passageway?" Owen asked, turning for the next room over.

Krew shook his head. "No. I'm not sure we have the time for that. Her magic came on fast last time and it's barely contained as is."

"*Your* magic," I corrected.

Owen's forehead creased as they both ignored me. "How do you feel? Do you have enough magic to carry her down there?"

Krew's eyes were on Owen's as he said. "I feel weakened, as if I had burnout last night, or gave a few drops of it away, but not like it's all gone. Were it not for the tub and waking up to Jorah glowing with magic, I'd think it didn't work at all. Or that I did give her only a drop."

"Wait," I interrupted, everything about this conversation finally sliding into place. "Do you mean to tell me we are going over the balcony?"

"I—" Krew began before his eyes landed on mine. "Yes."

"No. Absolutely not. I will not begin my first day with magic in such a reckless manner."

Krew smirked. "Honorable as that may be, and as much as I would like to keep arguing with you both, neither of you seem to be understanding that time is of the essence."

"Fine. But I'll take her just in case," Owen offered.

Krew dipped his chin. "That's probably best."

"And I'll do my best to catch you if you fall, Your Princeness." Owen gave the barest of shrugs.

He was joking right? I wasn't entirely sure, and this was not the time for such jokes.

They headed toward the balcony doors, and I vaguely noticed it had snowed sometime between the ceremony last night and this morning.

"Jorah, love," Krew said gently. "Please."

Seeing how concerned he looked killed my argument on my tongue. I looked to my palm and saw traces of magic and that faint buzzing starting back up.

As Owen lifted me into his arms I said to both of them, "We will not be making a habit out of this."

"Yes, Your Highness," Owen agreed.

And then he jumped.

CHAPTER 2

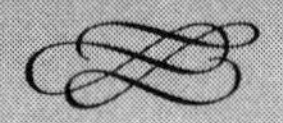

It took Owen and I longer to get to the ground. While Krew used his magic to form, as he'd explained before, something like a slide, Owen's green magic created what looked like stairs down. After the first lunge down, I determined it was just better to close my eyes and hold on to Owen rather than watch our descent.

As soon as Owen gently placed my boots on the ground, I felt better. I looked straight up at the balcony and fought off a shiver. "Never again."

Krew had my hand, pulling me toward the forest.

Owen formed a moving sound barrier around us as we headed farther in.

"So she broke the tub. With her magic?"

I swallowed hard, still not sure what to do with what had happened. It hadn't been a piece of paper I'd merely torn. It'd been a porcelain bathtub. "I really loved that tub."

"I'll get you another one. Within the next few days. I just don't want my father finding out," Krew offered.

Owen let out a curse and groaned. "That means I have to help you move the pieces, doesn't it?"

"Possibly," Krew said noncommittally. "We could also stage that I was upset and broke it. If we had a good enough reason for me to have been that angry. We can also lift it with our magic and not our muscles, you know. Either way, we can conspire what to do about the tub later. Right now, we have more pressing matters."

I sighed and looked at my palm to see the veins faintly glowing. I felt a dull buzz, but not to the throbbing extent I'd felt earlier—back when it had felt so strong, I felt it matched with every beat of my heart. "You mean like the matter of your magic being trapped in a vessel that is wholly unprepared to deal with it?"

Owen snorted. "Yes. That."

Krew didn't stop walking but pinned me with a stare. "Stop calling it that. It is not *my* magic any longer, Jorah. What is done is done. It's yours now."

"Well, what is done, should not have been done!" I argued, temper rising. "I was never meant to have this much magic, Krew. *You* were born for this. I was not. Not only am I unworthy, I am not . . . *ready*."

He stopped to look me in the eyes. "*No,* on the contrary I have never met a person more worthy of her power. But I promise you, this gets easier. It takes a week or so to get used to the feel of it." He gestured with his free hand back toward the castle. "Like back there. You probably visualized a little magic. And I should have explained this to you then, but we didn't have time. For you, a little is probably a teaspoon full or you pictured a quick shot of magic like you have seen before. Instead of picturing that, you need to visualize a strand of magic that is barely visible. Like a strand of hair. Little is relative. So when you are visualizing how to use your magic, you must be specific in what you picture and also the amount. You will learn over time how to do that, and what seems hard today will be second nature in a week or two."

All of that sounded exhausting. I just wanted sleep. I wanted to sleep for a week straight. After a long talk with Krew about what object hit him in the head hard enough to convince him to willingly hand me all but a drop of his magic.

I love you.

I squinted at him. "Stop talking to me in my head until I know how to respond back!"

He put his hands in the air in surrender. "Sorry."

"And we can communicate telepathically already?" Owen rocked back on his heels from where he had stopped too. "Quite the morning."

"Only half of us." I stomped forward. "All I wanted was a post-coital deep sleep of no fewer than eight hours. Instead, here we are. Traipsing in the forest for me to fail at using magic again."

"You didn't fail last time." Krew shot me a grin. "And the other half of that can still be arranged."

Owen tried and failed to cover his laugh with a cough.

I noticed we were quickly making our way to The Dead Lake. "I believe that is how we got ourselves into this mess. A lack of talking about important matters, like I don't know, the fact that we are apparently soul bonded and you can *hear my thoughts,* because we both assumed we had a few days before your magic would settle in me."

"He didn't know either, Jorah," Owen provided softly.

I snapped my head in his direction, expecting more jest and not for him to sound so serious.

"There hasn't been a royal soul bound pairing in at least three generations," Krew provided. "Granted, being a Valanova is powerful, but being soul bound is more so. That could've affected how fast the magic settled. I honestly have no idea."

"Or it could've been the amount of magic he gave you." Owen provided the thought we were all thinking. "Either way, we are working in uncharted territory here." He nudged my shoulder. "If you'd like to be pissed at Krew for not telling you he was giving you all but a drop of his magic or be mad at the amount of magic you now find you have, go right on ahead. But don't question the soul bonding. It's a testament to your relationship and connection. A miracle I was honored to have been there to witness."

I squinted at him. "Fine, but why do you have to sound so logical about it?"

Their laughter settled my nerves, my magic pulling back to a dull buzzing.

Once at The Dead Lake, my eyes automatically trailed to the areas I had healed while Owen expanded and thickened his sound barrier, just in case anyone should stumble upon us.

"That tree," Krew provided as we walked around the lake. "The tallest one there. The one that is half dead if not entirely dead already." I looked up at the tree in question as he kept speaking. "We need to remove those branches before they fall and damage the surrounding younger trees." Krew spun toward me. "So use your magic and do exactly that, Jorah."

I shook my head. "No. Not the forest. I don't want to hurt the forest too."

He took my hand and pulled it into his chest. "You won't, love. If anything, you are helping. We need to take care of this tree so that it doesn't hurt the others."

The buzzing increased. Even just thinking about using it again was rousing my magic. "You want me to just chop off branches with my magic?"

Krew nodded. "Yes. Exactly. Picture it however you'd like. A saw. A snap. Whichever. And then imagine the branch falling slowly, and your magic cushioning the branch's landing so that it won't hurt anything on the way down."

"That—" I shook my head. "My magic can chop down a branch and land it softly? That is too much. Can't I just send a breeze into the trees or something?"

"Breezes are harder to master," Owen provided. "Especially when to stop them, and it's hard to tell how aggressive of a wind you are making. Usually we start with object manipulation."

Like turning water to steam. Goodness. Did that mean I could also freeze things? I had this power, this power I felt burning in my veins, yet I had very little idea of the extent of what I could do with it. It felt like this power was a weight on me, so heavy I didn't know if there was any room in this body for me too.

"We will start with branches, love. One thing at a time."

I glared at Krew. "Are you hearing my thoughts again?"

"Only when your emotions are heightened. Or you are panicking."

I sighed. "So that's a yes."

Krew gave me a pitied look. "Listen. You need to use a small amount of magic maybe twice more and then you will feel better for likely the rest of the day. What you used earlier was not enough to numb the magic."

I shook my head, having no idea how we got to this point. "So we are moving branches."

He gave me a nod. "So we are moving branches. Maybe only two."

I tipped my head back to look at the sun through the branches. "At least I am not naked this time."

Owen choked on a laugh. "I see I was missing some information."

I took a step forward before turning back toward Krew, the magic now getting brighter and crawling up my wrists as if it knew and was ready.

"What?" he asked.

"This might be a silly question, but do you talk to your magic? Or how do you tell it what to do?" My cheeks burned with embarrassment. Talking with magic? How naïve was I?

Owen was the one to shake his head. "Not a silly question at all.

It's all about what you envision in your thoughts, in what you will the magic to do, and being specific in what you want the magic to do once released. So if it helps to think of it as talking to your magic, go right on ahead. Just make sure you envision the magic doing exactly as you want."

I took a deep breath. "Okay."

"Do you want me to help you like last time?" Krew asked gently.

I took in another inhale as I felt the magic's buzzing increase in intensity. It was hot enough now I felt no need for the coat I was wearing. My back muscles tightened as the feeling spread throughout me. "No. Let me try on my own this time."

"Okay."

I took three steps forward, remembering to breathe with every step. Taking one last deep inhale, I stopped and closed my eyes. I imagined two strands of magic the size of a hair. I imagined them cutting through the branch which was dead and softly carrying it to the ground without hurting any of the trees in the area in the process. I imagined it landing as light as a feather. And I imagined it not hurting the tree at all. The branch needed to be gone, but not the whole tree. The tree was going to be okay. It'd once been a huge, healthy green tree, and it could be that way again.

Don't hurt the tree. That was my last thought before I thought of the phantom touch I had felt earlier and visualized the magic leaving my body to do just that.

I again gasped as the magic left me, opening my eyes. Silver magic was racing along the ground toward the tree. It wound up the bark, circling around as it made its way to the dead branch. Just like I had pictured, the branch was cut off and then turned sideways as my magic wrapped itself around the branch and carried it softly to the ground. The branch landed in eerie silence, not so much as a rustle of snow beneath it.

"Well done," Krew complimented.

But my magic was not done. The same strands headed back for the tree, circling and circling. Round and round the stump it went.

I looked to Krew confused. What was it doing now? I thought I had specifically envisioned the magic not harming the tree. My heart skipped in horror as I realized it might cut down the entire thing and carry it to the ground also.

It continued circling the bark, and then all at once, it burst outward, multiple strands traveling along every branch and hitting every inch of the tree. It was as if the tree itself was now lightning.

And then with a final burst, the magic was gone, leaving the tree standing.

I gasped and took a step back. The tree was . . . gods the tree was *green.* And—and there were leaves. With everything white surrounding it, the tree was the only speck of green in the entire dead forest.

"Whoa," Owen commented.

I brought a hand to my mouth. I had done this? I had healed this tree?

I shook my head, tears gathering in my eyes. "I'm sorry. I went too far again."

I looked back to see Krew staring at me in awe. "You fixed the damn tree."

I was still shaking my head, though I added a shrug. "I don't know what I just did. I just didn't want the magic to hurt the tree. I wanted the tree to be able to be healed someday. I—" I took in a deep pull of air as I felt Krew's hand along my back. "I didn't know magic could heal the trees?"

"It can't. Not ours anyway," Owen offered.

"But mine can?" How was it possible someone who was just coming into their power could do something neither of them could?

Owen strode for the tree, reaching up and running his fingers along a healthy green leaf. "Before you became Enchanted, your will, your blood and tears, were healing the forest. Your magic must have taken on those same properties when you willed the tree to stay alive. Your Iron Will protects you from other's magic, but it must amplify your own."

My eyes went wide. "So I can heal the trees?"

Krew's eyes met mine. "It appears so. I don't know, love. I've never seen anything like this. It must be your Iron Will. Or maybe just your will to save the forest. I don't know."

"Beginner's luck?" I whispered as my eyes traveled up the tree, still in shock I had done this.

"There's only one way to test that theory," Owen grinned. "Do it again."

Krew shook his head. "We need to keep this a secret from my father for as long as possible."

Owen popped his shoulders up into a shrug. "Fine. Tell him you two had an argument in the forest and she cried by these two trees." He patted the bark of the dead tree next to the one I had just healed. "Do this one too. Then we will call it a day."

I looked at my palms, seeing and feeling no magic for the first time since it'd woken me this morning.

"Jorah."

My eyes went to Owen's.

"Do you remember what the first few days of training with me felt like?"

I smirked. "Yes. They were pure hell."

He rolled his eyes. "Well, this is a lot like that. Think of your magic as a muscle. You will be sore and a bit unsteady at times here at first. But as you gain your strength, it will get easier. We will teach you the right way. How to contain it, will it away, and how to use it frequently so that it truly becomes an extension of you. *You* run your magic, your magic does not run you."

I took a deep breath. It wasn't like I had any other options, was it?

Owen patted the tree next to him. "Come on. This one next."

"Can you at least move first?" I asked. "Please?"

He shook his head. "Nope. One of the first and most important lessons you will need to learn about magic is to trust your magic, to trust yourself. So I trust you. Send the magic into the tree. Not me."

I swallowed. "Can't that be tomorrow's lesson? I would really prefer it if you didn't sprout leaves."

Krew came to my defense. "Owen, she's barely slept."

"She can sleep after this," Owen promised. "Come on, Jorah. You can do this. One more tree. And then a nap."

I wanted to hate Owen for this. I wanted to scream that I had never wanted this power to begin with. But looking into Owen's green eyes, all I saw was how much he truly believed in me. There was no doubt in Owen's eyes. He knew I could do it. Even if I did not.

I took a deep breath and moved forward from Krew. The sooner we got this over with, the sooner I could go back to sleep.

I closed my eyes, envisioning what the strands of my magic had just done with the other tree. They had healed it. Healing the tree and not harming the forest at all in the process. I felt the buzzing of my magic pull to the surface, the heat of it along my skin. Just to see if it could, I pictured the magic leaving out of my pinky finger this time instead.

I opened my eyes just before willing the magic to leave my body to see the magic leave my pinky finger and head straight for the tree.

Both strands avoided Owen, winding around the bark just as it had on the other tree. Around and around it went, then burst into more strands which traveled along the branches, the thick ones first, then the smaller ones, and in a final burst, the magic was gone, leaving another green tree in its wake.

Owen looked above him and grinned. "Remarkable, Jorah. Remarkable."

"Are you sure you guys cannot do it also?"

Krew shook his head. "No. We can't."

A shot of green magic hit the next tree over, doing the same thing mine had, and I held my breath for a moment. What if it was the pattern of magic or something that they'd needed to see? But as Owen's magic burst at the end of its travel across the branches, nothing happened. The dead tree remained.

I rubbed my forehead. "This makes no sense." I also felt exhausted. All tension had left my body, and I felt as if I were a standing noodle. I was tired and confused, but finally, finally relaxed.

"We will figure it out later," Krew offered as he put a hand at the small of my back. "Let's get you back to our wing."

"Wait." I turned and squeezed Krew's arm. "My magic is obviously silver, but what is its shape?"

Owen put up a hand. "Now that is tomorrow's lesson. Releasing magic slowly is very difficult and hard to control."

I yawned. "Okay. Tomorrow then."

"I owe you some sleep and what I am sure will be a very lengthy discussion," Krew said playfully as we headed back toward the castle.

Those words had me wanting to voice a thought I just couldn't let go of. "Do you regret it? Forcing me into this power?"

Krew stilled and turned toward me. "Do I regret not telling you what I was considering? Yes. Do I regret how overwhelmed you feel right now? Absolutely, yes. Because you still see this magic as a burden when it was meant as a gift." He pointed with his free hand back toward the two green trees. "I regret how it went down, but no, I do not regret giving you this power. Look what you are able to do, love. Just look."

I didn't regret marrying Krew, or the fact that we were soul bonded, but I wasn't quite sure what this was yet. It didn't feel like a gift, but maybe it wasn't entirely a burden either. The thought of trying my magic on the lake was exciting, but I also dreaded it. Dreaded having to use my magic again soon. Dreaded all the unknowns.

"Will it take a few days for your magic to lessen?" I asked him softly. "Will you miss it?"

He shook his head. "No, I won't miss it. And I have no idea how long it will take." He held up his palm, his blue magic already running along the veins in his hand. "I want to practice with Keir tonight. I feel like I haven't lost much, just a few drops. What will likely take a few weeks to recoup. Not months like I was expecting." His eyes locked onto mine etched in concern, but he also looked . . . *happy*. "Everything is the same. The same and yet entirely different."

CHAPTER 3

Despite feeling an exhaustion that was bone deep, I knew I wouldn't be sleeping until Krew and I discussed this issue of our soul bonding. He could talk to me in my head. And as thrilling as that was, to be close to someone in a manner such as that, it was also intimidating as hell. What if I was mad at him? What if I accidentally checked out another man?

What did this all mean?

"Sleep or talk?" Krew asked me as we were finally alone again in his room.

I slumped down onto the couch. "Don't you have any princely duties to do today?"

He shook his head. "I am technically off the hook for the next few days while Father meets with parliament. I suppose I might need to make an appearance tomorrow sometime during the joint session and also at the wall to make it seem as if I am disloyal hunting. And I have a meeting with The Six later in the week. Otherwise, I am all yours, love."

My cheeks burned with heat knowing he meant that in more than one way.

He knelt at the floor in front of me, handing me a steaming cup of tea. "I cannot begin to understand how overwhelmed you must feel right now. And I know I am to blame for that, Jorah. I made a selfish decision to protect you with my magic. But it is also one I will *never* regret."

"Even if I come to regret it?" I asked quietly.

He gave me a small smile. "Even then. If it saves your life from my father like I intended it to, I cannot and will not regret this."

I knew his decision to give his magic to me had stemmed from his past experience of not being able to protect Cessa, Warrick's mother. I knew *why* he did it. I was just still shocked and stunned he'd actually done it. He hadn't told me. Or Owen, apparently. He just decided I needed saving and had done it. Giving away years of a magic that he had honed and worked hard to gain. Like it was nothing.

The rest of the realm can burn, but I made sure you will always be safe.

He hadn't given me this magic in a game of manipulation, it'd come from a place of love. In the way that he loved me so fiercely, he'd do anything to keep me safe. And though I was furious at him for this, for doing this without telling me, I was also a little stunned by how he loved me in his every action and move.

He was still eye level, kneeling in front of me. "Can you read my thoughts every second of the day?" I asked.

He smirked and gave his head a shake as he moved to sit next to me. He wrapped a hand around the back of my neck, massaging gently. "No. Eventually maybe? But I'd have to seek out your thoughts, it's not just there. If that makes sense."

I let out a long sigh. "No, it doesn't make sense, Krew. None of it makes sense."

His hand stilled. "Well, I can feel where you are, even if you are not in the room. I can feel the direction you are in, but in my head. And I know that sounds crazy. It's like some sort of tether between us. And when I focus in on that, in the direction I feel you, that's when I can hear what you are thinking. Though if you are feeling strongly, or in the case of this morning, about to panic, it seems to come chasing down that tether to me."

This was madness. I had never heard of any of this before.

"I know it sounds absurd. I need to find out more about soul bound couples, but there are very few living now. Over the generations there were fewer and fewer and now I'm not sure what information I can find. I should get Hatcher on this immediately, so we can learn more of what we are capable of together, but for now I'd like to keep this between us. At least for a few days until you have a better handle on your magic."

I gave him a smile of understanding. I didn't want anyone else to know I had magic for a while. "And why did you suspect we might be soul bound before last night? You could hear my thoughts even then?"

He gave his head a shake. "Not often, but my magic was regularly reacting to your emotions as well as my own. Even when my parents seemed to have a loving relationship, I hadn't ever seen that before, so I knew something was amiss."

"When was the first time you heard my thoughts?"

He sighed. I had apparently asked him a question he wasn't sure he wanted to answer. "Honestly?"

I gave him a nod.

"I swore I felt your panic the night you tried to run. My magic was . . . *inconsolable* until I found you."

My jaw fell open. "But that was before—"

"I know, love." His eyes never left mine. "That was before you cared for me in that manner. But my feelings for you were already there, whether I wanted to admit to them or not. I also swore I heard your thoughts the night of the fire."

I shook my head, considering all his words. I could be mad at him for how much magic he'd given to me in the bonding, but it was true that we had always been drawn to one another. Even back when I was still in Keir's Assemblage. Our souls seemed to somehow recognize one another even when we had rather they not.

"Here." He brushed a kiss to my temple and got up. "Close your eyes. Not for magic this time, but I am going to leave your side and go somewhere in our wing. I won't tell you where. Focus in, think of me, and see if you can figure out what direction I am."

I looked at him curiously. "Okay." I closed my eyes, willing to try this little experiment but unsure if it would work.

I heard a crackling sound and opened my eyes only to see that he put up a sound barrier around me and the couch. "That's cheating." But then I realized why he'd done it. I would have heard his footsteps and known what direction he was in. This way, I was truly blind, not knowing at all where he went. If it was on the bed behind me, out on the balcony, or in the neighboring room.

So I thought of Krew. My husband. My soulmate. I struggled not to focus on the images of the previous night, skin to skin, and instead just tried to focus on the intense look in his eyes as he had sliced open my hand and poured his magic into me. I turned my head slightly to the right. It felt like there was something there. Like he was there. With me. Like he'd always been with me, always occupied that space in my head.

"Are you—" I took a deep inhale and really focused, closing my eyes for a moment. "Are you sitting in Keir's usual spot at the table?"

He let the barrier fall and said, "Very good, love. Yes, I was."

I gave my head a shake. I wasn't sure what was more terrifying. The fact that I felt Krew in my head or the fact that I had turned a dead tree completely green earlier. "Once more," I demanded.

Krew laughed as he leaned up against the doorway. "Why don't you try to say something to me instead? But not out loud. Through our bond."

I closed my eyes, focusing in on the tiny space where I had felt Krew. I tried to think of it like a tether as he'd said, like a rope connecting the two of us.

I am tired. Entirely overwhelmed. I want to shake you, but I also love you.

Krew was grinning and back at my knees, kneeling before me.

"I love you too, my wife."

"Why did you do this to me?" I whispered. "You knew I was anxious enough about only a drop of magic, so why would you think giving me all but a drop of it was a good idea?"

Krew took my hand. The scar from the cut during our bonding was almost gone. It looked like it had been weeks when it had only been but a day. He gently trailed his fingers over the mark before kissing my palm. "Because you are the absolute best person I have ever had the honor to know. And if magic really is an extension of ourselves, we need a whole lot more of you, your light in this realm." He switched hands to do the same with the other. "You might not accept this gift now. And if you'd like to be mad at me, go right on ahead. I understand now how you'd feel forced into it, but please know that was never my intention."

I let out a sigh. "Can our magic combine?"

"I think so, yes. We can try tomorrow if you'd like."

"If you still have yours?" I added.

He gave me a nod. "I'll still have some. It's just a matter of how much." He paused and rubbed my arms, still in his shirt. "How are you feeling now?"

I took a deep breath and tried to send the word to Krew. *Exhausted.*

For some reason, learning how to talk to Krew telepathically was a lot easier than using magic. Maybe because there were less variables. Less tubs to snap in half.

"Let's go to bed then," he said, holding a hand down for me.

I knew all of these issues couldn't be fixed no matter how much we talked them to death. "You'll stay? In case I wake like before?"

He pulled me to standing and kissed me. "I'm not going anywhere. And any time in the next week I am not at your side, Owen will be. We are with you, love. Every step of the way."

* * *

I WOKE WARM, but not from the buzz of the magic. It was Krew. I was tucked into his chest while he read a letter in his hand. If I had to guess, it was late afternoon. I'd slept for hours. Glorious hours of deep sleep and no magical interruptions. And I likely would have slept on through the afternoon and night were it not for feeling hungry. In our haste to use my magic and then discuss things, I hadn't eaten this morning.

Krew brushed a kiss to the top of my head. "Hey."

"Hi."

"How do you feel?"

I sat up and looked at my palms. No magic was visible beneath the surface. I somehow knew it was there waiting though. Just like I knew what direction Krew had been in. Instinct told me so.

"At least I'm not naked and glowing this time," I offered, "but I'm starved."

"Would you like to take a shower and relax while I get you some food brought up?"

I gave him a nod. "That'd be nice, thanks."

He let out a sigh. "Owen wants to discuss our gameplan for keeping you away from the king later. He wanted you to be in on the conversation. If you feel up to it. Or if it's too overwhelming, we can handle it on our own."

I sighed. "I'll be there."

Krew paused. "Renna knows something is up as well. She's

been pestering me. She tried to come up here earlier, but Owen somehow deterred her."

I stood, ready to get under the hot steam of the shower water. But not ready to see what I'd done to the tub again. "Might as well have her in on the conversation too?"

"Are you ready for that?"

I gave him a shrug. "No. I'm not ready for anything."

Within the hour, I had eaten some soup and a sandwich, and Owen and Renna arrived. I stayed quiet, listening to Krew quickly and concisely bring Renna in on the events of the past day. As much as he could between all her questions, anyway.

"So you are going to get married before the Assemblages are over?" Renna asked, eyes big.

Owen shot her a grin. "They already are."

Renna's eyes went even bigger. "Why does Jorah look like she wants to kill someone then?"

Krew gestured with a hand. "Yes, well, that'd be me. Her husband. Because I gave her more than just a drop of magic and she's not quite sure what to do with that yet."

I closed my eyes for only a moment to send Krew a thought down the connection to him in my mind. *Kill you or kiss you, I just cannot decide.*

Krew burst out laughing, causing Renna to look at him like he had grown horns.

My vote is the second option.

She stood up and immediately raced for me. Looking at my palm, which was all but healed, and then grabbing for Krew's to do the same. "I don't believe it."

"I didn't either," Krew said gently.

She took both of my hands. "Soul bound?"

I gave her a nod. "Yes. Are you ready for the weirdest part?"

Her beautiful forehead creased. "You mean there's more?"

I whispered though there was already a sound barrier around

the room. "Not only did he give me more than a drop of his magic, he gave me *all* but a drop of his magic." Those were not words which could be thrown about at a normal volume. I cleared my throat. "And I woke to the magic already there, burning along my skin, and I may or may not have broken a tub and turned a tree green."

Renna's breath caught and she spun for Krew. *"What?"*

Krew gave her a shrug like it was a minor offense. "I'd rather work to recoup my own magic than worry if she had enough to deal with my father."

Renna just stood there a moment, in full shock, and then she was there wrapping her arms around me. "Oh, honey. I get it now. I so get it. You go right on ahead and kill him, I'll grab the shovel."

"So, I've never been happier," my voice cracked, "but also never been more scared, Renna." I felt the dull buzz of my magic flaring to life. I was very quickly going to have to learn how to keep my emotions in check at all times. "How am I supposed to keep this from the king? How did I ever believe I could?"

"Well, we aren't due for a ball for another ten days," Owen offered. "That helps."

"You are going to have to have some lessons in willing your magic away too," Renna offered. "Think of it as reassuring your magic that you are in fact fine and do not need it yet."

I kind of liked the thought of that, but I had no idea how to do it. Then again, before this morning I'd had no idea how to use magic or talk to Krew telepathically.

"What about her blood?" Renna asked. "Won't the king somehow know she is Enchanted now?"

Krew shook his head. "We took vials of blood from her leading up to our ceremony. I have a stockpile of blood for now. If Keir and I can convince our father to end the Assemblages by summer, we may have just enough to distract him for long enough."

"I am still so upset I was not at this ceremony," Renna squinted at Krew and then at me before spinning to Owen, "and he was."

Owen brushed a nonexistent speck of dust off his shoulder. "Priorities, Renna."

"Until that first ball though," Krew added, "we keep Jorah away from my father, agreed?"

"Agreed," Owen nodded.

"Do we have a plan for that?" Renna asked. "You know the first week after the magic settles is hard." She shook her head and mumbled to me, "Sorry, Jorah."

"When have you ever known me to not have a plan?"

Owen snorted. "The night you saved her."

Krew's eyes met mine. *My best plan yet.*

I rolled my eyes. He was entirely too smug.

Krew's attention switched back to Renna. "I have staged a disloyal arrest for tomorrow. For someone who isn't truly disloyal at all. So if Father wishes to torture the man, there will be no important information given. But it should be a nice distraction for him. Add in the heavy sleeping tonic he is getting this week, and he should not notice Jorah's training sessions in the forest at night."

So I was training with magic instead of my body now. And I would be training with Krew instead of Keir and Krew. "Wait," I gasped. "You are going to send an innocent man to get tortured as a distraction while I learn how to use magic?"

Krew shook his head. "No, love. I set up a rapist. It's beyond time he's off the streets of Rallis. He more than deserves whatever he gets."

I rubbed my hand across my forehead. "There has been so much to take in about this day that I honestly have no idea what to even do with that."

Owen laughed and crossed his arms. "So tomorrow would be a better day to tell you that Keir and Krew are also bribing the king's mistress?"

I sat down on the couch.

"Owen," Krew snapped. "Stay on task. Yes, we can discuss that tomorrow. Or the next day."

For the next twenty minutes I sipped a tea and listened to Owen, Krew, and Renna talk about the specifics of me avoiding the king. Everything from which hallways we should avoid and who we could or could not speak to.

I wished more than anything it were possible to skip a week. I just wanted to know how to control and use my magic safely. Everyone made it sound like it was so simple, a totally easy feat.

I feared it'd be far more difficult than that. I felt as if this power raging within me would blow me to bits at any given moment.

By the time Renna and Owen left, I was feeling exhausted all over again. Was it the magic? How had Krew walked around with this much magic and stayed upright?

"Ready for bed, love?" Krew asked from where we lounged on the couch next to one another.

"Yes. Why am I so tired? Is it the magic?"

Krew nodded and pulled me to standing. "Yes. Your body is getting used to its presence. The first few days will be tiring. Add in the fact that it was quite a bit of magic, and yes. You are going to need a lot of sleep this week."

I looked to the bed, our bed. We had shared it every day for months, and yet tonight I was terrified. Not to sleep *with* Krew. Not to sleep *next to* Krew. I had planned on being in that bed wrapped up in Krew as often as possible before the magic settled. But now I already had the magic, and everything was new and different.

"What is running through that cunning head of yours?" he asked gently. "You may ask anything you want, and I will not make fun of you for it."

"Can I—" I shook my head. "Can we—" I swallowed. "What if I start glowing in the heat of the moment?"

His lips twitched. "Do you think that would truly deter me?"

A ghost of a smile raced across my lips. "Well no. But what if my magic begins to burn my skin like this morning?"

He shook his head. "That was different. Your magic needed to be used and then your panic in finding it there worsened it. Your magic can begin burning and glowing in response to your emotions, yes, but other than when it settles, it typically only reacts that strongly when it is trying to protect and save you. Think of it like a built-in defense mechanism. And pleasure, love, is not something you need saving from." He brushed a gentle kiss upon my lips. "You do not need to be saved from me, I can promise you that."

I took a deep breath.

"But if you'd rather wait, I will not rush you. You've had more than enough of trying things out for the day."

I shook my head. "That was not part of our marriage terms."

"Neither was this much magic," he argued.

"Still," I admitted. "The magic terrifies me, but for some reason, our bonding doesn't." I placed my hand on his chest. "This? This doesn't. It just feels right."

He trailed a finger slowly across my hand and up my arm. "Do you feel your magic burning now?"

"No."

He moved his hand up to my cheek, trailing down and across my collarbone. "How about now?"

I fought off a shudder. "No."

He leaned in to kiss my lips before running his nose along my jaw. "Do you want me to stop?"

"No."

His lips crashed into mine. "I'm going to keep asking. And I need you to tell me when you need me to stop."

"And if I don't?" I whispered.

His eyes seared into mine. "Then we don't."

CHAPTER 4

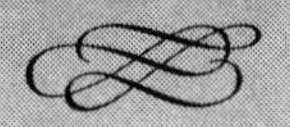

"So, how do I make sure I don't mess up around the king?" I asked Owen and Krew as my boots crunched the snow beneath us. It was early. So early I could barely see a thing. "How will he not see my magic crawling across my skin in his presence? Because emotions are always high around him."

Now at the lake again, Owen expanded the moving sound barrier further out into our surroundings. "I think Renna did a great job of explaining it last night. Think of it as assuring the magic you do not need it yet. This is something the majority of Enchanted in Savaryn have had to master. We have a select few ways we are to use our magic every day, but the king and Krew's grandfather for decades have told us to use it sparingly. Rarely."

"Doesn't that go against the ultimate goal of being the most powerful country in the realm? If his army isn't as powerful? A bit counterintuitive?"

Krew shook his head. "No, my father doesn't give a damn about Wylan. He only cares that he is the most powerful Enchanted in the realm. The other countries were hit hard with the disease, and he keeps the rest of Wylan in check with false information about our magic and fear. So he is the most powerful Enchanted in the realm right now." His eyes went to mine. "But not for long."

I gave my head a shake, thinking how awful it must be to be Enchanted and constantly fight the urge to use magic, thinking using too much would somehow make them magicless, make them belong in Rallis. Feeling the constant pull to use magic, but always having to weigh whether it was a worthy enough moment for it or not. "I have so many questions I don't even know where to begin. What does the fact that I now have magic do to my Iron Will? Can magic now be used on me?"

Owen flicked a finger and a breeze of wind hit Krew and me. Krew had my hand in his, the magic seeming to go around the both of us. "Looks like not." He and Krew exchanged a look, Krew giving his head a shake.

"What?" I asked, looking to my palms and seeing my magic flaring to life. It had gone from a dull buzz to a strong buzz now, as if in defense of magic being attempted on me. A built-in defense mechanism. Just like Krew said.

Owen's eyes were on mine when I looked back up. "With your Iron Will giving you protection from other Enchanted's magic and the amount of magic you now wield, you are quite the weapon. Which is irritating to Krew because he only wanted you safe."

I thought back to Sasha Girard telling me I was the counter to the king's power. Would I be able to get us close enough to the king to kill him if my touch was still immune to magic?

The buzzing was getting louder though, and I was beginning to faintly glow.

"Okay, love," Krew said gently. "There is a very large trunk down over there. It will take more than just a little magic to move it, but could you move it over here?"

It was a massive tree trunk, over half the height of me. Had the forest been alive and not dead, I was sure it would be crawling with moss or fungi by now, a great hiding spot for creatures.

Instead, it was just black and sitting there stuck. But Krew thought I could move it? Granted I knew that was what we were out here for. For me to use my magic a few times early this morning before anyone else was up.

He added, "Imagine maybe twice as much magic as you used yesterday. And try not to heal it, all right? It's been dead for years. You can will your magic not to hurt any of the other trees in the process of moving it, but try not to heal it."

I looked at my palm, knowing I should use magic, but also seeing if I could somewhat calm it. *Not yet. Not yet.* Now I knew why Krew and Owen always told me to breathe. Keeping deep breaths of air pumping into my lungs helped calm my magic immensely.

Within a minute, the glowing had faded, and the buzz disappeared entirely.

"Nicely done," Owen gave me a nod. "But that doesn't mean you're off the hook for using magic." He placed his hands on his hips. "Krew is going to be busy later in the day for a few hours and you and I are going to work a little on a combination of doing what you just did, and then bringing your magic to the surface on command. The better handle you have on that, the better you will be around the king. And then tonight after the king is asleep you can start training with the princes. But for now, you still need to use a little magic to get you through the rest of the day comfortably."

"Will this all be just as much fun as training is?" I groaned.

Owen cocked his head. "Seems likely." He paused. "And we will get back to our training eventually too, but you are off the hook for this week anyway."

I tipped my head back to the hazy sky beginning to peek in from around all the branches. "Great."

I stepped toward the downed trunk and decided I might as well get it over with. If I used my magic twice today, maybe I could be done for the day again. Relaxed and ready for more sleep.

I closed my eyes and imagined two slightly thicker strands of magic heading to the trunk of the tree and moving it toward us gently, not hitting any of the other trees, and not going too quickly. I imagined only enough magic to move the trunk, not enough to hurt anything in the forest. And then I willed the magic now buzzing in my palm out toward the trunk.

Magic shot out of my hand and traveled along the ground, wrapping around the ends of the trunk and slowly and gently beginning to move the trunk.

I slid it right to where Krew had gestured, the magic disappearing as it did.

Owen's eyes were on Krew's and not mine, when he said, "Good work."

I looked at both of them. "That seemed easier today. What's with you two though?"

Neither of them said a word for a moment. And then Krew's eyes finally came to mine. "I wasn't sure if you'd truly be able to move that or not." He paused. "It was quite heavy. Did you only imagine twice the amount of magic as yesterday?"

I gave him a nod. "Yes. That's what you said to do."

Krew gave his head a shake. "With your Iron Will in combination with the magic I gifted you, I am not sure if we truly know the extent of your power yet."

I sighed. "Great. I just love being an experiment. It's my favorite."

Krew held up his hands. "It does not matter for now, love. One day at a time."

"Tell that to the tub," I mumbled.

"Let's try to do a slow breeze," Owen offered. "So you can find out what shape your magic travels in."

Now that I was dying to know. One more time using magic,

and then I could go eat some breakfast and take a nap. I still absolutely dreaded using my magic, and I had no idea how long it was going to take, if ever, for that feeling to go away. Could I just use it a few times a day and then suppress it the rest of the time?

"Imagine a slight breeze, going only the distance of the lake, and then it dissipates," Owen offered. "But imagine the magic leaving your hands slowly. The softest and slowest breeze you could possibly imagine. You'll really have to concentrate."

I shook my head and took a deep breath before shaking out my hands. "I'm nervous what it will be. What if it is a huge rat?"

"Could be a lion," Krew argued.

"Or another wolf," Owen stated.

"Or an insect," I added with clear disdain. "It could be a centipede."

Krew chuckled. "Just try it, love. I doubt your magic takes the shape of a rat or a centipede."

I fought off a shiver. "Okay."

I closed my eyes, feeling the pull of my magic increase. Whether it was because I was so nervous or because it knew I was about to use it, I wasn't certain. I wanted to think about the lake and healing it but knew I couldn't. I wanted to fret over whatever shape I was about to see but had to push it all away. I inhaled and focused in. I first imagined the breeze, slow and lazy just like I had seen Owen and Krew do before. I imagined it blowing slowly and gently around the lake in a circular pattern twice before disappearing at the far edge of the lake.

I took a deep breath and then released my magic toward the lake.

I opened my eyes to see my magic rising from my pointer finger slowly, whisps of silver magic slowly rising out of me. And then gently, a bird of sorts shot to the sky. I barely caught it, as the magic was still moving faster than I intended and then it was gone in a flash. All I knew was that it was somewhat birdly shaped.

"One more time," I demanded, taking a moment this time to really think about how slow I wanted my magic to move. As if dipped in molasses and slowly rolling toward the lake before making three slow circles and disappearing. I again willed the magic out of my hand.

At first, I thought it was a raven just like Keir's. Though it wouldn't matter, I would've preferred to match Krew's wolf over Keir's raven. But then, as the second attempt did move much slower, I saw that this bird was much larger than Keir's. It wasn't a raven at all. As it circled around the lake, I found it was actually a hawk.

In a flash, Krew's magic also took to the sky, charging along the ground in wolf form before joining the breeze my magic was circling. Our magic joined on the last circle my hawk flew, the wolf running around above the surface of the lake and my hawk just above it as the silver and navy intertwined.

"We've got a wolf and a hawk," Owen said with a laugh. "Thank the gods it wasn't an owl."

"I was more worried I'd match Keir's raven and that'd be awkward as hell." My forehead creased. "Wait. Whose magic is the owl?"

"My father's," Krew bit out. "Not that it ever moves slow enough for you to notice."

I thought of the way the king was always perched in a balcony, scanning and watching. I should've guessed that before now. He was a scavenger, through and through. "So we've got two birds, a wolf, and a bear," I offered. "I don't know what shape I thought it'd take, but I never considered a hawk."

"As much as you like the forest, it doesn't surprise me any," Owen laughed. "The wolves can be the guardians of the forest; you can take watch above it."

"How do you feel?" Krew asked me.

I was still smiling over Owen's comment. "Relieved. Relieved I'm not a rat."

He laughed. "No. I meant magic-wise. Do you need to go once more, or are you good for breakfast?"

I had no idea if I was good or not, but I found I shook my head. "No. I'm fine. And starved."

"You know what this calls for?" Owen asked.

Krew pinned him with a glare. "She is going to be exhausted this week with the magic settling in. She is absolutely *not* making you cookies."

"No, no, no." Owen shook his head. "Not where I was going."

I laughed. "Bacon. He meant bacon."

Krew rolled his eyes. "What is with the two of you and bacon?"

Owen rubbed his hands together. "What's not to like?"

* * *

I SLEPT for a few hours and then Owen demanded I work on pulling my magic into my palms and then calming it. Krew was off dealing with the arrested disloyal who he had set up. I wasn't sure if he'd be gone the rest of the day or just a few hours. Silvia had, of course, known about the wedding and the bonding taking place, as she'd gotten me ready for hours on my wedding day. While overjoyed and excited to be in on the secret, she'd promised to give me space these first few days while I adjusted to the magic. I only wished Owen had followed her example.

"I don't want to break anything!" I argued with Owen. "Can't we do this outside?"

He shook his head. "Not at this time of day."

"Well, I'm not confident in it enough to use it in Krew's wing. And I was about to go take a shower."

"You won't be using it, you'll just be calling it forward and then calming it," he offered.

I glared at him. "Unless I cannot calm it."

He reached a hand down to where I was reading at the couch and pulled me to standing. "You have to get past being afraid of your magic, Jorah. The sooner you do that, the better you'll feel."

I gaped at him. "Excuse me? Krew just handed me over all but a drop of his magic, when I had been terrified for even a drop of it, and I am just supposed to accept it, no reservations at all, when this is something I have feared for the majority of my life?"

Owen put a hand on my shoulder. "I get it. I do. But being afraid of your magic is only going to make you miserable. My hope is the more used to it you get, the easier it'll be."

"And if it is never easy?" I snapped.

He wrapped his arms around me. "Hey. I get it. We will cross that bridge when we get to it. Right now I am only asking you to try to bring your magic up, then press it back down. That's it. Come on, you're a natural already. You've got this."

"Owen, I busted a tub, and healed a tree without even meaning to."

He shrugged while still hugging me. "Minor details."

Already feeling somewhat angry at him, and Krew, and everything they were asking of me these last two days, it took very little effort to let the magic come to my palms. In a dramatic flair, I let it continue, weaving up my arms and down the rest of me.

The very odd and somehow good news about all this was that it had a warming effect on my skin and I did hate to be cold.

"Okay, now calm it," Owen commanded.

I closed my eyes only because I couldn't stop glaring at him. I repeated what I'd told my magic earlier. *Not yet. Not yet.* As I opened my eyes back up, I repeated it again, taking a deep breath as I did.

It took about a minute, but as soon as all traces were gone, I looked back to Owen. "Are you happy now?"

He grinned. "Yes, but no. By the end of the week, you need to be able to do that in seconds, if not faster. Try again."

I rolled my eyes. "I loathe you right now."

"That's fine," Owen offered. "I can take it. My job right now isn't to be your friend, Jorah. My job right now is to be your guard and keep you safe from the king at the next ball. Plus, I thought we had already established that I'm pushy."

As frustrated as I was, I couldn't help but smirk.

So he walked me through the same thing again, and again, and again. By the fourth time, I was faster, but a sheen of sweat had broken out on my forehead. It was exhausting playing with my magic, tempting it, but then keeping it at bay. And if it was exhausting doing so in a safe space, I couldn't imagine what being around the king would do to me.

"Go take your shower, Your Grace," Owen said as he turned me toward the bathroom. "Then I'll let you take another nap."

I stomped toward the shower. "And here I thought marrying into the royal family would've given *me* the power to boss *you* around."

CHAPTER 5

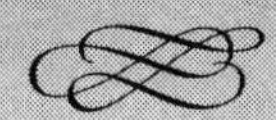

After Owen had convinced me to practice tempering my magic twice more that afternoon, I'd been too exhausted to even make it through dinner. Falling asleep while eating with Krew, he'd apparently moved me to bed and left to practice with Keir.

I woke to voices a few hours later. Owen and Krew. They were in front of the fire, speaking softly. I was sure to keep both my magic and my emotions calm, wanting to know what they were whisper-yelling about.

"But is it enough?" Owen snapped. Very rarely had I heard him take that tone with Krew.

"Won't *she* know if it is enough or not? She seems to be doing fine today," Krew defended.

Owen shook his head. "She has no idea if she's fine or not. She moved that trunk like it weighed next to nothing today. We have *no* idea what she is capable of. None."

From what I could see, Krew grabbed at his hair. I didn't have to pull on the invisible tether between us to understand he was worried.

"She is still scared of it," Owen continued. "As long as she fears it, suppressing it too much can make her dangerous."

I fought to keep my emotions calm and even. I felt my magic rising to the surface. Their words were similar to what they had told me earlier that day in the forest, but I hadn't realized just how serious of a problem this apparently was.

Though my magic calmed on command, becoming easier with every time I did it, I must have thoroughly failed on the emotional side of it. Because I felt Krew send through the bond to me, *Did we wake you?*

Yes.

"Then we have the matter that your magic has presumably done nothing, gone nowhere, only slightly dipped, yet at the same time Jorah is powerful as shit."

"Owen," Krew hissed.

"Tonight Keir went half power at you, and you held your own. I am . . . *disturbed.* Tomorrow when he goes full blast at you, we will see. Maybe by then you'll be weakening."

"We woke my wife," Krew offered.

Owen looked back to where I still laid still. "How'd you know?"

Krew's eyes were on mine when I opened them up.

"Oh right. Because you two talk with everything but your mouths these days," Owen barked. "Sorry, Jorah."

I yawned. "Can you worry yourself into a tizzy tomorrow, please?"

"I'm not worried," Owen snapped.

"Oh?" I asked, and to Krew I added, *He is so worried.*

He is.

"I am just . . . there is a lot going on. That is all."

I yawned. "Go to bed, Owen Raikes. We will handle it in the morning. Bright and early, I'm sure."

"Yes, Your Highness." Owen sent me a smirk and then left.

I stretched and moved to resituate the blankets, ready to go right back to sleep. Tomorrow. We could figure it all out tomorrow.

I'm going to shower quick. Want to join me?

I jolted. Was he going to flirt with me through our bond? At completely inopportune times? Of course he was. I was doomed. Irrevocably doomed.

But I'm warm.

His response was immediate. *You could be warm in here too.*

I curled in tighter to the covers and could almost feel him laughing. After a minute, while still in the shower, he asked, *How much of that did you hear?*

I considered my answer. *Enough.*

Please don't worry. It may take a week or two to figure out how our bonding affected both of our magic, but all in due time, love.

I wasn't so sure about that. I was trying not to let Owen's comment fester, but I wasn't sure I was accomplishing it. Was I dangerous?

Long after Krew was out of the shower, long after I'd used my touch to map his body, long after he'd fallen asleep, I remembered those words. I was powerful, yet no one knew how that paired with my Iron Will would affect things.

One time. I'd used my magic one time and felt good about it. Yet even then I'd done more than intended. I was looking forward to the day this power felt like a gift and not a burden, but I wasn't sure that day would come anytime soon. If ever.

* * *

IT FELT like the exhaustion was going to be a permanent companion to my new life. I carried it with me wherever I went, my own personal shadow.

I used magic two times the next morning, successfully, but almost wincing as I had. What Owen had said rattled me. I didn't trust my magic. At all. And I was beginning to wonder if Krew's so-called gift was a waste. If I'd end up suppressing my magic so much that I'd become just like all the other Enchanted in Savaryn. Weakened by not using it enough.

Maybe I preferred to be that way.

The rest of the day I practiced calling my magic to the surface and then calming it repeatedly. In the shower alone, I'd done it six times. It was far easier than I thought to will my magic to stay away. That wasn't the hard part. The hard part was using it. And not doing something with it that was . . . extra.

Silvia came in to check on me and braid my hair, and though I had been beyond nervous, for the twenty minutes I had seen her and chatted with her, I'd kept my skin clear of all traces of magic. It wasn't that it truly mattered because she already knew I had magic, but it was a nice trial run of being around someone and containing my magic. It was almost as if my magic was beginning to know the rules of this little game too. The need to stay hidden for a while.

I turned the corner after chatting with Silvia to find Owen's sound barrier up around the room next door. Assuming he was just ranting away like the night before, I stepped into his barrier, making it fall.

My palms burned only slightly. I had half a mind to put a barrier up to replace it myself. But I didn't want to break something. So I willed the magic down and let Owen replace it.

Keir was there too, as were Krew and Renna.

"How are you feeling?" Keir asked.

It was nice of him to ask, I just wasn't sure they wanted my actual answer. "Fine."

How are you really feeling?

My eyes went to Krew's as I sent him the truthful answer. *Like there is barely enough room in this body for me anymore.*

He stood and walked over to me, brushing a kiss to my temple. "Sit in my seat?"

I gave him a nod as he headed over to the bar area, pouring himself a drink and me a hot tea. "What'd I miss?"

The table was quiet, all of them looking to someone else, all eyes avoiding me.

I snorted. "If you were talking about me, that's fine. I'm used to it at this point."

Renna shook her head. "No, Jorah. We weren't talking about you. We were . . ." She took a deep breath. "We were talking about the fact that the princes have bribed the king's mistress to get the king extremely drunk and then take the ring off his dumb thumb."

"When?" I snapped. "When is this happening?"

"Soon," Keir offered with an apologetic smile. "We figure the more he's distracted this week and next, the better."

I vaguely remembered Owen saying something about the princes bribing his mistress, but I had naively assumed it was related to the stronger sleeping tonic he'd been receiving this week.

I stood without another thought, my eyes going directly to Krew's. "So let me get this straight. While you are possibly about to lose all but a drop of your magic, you are going to bribe someone we do not trust, to get an object that may or may not hold your mother's magic?"

"It has to be the ring," Keir argued. "It has to be. It's the only object which never leaves his side."

Krew handed me the tea, but I was too busy glaring at him to thank him. I switched my attention back to Keir. "I don't doubt that it could be the ring. I doubt the timing of doing this now, when Krew's magic is supposed to be weakened. I don't trust her, whoever she is. And I do not think this is a wise move. Not now."

Keir gave me a shrug. "But if it works . . . ."

I felt the hum of magic at my palms and took a deep breath. "If it works? If it works what? You're going to take down the king yourself? Because Krew can't. His magic is trapped in me."

"Jorah," Krew warned.

"I know, I know. You don't like me calling it *your* magic anymore."

"No," Renna said calmly. "You're glowing."

"Rather aggressively," Owen added.

I looked down to see they were right. "Dammit." I closed my eyes and took a deep breath, willing the magic to subside. I opened my eyes, looking at Owen. "There. Happy?"

"Uhh, no," he answered.

I rolled my eyes. "Go figure."

"You're going to need to use a little to get through the rest of the day," Owen told me.

"I'll be fine," I snapped. "Let's get back to this reckless plan of the ring. Which apparently is going to happen soon."

"Fine. Use some magic first," Owen demanded.

I squinted. "Excuse me?"

"Use some magic."

I shook my head. "No. I told you, I don't want to break anything else. And I already have used it today. That was why you pulled me out of bed at dawn this morning. I have done every single thing you have demanded for the last three days and I'm sick of it." The tears of frustration pricked my eyes. I was so tired of this. So tired of them having me do this or that, so tired of them trying to figure me out. When I'd never even wanted this to begin with.

"Leave her alone, Owen," Krew snapped.

"Jorah," Owen warned, ignoring Krew entirely. "You can't just suppress it all the time. You are going to have to start using it more frequently."

"Fine. I'll use it tonight. In the forest. I can't use it up here."

Owen narrowed his eyes. "Can't or won't?"

I clenched my jaw and willed my magic away so it didn't just further prove his point for him. "Both. Both, Owen."

I grabbed my tea and left, pulling down the sound barrier of Owen's with me when I went.

CHAPTER 6

"How long are you going to be pissed at me?"

"A while," I admitted to Owen.

Krew held open the back kitchen door for me. It was late. Atrociously late. It was after midnight. And I was so tired I felt like a walking corpse. But here we were. Going back out to the meadow to train.

"Well, if you want out of this like the badass I know you are, you aren't going to get there by getting coddled."

I stopped dead in my tracks and willed my magic to stay put. I thought I had been mostly past this little tiff with Owen. Up until the word *coddle*. "I'm sorry?"

Owen gave me a shrug. "It's the truth."

I squinted. "Who exactly is *coddling* me, Owen?"

His eyes were no longer on me though, they were on Krew, the two of them stuck in a stare down.

"You think Krew is coddling me?" My voice went up in pitch as I asked the question.

Owen's eyes briefly hit mine before going directly back to Krew's. "Yes. Whether it is intentional or because he is distracted with becoming soul bound to you, or maybe even just distracted *with you*, I'm not sure."

"Owen," Krew warned. "Push too far and insult *my wife* and we will have a problem."

The way he'd sliced through the words *my wife.* I fought off a shiver.

"You know she needs to be using her magic more frequently. You know she has to learn to trust it," Owen argued.

Krew took a step forward with a look on his face that had Owen backing up. "And what you do *not* know is what she feels like, what she's felt like every day since I gave her magic. You don't feel how overwhelmed she feels, but I do. I *feel* her panic. I *feel* her fear. She is terrified, Owen. And has been terrified every waking moment since she found the magic crawling across her skin."

Owen was quiet a moment, thinking through Krew's words. "Your guilt is not helping her, Krew. Both of you need to understand that what was done is done. Jorah is powerful. And she is strong." Owen's eyes switched to mine. "You were strong far, far before you ever had the magic. You are going to be okay. We are going to get through this. All of us."

I wasn't sure who he was trying to convince. Me or him. I was also entirely sick of hearing *what was done was done.* If I never heard that phrase another day in my life, that would be splendid.

The rest of the walk was quiet, though I could feel Krew stewing next to me.

Do you really feel guilty?

Yes. I had no idea you'd be this terrified with my magic or I might have only given you half. But Owen has a point. His delivery of it is horrid, but he has a point. I was trying to give you time and space to come to terms with everything.

Keir was already in the meadow when we arrived.

"Took you guys long enough!" he hollered in jest.

"Sorry," I offered. "It's my fault."

Keir tipped his head to the side like he didn't believe me.

"Krew and Owen had to have a little argument about who is and is not coddling me."

Keir looked to each of them and back to me. "And both live to tell the tale? Well, you've got your magic suppression mastered, I see."

I couldn't help but laugh, thankful for Keir cutting through the tension.

Krew rolled his neck to the side, his magic already slithering along it. "Let's go first, brother. Then I'll practice with Jorah."

Keir gave him a look. "And you are sure you want to do this full speed?"

Krew nodded. "I've never been more sure."

Owen nudged me with an elbow. "Let's go watch where we did last time. Watching them this time might give you some ideas for how you can use your own magic."

With as much sarcasm as I could possibly muster, I said, "Can't wait."

"I'm sorry I've been such a hardass," Owen said gently as soon as we were settled against the tree trunk. "I know you are struggling. I just want to fix this for you, and I know the faster you trust your magic, the better off you'll be."

My palms heated. It was crazy how tied together my magic and my emotions were. "I don't know how to just flip the switch and do that, Owen. I'd love to. There have been times I wanted to try something. Put up a sound barrier when I knock yours down. Or try to fix the lake. Or try to make an orb just to see if I could. But I am scared, Owen. Every time I've used magic, I've done something extra."

"Not every time."

I looked to him, my eyebrows pulling together.

"The second tree you healed. You did exactly what we asked you to do and nothing more."

I considered his words.

"And that was right after you healed the first tree. See what happens when you use it regularly? It's easier to control."

I sighed. But what if it was worse? What if the more I used it, the more dangerous I became? Wasn't that how Krew became this powerful to begin with?

"Owen," Krew barked from where he and Keir were about to begin. "Can you stop scaring my wife so I can focus?"

"Yeah. My bad." He put an arm around me and gave me a one-armed hug. "I might be hard on you, but I love you and I want you to be safe. Learning how to use your magic correctly is important. And it's a luxury very few Enchanted have been given. We are teaching you the right way."

"Owen," Krew snapped.

"Got it," Owen hollered back. He winced as he looked at me. "Okay, done talking now. Promise."

"Doubt it," I mumbled.

Keir and Krew took off, their blue magic lighting the night sky.

In between throwing magical orbs and what looked like bricks at Keir's head, Krew sent down the bond, *You okay, love?*

I snorted. *Yes. Please focus.*

He grinned and sent another brick at Keir's head.

As they picked up their intensity, at first all I was thinking of was how Krew seemed to be holding his own. He certainly didn't move or act like he had only a drop of magic in comparison to Keir.

But then my magic started to slither. Every time Keir would manage to hit Krew, even just blowing him backward, my magic would react. The first few times I took some deep breaths and calmed it. I kept repeating to it, *Not yet. Not yet. Not yet.*

I didn't know if it was happening because Krew's magic still recognized his feelings and wanted to protect him, or if it was because we were bonded and *I* wanted to protect him.

Five minutes later, I was beginning to sweat with how many times I'd had to shove the magic down. "Owen," I hissed.

He turned toward me, looking me over. "What's wrong?"

I turned away from the magic and reached for the bark of the tree trunk, trying to focus on how scratchy and cold it was. My whole body was throbbing and buzzing and it was taking everything in me to suppress it. "My magic. It wants to help protect Krew."

Owen cursed. "Let's get you out of here and then you'll need to use a little magic, okay?"

I looked down, seeing my skin glowing. I was suppressing my magic actively now, and still I glowed.

What's wrong? Krew asked down the bond.

I ignored him. It was all I could do not to burst into flames with the pull of my magic. It wanted to help. It wanted to protect. It wanted . . . *out*.

I sucked in a breath and tried to breathe. If Krew felt me panicking, I was only making things worse. I needed to get calmed down somehow, even though I felt anything but calm.

"Come on," Owen offered out a hand down to me, where I was still hunched over, hanging onto the bark of the trunk.

I reached for his hand, but when I did, everything seemed to happen at once.

Though I couldn't see what the princes were doing behind us, I could feel Krew through the bond. Keir had sent a wave of magic in one form or another at him, a cheap shot. And Krew, likely distracted because of what was going on with me, went down with the magic, grunting as if he had the wind knocked out of him.

And hearing Krew in pain made me see red. I knew they were practicing. I knew they had done this a thousand times, but I was immediately enraged. I considered sending a barrier of magic around Krew to protect him, much like a sound barrier, just to get Keir to back away from him for a second so I could breathe and get my magic under control, but when I reached my hand out for Owen, the magic left my body. I'd just thought it and the magic left to deliver.

I spun and watched in horror as my silver magic raced along the ground. As soon as it reached Krew, it put him in a semicircle, just like I'd imagined. But to do so, it also hit Keir with magic to get him to back away. Also like I'd envisioned. But instead of Keir having to back up, it threw him backward in an effort to separate them, and he hit the trunk of a tree twenty feet away like he was a rag doll and not one of the tallest men I'd met. As he fell to the ground, I only hoped he hadn't broken anything. Like his neck.

Skin still glowing, I put a hand over my mouth. What had I just done? Had I just killed Keir?

Krew was stuck in my magic barrier while I raced for Keir.

Please be alive, please be alive, please be alive.

Owen was with me stride for stride.

As soon as we got there, Keir was there, rolling on the ground. "Damn, Jorah."

I dropped to my knees. "Keir. I'm so, so sorry."

"He's okay, Jorah," Owen said gently. "Now could you—uh—let Krew out?"

Keir slowly sat up, giving his head a shake. He looked toward where Krew stood, stuck in my magic protection, and let out a laugh.

"This is no time to laugh," I chided. "I thought I killed you."

Owen put a hand down for him, and Keir winced as he took it and hoisted himself up to standing.

Then Owen was lifting me up too. "Jorah. You need to imagine your magic either disappearing, kind of like blowing out a candle, or send more magic at it to break the dome of magic around Krew."

I shook my head. "No! Do you see what happens when I use magic? People get hurt."

Owen took me by my shoulders. "Your magic, likely your bond, was making you feel the need to protect Krew. That was our fault for overlooking it. Not yours. Now focus, please. Send some magic at that dome so Krew can come over to you."

"Can't you do it?" I begged.

Owen shook his head. "No. I tried while we were running over here. It just bounced off."

Come on, love. You can do this. Let me out so I can help.

I closed my eyes but winced as I let out a single strand of magic and sent it toward Krew. Immediately the dome fell and he was free.

Within ten seconds he reached me and wrapped me in his arms.

"I'm so sorry," I gasped.

"Shhh. I'm sorry I didn't realize sooner what was going on," he whispered into my hair.

"Is—" I choked on a sob. "Is Keir really okay?"

"I'm fine," Keir said gently from the left of us. "Seriously. Knocked the wind out of me and that's it." The way he was holding his side didn't have me convinced.

I again shook my head. "What about your ribs and your back? You hit that tree so damn hard. Which I did not imagine in my head, I might add! I wanted you to back away from him, I never thought to do that." Then I pinned a glare on Owen. "You told me I was a natural. And then this happens. See?"

Owen dipped his head to his shoulder. "You are a natural, but this much power is not natural."

"Not helpful," Krew commented as he ran a hand through my hair. "Breathe for me please, Jorah."

"I can't," I gasped. "I almost killed Keir. Something *I* never willed to happen!"

Keir's voice was quiet as he said, "Are you guys seeing this?"

I turned, confused, and looked down to where he was looking. My tears, everywhere I'd cried, were glowing silver.

"Your tears had power before you became Enchanted," Owen offered as he and Krew exchanged a look.

"I need to get you out of here," Krew offered. "Before you heal the entire damn forest on accident, and I have to figure out how to explain it to my father."

"She needs—"

"I know," Krew snapped. "I know, Owen."

He scooped me into his arms and using his magic, we shot to the sky.

* * *

THE TRIP up the balcony was equally, if not more so, terrifying than the trip down. I wasn't sure which was worse.

As soon as Krew placed my feet down, I slumped to the ground in front of the fireplace, overcome with the emotions of what had just occurred.

They told me I just had to will it to happen. But I'd never willed Keir to get hurt. I'd been mad Krew was hurt and the next thing I knew, Keir was being slammed up against a tree.

Krew quickly shut the balcony door and put up a sound barrier. He got on the ground with me, wrapping me in his arms. "Listen to me please," he said gently, taking one of my hands in his.

I sniffed and wiped at my eyes.

"None of this is okay. None of it. But I need you to use your magic again."

"What?" Of everything I was expecting him to say, that was not it.

"You haven't been using it enough. You're doing excellent at suppressing it when you want to, but when you do use it, you haven't been using it enough. So tonight when your magic was reacting to a threat to me, it overreacted. This happens all the time to the Enchanted in Savaryn. You have to use it more often, love. So it's easier to control."

"I—can't." I shook my head.

"You can. You have to. I thought you were using just enough so your magic was there but not pulling at you. I was mistaken."

I shook my head. "No."

Krew used his magic to put the fire out. "Light the fire, Jorah."

"No."

"Yes."

I kept shaking my head. "No! When I use my magic people get hurt. Or objects. Like the tub."

"If you don't start using more of it, you will be the one getting hurt, Jorah. You will fear it so much, it will take over your life."

"Hasn't it already?" I snapped back.

He pointed at the fire where he sat on the floor with me. "Light the fire. Don't make it harder than it is."

"Harder than it is? If you were going to be a prick, you might as well have just let Owen bring me back up here."

Krew tipped his head back frustrated. "Yes, well, Owen was right. I was trying to give you space, but you definitely weren't using enough magic. Tonight proved that. Your magic should never explode out of you like that. Not if you are using it correctly."

"I don't know how to use it at all, let alone how to use it correctly."

Krew gestured again toward the fire. "Well, we will remedy that. Right now. You are going to start the fire. And then put up a sound barrier. And then do it all again. Again and again until you feel so tired you cannot move."

"I'm already that tired." Tears spilled out and down my cheeks. "This is why I only ever wanted a drop!"

He clenched his teeth in frustration. "Start the fire."

Did he finally see now what a waste giving away his magic to me had been? "Are you mad at me? For almost hurting Keir?"

"Start the fire," he said more firmly.

I couldn't even see him before me because everything was so blurry. I scooted back away from him, yanking my hand that had been in his away.

I closed my eyes and took a deep breath. I really hoped I didn't set the entire damn castle ablaze. I thought of my magic, pulling it into my palms, willing it to warm me. Then I thought of just the fireplace and the wood in the fireplace. My hand was shaking as I tried to move it off my lap.

I opened my eyes only briefly to look at the fireplace one last time, just to make sure I didn't overdo it, but then Krew was there, scooting in behind me and wrapping a hand around my eyes. He whispered, "Just start the fire."

"I'm scared."

He moved to put his face next to mine. "I know. I'm here. Just start the fire, love."

While I imagined only two logs out of the five lighting up, he grabbed my still shaking hands and lifted one palm out while gently rubbing the top of my hand with his thumb. "Start the fire."

Tears going nowhere, I did as he asked, willing the magic to leave my palm but only light two of the logs. A phantom touch raced across my skin.

I couldn't see, Krew's hand was still over my eyes.

"And now the sound barrier."

I took a shaky breath and I shook my head. "No."

He ran his thumb over my hand. "Yes. A sound barrier. You've seen them hundreds of times. Walked through dozens of them. You know exactly what they look like."

I pictured one in my head, but with thin strands of magic, not thick ones like I had seen Owen create. Just a small thin one.

Krew's fingers of his free hand ran through my hair. "The sound barrier. Go ahead."

I released the magic, still blind, wincing and hoping that the entire wing wasn't on fire and the sound barrier didn't break anything.

Krew lifted his hand off my eyes but settled it lower around my shoulder. "Look, love."

I opened my eyes to see the fire lit, the two logs exactly as I had wanted, and a thin sound barrier at the door. Nothing was broken. Nothing was burning.

"How do you feel?" he asked.

I didn't want to answer that.

"Say it out loud."

I sighed. "Still terrified."

"Okay, so we do it again," he said gently, and with a flick of his finger, the fire went out and the barrier fell.

"I could do this a hundred times and might still be terrified," I admitted, my voice still thick with emotion.

"I know, but go again."

Seeing there was no point in arguing, that he was just going to keep forcing me to do this over again, I moved to close my eyes again.

Krew squeezed my shoulder. "No, not this time. Keep your eyes open. See that you are in control."

What had Owen said? *You run your magic, your magic does not run you.* I took a deep breath and looked at the now extinguished fire. I thought again of just the two logs and how I wanted them to be started on fire. Within a minute, I had the fire burning and the barrier back at the door.

"Again," he whispered, brushing a kiss to my cheek.

I sighed.

On and on we went. And what had to be a dozen times later, he had me do both at the same time. Which I somehow managed to do without sending the whole castle into flames.

"Do you feel better?" Krew whispered in my ear.

"I don't know." I yawned. I was tired before we even left for the meadow, so now I was beyond tired. "Do you? You're the one forcing me to do this."

He moved my hair to gently massage my shoulders. "For now. But tomorrow you will have to do this again. And again. And again. Until these two things are so normal that you barely even have to think about it."

"Can I train with just Owen tomorrow morning?"

His forehead creased. "Jorah, I was never mad at you. Not for a moment. Not for what happened with Keir, none of it. I was only ever mad at myself."

I gave him a shrug. "Okay, but if tonight showed us anything, it's that my magic reacts strongly not only when I haven't used enough of it, but also with you around. I need to learn how to control it on my own. Without you there to help."

He brushed a kiss to my temple. "Whatever you need, love. But can I come toward the end?"

I stood, wiping my palms on my pants. "Also, learning how to wield a drop of magic in ten days was in the realm of possibility, but I'm not sure this is, Krew. And asking me to figure out how to be in total control of this much magic and then turn around and be around your father isn't fair."

"No, it's not," he agreed.

I walked toward the bed, kicking off my boots on the way. "Well, you might have to scheme my way out of the next ball at this rate. We need a backup plan."

CHAPTER 7

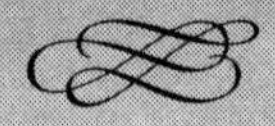

Owen had me moving a moderately sized fallen branch around in patterns with my magic. I had to keep a steady stream of magic coming from my hand, and it took more concentration than anything I'd tried before.

"Good. Now zig zag," Owen commanded.

I groaned, reaching up to wipe my sweaty forehead with my free hand. Between last night and this morning, I had used far more magic than ever before. I still feared my magic, the weight and power of it all. The fact that I never seemed to *not* feel it there waiting; not once had I felt it dip or lessen. But using it was at least becoming easier.

Minutes later, when Owen finally let me have a break, he tossed me a canteen for a drink of water.

"What else do you want to try?" Owen asked. "More breezes? A moving sound barrier?"

My eyes were on the lake, wondering what I could do to the lake with my magic to heal it.

Owen turned and looked over his shoulder at The Dead Lake. "We should probably try to not do anything too obvious today."

I glared at him. "You're the one pushing me to use my magic all week. Now I finally want to try something and you tell me no?"

Owen winced.

"What is the point in having all this damned magic if I cannot heal the forest?" I snapped, taking a step forward.

I called the magic to my palms, a trail of heat warming my veins as I did. I imagined the lake clear, the toxins gone, the water clean. And then I sent the magic out.

It raced along the ground before striking the lake water. There was a small ripple, slowly circling outward, but the lake stayed the same.

I look another step forward, instinct telling me I needed to be closer to the water, maybe even stand *in* the water.

As my first boot hit the water, Owen said from behind me, "What are you doing?"

I shrugged. "I don't know. I just felt like maybe I needed to stand in it for it to work."

"Your boots will be nasty."

I was already calling my magic back up. "If it fixes the lake, totally worth it."

I heard his snort just as I willed my magic out again, the same as last time but with more strands of thicker magic.

The ripple was much, much larger this time, but the lake remained black as night.

"Can I try it with more?" I asked.

I felt through the bond that Krew was coming closer, he must have been about to come join us.

"I don't know, can you?" Owen responded.

I called the magic into both palms. I focused on the water but kept my eyes open. I thought of multiple strands of thicker magic weaving their way through the water and healing it. Making it pure and clean again. Enough magic to cover every drop of the lake. And then I willed the magic into the water.

The magic poured out of me, as if glad to have an outlet, racing along the water and weaving throughout. As the magic dove beneath the surface to reach the bottom of the lake, the entire lake started to glow. I took a deep breath and focused in, that same instinct telling me to keep sending more magic, a constant stream until every drop was covered in my magic.

As soon as everything was covered, I stopped sending magic into the water and my magic burst outward taking me by surprise and almost making me fall. And following my wave of magic, a low wave of the tar looking water also rippled across the surface of the lake, slapping at my boots.

All that, and yet the lake remained black.

I spun back around toward Owen to find both Owen and Krew looking at me with concern etched on their faces. "What?"

Krew gave his head a shake. "I said you needed to use magic more and more often. I didn't mean you needed to bring yourself to the brink of exhaustion every day."

Owen mumbled to Krew, "Her nose isn't bleeding."

I brought my magic to a palm, making sure it was still there and ready. It immediately warmed me, and then I shoved it back down. "That wasn't the brink of exhaustion, I don't think."

"That was a lot of magic," Krew commented.

I gave him a shrug. "So maybe I will not accidentally injure anyone today with my magic?"

He gave his head a shake. "No. You will practice fires and sound barriers today numerous times and that will never be an issue again."

He came toward the edge of the water and offered me a hand, helping me step out of the lake.

"Is it me or is the lake not as thick?" Owen's forehead was crinkled as he looked in our direction.

Krew grabbed a nearby stick and stuck it in the water, trying to stir the water at the edge with the stick. "I think it might be a little."

I looked at the lake and fought off a smile. I was still terrified of magic. Of what I could do. But this? This was a safe area I was willing to repeatedly use my magic if it meant that eventually I could fix the lake.

* * *

I WOKE THE NEXT MORNING, stretching and looking to my hands. They were clear. I'd used so much magic the previous day between the lake and all the fire and sound barriers Krew had forced me to do throughout the day, and again that night at practice with Krew and Keir, that I had been granted one morning to sleep in without heading out to use my magic before the king was up.

Owen and Krew were nowhere in sight, but I knew they were around somewhere.

Judging by the direction I felt Krew down the bond, he was likely in the throne room. Knowing they'd demand I start the fire and put up a sound barrier at least once now that I was awake, I did both of those things with only slight terror. Wouldn't it be my luck the one time they were not in the room with me for this, I lit the castle on fire?

But in the fireplace, only the two logs burned. The silver sound barrier stood steady at the door.

Good morning, love.

Good morning, Krew.

Did you start the fire?

Yes.

Sound barrier at the door?

Yes.

I'm with Father and Keir. We have to take him to see your trees. I'll be back hopefully within an hour. Owen can call for your breakfast when you are ready.

Thank you.

I decided I should shower first as Silvia would come by later and if I could charm her, maybe even braid my hair in my favorite way.

As I stepped out of the shower and brushed my teeth, I thought I might try to read a little while I waited for Krew. These last few days I had done so very little for myself. It'd been too . . . chaotic. I'd either been stressing or sleeping and that was about it.

Heading into the closet which housed all of my clothes and also Krew's, and had long before we ever wed, I remembered how comfortable Krew's shirt had been to wear that first morning my magic had settled.

Knowing it wasn't likely I'd be leaving Krew's wing today except for maybe a quick forest trip, I grabbed a black shirt and threw it on, this time with undergarments, of course. I was feeling the need to be cozy, not risqué.

For now, I left my hair around my shoulders to air dry.

I drank my tea and read while eating a muffin Owen brought in, content to just be. My magic was still there, but the pull of it was not so consuming that I couldn't concentrate on my book. Owen had to go talk to some other guards, so I was alone, alone with my book. A lovely place to be.

After about an hour, I decided I should put out the fire and sound barrier and do one again. I didn't know if Owen and Krew were right about how often I needed to use my magic, but I just knew I never wanted what happened with Keir to happen again. So if that meant I needed to do small things like this often, I would have to learn to accept it. I didn't have to like it. I just had to do it.

I called my magic up and did just that. I put out the fire, took out the sound barrier and then started it all again. Feeling warmed from my magic, I took a break from my spot at the couch to look out the balcony. Feeling that Krew was already back at the castle from his trip to the forest with his father, and deciding I was already warm enough from my magic, I threw on my slippers and went out to the veranda.

Though there had been a light dusting of snow last night, the days were ever so slowly warming up. A tease of spring on the horizon. I thought of what the king must be thinking about the trees I'd turned green. Looking at the forest beneath me, which looked like it'd been sprinkled in powdered sugar like a pastry, I imagined what the entire forest would look like in spring if it all weren't dead. Not just two trees, but all of it. It'd be breathtaking.

I only hoped if I was forced to carry this much magic and power, I had it in me to do this. To fix the forest. If I had to feel this constant fear, maybe something good could still come from it.

I turned my face toward the sun and took some deep breaths. Life was still beautiful. Chaotic. Terrifying. But beautiful. And being bonded to Krew was everything I'd hoped for and more. I might resent the magic, or the amount of magic, but I still wouldn't have changed it.

I let my sound barrier around Krew's room fall as Owen and Krew arrived, wanting to hear their voices if they went in the other sitting room. Knowing one or both of them was going to command me to eventually put it back up, and tired of both of them bossing me around all the time, I did it without prompting, sending my magic along the floor to do just that, this time encompassing all of Krew's wing.

Krew and Owen were talking about whether or not the king bought their story about the trees. Apparently, news of the trees turning green had brought a bunch of people to the forest to see them, and they were debating whether it was safe to train at the forest that night or if we should go elsewhere. I listened but kept taking in the scenery. Imagining the day I could stand here overlooking a green and healthy forest, listening to birds chirp.

Krew was saying something and then trailed off mid-sentence. I turned over my shoulder to see what the issue was, to find him standing there at the foot of the bed gawking at me. Even in just his eyes, in the way those grayish blues met mine, I knew the intensity of how he felt toward me. And I wondered how I hadn't noticed it long before I did.

Owen peeked his head around the corner to look at me. "Are you talking to him in his head again?"

I shook my head, turning to face them. "Actually no."

Krew shoved Owen away like I was dressed indecently.

I snickered as I made my way over to the two of them, sliding out of my slippers once inside the door. "It's not like he hasn't seen me in far worse, Krew. I'm fully covered."

"That may be, but not for long."

I rolled my eyes as Owen started backing away for the main door. "Right. I'll just disappear now. We can finish this later."

Just to be a brat, he broke my sound barrier with his magic as he went, the door clicking behind him.

Krew opened his mouth to say something, but again not wanting to hear anyone boss me around for at least another few hours, I sent the sound barrier right back. That had likely been Owen's reason for breaking it to begin with, to force me to do it again.

Krew grinned at me and used his own magic to shut the veranda doors behind me. "I was only going to say that I could get used to this."

"Me in your shirt?" I shrugged. "I knew I wasn't leaving this room today anyway, so I figured why not be comfortable."

He crossed the space between us in two strides. "That too. I meant because there you were looking at the forest, stunning me in my own shirt, yes, but also happy. I felt that you were *happy*. I haven't felt that from you all week."

"Yes, well we've had quite the week, haven't we, husband?"

His lips raced to meet mine. He was an artist, pushing and pulling at my skin as he brought me closer and kissed me hard.

"Krew," I gasped, trying to pull away. "It is the middle of the day, Silvia might come in at any moment."

He was not to be deterred though. "Owen's handled far worse. He'll handle it."

CHAPTER 8

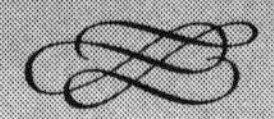

This was the first trial. The second would be tomorrow when I was to play cards with Renna, Molly, and Gwen and try my damndest to not give away that I had magic. Not that any of them would truly care, so it was a safe trial. But for now, I was practicing in the dead of night again with Krew, Keir, and Owen.

"Okay, I have an idea for the last part of tonight," Owen offered.

Keir and Krew had practiced earlier, Owen and I showing up later. And to everyone's confusion, Krew still seemed to have all but a drop or two of his magic. We didn't know if it had to do with the soul bonding or if Krew's magic would just be gone some morning or what.

I also wasn't sure when Owen was sleeping this week, but it was safe to say all of our schedules were thoroughly messed up.

I sighed. "Judging by the look on your face, I already hate it."

Owen crossed his arms. "You've gotten much better at moving objects. And much better about using magic more often. Now I need you to work on using magic at or near people."

I didn't even need to think about my answer. "No."

"Jorah," Owen began.

"No."

He cocked his head in my direction. "Listen, what happened with Keir happened because you were feeling protective over Krew, likely because of your bond, and hadn't used enough magic since acquiring it. This is going to be a controlled environment."

"I almost killed Keir," I reminded him.

Keir shook his head. "Nah. It'd take much more to kill me, honey."

I rolled my eyes. "Okay, I inadvertently *attempted* to kill Keir."

Owen swiped at the air. "Whatever. I just want you to put up one of those barriers again. Like you had around Krew. And I want to test it to see how strong it is. Though the concept is not new, that one was strong enough that I'm wondering if you put a steady stream into it, if you could keep another Enchanted from shattering it." He paused. "The other night it was just easier to have you take it down, since you were the one who cast the barrier. But tonight, I want you to focus on keeping it up, strengthening it. As long as you can."

I took a deep breath. If I was strong enough to will it there and will it to stay, it could give us a huge advantage with the king. No one needed to say it out loud, but we all knew it. If I was as strong as they thought I was, this could be helpful. "Fine. But no one will be in said barrier."

Owen shook his head. "Nope. Krew will be."

My eyes tried to leave my head. "Have you lost your mind? My magic went insane last time. It's like it still recognizes him or something."

Krew put a hand at my lower back while Owen and I continued to argue.

Owen tapped his chin. "But it is important you use magic around people and on people, Jorah. It'll help you learn to trust it. I don't think you fear it quite on the level as you did when you chucked Keir across the meadow, but I don't think you really trust it yet either."

He was right, but I wasn't about to tell him so.

"Okay, fine." Owen put a finger in the air. "I'll go in the barrier. Krew can coach you through it, and Keir can try a variety of things to take it down. Normally they are pretty easy to break through, so I don't know if the other night was a fluke of your magic or your Iron Will or what."

I tipped my head back to look at the night sky. I'd tried the lake again this morning, and not even the viscosity of the lake had changed this time. It was safe to say it was going to take a substantial amount of magic to fix the lake, if magic even could. "I would like to sleep before dawn tonight, so let's get to it."

Owen bowed. "Yes, Your Highness."

I rolled my eyes.

As soon as he got to the middle of the meadow, I called my magic up. I wasn't even mad about that part because the night breeze kept clawing at me, sending shivers along my neck. The warm hum of my magic was a welcome respite to the chill.

I took a step forward. I'd been working with Owen on releasing magic through my palm and not my fingers, so I did that, sending the magic along the ground, and then to encase Owen just like it had with Krew, in a dome shape around him.

"Ready for Keir to try to shatter it?" Krew asked. "You might want to send a steady stream of magic on it, keeping in mind that you are strengthening it."

"Let me try to break it first?" Keir asked. "I want to know how strong this thing is."

I gestured with a hand. "Have at. Bonus points if you knock Owen on his ass."

"I heard that!" Owen hollered. "You didn't make this thing soundproof."

I looked back to Krew. "Oops."

Keir's magic took to the sky. It wrapped around my magic and looked as if it were trying to squeeze it, but then all the blue magic just disappeared.

"Hmm," Keir muttered to himself. "One more time, hang on."

This time more of Keir's magic traveled along the ground and then gathered at the top of the dome, striking it through the middle. The dome shattered, a silver flash the only indication it was gone.

Keir gave Krew a look. "I had to use quite a bit of magic to do that. And she wasn't sending more."

Krew's eyes were on me. "Can you put it back up and then try to steadily strengthen it while Keir goes again?"

I gave him a shrug. "I can try."

Owen sat down, propping a foot up to hold his elbow. "I'll just be over here. In a bubble."

With one hand sending magic to form the barrier, I used the other hand and sent a sound barrier, muting Owen's comments for this round.

Krew chuckled next to me.

And then I kept a slow stream of magic heading at the dome. I visualized strengthening it as if surrounding it with a brick wall. My magic weaved around and around the barrier, constantly in motion. Soon the magic was so thick, it was getting hard to see Owen within.

"He can still breathe and stuff in there, right?" I asked Krew while keeping my eyes on the dome, focusing on where I was sending my magic.

I could hear the amusement in Krew's tone. "Yes."

"Ready, Jorah?" Keir asked. "If what I tried last time doesn't work, I'm going to throw a whole bunch of stuff at it, just like I do when training with Krew."

"I guess?"

That must have been good enough for him because more blue

magic took to the night, racing in to wrap around my magic. He sent enough that it looked like he was trying to squeeze the dome and also break it at the same time. Neither happened, though I did seem to feel the pull to send even more magic to defend the advance.

"Easy, love." Krew wasn't touching me but was only inches from me, so his voice was almost a whisper while he encouraged me. "Keep it steady."

Keir said to no one in particular, "Well this is just getting embarrassing now." And then he was moving, throwing balls of magic, trying to send a breeze hard enough to move the dome, and throwing what looked like a massive chain of magic at the dome.

Each time he switched to do something, I was convinced the dome would shatter, but it held on.

Still sending a slow stream of magic with one hand, I wiped at my forehead with the other. Between the magic I had used on the lake earlier, and the seven hundred times I'd started and put out the fire today, I was feeling more exhausted than usual. Sure enough, my hand came back wet. I was sweating, trying to focus on the dome and keep it strong.

Keir was now hailing down on the dome with his magic, his blue attacking my silver at every angle. And then in a quick move, what looked like a dagger made out of magic struck through the layers of the dome. Once it broke through, the whole thing shattered.

Owen stood up and clapped. "Well done!"

I was fighting off the urge to grab my knees. I looked over at Keir, who was also breathing heavily. Granted he had just practiced with Krew, but still. At least I wasn't alone in being winded.

"That was impressive," Keir offered.

"I didn't do anything extra? Like turn the grass green or something?" I asked hesitantly.

Krew placed his hand on my back. "No. Or I don't think so anyway. Time will tell."

Owen was walking over. "We should go again except this time have Krew add his own magic. And then see what happens."

Krew shook his head. "Maybe tomorrow we can practice more. Jorah is already sweating. You know she already used a lot on the lake this morning."

"Fine. Ruin my fun," Owen whined.

I wiped my hands along my pants. "And by fun, you mean strategizing how to best use my magic?"

Owen held up his fingers with a short gap between them. "Maybe a little."

By the time my head hit the pillow, I was again utterly exhausted. I was beginning to not fear my magic as much, as long as I could use it sporadically throughout the day. But I still didn't trust it. I had no idea how to.

I wasn't sure if I ever would.

* * *

Owen nudged me with an elbow as we neared our old practice room. He put up a small traveling sound barrier around us. "You good?"

I took a deep breath and made sure my magic was pushed down. "Yes. I just hope Krew stays out of my head for the next few hours like we all agreed."

"Remember, this is your practice run. If you mess up, it's just with your friends, so we should be fine."

I gave him a nod. "I know. Though I'd prefer for Gwen to not know. Not sure I totally trust her not to run to the disloyal with it. But not inviting her also felt rude."

Owen opened the door to the room. "Yes, well, eventually the disloyal are going to find out. Hopefully it is on your terms and not hers, though."

We were the first ones there, purposefully having arrived early. As soon as he shut the door behind us, I used my magic to move the massive table over for us to play at. I also lit the fire. And then moved the chairs too.

Owen turned to me, eyebrows up.

"What?"

He tilted his head to the side. "You used your magic. Without prompting."

I pinned him with a glare. "Only because I am so sick of you and Krew demanding me to use my magic all the time. It's nauseating how often I am bossed around. I just cannot stomach it anymore."

Owen's eyes went to the window a moment as he thought on that.

I sighed. "Look, I know you want it to be simple and easy for me to trust my magic. I know you want it to happen the quicker the better. But I don't trust it. I threw a person at a tree as if they were a mere doll. I snapped an entire bathtub in half. So no, I do not trust it. Not even a little. I might not fear it as much as I did at first, but that doesn't mean I'm there yet."

Owen threw an arm around my shoulder. "We have time, Jorah. It's okay. You're powerful as hell. It's okay not to know what to do with that. Particularly when you never asked for it to begin with."

As I pulled back, I told him the truth, wanting both he and Krew to get it through their thick heads. "We don't have enough time. There is a ball in four days."

I heard the door creak open, and instinct had me making sure all traces of my magic were gone.

Fortunately, it was only Renna anyway.

"Hey."

She grinned and headed right over to the table. "Hey, Jorah. Ready for a good old fashioned butt whooping?"

I shrugged. "We'll see."

We grabbed our seats and I began shuffling the cards. The feel of the cards in my hand gave me a weird sense of peace. That though so very much had changed in the last few weeks, some things would always be the same. I was still Jorah. I still knew how to play cards. And trash talk.

We heard Molly before we saw her, jokingly telling her guard today was the day she would finally win.

"Bold of you to assume that already," Renna teased.

"Bold of you to doubt your oldest friend," Molly fired back while placing her hand over her heart. "I am wounded."

She sat down on the other side of me. "How are you two today?"

I saw how genuinely happy Molly seemed these days and I wondered how things with Keir were going. I almost wanted to ask Keir. Almost. But if things were going well, I was just going to stay out of it.

"I'm tired, but good," I offered.

"I am bored, Molls. Bored out of my mind," Renna provided.

"We should go for a walk in the gardens soon," Molly supplied. "It's been my new thing. Reading and walking in the gardens. Because the two of you are too preoccupied with a certain prince."

Renna choked on a laugh, and I knew she had to be thinking of the fact that Krew and I were, in fact, now married. Meanwhile I just felt bad Molly didn't know.

"Sorry I'm late!"

We all turned to see Gwen coming in.

"You aren't," I offered. "Only boasts and empty promises are being made."

Gwen laughed. "I'd rather win first and boast later."

Now that I believed. She was the youngest woman at the table, but she'd never been afraid to ask the hard questions or go after what she wanted. Whether that was because she was a disloyal or because that was just her personality, I didn't rightly know.

I didn't hate Gwen, nor was I even remotely still mad at her for how everything played out while I was in Keir's Assemblage. I just didn't know if I could ever fully trust her. She was ambitious in a way which made me wonder when it came down to it if she would choose those ambitions over protecting her own friends. If she would use anything and everything to her advantage.

"The next ball is going to have another play," Molly provided a few turns in. "I was kind of hoping for the acrobats again."

"Keir said there are plans in the works for a tour of the kingdom with the Assemblages too," Gwen offered. "Won't it be fun to travel to all the levels of the kingdom?"

I exchanged a look with Renna. Were they just being chatty and sharing information to be nice? Or was each sharing a piece of information they had in an effort to show how much they knew? How close to Keir they were?

Women were a weird species. I was one and even I wasn't quite sure I had us figured out.

I hadn't known either of the things they mentioned, but with all the discussions we'd been having the past few days about the trees I healed in the forest, I wasn't mad. And then Silvia had been fitting my gown for the ball that I may or may not go to depending on my control over my magic.

There had just been a lot going on.

After Molly's turn, she whispered, "Have you seen the king's mistress?"

I shook my head.

"I only saw her from afar, but she looked . . . *young.* Our age."

I tried not to gag. "Well that's . . . ." I decided it was best I just not finish that.

Molly wrinkled her nose. "Wouldn't it be just *odd* if the princes' new stepmother was the same age or younger than they were?"

I ran a hand down my face after taking my turn. "That's disturbing. We need a new topic."

Renna kicked me under the table as if to ask if I was good with my magic. I sent her a look saying that I was fine. A bit disgusted, considering we were also discussing a potential future mother-in-law of mine, but fine.

Tea and snacks were brought in while we continued to play, well into the hours of the afternoon. It was a long and close game, but the rhythm and mind-numb of a decent card game was a welcome change to the worries as of late.

The card game finally ended, and I had barely snuck away the winner. But even that felt good. The focus and clarity to win a game of cards without panicking about my magic.

"Renna, would you rather the Assemblages run until summer or end soon?" Gwen asked. We were asking each other "would you rather" questions, a game Molly had started us on since none of us had been in a hurry to leave.

I tried not to smirk because I already knew her answer. "Well that's an easy one. End soon. The sooner the better."

It was Renna's turn next. "Jorah, would you rather go to a ball or a royal family dinner?"

"Umm, I'll just go with no? Can I choose neither?"

Molly laughed. "No. You have to pick."

I sighed. "I guess a dinner, but only because there aren't all those extra watchful eyes whispering about how I could possibly still be here because I'm from Nerede."

Gwen nodded from across the table. "I'm with you there."

Molly added, "The king calling you 'Jorah of Nerede' like it's your title definitely does not help matters."

It was my turn to think of a question next. So far I'd done all desserts and I didn't see a reason to veer from that. "Hmm. Gwen. Chocolate truffles or chocolate cheesecake?"

"Gah!" Gwen moved her head back and forth from one shoulder to the other. "Truffles. If I have to pick, but only because they are easier smuggled."

I laughed. "Gwen! You aren't supposed to steal them."

She glared at me. "Don't even try to tell me you haven't at least thought about it."

My shrug apparently showed my guilt on the matter.

"Jorah," Molly began. "Would you rather have a crown, or would you rather heal the forest?"

I grinned. "The forest."

Renna added, "I got to see the trees you healed, by the way. News of your work is traveling fast."

Gwen asked quietly, "It's really your tears?"

It wasn't entirely a lie, but I still felt bad telling her, "Krew makes me cry and then I randomly heal things. Flowers happened the first time. It has to do with my Iron Will, but we aren't sure exactly how. I still don't quite believe it all myself. And now I'm the king's blood bank while he works to figure it out."

Gwen gave me a pitied look. "So even if you were to go home, you are likely not going home?"

I gave her a shrug. "I imagine not."

Molly clapped her hands gently. "We got way off topic. Okay, whose turn is it? Gwen's?"

Gwen gave her head a shake. "Right. Sorry." She paused. "Molly, would you rather have a crown or more magic?"

I sucked in my breath. Though it was true the questions had been getting more serious, that had been somewhat rude. "Gwen."

She shrugged. "It's no more serious than what she asked you."

Molly looked down at her teacup. "Except that when I asked Jorah her question, I already knew her answer because I know her that well."

An awkward silence fell on the table as Molly's point struck home.

"Well?" Gwen asked softly. "Are you not going to answer it? It's a valid concern."

Molly stood, the tears very obviously welling in her eyes. "No, because if you knew me, truly knew me, you'd know it's not a valid concern because I want *neither*. If you truly knew who I was, you'd know I just want to find the love of my life. That's simply it." And then she stood abruptly, turning toward me and Renna. "Thank you for having me."

As soon as she was gone, Renna turned on Gwen. "Why did you even have to go there, Gwen? It screams of jealousy."

Gwen shook her head, her cheeks going pink. "It's a valid concern. I just don't think she's right for Keir at all!"

I pushed my magic down, knowing the emotions in the room could be a cause for it to flare. "Was anyone other than yourself ever good enough for Keir in your opinion?" I asked gently. Seeing she got even more red in her face, I added, "And I'm not harboring any judgement or ill will against you because of things with Keir. I am happy with Krew."

Gwen stood, blinking hard as if fighting off tears of her own. "I do think I am best for Keir. Because I know how I feel about him, okay?"

Renna gave her a nod. "Okay, that's fine, honey. Let's just try not to tear others down in order to get what we want, all right?" she paused. "At the end of the day, it's not your decision. It's Keir's. And that might be horrible, but it doesn't make it any less of a truth. You don't get to decide for him. He has to choose you back."

Gwen stepped back, her chair almost tipping over behind her. "I don't know how to do this, okay? Jorah says she loves Krew right in front of you, Renna, and you act like it doesn't bother you. If Molly said that about Keir in front of me, I'd probably burst into tears. I don't know how to do this. I don't know how to be friends with her when she's trying to take him away from me!"

Renna and I looked at each other, not knowing what to say. Part of me wanted to just tell her everything. That Renna and I had never been in competition with each other. Would never be. "Gwen."

"I'll just go," she said, wiping at her eyes as she left.

Renna slumped back in her chair. "It had been such a fun afternoon until the end there."

I did the same. "I agree."

"You know what being in Keir's Assemblage was like. Do you think he will take those two down to the end?" she asked quietly.

I let out a sigh. "I don't know. I don't talk to Keir about it because we have an amicable sort of peace going on currently and I don't want to mess with it. But for both their sakes, I hope the Assemblages are done soon."

With everything else going on, Krew and I secretly getting married and bonded, and the well of power I now had in becoming one of the most powerful Enchanted in Wylan, I had almost forgotten about the Assemblages in recent days. While Krew's Assemblage might be only a farce to keep up appearances, Keir's was still very much in the air. Who he chose could very well become the next queen.

I wanted him to find the happiness Krew and I found, but I also selfishly hoped he chose wisely.

For all of us.

CHAPTER 9

"Tiny!"

I missed that never-quiet voice and the big man who carried it. I'd learned the hard way the king didn't like the friends I kept. After he sent a message by starting a fire in the kitchen, I'd done my best over the last few months to stay away from the kitchen and the kitchen staff.

But every once in a while, like today on our way back in from feeding my friend of the wolf variety, Rafe, I'd slow down just to observe the hustle and bustle.

"Chef," I greeted back. "How are things?"

"Well," Maurice rubbed his chin, "but George will not stop moaning about how he misses your cookies."

My eyebrows shot up. "Still? But I taught you the way."

He swatted the air and leaned in to say quietly, "You and I both know I don't make them as well as you do."

"Nor as often. I will have to make a batch sometime soon and send them down," I offered.

Tilly, the baker, looked at me over her shoulder, "Or you could just make them here."

I let out a long sigh. "I could, but I also cannot."

"Because?" Maurice baited, then more quietly he added, "I told you not to worry about us."

"You know why, Maurice." I paused. "But for what it is worth, I miss all of you too."

"Stay safe," Jakob said with a smile as he stirred something on the stove. I hadn't even realized he had been listening. Then again, the kitchen staff was always listening.

I gave him a smile. "You all, too!"

Owen and I took the secret passage back up to Krew's wing, as we had since the bonding, just in case we should run into anyone unexpectedly.

"We could maybe try to get up early and you could spend some time with them before breakfast," Owen offered quietly.

I again heaved a sigh. "I'd love to, but I don't wish to risk it. I miss them, but it's not worth it. I want them safe."

Owen was quiet for a set of stairs while I wrapped my coat tighter, the narrow hallways always feeling so blasted cold.

"I feel as if you have become even more isolated since the bonding," Owen offered.

I shrugged. "That's likely true, but at least I understand *why* I am more isolated."

Owen gave his head a shake. "Having magic was never supposed to make you even more isolated, part of the reason Krew did it was to give you the confidence that you are safe."

"Am I though?" I paused. "I know you want me to trust it, I get it Owen. But you also need to accept that it might be years until I do. Or never. It might be never."

Owen stopped and turned toward me. "Okay. I get it. I just want to fix it and I don't know how."

I gave him a shrug. "You can't. You just can't."

* * *

THAT AFTERNOON Krew asked me to sit in on a meeting with Keir, Renna, and Owen. Krew was still meeting with The Six regularly, but I was trying to stay away for now. It was one thing keeping my magic down while playing a harmless game of cards with my friends, it would be a whole other thing to keep my magic calm while scheming to take down the king. In a group of people who didn't all know I had magic.

Renna was the last to arrive. As soon as she came in the door, for what was likely presented as a date with Krew, Owen put up the sound barrier at the door.

Renna plopped down in the seat at the oval table next to me, and immediately blurted out, "Tell her or I will."

I turned toward her. "Tell me what?"

Krew closed his eyes. "Dammit, Renna. It's not like we were keeping it from her intentionally. What do you think we are all here for?"

Renna narrowed her eyes at him. "I almost had to lie yesterday, and I will not do it again. Yes, she's struggling under the weight of all that magic, but she should know. She should've known all of it when we first told her about this."

I calmed my magic and switched my attention to Krew. "Tell me what? About the ring?"

Krew gave a nod. "Yes. The plan to get father's ring is happening tonight, Jorah."

Keir let out a sigh. "Annnd it's Nara."

My forehead creased. "What's Nara?"

Keir's eyes were on mine as he said, "She is the king's new mistress."

It was a good thing I was already sitting down, or I was sure I would have fallen over. "You mean to tell me quiet and kind Nara is the king's new mistress?" Then horror dawned on me as the blood fled from my face. "Willingly or unwillingly?"

Renna grabbed my wrist and squeezed. "Willingly."

Nara. Nara who was my age. Who had just been in Keir's Assemblage? Who had likely kissed Keir? She was now sleeping with the king? The king who hated the lower levels?

I guess the king took that whole property of the crown bit seriously.

Krew brought a cup of steaming tea over to me and sat down next to me. "She is not a disloyal either, nor does she even know about the disloyal at this point, which is why we thought it might be better that way."

I shook my head, still not understanding all of this. Nara. The king's mistress? Granted she was gorgeous, but it just seemed so out of nowhere.

Renna spun toward me. "She wanted out of Rallis, Jorah. The king offered to give her lodging here in exchange for . . . *her companionship.*"

I swallowed hard. "I think I'm going to vomit."

She gave me a nod. "I will with you. But Nara wasn't after a crown, as much as she was after a more comfortable living, so she agreed to the king's terms."

I gave my head a shake. "But he's more than twice her age!"

Keir's tone matched the disgust of my own. "We know."

"The princes found out about it and tried to remove her, thinking she had not been willing," Renna continued. "But she told them to leave her alone. That she had no desire to go back to Rallis."

I thought back to all the card playing. How cheerful and happy Nara always was. Had it been because she was in the castle? Living out a dream of becoming a princess, and she had wanted to continue doing that, even if it meant some sacrifice on her part? "Nara is smart though, definitely smart enough to know better."

Renna tilted her head. "Yes, I agree. But you also know that the king can be charming and persuasive if he wants to be."

I rubbed a hand across my forehead, shocked my magic had

stayed hidden beneath my skin for this. This was all extremely *disturbing*.

"So then I convinced her to try to get the ring," Keir provided. "I was honest to an extent. I told her we were worried that it may hold part or all of our mother's magic, and that we needed to get the ring away from him in order to see."

I held my hands out in a gesture. "So the king is charming her, and she's falling for it, but you think she will just take the ring and not turn around and tell him? Not use it against you?"

Krew's eyes met mine. "It is a risk. A huge risk. Nara was friends with the two of you on at least some level, so we thought she was at least halfway trustworthy. And we also thought it best to use someone who didn't have information of the disloyal that could be found out. We figured if she blabbed to our father, at least it would only be about the plan for the ring, not all the other plans."

I rested my head on my hands. "This is madness. I mean, I love Nara. Consider her a friend . . ."

Renna finished for me, "But don't trust her enough to send her into the king's bed?"

I gave her a nod. "Nor do I hate her enough to wish that upon her, willing or not." I still just could not wrap my head around how she could have agreed to what the king offered her. But being from Rallis, she had always been on the cusp of being in the upper levels. The king needed someone to warm his bed and she was offered the chance to skip Savaryn and go straight to the top of the kingdom. It had evidently been an offer too tempting for her.

I calmed my magic and moved to pinch the bridge of my nose. "And this master plan for the ring is revolving around the fact that you think Nara will be more loyal to the two of you than the man who just offered her everything she apparently wanted?"

Keir winced. "More or less. But to be fair, she and I had been good friends. She knew I struggled under the weight of my father's decisions."

Krew added, "So we went ahead with this plan working off the assumption that she's a good enough person to do the right thing."

I wanted to bang my head against the table slowly. This was one of the more reckless plans Krew had ever developed. And I knew why they were doing it. They wanted to figure out which object held their mother's power. Because once we knew that, we could level the playing field. And when the field was even, Krew wouldn't have to give up his life in order to kill his father. He'd be able to do it outright.

Particularly since it seemed he was just as strong as ever.

My eyes went to Krew's. *I know why you want to do this, but I do not like this plan.*

I know, love. We just felt it still worth the risk. I didn't want to tell you until I knew for sure it was happening. And Keir and I decided the afternoon of the day of our bonding. I was a bit distracted that day, but I should've told you anyway. I'm sorry.

"They're doing it again," Owen deadpanned.

"Doing what?" Renna asked.

"Talking without words," Owen provided.

Keir's eyes went big as they bounced between us. "Really?"

Krew gave him a nod. "Yes. And Jorah does not like the plan."

"I agree with her. Also that is creepy," Renna laughed, looking between us. "What if he flirts with you when you are talking to someone else?"

Tempting.

I rolled my eyes. "Then I will do my best to ignore it?"

Or you could whisk me away to a secluded corner, unable to deny me for a moment longer.

I glared at Krew. "Enough. Let's get back to this obnoxiously flawed plan."

The rest of them were just sitting there.

I put my hands out in a gesture. "What? You all really think this idea is going to work perfectly? Not considering one of the seven thousand different ways it could go awry?"

"No," Keir said quietly. "We are all just wondering about the bond but don't want to pry."

Renna smiled at me. "What the two of you have is incredibly rare and intimate."

I never considered that. Of course they'd be curious. I would be too in their positions. Most days I was too busy trying to figure out how to control my magic that I tended to forget that what Krew and I had was not the norm. Far from it.

Krew took my hand and gave it a squeeze. "Well, I felt her stronger emotions even before we were bonded. I think it had more to do with where I was at with my own feelings than hers. Since she still loathed me at that point."

"How soon did you begin to feel her emotions?" Keir asked him.

Krew gave him a look. "You don't want to know the honest answer to that."

Keir cocked his head but didn't appear bothered, just thoughtful. "Fair enough."

There was only a brief awkward pause before Renna's voice ended it. "Jo and I are only heart bound, of course, and we cannot speak telepathically, but I can sometimes feel her emotions too. The extreme ones. She doesn't have to tell me how she feels, I just know. So I get it."

Krew added, "As soon as we were bonded, as odd as it may sound, it's like there became a space in my head that is no longer my own. It's not like the space she takes up when I have thoughts of her, rather it's like there is an actual place in my head which is just *ours*. It's a fluid sort of space. The best way I can explain it is an invisible tether giving me an immediate way to access her and her emotions. I don't have to *see* her to make sure she's safe, she's always with me instead. If something were to happen, I'd immediately know."

Though it was all new, it didn't feel all that weird either. Maybe it was because Krew and I had a connection for a long time before we were ever bonded, I wasn't sure. But I did feel bad that Renna and Jo couldn't also communicate telepathically. I didn't for a second believe that Krew's and my relationship was somehow stronger or more special than theirs. There had to be a better explanation than that. Maybe it was just the amount of magic he gave me that had somehow triggered the soul bonding instead of the heart bonding.

Krew added, "And through our bond, I can feel the direction she is in. If I really focus, I can figure out the specifics. But it doesn't take much work to know if she's in the forest or in the castle or training with Owen."

Renna tipped her head to the side. "Impressive."

Owen gave a nod in agreement. "And the talking. Is there a distance it won't work?"

Krew gave a shrug. "Your guess is as good as mine."

"Great, more experiments for us to try for Owen," I groaned.

Renna stood to grab a drink. "And we still have no idea why Krew didn't seem to lose any of his magic?" She reached for the whiskey bottle and helped herself to a small glass of it.

Krew gave his head a shake. "No."

I knew he'd gone to John Nottle, the same sage who had married us, and asked why his magic had not seemed to lessen at all. John was just as confused as we were, though he wondered if Krew's selfless motives were at play.

Each day we all kind of just waited around for Krew's magic to vanish or slowly lessen. And each day Krew woke up the same. As if he'd given me only a drop or a few drops.

Meanwhile I was living proof that he'd given me much more than a drop. I wasn't just Enchanted; I was strongly Enchanted.

I sighed, drawing Owen's attention to me. "Stop sighing, Jorah."

"I just want to ask about the plan tonight, but also do not know if I even want to know," I admitted.

Renna sat back down beside me, setting a glass that matched her own next to me. "Here, you might need something stronger than the tea for this."

I smirked. I hated the taste of whiskey, but I appreciated the gesture. "Thanks, Renna."

Krew launched into explaining all of it, leaving no details out. Evidently, Nara and the king liked to partake in alcohol before their . . . *festivities*. So she was going to make sure he was good and drunk, passed out completely, and then she'd pull the ring off. If she could. They had a backup plan which involved a bath, but I put up a hand and told Krew to explain it to me if we needed it.

It was all still so very disgusting to me.

Nara often stayed the entire night with the king, so they had a secret pouch in the lining of her robe. If he woke up and immediately noticed the ring was gone, he could get angry, but he wouldn't be able to find it. Neither on her or anywhere else in his bedroom. Nara would ensure that it appeared she was as drunk as he was, that way her confusion about it was all the more believable.

But rather than Nara getting caught by suspiciously delivering the ring to either of the princes afterward, they had a drop off location set up. She'd never be seen so much as speaking with either prince.

I rubbed my forehead again. "So let's be irrationally optimistic and say that this little plan works. Nara gets the ring, and the ring is in fact the object holding your mother's magic . . ." I tried to find the proper words to express what I was thinking. "What will you do when the king goes on a rampage trying to find it to get it back? We have a ball coming up quickly. Not to mention he might hurt Nara and blame her if only because she is the nearest scapegoat."

Krew's voice was laced in determination. "We have another ongoing disloyal hunt in the works which will get the king in the throne room and away from Nara tomorrow morning. As for the ring, we will get that ring out of Kavan Keep and away from the king for as long as it takes."

As long as it took . . .

To kill him.

CHAPTER 10

I was convinced the magic had turned me fully nocturnal. I stayed up until almost dawn most nights with the princes. Whether it was practicing my barriers or using my magic in other ways. I used enough at night now that I was allowed to sleep in for the mornings. Owen needed sleep too, after all.

But not this morning. There would be no sleeping until lunch today. Not when I was waiting to find out if Nara was successful or not. And knowing what she'd had to do, that she'd had to get the king drunk and likely slept with him too, it made me queasy just thinking about it.

I'd barely slept.

Worst case scenario, the king killed Nara on the spot. Best case scenario, we got the ring. But even if they managed to pull this off successfully and get the ring, there was still no guarantee it was the object which even held the queen's magic.

Short of stripping the king down to naked and removing all jewels except the familial kind, there was no way for us to really know what object it was. Enter Nara onto the scene. To do exactly that.

With a sigh, I threw the covers back and got out of bed. This was useless. I wasn't sleeping until I knew whether Nara was okay. The sun had barely lit the sky a purple color, so she should be waking up soon.

I almost wondered if it would have been better to have her steal the ring and then just disappear. But then again, Nara would not have agreed to that because she preferred to not leave the castle at all.

I turned the shower water almost as hot as it could go and let it pour over me. Krew had still been asleep when I got up. I didn't wish to wake him, but I also didn't care that much if I did. It was his reckless plan which was waking me in the first place. That might be petty, but at this early in the morning, I didn't really care.

With a deep breath, feeling my magic churn under my skin, I released the magic to turn the droplets to steam. This time it went much better, the droplets turning to steam before they could hit my head.

The tub I broke the first time I'd tried to use magic had been replaced. The new one almost identical to the old one, which now sat in the bathroom. I hadn't used it yet, but I was fairly certain it was even bigger than the old one. Likely big enough for two people.

Krew had told the king he was arguing with me and broke it in anger. If he knew his son at all, he would know that Krew would never do that, but the king seemed to like that Krew and I were arguing. In fact, we were considering staging a fight at the ball to get me out of there sooner.

I just hoped I was beyond the days of splitting a tub in half. The ball was tomorrow. And that was only if we lived past this day and this plan to get the king's ring. I was better at controlling my magic, and containing it seemed natural now. But could I stage a fight with Krew and contain it? That was the question. My magic seemed to want to defend him. So it could all be problematic.

But alas. One flawed plan at a time. Hopefully leading us all the way to the king's demise.

Are you in the shower?

I rolled my eyes. *No. Owen is in the shower in your wing while I am off gallivanting in the forest solo.*

I could feel Krew's amusement. *A simple "yes" would have sufficed, love.*

Fine. Yes, I am in the shower.

You barely slept.

I am aware.

May I join you?

I turned another batch of water droplets to steam. *Can you at least check on Nara first?*

Of course.

It was odd that even just knowing he was awake to wait with me made me feel better. Was I still a little mad at him and Keir for this whole foolish plan? Yes. But I also knew both princes didn't wish any harm to come to Nara. They'd seen an opportunity and took it, while trying their best to ensure she had a way out if she wanted it.

I felt Krew before I heard his voice. "Raincheck on the shower I'm afraid, love."

I didn't have time to be disappointed as worry washed over me immediately.

"They are still sleeping, as of right now, but I am going to head downstairs and be ready for when our faux disloyal arrives. They sent word to the wall they are running a little bit ahead of schedule."

I took a deep breath. "You will let me know once you know Nara got out safely? Ring or not?"

He peeked his head in the shower. "Of course."

I stepped back into the water, closing my eyes to let the water fall over my head. "Either way, your father is sure to be extra irritable today. Please be careful."

Krew didn't say anything, so I opened my eyes. To find him gawking, his eyes taking care to roam over all of me.

"Krew."

His eyes found mine at the same time his lips turned at the corners.

"Please be careful."

He sighed and said more to himself than to me, "Maybe I do have five minutes?"

"Krew."

He leaned against the shower wall, crossing his arms. "Fine. Spoilsport." He looked in no hurry to leave. "But this," he made a circular motion with his finger, "this is definitely happening later."

I glared at him through the water. "Let's just get through this morning first, Your Grace."

With a flick of his finger, his magic shot toward the water. I was confused why he needed to turn it to steam, or if he was just using some magic to prepare for what was sure to be a taxing morning, when I felt the water hit my back. It was freezing. So cold I was shocked it hadn't turned to tiny ice pellets.

I gasped, my entire body tensing. "That was rude."

With another flick of his finger, more magic was flying toward the water.

I squealed, having learned my lesson, but couldn't get away fast enough. Yet this time, the droplets of water that slid down my back were even hotter than I had it set.

I sighed with relief.

Krew's smile stunned me from where he stood, still leaning up against the shower entrance. "I love you. I'll be back as soon as I can this morning."

I took a deep breath. "I love you too. Please be careful."

"When am I not?" he said over his shoulder as he turned to leave.

Not wanting to exert the effort to yell, I sent to him, *I don't know, every time you jump off your balcony?*

I heard his laugh and then his magic was there at my feet, waiting to attack the water again.

"Krew," I warned.

His magic launched toward the water, turning the water in the air to freezing again.

I tried not to squirm, but it was so cold as it pelted my skin, I couldn't help it. The noises that came from my mouth were certainly not human either.

Once out of the shower, I quickly brushed and dressed, ready to face the day.

And hope like hell it brought something other than tragedy.

* * *

I WAS READING in front of the fireplace in my favorite chair. Owen was there with me, both of us having breakfast in Krew's wing. The stress of the day even had us eating our breakfasts in the sitting area, not at the table.

We couldn't be bothered to be proper with everything on the line.

"Anything yet?" Owen asked for what had to be the hundredth time. He'd, of course, made me put up and take down the sound barrier at the door multiple times already.

"No."

Owen groaned, twitching his foot at the ankle.

I was content to read, but Owen apparently wasn't. "Would you like to play cards while we wait?"

He sighed. "I'd love to, thanks."

I put my book down, placing the piece of parchment in it to save my spot.

Nara is okay.

I gasped. Finally. Finally, Krew was checking in.

I closed my eyes and felt for the bond. He was walking somewhere within a different wing in the castle.

Father was not happy. Yelled at her and from what we have been able to find out, may have thrown a book at her. But she is otherwise fine.

I took a deep breath and opened my eyes. Owen's green eyes wide and on mine.

And the ring? I asked.

I don't know for certain yet, but if my father was that mad this morning, it is likely she was successful.

I switched my attention to Owen. "Nara is fine, though the king likely scared the hell out of her. The ring we aren't sure about."

His sigh of relief matched the way I felt too.

Thank you for letting me know.

Thank you for not hating me for this.

"And our disloyal apprehended?" Owen asked.

Owen is asking about the faux disloyal.

I could feel Krew's disgust as he responded, *Currently dealing with it. Taking him into the mountain as we speak.*

I relayed that information to Owen for him.

I hopped up to grab the cards. Silvia would be in later, but until I knew for sure about the ring, I wasn't sure I was going to be able to go back to sleep.

Owen shuffled the cards. "Do you know how nice this whole speaking telepathically would have been for Krew and me these last two years?"

I laughed. "Well, you do want to become bonded to him still, do you not?"

"Well yes, but I can't be soul bound to him if you are. Plus Krew was checking with the sages about an Enchanted having more than two bondings. John suspects their power will lessen the more bonds one person holds."

I giggled. Here Owen wanted to use this as a weapon to have a means of more productive communication for all things in the disloyal underground.

"What?" Owen asked.

"It's just that you see it from a strategic standpoint, and Krew mostly uses it to flirt with me or check in to see how I'm doing. It's very innocent compared to how you would want to use it."

"Innocent?" Owen asked. "Not the word I would use."

I put a hand up. "Fine, but you knew what I meant." I paused. "Do you really think Krew's magic will remain? It won't lessen any further?"

Owen leaned back from the cards he'd been about to deal. "I think we have no idea. And we have no idea because no one has ever been foolish enough to try to give all but a drop of it away. Until now."

"To a vessel who didn't even really want any to begin with."

We stared at each other for a second and then we were laughing. Soon I had tears rolling down my cheeks. Maybe it was the lack of sleep, maybe it was the absurdity of it all. I wasn't sure. The first Enchanted in who knows how long who wished to give all of his magic away managed to give it to someone who didn't really want it to begin with? What were the odds?

Owen picked up the cards and dealt them, Silvia came in shortly after. We convinced her to play a few hands with us before my gown fitting.

If I was going to have to wait the day away to find out about the ring, then at least I had good company.

* * *

The tar-looking water sloshed over my boots. I sent another wave of magic into the lake, stronger this time, doing my best to maintain a steady stream flowing out of my palms. It took far more concentration to have a continuous flow than it did for merely sending it to move objects. I wasn't perfect at it, but I was slowly improving.

It'd been an exhausting day. Nara had been essentially locked in her room for the day while the king looked everywhere for his ring and decided if she was to blame or not.

We didn't have the ring yet because she hadn't been able to take it to the drop off point. And the king was angry, but based on what Krew said, not as angry as he would have expected if the object held their mother's magic. Then again, maybe the king was just trying to make it appear he wasn't overly bothered.

Whatever the reason, I was over this day. I was over this plan. I was over the king remaining in power. I wasn't skilled enough or strong enough to attempt to take him down myself. Nor was I sure I was brave enough or naïve enough to try it on my own. But I needed something good to come from all this.

There were so many different plans in motion that I was lost. Like a dance I didn't know the steps to, I was just being dragged along.

But I didn't want to be. I wanted to know the steps, to help. I wanted the king gone too; I just didn't know how to accomplish that.

So here I stood at the lake. If I wasn't going to go to bed with the knowledge of the results of the princes' stupid plan, at least something good could come from this day. I would try to heal the lake. Again.

"Jorah," Owen warned. "I think you've used about enough for the day."

I ignored him entirely.

Krew was standing next to him and added silently, *You didn't sleep well last night, love. Don't overdo it.*

I ignored him too. Sometimes if I used enough magic, my skin would slightly glow. It was an adrenaline high I was beginning to like. But following that high, I usually crashed into a deep sleep. And that was what I was going to need tonight. To use so much that I could just sleep. Sleep and not worry. About Nara. About the ring. About the king. About the ball. I needed eight hours of no worrying.

So I sent even more magic into the lake which was now completely and wholly covered in silver magic.

"Jorah," Owen barked, this time sounding pissed. "Knock it off."

I didn't stop the magic flowing from my palms into the lake. "First you tell me I don't use enough, now you tell me I use too much. Which is it?"

I was facing the lake, not him. But I heard his stomping toward me as he said, "There is such a thing as burnout, you know."

"Just a little more," I offered. "Please. I need something good to come from this atrocious day."

At least dial it back please, love.

Having not heard Krew speak to me, Owen said even more angrily, "Jorah! Stop it, dammit. Right now."

I stopped with one hand, only to use it to send a breeze at Owen that would knock him down. At the last minute, being afraid that I would chuck him like I had Keir, I sent out even more magic to catch him. Just to be safe.

He grunted as my magic knocked him off his feet. And sure enough, he looked as if he landed in a pillow of my silver magic.

"Not funny."

I snickered. It was a little funny.

Jorah.

Uh-oh. The full name comes out.

"You are far too contumacious for your own good," Krew grumbled as he moved toward me.

I squinted at him and spun, my back now to the glowing lake. "Is that even a word?"

"I—" He ran a hand down his face. "I don't know!"

I tried not to smirk at his honesty. He was clearly frustrated with me. Now was not the time to laugh.

Krew glared at me. "Stop. I know you are mad because of the plan to get the ring. I know you didn't like it. I know it's been a waiting game all day and we still don't know all the answers. I'm frustrated too." He'd been walking while he spoke to me, and now he was right in front of me. "Stop, Jorah. That's enough magic for one day."

I shook my head. "No. No it's not. The water hasn't changed yet. And I'm not skilled enough to use this magic for anything else, so let me at least try to do this."

He put a hand on my arm, and I found that not only the lake was glowing, but I was also lit up with my magic. "You can try again tomorrow, love. But that is enough for today."

The tenderness of his words had me finally cutting off the magic. At almost the same time I did, I felt it. The thin line of blood trailing out of my nose.

I guess I had used far more magic than I thought despite using it in less time than it normally took Krew and Keir to practice. I'd only seen this once before, when Keir had used so much magic putting out the fires in Nerede that he'd also bled from his nose.

I wiped at it and took a step forward. There was no adrenaline high this time. There was no change to the lake either. All that remained was a bone deep exhaustion.

"Are you all right?" Krew asked gently, handing me a handkerchief from somewhere.

I let out a long sigh. "I'm scared. And worried. And tired. So no. I'm not all right."

"Here, let her sit a moment," Owen offered, as a tree trunk was moved toward me laced in green magic.

I gladly sat down, my eyes looking upward to try to find the stars from around the branches. I kept wiping at my nose, but it was slowing already. "Aren't you going to say I told you so?" I asked Owen.

He shook his head. "No. This is a lesson I hoped you'd never have to learn. It doesn't feel good when you reach the level of burnout. Better get a little food and get to bed."

"Just to await the ball tomorrow. Can't wait."

Owen sat next to me, nudging me like he always did with his elbow. "I have no doubt you'll heal this lake someday, Jorah. Maybe it isn't about the amount at once, but how often you try. Maybe on try ninety-nine it works, I don't know. But I think even the forest wouldn't want you to kill yourself in trying to save it."

One lone tear escaped out my eye. "Okay."

"And I know you are worried about the ball, unsure if you should even go, but I know for a fact you have grown leaps and bounds with your magic this last week, Jorah."

"I—"

I couldn't even argue before Owen was cutting me off. "I don't care if you don't trust it yet. You can contain it as well as any Enchanted I know. And you are using enough of it throughout the day now." He paused. "You're ready."

His words were too much to bear. Far kinder than I deserved. "And if I walk in that ballroom and see the king, unable to keep my magic from showing, and he finds out in the first few moments I have magic?"

Krew provided, "Then it's a good thing I still have my magic too, love. It will be handled, one way or another."

CHAPTER 11

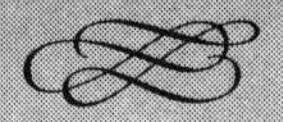

I woke to a knock and my breakfast being brought in by George and Owen.

"Sorry I woke you!" George said with a hand in the air.

Realizing the food he brought in was my breakfast and lunch both because I'd slept until mid-day, I waved him off. "Don't be, George. It is beyond time I face the day." This dreadful day I had been worrying over since the bonding.

"Let us know if there is anything else you need," George said with a quick smile before leaving.

Owen put up a sound barrier as soon as he was gone.

I sat up and stretched my neck. "Why'd you let me sleep so long?"

Owen put his hands on his hips a moment. "Because I've been running you hard this last week. Krew said you barely slept two nights ago, so I wanted to be sure you were rested enough for today. Burnout can take a few days to recover from."

I looked outside a moment and back to him. "Wait. So you are actually going easy on me?"

Owen grinned. "Only for today, honey, but the good news is that we now have the ring."

My breath caught. "We do?"

He tilted his head toward a shoulder. "Well in a manner of speaking. It is currently en route with Krew. He is personally taking it to Hatcher to have it tested."

The smartest part of that entire damn plan was to get the ring from the drop off location in the gardens and out of the castle as quickly as possible. The king would not be finding it in Nara's room or either princes'.

"Wait. Can you still talk to Krew now? Even though he's probably in Savaryn by now?"

"I'll try." I felt for the bond, and knew Owen was correct that Krew was not in the castle. *Good morning.*

Good morning, love.

You have the ring, I hear?

What? I wanted to be the bearer of good news. Dammit, Raikes.

I laughed.

Owen offered, "Still working, huh?"

I nodded to Owen before asking Krew, *How does it feel?*

Like a ring. I don't know. Nothing about this ring reminds me of my mother. Nothing at all. But that doesn't mean her magic isn't still somehow trapped in there.

I considered that. *Be safe today.*

Always. I'll return to you soon. Hatchet will likely need a few days with the ring before we know more.

Owen's voice had me snapping back to the present. "Renna is on the way to eat with you before Silvia begins with ball preparations."

I didn't have time to be surprised as he explained, "She and Krew have fine-tuned their plan to get you out of the ball early."

I groaned as I stood, slipping my feet into my slippers and

stomping into the lavatory. “More plans.” Though I guess I had in a way asked for this when I told Krew I didn’t know how to get through the ball.

I could hear Owen’s chuckle from behind the door.

Freshened up and fully awake, I devoured my breakfast. What was it about using a lot of magic that made me absolutely ravenous?

Renna filled me in on Gwen and Molly’s tiff while we ate. It appeared things were not blowing over where they were concerned.

I sighed. “So there is the threat of drama tonight. And not just from myself.”

Renna winced. “About that. Are you ready to hear our very simple way to get you out of there tonight?”

I put down my tea. “Yes. Let’s have it, you schemers.” I know I had somewhat asked for this, but I wondered if the best way to go about this was to have me simply leave early feigning a headache or something. It didn’t need an elaborate plan.

Renna swiped a hand at the air. “It is all really quite simple. We will appear to be having an intimate moment in the hallway. We will make sure to be seen by one of the king’s spies. And then the spy will relay that information to the king. Should take no longer than a few minutes. And then Krew will come back in and you can appear to be jilted by his lack of affections, and he will dismiss you.”

I squinted. “How intimate will this moment be?”

Renna was shaking her head. “Not intimate at all. He won’t even touch me, Jorah. Though we’ve always conspired to make me one of his frontrunners, he has never crossed any lines with me. We are not about to start now that both of us are happily married. He will likely have a hand above the wall at my head. So it appears we could be kissing, though we will not be.”

I could remember myself being in that position with him on

more than one occasion, so I understood exactly what she was referencing. The plan itself wasn't awful, I just wasn't sure I was ready for all that tonight. But then again, it sounded like the plan was already in motion, I was simply being informed about it.

"You will not even have to see it," Renna reminded me as if sensing my hesitation, "you just have to have one tiny conversation afterward with Krew where it does not look like he is about to whisk you to his bed. Can you give me that? One conversation where the two of you don't look madly in love?"

I rolled my eyes. "Please. We've had to pose often the last few months. I am used to putting on a show, Renna. That part I'm not worried about. I'm worried about my magic staying out of view with this plan."

She cocked her head. "You mean back when you were merely pretending to be in love?"

I nodded.

She grinned. "I'm not sure that was a show for anyone, Jorah."

A short laugh escaped my lips. "Okay. Point made. But I am still halfway flummoxed with that plan to get the ring, so it shouldn't be all that hard to pretend to be angry with him."

Renna took a drink of her water. "Just not fully flummoxed or your magic might flare."

"So half flummoxed it is."

We looked at each other for a moment and then both burst out laughing.

Owen soon kicked out Renna to take me for a quick walk. We went to our training room, and he had me use magic to move various objects in different directions, making sure I had used enough magic to keep it contained later.

By the time I made it back to Krew's wing for a bath, I was slightly sweaty. And feeling ready to get this ball over with. I didn't even have to stay the whole night.

And we'd get to toy with the king.

I could do this. Right?

* * *

Silvia helped me into my blood red gown. The upper half was tight and corseted, the lower half a draping velvet. Feeling nerves, I kept rubbing my palms along the smooth velvet at my thighs.

"You look lovely," Silvia offered as she ran her fingers through the curls down my back.

I smiled at her through our reflections in the mirror. "Thank you."

Her eyes darted to the door and back to me, like they had often while she applied finishing touches. I wasn't sure if it was my nerves rubbing off or what, but Silvia seemed bothered by something.

I sent a sound barrier around the door to the lavatory just before catching her wrist and squeezing lightly. "What's wrong, Silvia?"

She hadn't seen my magic before, and her eyebrows reached to her graying hair as she gave her head a shake. "Nothing."

But the crow's feet at her eyes weren't showing when she smiled, so I knew better. "If you know something about tonight, please tell me."

She again shook her head. "No, it's not that."

I spun around to look at her, wondering if I should believe her or not.

She sighed and looked at the ceiling. "I am just worried about you. That's all."

"Me?"

She snapped her head and gave me a look my mother had on numerous occasions. She leaned in, grabbed me by the shoulders, and whispered, "Your magic, darling. Will you be all right tonight around the king? Now that you have magic?"

I gave her a shrug. "I'm not honestly sure how I will keep it from him." I hadn't told her I now held all but a drop of Krew's magic and was quite powerful. It was nice that I'd never had to hide my magic from Silvia, but I wasn't sure I should tell her everything either. Particularly when not knowing the truth could help keep her safe. I felt I could be honest with one thing though. If only so I could have another safe place to vent. "Krew and I are soul bound. I've found my magic feels the strong need to protect Krew as well as myself."

Silvia's eyes went wide and her hand fell away from my shoulder in order to cover her mouth that had fallen open. "Soul bound?"

I gave her a nod. "Yes. So it's not quite so simple as me keeping my magic contained."

She gave her head a shake. "I knew that you somehow felt . . . *strong*."

That was when I noticed the tears swimming in her eyes.

My forehead wrinkled. "I am truly sorry I didn't tell you before now. I've been a bit distracted since the bonding. Figuring out how to use my magic and how to do so safely."

She shook her head. "No. It is not that." She wiped at an eye and gave me a smile laced in sadness.

"Silvia?"

"It is only that I cling to the day in which the two of you rule this castle and not that man." She paused to wipe at another tear. "I have clung to that day for years. Since the first bruises showed on Katarina." She gasped out, "But this, my darling. This gives me hope anew. Hope that this bond between you and Prince Krewan can heal Wylan. For good."

"All because we are soul bound?"

She laughed. "No. Did you know the king was heart bound with his final two consorts from his own Assemblage?"

I shook my head. "No. I did not know that."

She smirked. “He wanted a soul bound pairing and for a while believed it could make him stronger. Katarina always suspected he was bound to a few of his mistresses as well. He never was soul bound to anyone.” She paused as if looking into the past to dig up more memories. “His obsession to become soul bound only lasted a few years. He gave up altogether, not wanting to waste his magic. Not wanting to do the work of recouping it again and again.”

That must have been how they found out the bonds themselves became weaker the more you had. Through the king. But he’d found a different way to become stronger anyway. And given this information from Silvia, I wondered if John wasn’t right. If Krew’s selfless motives had caused or triggered the soul bonding. Because the king would have always been far too selfish for such a thing to work.

“In my lifetime,” Silvia continued, “I have only known three soul bound couples.” She paused. “But there is a common theme among them.”

“Which is?”

“That soul bonding is *never* a mistake.” She smiled a real smile this time and looked down her nose at me. “And don’t you find it a poetic sort of justice? That his son would have something the king wanted but failed to have?”

While this news made Silvia rather hopeful for the future, what she’d said filled me with even more dread. This would be just another reason for the king to take an *interest* in me if he knew.

I needed to keep my magic far from view tonight. Far from the king. Until the moment we used it to remove him from that throne.

* * *

KREW HAD BEEN GONE MOST of the day dealing with the ring and then meeting with his father. While he quickly showered and readied himself for the ball, I had a book on the floor that I was moving back and forth and in patterns with my magic, just like I had done with Owen this morning. I was only using a small amount of magic, not wanting my skin to even remotely glow, but wanting to use enough that my magic would be easier to control throughout the night.

The goal was to only be down there a few hours. I had survived countless balls and conversations in that ballroom as a magicless and vulnerable woman from the lowest level in the kingdom. So I should be able to play my part despite the fact that I was very much now a weapon.

I felt Krew through the bond before I physically felt his arm around my waist as he pulled my body into his chest.

I stopped the flow of magic and took a deep breath.

Krew kissed the back of my head. "You can do this, Jorah love. And if you cannot, *we* can handle this."

I closed my eyes and just stood in his arms a moment. It was not lost on me that one of Krew's hands was traveling along the velvet portion of my dress toward the slit in my leg.

"Krew," I groaned. Turning to face him. "The top part of this dress is literally a corset. So don't even think about it."

He cocked his head. "My wife is dressed like this, and I am not supposed to even *think* about it?"

I squinted. "Considering the importance of this night, yes."

His lips gently pressed into mine as he sent down the bond, *Theoretically, it wouldn't have to come off, but fine. I hear you.*

I tried not to laugh directly into his face.

"Renna brought you up to speed with our plan?" he asked as he reached for my hand and brought it up to place a kiss on my palm.

I inhaled deeply. "Yes."

He looked into my eyes. "It will not be real, Jorah. Not a moment of it. Just close proximity and conveniently located." He paused. "There is nothing, not a thing in the realm that could tempt me otherwise." He found my other hand and did the same, bringing it up to kiss my palm. "You have all of me, love. There's never been a competition within my Assemblage, it has always been you."

I kissed him hard. "I know." After a moment I added, "And you'll try to stay out of my head so I can make it through the night?"

I will behave.

Thank you. Out loud I added, "I am going to head down with Owen now. Wait a few minutes before you leave, will you?"

Just as I turned to leave, he grabbed my hand and tugged me back into him. "Yes, but I want it noted that I am looking forward to the day where we come and go to events as husband and wife."

I was too, but it felt likely the Assemblages would drag on another month or two. The princes were to cut one more consort before the tour of the kingdom. Down to three each. So close to the end of the Assemblages, and yet so very far.

Before allowing me my leave, Krew kissed me once more. His lips were gentle while his hands were far more frenzied. It was as if his hands couldn't decide which part of me he'd like to touch most. I found I forgot all about my nerves for a moment, wishing we had the time for his hands to finish their mapping of my body.

But we didn't. I only had to survive a few hours downstairs and that could come later. It would be that much sweeter without the looming ball too.

Later, I promised us both as I kissed him one last time.

As Owen and I took the stairs down, a thought hit me. Though I entered the ballroom as Krew's consort, one of his four, I also entered the room with confidence. Not the confidence of being Enchanted, but rather with the confidence and knowledge that Krew had chosen me. There were no lingering what-ifs to worry on. He chose me.

And no matter how convincing Krew and Renna were tonight at distracting the king, Krew's Assemblage would end in only one way: with a Wylan crown on my head and a ring upon my finger.

I may never be queen, but I already was *a princess*.

CHAPTER 12

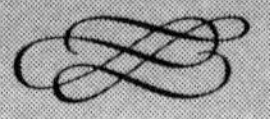

"Rinaldi. How are you tonight?"

He put his tray in my direction, my lone water flute already waiting.

"Thank you," I smiled. We'd gotten into this routine. He knew I'd find him first, and so he only had just one water waiting and ready.

"I am well, Miss Demir. If I do my job correctly tonight, I may even be able to sneak in the back for the play."

I grinned. "Oh yes, the play. Were you able to sneak in for the acrobats?"

He gave me a quick nod. "Only for a moment. They were spectacular."

"I quite agree."

Molly arrived at my side, and with a quick nod, Rinaldi headed off to grab her a champagne.

I looped my arm in hers as we walked in the direction of my window. Rinaldi would know to find us there. I whispered, "I am a wreck, Molls."

She gave her head a shake and looked at me. "What, why?"

I took a deep inhale and made sure to push all the magic down for the third time since walking in the ballroom. "Things are happening tonight. Multiple things. And I feel . . . a bit out of sorts."

"Well get yourself together, woman," she chided. "Of the two of us, you are supposed to be the one madly in love and well on the way to locking down a Valanova heir."

I laughed, having not expected her to say that. "Well, I do have to appear mad at Renna later, so I was rather hoping to pull off the pouting consort all evening."

Molly's nose scrunched. "Not your best look, I'm afraid."

I choked on a laugh.

Molly squinted at me. "Wait. We aren't really mad at Renna though?"

I shook my head. "Not at all."

Molly thanked Rinaldi, who had returned with her champagne. "We are the women who switched. Though things are obviously tense in my Assemblage, I was hoping yours had avoided it."

I tried my best not to pity her. I knew she'd hate it. "It has. For the most part. It just needs to appear that there is more tension than there really is."

"Ahhh," Molly added. Her eyes seemed to fly to the king's balcony, and I knew she had things figured out.

"Is there anything I can do to help with the tension in yours?" I asked quietly.

She took a generous drink of her champagne. "No. Keir just has to decide what he wants. But I don't think he's ready to make any decisions yet. He needs more time. So we are all stuck."

I almost wished I could put up a sound barrier and ask her more questions, but I couldn't. Deciding we were far enough away from the others, I asked, "And you don't? Need more time?"

She shrugged. "I would honestly take more time also. I know our relationship was not love at first sight. Particularly since I was not even in his Assemblage to begin with. Things have rather moved at a snail's pace. But he listens to me ramble for minutes about my books. Attentively. Asking me questions and walking in the gardens with me daily now that he knows what time I'm usually there."

No wonder she liked the gardens so much.

She looked me in the eyes. "Why would he do that if he didn't care for me at all?"

"He wouldn't," I offered, knowing exactly how busy the princes had been as of late. If Keir was still finding time to see Molly every day, she definitely mattered to him. I also knew for a fact how I cherished my friendship with Molly for the sole reason of her not being in the know on all the disloyal happenings in and around the castle. Keir might feel similarly, though I selfishly hoped it was more than just that. "And," I added, "if there is one thing I know, it is also how good of a friend you naturally are."

She tilted her head. "Particularly to those who try to keep me at an arm's length?"

I giggled. "Yes, that. And I also feel as if Krew and I became friends before we crossed the line over to more. Not all love stories read the same, Molls. Yours doesn't have to fit the mold; it only has to be *yours*."

Her eyes went misty as she wiped at her eyes. "Stop making me cry, dammit."

"Well stop cheering me up, then."

We were quite the pair tonight. And I was so tired of keeping things from all the people I cared about just to keep them safe from the king's wrath. I wanted to tell her Krew's Assemblage was all but over. I wanted to tell her I now wielded magic. I had so many things to say and not enough safe spaces to say them.

* * *

WE WERE SEATED for the play. Krew had Renna on one side, me on the other. That was normal for events such as these. What was not normal was the whispering Krew and Renna were doing while the play started up. The king was perched above us in this room, and I had successfully looked his direction only once the entire night. So far, my skin had stayed free of all traces of silver.

The play was a dramatic one of sorts. It was about how the magic was gifted from the gods to protect the lands. The part I found most hilarious was that one of the gods was portrayed by a woman actress. I was sure the king had *not* approved that portion of the play.

Krew again whispered something toward Renna, and I slumped away from him. Trying my best to appear jilted by his lack of attention. The jealous lover.

I felt Krew down the bond. *Are you all right? Too much?*

I'm not truly mad. I am annoyed but really just trying to appear to be mad. Body language and all that.

He smirked next to me and reached a hand over to squeeze my hand a moment.

I squinted at him. *Though if this were real, I would definitely be slapping that away.*

Renna kicked his foot gently. I realized it must be entirely too obvious that Krew and I were communicating. I'd been nervous all night to say a word to Krew that wasn't out loud, wondering if the King or the other Enchanted in the room would somehow sense it. Like the way I could feel the buzz of magic.

I straightened my shoulders and continued ignoring Krew. We didn't need the king figuring out we could communicate wordlessly. I was already halfway through this night, I just needed to be able to get through the play and then I'd be dismissed early. I was almost there.

So I settled in, leaning as far away from Krew as I could, and watched the play, letting myself get lost in costumes and scenes.

It wasn't half bad. I didn't know how I felt about some sort of deities just gifting a third of the population of Wylan this magic without considering the evil that could be done with it, but the overall theme of the play was meant to be uplifting all the same.

Another of the actors posing as a god, this one male with a long beard and wearing a white robe, took to the stage as the rest of the scene stilled behind him. "Magic in this realm was never intended to harm, it was always intended to protect both the lands and the people in them."

I almost wanted to laugh. If a god or gods did give us magic to protect, we'd gotten it completely wrong. In what messed up realm would the kingdom then be divided with the most vulnerable population kept at the coast and the first line of defense should anything ever happen? We were not being protected; we were being lined up for slaughter.

I wondered about the other countries and how their magic was divided among them. Was there a hierarchy assigned in every country in the realm? Because if that were the case, the magic might have done more harm than good.

The room was clapping, so I found myself following suit. The play overall had been entertaining enough to watch, but I kept coming back to that *to protect* line.

Some Enchanted I knew, like the princes or Owen, did use their magic to protect. Others, like the king, used it as a scepter of control. It seemed there had been no prerequisite to become Enchanted, and though the magic may have been intended to protect, it had twisted into an uglier reality, one of oppression.

Krew and Renna stood, Renna's arm was in Krew's and I knew it was officially time for their distraction plan. Krew didn't say a word to me through the bond, but his eyes caught mine for only a moment and I knew what he was telling me. The night was almost over.

I left my seat by myself, wanting to wait for Molly. If she was on Keir's arm, I'd of course just give her space.

Isla, wearing a gorgeous purple gown, gave me a tight smile. "Welcome to the rejects, Jorah." She gave me a sigh. "It is not so bad once you get used to it."

I fought the urge to allow my mouth to drop open. She'd never been rude to me, but she'd never really been nice to me either. "I'm sorry," was all I managed in a response. I supposed if this were all real and I really had just been replaced by Renna, I might actually feel better with her words, a sense of camaraderie. As it was, I felt awful.

Molly did end up being on Keir's arm, so I slowly walked with Isla in companionable silence as we all filtered out in knots or pairs leaving the theatre to go back to the ballroom. I felt annoyed and guilty for this whole charade but also for not getting to know Isla better. I hadn't trusted a soul when I arrived at this castle, and I hadn't wanted any friends. Molly and Renna had somehow wiggled themselves past my defenses anyway. Gwen too for a while. But I had also always known that only two of us would get to stay while the rest of us would go back to our little corners of the kingdom. So what would have been the point?

Had I known things would end up the way they did, I might have made more of an effort to befriend more of the women in Krew's Assemblage once I switched over. But back then I had thought I was merely faking it to my freedom.

How wrong had I been?

Still lost in my thoughts, I heard forceful footsteps behind me, noticed the sea of people moving aside, and Isla and I automatically did so as well.

It was the king, heading back to the ballroom. Or so I assumed. I tried not to look his way or draw any attention to myself. I just shoved my magic down as far as I could and hoped like hell it behaved.

"Jorah of Nerede," his voice said as he came to a stop before me. "May I have a word?"

I gave a bow as my eyes automatically flew to find Owen. "Of course."

What could he possibly want right now? I wondered if I should alert Krew down the bond what was happening, but I didn't feel brave enough to do so a mere foot from the king. Owen was there and moving in closer. He wasn't going to let us out of his sight. And though I couldn't read Owen's thoughts, I knew from a glance he seemed to be telling me that I was okay, that I had this. Whatever *this* was.

The king offered me his arm and led me around the people, along a side wall of the massive ballroom. I thought for a moment that we were going to take the grand staircase up to his balcony, and I was just his escort for the time being, but then we stopped before the stairs.

"I have yet to see you in person to say the trees in the forest are remarkable," he offered with a smile. "Truly remarkable."

I pushed my magic down again, trying to wrap my head around how Nara would have wanted to sleep with this disgusting excuse of a man. "Thank you, Your Grace."

"You continue to impress," he said with a nod. "And I am happy to see you've found your place in this castle."

"Thank you." The more compliments he showered over me, the more suspicious I grew. What was he up to? Was he out of my blood again? He had to want something from me, the question was, what?

"I've something to show you," he said calmly. "Call it a peace offering after the fires in Nerede I know you were not pleased with. A peace offering and a promise that no matter what happens, you are always welcome at Kavan Keep. With everything you've done and provided in trying to heal the forest, it is the very least I can offer you."

Was he about to offer me the same thing he had Nara? If so, I was going to vomit all over his boots. That was not an offer I would ever entertain, and he surely had to know that.

His guard opened a side door I hadn't even realized was a door, the paneling matching that of the rest of the room.

The king patted my hand in the crook of his arm.

I was so focused on pushing my magic down and willing it to stay there as the king touched me, I barely noticed we went out of the ballroom and into the hallway.

I turned to look back over my shoulder. My eyes locked on Owen's green ones where he was still stuck in the ballroom as one of the king's guards shut the side door behind us.

When had this night gone so wrong? All I'd needed to do was avoid the king and appear jilted by Krew to get out of there early.

Instead, I was stuck with the king. The king and the magic hiding within my veins.

CHAPTER 13

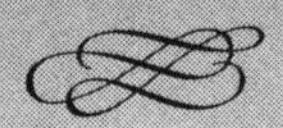

As I continued walking on the king's arm, I kept shoving my magic down, glancing at my hands and wrists to be sure that all traces of silver were gone. It'd just take one little flare, one flare and then the king would know.

And of all the ways he could find out, being alone with the king when it happened seemed like the worst possible scenario. But I needed to keep my cool for both my magic and for the bond with Krew. So I kept taking deep breaths and trying to stay calm.

It didn't take long. As we turned the corner, it all slid into place. I stopped in my tracks, my hand in the king's arm falling to my side.

Krew and Renna.

I could barely see Renna from around Krew's frame. But I could see her hands on his tailcoat, the pink of her painted nails against the black of his coat. Krew's forearm rested against the wall over her head while he leaned over her.

It wasn't real. It wasn't real. It wasn't real.

I took a deep breath and fought with every breath in me to keep my magic down.

Krew and Renna's plan had backfired. Not because the king didn't believe them, but because I was being forced to see it. Forced to see it and not use magic. I knew it wasn't real. I knew they were likely bickering about something in that sibling way that they often did. But it didn't erase the reality I was seeing with my own two eyes of how very real it *did* look.

I wanted to scream. To cry. To use my magic and send a breeze throughout the entire castle with my frustrations.

But there I stood, shoving it all down. Unable to do a thing other than breathe.

"What the hell?" Krew snapped as his eyes flew to mine and he slowly turned around.

I couldn't look him in the eyes. I just couldn't. I slammed my eyes shut and swallowed hard. I also couldn't dare cry. My tears would glow with my magic. So to the king, I managed to get out, "I believe this was a lesson I have already learned. Two-fold, Your Grace. A third time feels entirely unnecessary."

The king placed a hand on my shoulder. I opened my eyes and willed the well of tears there to somehow stay in my eyes. If even one of my tears fell this would all be for naught.

"This is not a lesson, dear, but rather a show of good faith. I know you appreciate transparency and honesty. This is me letting you know what has been going on behind your back."

The king thought he was doing me a favor?

From around the king, I could see Krew's magic flaring. He was furious. And the king's hand was still on my shoulder so that was not helping matters.

I heard Owen before I saw him. "I am getting really sick and tired of these games." He grabbed one of the king's guards, shoving him against the wall and holding him there. By the throat. "Lock me out of a room from the consort I am here to protect again, and it may very well be the last thing you do."

The king rolled his eyes. “Calm down, Raikes. I meant no harm to the girl.”

I tried to focus on Owen. Not on Krew. Not on Renna. I couldn’t even look their direction for fear of losing control of my magic. Feeling a tear about to spill over and knowing it would release the whole dam of them, I turned to the king and did something that I never in a million lifetimes thought I would do to this man. I begged. “May I take my leave now, Your Grace?”

He gave me a nod and patted my shoulder once more. “Yes, of course, Jorah. Goodnight.”

“Jorah.” It was Krew’s voice, and I could hear the real concern. He was not acting.

But at this point, neither was I.

So I fled. I walked as quickly as possible to the first corner, ignoring the king and Krew’s harsh words to one another behind me, and then as soon as I was out of view, I was sprinting for the stairs.

Hearing footsteps behind me, I never slowed. I needed air not shared by the king. I needed to erase from my memory how real Krew and Renna had appeared. I needed . . . to use this power burning in my veins. To release my magic and have it ease the burden of this pain.

Up the first set of stairs, the footsteps caught me.

“It’s me.”

Owen. Thank gods. “Owen,” I gasped. “I couldn’t take the chance the king would follow me to the elevat—”

“I know. I know.” And without another word, he scooped me into his arms and raced us up the stairs. Considering I had been in heels and he had been in boots, he was still faster, even carrying my weight.

As soon as we were in Krew’s wing, I lit the fire. It blazed a bit more than I had wished, but at least I hadn’t lit the entire castle on fire. Because right now? Right now, I felt like letting the entire castle burn.

I knew Krew and Renna had been acting. It had been exactly as they had told me it would be. But the fact remained that I was never supposed to have actually *seen* it.

And I was so sick of being in this castle and having to see someone I cared about in the arms of another. Real or fake, it played on all the insecurities I'd had with Keir. I was also so damn tired of being a pawn in someone's master plan. I didn't know which made me more infuriated, to be honest. I was just irrationally pissed off at everyone and everything.

I needed to use magic. A lot of it. I was frustrated and so tired of these schemes and plans at every turn. There should only be one plan: take down the king. The rest of them didn't matter, and particularly if they harmed others in the process.

I sat on my bed feeling utter defeat. We'd had this grand plan to get me out of the ball early, and though it had technically worked, it had also backfired in the worst way. As all our plans around the king did.

I was not just playing the part of the jilted lover, I'd become her. And while I was feeling sorry for myself, I was angry that yet again I was to be a dirty little secret.

Owen was blurry before me. "Jorah."

It sounded like he was so far away. So very far away.

"Jorah," he snapped.

I gave my head a shake, realizing the reason I hadn't been able to hear him that clearly was because of the buzzing of my magic. "What?" I croaked out.

"You need to use some more magic. Make a dome. Put out the fire and restart it. Make a sound barrier. Move a book around. Something. Anything. Please."

I didn't know much, but I did know that when I was this upset, this was not the place to use my magic. I would break something.

And the king wasn't yet asleep so Owen couldn't just jump off the balcony with me either. Not yet anyway.

I looked at my palms to find them glowing brightly. All of my skin was for that matter. I was brighter than the first star that graced the night sky. The buzzing wasn't yet pulsing with every beat of my heart though, so there was at least that. I had no desire to use my magic, but I had no desire to push it away either.

"Jorah," Owen begged.

The door slammed open and Krew and Renna came in.

Seeing them together after everything I had just been forced to see made my anger go nowhere. Rationally, I knew the entire thing was innocent. But I was really tired of the king's attempts to rattle me *working*.

"Jorah," Krew said as he rushed toward me.

But then he was being shoved away from me. Not by my magic. Or any magic of any sort. Just by the brute force of Owen.

Krew cocked his head and moved to shove back, his magic lighting up his veins just as mine were steadily glowing now. "She is *my wife*."

Owen's own magic began snaking along his veins. "Then try acting like *her husband*." He stopped to purse his lips. "You only go near her if she wants you there. I have sat by Keir doing this to her too many times to count. Real or not. So give her a gods damn minute."

"I know," Krew bit out, voice going emotional. "You know what I feel for her. It wasn't real."

Owen leaned in. "Well then you were the absolute fool who forgot to consider in this plan how your father might delight in torturing her with it."

Krew's head snapped back before moving his eyes to mine. "Jorah." *I'm so sorry.*

I closed my eyes and took a deep breath. This wasn't okay. I wasn't okay. And I wasn't going to just pretend otherwise. I felt an exhaustion bone deep. As if I hadn't even slept a full night upon arriving at this wretched castle. After overdoing it last night and the nerves of the day, having to keep my magic at bay for the whole disaster of a night, having to physically touch the king, I was shot. Emotionally. Physically. Mentally. All of it.

Owen didn't remove a finger from where he held Krew back from me. "Jorah, honey, do you want me to let him go or do you need a minute?"

I kept my eyes closed. "Just need a minute."

Owen let go of Krew but stood between the bed where I was and where Krew stood. Owen had been with me through far too many of these situations. He knew exactly what I needed. Space.

"She needs to use her magic," Renna said gently.

"She knows," Owen snapped. "And she already did use some."

Feeling someone in front of me, I opened my eyes to see Owen there again crouching to be eye level with me. "Can you please just put out and restart the fire for me? You don't have to use a lot. Just the usual."

I flicked a finger and did as he asked. Only because he looked so worried it was hurting me to see it. The fire was out for what felt like a half a second and then the fire was back to roaring. As hot and bright as it could possibly be within the fireplace. And it did nothing to the glow of magic on my skin. I was about to put up a thick sound barrier when the door swung open again.

Keir came storming in the room right toward Krew. "What the hell was that? You have to be kidding me!"

My eyes went to his as he took in my glowing form, still just sitting there on the bed. I only needed one minute to gather my thoughts and wits, but apparently, I wasn't going to be allowed even a moment.

"Sorry if I am late to the party here, but I was busy dismissing *your* consorts, brother." He paused. "Have you lost your damn mind?" Keir gestured with a hand toward me as his attention stayed on Krew. "Did you learn nothing?" He looked from Krew to Renna and back again. "How could you force her for even a moment to see something like that again?"

"We just wanted the king away from her," Renna said as she fought off tears of her own. "We never meant for things . . ." she swallowed, "to get that far. Or for her to see it."

Krew didn't get defensive or angry. He just stated, "Father tells me all the time I should bounce between women and not become too attached to just one. I thought he would approve if I made it appear I was doing just that."

Keir shook his head. "Unbelievable."

Owen got up from where he'd been crouched in front of me and walked toward the three of them holding his fingers up like he was pinching the air. "I am *this* close to kicking all of your asses out."

I was tired of hearing them bicker. Tired of the excuses. Tired of the outrage. Tired of it all. It changed nothing. I'd been forced to see it. And it hadn't been real. But just because it hadn't been real, didn't mean it didn't hurt a little.

I'm so sorry, love.

I ignored Krew. I wasn't ready to speak yet. Out loud or otherwise. I wasn't ready to do anything. I was somehow still cold despite the magic traveling along my skin, likely because I was just that exhausted. Or maybe it was a side effect from the burnout the night before. Either way, I wanted to sleep and not have to listen to the people around me at each other's throats after another stupid plan. I just wanted a new day where all these jumbled up feelings made sense. Some clarity to organize and categorize them all. Because the weight of it all was just too much for me to bear right now.

My magic pulsed once as if begging me to let it help.

So for once, I let it. *Okay.*

As one lone tear rolled down my cheek, my magic left my palm.

Before I could blink, it formed a dome around the bed. I'd made sure it was both a sound barrier and magical one. So I could drown out all the chatter.

What I hadn't been consciously aware of asking my magic to do was to crawl along the blankets and warm them. I'd had a fleeting moment of wanting to be warm, and my magic had responded.

"Jorah!"

Owen was there but I could barely hear him.

I reached for my heels, gently taking one off and then the other, dropping them onto the floor. I gave him a tired smile as I moved to get under the covers. To Krew, I said, *Please tell Owen I just need a minute. That's all.*

Owen gave me a nod of understanding as Krew did just that.

Minutes later the lights were turned off. The dull sounds of their voices finally left. I knew Krew and Owen remained, but they left my dome of magic around me without even trying to break it.

In minutes, under the glowing covers and warm protection of my magic, I fell asleep.

CHAPTER 14

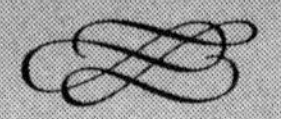

I woke to the sunlight pouring through the curtains, which were only pulled halfway. Seeing them through a silver webbing of magic, I jolted awake, remembering how I had gotten myself in this position.

My magic was still up. The dome was still standing, the blankets still warm. And it was morning. How was that possible? When I had released my magic, I had intended for the dome to be strong, but I'd kind of assumed Owen or Krew would just break through it eventually.

But here it was. Hours later. And since I'd been asleep, it wasn't like I had been feeding a constant stream of magic into it. It'd just been one burst of magic. A powerful one, evidently.

On my side of the bed, leaning against the wall, sat my tormented prince. My husband. And I wasn't sure he had slept at all. Particularly not if he was sitting against a wall.

I turned my palm up and used my fingers to will the dome to fall, like snuffing out a flame of a candle.

The morning brought with it sunshine and the clarity of being rested. Though I felt entirely better and calm from sleeping what had to be close to eight full hours depending on what time it was, I was still bothered and hurt by the night before.

I wasn't just over it now that it was morning and the sun was shining. But I did understand why they did it. I was even partially to blame for asking for a way out of the ball to begin with.

And I was also beyond ready to get out of this damn corset.

Krew didn't speak a word to me. Not out loud or in my head, he just watched, head against the wall.

"Good morning," I said quietly.

"Good morning."

After a quick trip into the lavatory, I sat on the bed across from him, unsure what to say or what to do. What he'd done was not okay, and I was pretty sure he knew that, but I also didn't want to start the day with an argument either.

"Where are Renna and Owen?" My voice came out at almost a whisper.

"Renna is in her room, though I am not sure she slept much either. Molly and Jo are with her. Owen is likely still asleep on the couch in the other room."

Realizing that Renna probably assumed I loathed her now, I knew I needed to see her first thing. The issue here wasn't that I hadn't believed it was fake. It was just that I was hurting and needed a moment alone, but none of them would even give me space. So my magic had made it happen for me.

My magic.

It had helped me. It'd fed off my emotions and had protected me. It'd given me exactly what I needed.

I stood and looked for the door.

"Where are you going?" he asked quietly, though his voice sounded rough.

"I would like to go see Renna right away, but I was going to ask whatever guard outside the door to send for Silvia."

His forehead creased.

I gestured to my body. "So I can get out of this damn dress."

"Let me."

I moved to shake my head, knowing that we had a lot of talking to do before any undressing of any kind, but he put up a hand. "Only help you out of the dress. I will not touch you until you wish me to."

The anguish I felt through the bond and saw in his eyes had me nodding.

It wasn't until I agreed that he finally moved from his position against the wall and approached me.

I turned my back to him so he could undo the lacing. Fortunately for him, the loosening would be less tugging than the tightening had been for Silvia.

He gently lifted my hair and placed it over my shoulder, taking care not to touch my skin as he did.

I fought off a shiver, my back muscles tightening.

Krew started pulling on the strings as quickly and gently as he could. At what I assumed was about the third pull of string, I felt the corset loosen around my lower back.

I let out a sigh of relief.

"How is it possible you slept in this thing?"

I gave my head a slight shake. "I am not entirely sure."

Four more rows upward, I grabbed at my chest to hold everything in place. I took in huge pulls of air now that my lungs were finally free.

"Can I just cut if off?" Krew asked, sounding rather bewildered. "All that did was loosen. How do I get it off?"

I tried not to smile. "There are some clasps at the front that I will have to undo to finally be rid of it. Loosening it was all I needed." I spun and looked at him. "I'll change and be right back."

"Will you consider eating breakfast before you go?"

He knew he'd messed up. He knew how hurt I'd been. And here he was trying to make sure I ate breakfast and took care of myself after he'd been the one likely up all night watching me. "Can you send it to Renna's room?"

"Of course."

I inhaled deeply. "I'd like to go there right away and make sure she knows I don't hate her."

His eyes didn't leave mine, and we just stood there in an awkward silence as the moments ticked by.

I reached out my free hand to his wrist. "I don't hate you either."

He closed his eyes. "I know. It is your disappointment that I cannot bear." He gestured with his head toward the lavatory and closet. "Go change out of that deathtrap of a dress. We can talk later."

My hand fell from his wrist as I did exactly that.

I brushed my teeth and didn't bother to fix my hair at all. I wanted to speak with Renna first. Then I would face Krew. I didn't want to make him feel worse than he already felt, but I felt like I also needed to be honest.

I wasn't looking forward to it.

As I came back out into our bedroom, Owen was standing there waiting. "Can you—"

Knowing exactly what he was going to ask since we missed our morning training session, I immediately released my magic. At as close to the same time as possible, I sent tendrils of silver to the fire to put it out and relight it, as well as a sound barrier at the door, and then for extra flair I moved the book on the footrest around in a circular pattern. And then while keeping the book moving, I took down the sound barrier and again put out and relit the fire.

As I looked back at Owen, his eyebrows were up as his eyes were on Krew.

"Are we good now?"

Owen dipped his chin. "Yes."

"Then shall we?"

He rocked back to his heels. "We shall."

Out in the hallway, we made it two turns before I stopped in my tracks.

Owen immediately put up a sound barrier around us. "What is it?"

"Nothing." And then I threw my arms around him in a hug.

Not having expected it, his arms were just stuck, mine around him. "Thank you for trying to help me last night. I just needed a minute of space, and you were the only one who seemed to understand that." Him and my magic. "I wanted to give you a hug right away this morning, but I didn't want to further torture Krew any."

"Speaking of, how much longer will we be torturing him today?"

I pulled my arms away and began walking again.

Owen put up a finger as he fell into step beside me. "I only ask to prepare for his level of *sulking*. You had every right to be upset."

If I remembered right, Owen had also been upset. He'd held one of the king's guards up against the wall by the throat. "Will you be in any trouble at all? For defending me?"

He shook his head. "No." After a few footsteps he added, "Do you want to talk about it?"

I sighed. "Not really. I need to make sure Renna and I are fine and then I need to talk to Krew. So I'm afraid there will be far more talking this morning than I currently feel like."

Minutes later, we arrived at Renna's door.

I put up a hand to knock, but the door swung open before I could even touch it.

A puffy eyed Renna opened the door. She at least did look more rested than Krew, but she still looked like hell. And I had never seen her look anything other than flawless. It was a bit jarring.

"Hi."

"I'm so sorry," she blurted out.

I smiled at her. "I know. Can I come in?"

She nodded, taking a shaky breath.

As she stepped back so we could enter the room, I found Molly and a woman I assumed to be Jo already in the sitting area of Renna's room. A room quite similar to my first one at the castle. And our breakfast had apparently already arrived, waiting under silver trays.

This had to be the absolute worst way to meet Renna's wife, since I was the reason Renna was crying, but here we were. "Hi. You must be Jo."

"Hi, Jorah," Jo said not unkindly.

"Molls," I greeted.

Molly gave me a little wave as her greeting.

I sat on the end of Renna's bed, as sitting next to Jo on the couch felt too rude to someone I'd just met. And Molly was already in the chair.

Renna sat next to me, grabbing ahold of my hand. "Jorah, I'm so sorry." Her voice cracked halfway through her apology. "I am *so* sorry." She took a deep breath. "If I would have seen Jo in the hallway with someone, real or not, I would have lost my mind."

"I—"

She cut me off. "I need to say out loud, whether you believe me or not, that other than hold onto his jacket, I did not even touch Krew. I have never kissed Krew."

"I—"

"I know given your relationship with Keir and how many times you saw him kissing other women that what I am saying might be hard to believe, but I am telling you that I would never cross any lines with Krew, no matter the plan."

I looked at Molly sitting in the chair with a book in her lap and mouthed, "Sorry."

She gave me a shrug.

Renna kept going. "He just wants you safe from his father, Jorah. More than anything, more than he wants his father dead even. He wants you safe."

I assumed Renna's room was safe to talk freely since her wife was often with her, but not taking any chances, I pointed at the door and put up a sound barrier just to be sure.

"Oh my gods!" Molly's eyes were wide and her mouth slightly open. *"You have magic."*

I tipped my head back to the ceiling before looking back to Molly. "I have wanted to tell you all week, but I couldn't. Or I didn't. But I wanted to. And I'm sorry I didn't sooner. Can I explain in a minute? I need to talk to Renna for a few minutes and just wanted to be sure this was a safe area to speak."

Molly nodded, speechless for what had to be the first time in her life.

I turned back to Renna. "I know it wasn't real. I know why you both did it. But the fact remains that instead of being asked if this plan should be done or not, or having a say in it whatsoever, I was kind of just informed of its happening."

She finally went quiet, letting me talk.

"I also know the intentions behind it were pure, but it never should have happened, Ren. Not because of my messed-up history with Keir, but because it was just one step too far in trying to distract the king. And it was another step too far because you and Krew are both married, and not to one another."

Jo raised her hand. "I also disliked this plan. For the record."

Molly's voice was high as she said, "Wait! You and Krew *got married*?!"

"Sorry, Molls. I'll explain everything in a minute."

I turned my attention back to Renna as she wiped her eyes.

"I know we can't go back and do it over again. But I also know that if we could, we'd all do it differently. It is over and done with,

I get it. But just because I knew it wasn't real, didn't mean it didn't hurt."

She nodded. "I understand that."

I winced. "And I just needed a minute to gather my thoughts after having to contain my magic around everyone all night. I still have no idea how I pulled it off. No idea. But then as soon as Owen and I got back to Krew's wing, the both of you arrived. Then Keir. And then all the bickering and arguing. It was all so . . . *loud*."

While I took a deep breath, Renna said quietly, "And you needed space."

I gave her a tight smile. "Yes. So I created a barrier around myself to drown out the noise. Not because I hated you all, just because I wanted to be alone while I dealt with my hurt, while I got myself calmed down, while I gave myself the space to breathe."

Renna grabbed at her chest. "I am relieved. Owen told me that was probably the case, but—"

Jo interrupted with, "But you still stayed up most of the night and made Molly and I stay up with your moping ass?"

Renna gave her a nod, her chin crumpling as more tears formed in her eyes.

I squeezed her hand still in mine. "I don't hate you. I don't hate you even a little. Please just try to include me in these plans in the future. I know you and Krew have been conspiring together long before I came along, so it isn't natural to have me in the mix. I get it."

Renna shook her head. "But I love you both so much. I wouldn't change a thing."

I shook my head. "Nor I. I'd just like to focus all our energy onto the king. Because in the grand scheme of things, last night's plan hurt more than it helped. Krew is protective of me and I know that, but the only plans in play now should be toward the king. Not me. Krew gave me enough magic to ensure I was protected. So let's focus on what really matters. Getting the king off that throne."

I got up and moved closer to Molly. "And I am terribly sorry I never told you what was going on. You have been nothing but a great friend to me. For the longest time I told myself that keeping you in the dark was keeping you safe. That if you didn't know anything, the king couldn't hurt you." I sighed and wiped at a tear. "But I know all too well what that feels like, and I am so sorry for doing it to you. It should be your choice. So I'm offering it to you now, Molly. Would you like for me to share what has been going on? Knowing that it might make you more unsafe than you already are within the walls of this castle." I paused. "And also will you forgive me for being a horrible friend?"

She stood and hugged me. "Of course. And of course I want to know. Of course!"

I smiled at Renna and gestured with my head to the breakfast still waiting. "Well let's eat and I'll tell you anything you'd like. Where would you like me to start?"

Molly gave her head a shake. "Uh, the beginning. You know I like a good story."

So for the next hour, we ate breakfast. I talked to Molly while the rest of them ate, and then I ate while Renna took over and explained the rest, even including the Nara situation.

"So she's still here?" Molly exclaimed.

Renna winced. "I'm afraid so. Apparently she was the young woman you saw from a distance."

Molly just sat there a moment, looking in the direction of the window while also not really looking at anything in particular. "I can't believe it was Nara. This whole time. The king is creepy." She gave an exaggerated shiver. "How can she bring herself to see him naked? And not only see him naked but actually touch him?"

Renna gestured with a hand. "The realm may never know."

Molly took a drink of her coffee. "And I always knew about the disloyal. Heard it whispered about even in Savaryn. Particularly living so close to the Rallis wall. But I didn't realize exactly how many of us are disloyal to the king whether we label ourselves as such or not."

Renna grabbed at her chest. "Did you not know about Keir? I'm so sorry if I ruined it. I should've let him tell you, but once we got explaining, I figured you might as well just know it all."

She shook her head. "No. I knew Keir was conspiring to get his father off the throne. So I assumed he was working with the disloyal. Not surprised at all to find out he's been behind them all along." She paused. "I assume Jo already knew all of this, but will the two of you get in any trouble with the princes for bringing me up to speed?"

Renna looked to me.

I sighed. "I don't really care, Molls. I just do not care. If the king forces me to keep everyone I love at an arm's length, then he forces me to stop living the most vibrant part of my life. There is being safe and then there is ceasing to live, to love. I'm tired of riding that fine line."

With one more sip of my tea, I stood. "And I have a long overdue conversation with my husband to get to, if the three of you do not mind."

Renna's eyes went huge. "You didn't talk to him first?"

I shook my head. "No, I came here as soon as I was awake and out of that damned dress."

Renna's eyes went even larger, if that were possible. "He's going to be a wreck."

"I'm aware," I said lightly.

"Renna," Jo groaned. "Let them handle it on their own."

Renna put her hands in the air. "Right, right. Just not used to another woman being around to deal with Krew's mood swings."

"Sounds like the three of you all need naps anyway," I smiled, not really bothered. "I will see you all soon, I hope."

Out in the hallway, I gave Owen a tight smile.

He put up a moving sound barrier over us.

"One down, one to go," I told him. "Molly was there too, and I may or may not have just brought her up to speed on everything."

Owen gave me a shrug. "She's dating Keir. Best friends with both you and Renna. I always kind of assumed she knew more than she let on anyway."

I gave him a nod. "Exactly. So what was the point in keeping things from her?"

I was quiet the rest of the walk back to Krew's wing, trying to figure out what I wanted to say and how I wanted to say it. I didn't want to punish Krew or make him feel even more awful, but I wasn't about to act like everything was perfect either.

I took a deep breath as the door to Krew's wing came into view.

"Good luck," Owen said as he dropped our sound barrier.

"Thanks."

* * *

I ENTERED our wing by myself, looking for Krew. He was freshly showered and sitting out on the veranda. In the cold. It wasn't raining. Or snowing. But it wasn't all that nice outside either.

I went outside and sat down next to him, taking in how pretty the forest looked at this time of day. I had this vision of the forest vibrant and green, Krew chasing Warrick across the meadow, the king nowhere to be found. It didn't matter if Krew was then king or Keir was. It was just an image that I didn't want to let go of.

Tears pricked my eyes.

"Did your conversation with Renna not go well?" Krew asked gently.

I shook my head. "No. It went fine. I mean, you might be mad at me because I filled Molly in on just about everything, but it went really well. That isn't the reason I was getting choked up." And then down the bond, I added, *I miss Warrick.*

He closed his eyes and took a deep breath. *Me too. Father wants us to plan a trip to Nerede soon so you can fish for disloyal information. So we should be able to see him soon.* He stood and held a hand toward the door. "Shall we?"

I stood with him.

Once inside, we settled on the couch. Krew gave me space but turned slightly toward me. He reached for my hand but then stopped, as if unsure. "Tell me how to fix it." His eyes tore into mine, and I knew he hurt. He hurt because he knew he'd hurt *me*. He moved to rub his forehead with both hands, resting them on his temples. "I watched Keir do this to you on repeat and I promised myself I would never do it. And yet here we are, married less than a few weeks and I did. Just tell me how to fix it, please."

I reached over to put my hand on his shoulder. "You can't fix it, Krew. You just have to learn from it."

Krew tipped his head back to look at the ceiling. "I thought that Renna and I could get my father away from you. And seeing you struggling this much under the weight of the magic, that was all I really wanted for you. To get him off your back."

I sighed. "I understand all of that Krew. I understand the motive was to protect me. It doesn't change the result. It was too far."

"I agree."

Unable to speak at a normal volume, I whispered, "Please don't make me beg your father for anything else *ever again*."

He closed his eyes and tilted his head as I felt his pain down our bond. "I won't."

I leaned against the back of the couch. "And you didn't even ask me if I wanted you and Renna to do this. Before the bonding, I probably would have been all for it. But we are married now, Krew. And that means something to me."

His eyes flew to mine. "It means something to me too." His voice cracked. "It means . . . *everything* to me, Jorah."

"Okay, but you've got to stop all this constant scheming, Krew. I wasn't that thrilled about Nara. And I'm still not. So we go directly from that into me getting informed about the situation with Renna. I wasn't allowed the courtesy of being included in the planning. I was just told how it would all happen. All of these plans are exhausting, Krew. The only thing that matters is taking down your father. It could be a week. It could be a year. It could be five years. Let's focus solely on what we have to do to take him down and then the rest of the time let's live our damn lives." I paused, the tears finally spilling over. "I don't want to waste however short of time I may have as your wife with pointless plans that wouldn't matter at the end of the day anyway. I want to build a life with you."

I saw a tear slip down his own face. "I want that too, love. That's why I decided we should act on the Nara opportunity. It's why I feel an urgency now to remove my father from power."

"I get it," I agreed. "Let's just not waste our time on plans that don't matter long term. I want him gone too. But I also want to recognize myself in the mirror when he finally is."

Krew's eyes went to mine. Though I could feel his emotion down the bond, I wasn't certain I had ever physically seen anyone so full of self-loathing. He looked absolutely miserable. "I am sorry, Jorah. Truly. Sorry that out of my own insecurity of needing you safe, you were hurt in the process. It wasn't fair to you. I shouldn't have to hurt you in order to keep you safe. No matter how badly I do want that."

"In the future can you at least talk to me about these plans? Before they are already set in motion. I falsely assumed my days of being in the dark were over."

He sighed. "Yes. Absolutely. You were just struggling with how much magic I'd given you, and I didn't want to make things worse."

"Well by not including me in the planning of either the scheme for the ring or the Renna situation, not only was I left out, but I was also hurt. So it definitely made things much worse. I know I could barely keep my eyes open most days and that is on me, but it feels like I missed out on so much."

He gave me a nod and closed his eyes a moment. "I get that. I have no desire to keep things from you, love. Not ever."

"I'm sorry my magic kept you away from me all night. That wasn't my intention. At the time I just needed a moment of space and quiet and everything was so loud and in my face. I didn't mean for it to be all night," I explained. "But you could have easily broken the barrier and gotten to me, so why didn't you?"

"I felt how helpless and hurt you were. Combine that with seeing your magic was protecting you and providing for you what I could not, and I didn't want to break the barrier until you were ready for it to be broken. I told Owen, Renna, and Keir to leave it up. It should have been your decision on when it came down."

"Oh." That was kind of him. The barrier had been powerful, but Krew was fast enough and strong enough with his magic that he could have had it down in a few minutes. Instead, he'd stayed up likely the majority of the night, sitting on the floor outside of the barrier and allowing me some peace despite it torturing him to do so.

That thought had me moving to crouch in front of his legs. "Krew?"

"Yes, love?"

"May I have a hug? The magical kind that must last a full minute or longer?"

He closed his eyes and inhaled a deep breath. *I thought you'd never ask.*

And then I was being pulled onto his lap, my head against his chest while he held me. The seconds began ticking by. By the end of a few minutes, I felt his breathing even out and slow. So much so, I was afraid he was going to fall asleep right there with me in his lap.

"Krew."

"Mmm?"

"Let's go to bed," I offered while standing.

While he headed to the bed, grabbing his shirt and pulling it over his head, I pulled the curtains closed. "Will your father bother you for anything or can you sleep for a few hours?"

"I effectively told him this morning I was busy cleaning up another one of his messes."

I'd ask him later how all that went; for now, I was just grateful he could rest.

So in the middle of the day, I slid into bed next to him. I wasn't all that tired, but I knew Krew needed it. He needed me by his side after not being able to be by mine all last night.

"I love you," he whispered sleepily, brushing a kiss against my temple.

"I love you."

As I laid there considering everything and wondering for the thousandth time what might be the best possible way to get rid of the king, I realized that if Krew and I didn't figure this out, Krew's insecurities about the woman he loved being hurt by his father might be the thing that got him killed. My biggest fear was that in trying to protect us all, he'd never even make it to the showdown with his father.

And of all us, he deserved to be standing there when the king was no more.

CHAPTER 15

As dawn turned the sky to a blueish purple haze, my feet pounded into the hardened grass in the forest. In those first few days while I slept a ton and avoided my magic, Owen and Krew had jogged a trail through the forest for me, so that I didn't have to worry about random sticks and twigs tripping me up, and so that we could be out of the open view of the meadow. Now a worn path of a foot's width ran before me cutting into the dirt and leaves.

Owen's footsteps were right on mine, and I knew at any moment he was going to tell me to move my ass in that way that only he could, so I picked up speed and flew up the pathway.

Finally meeting the tree we were running to, I grabbed my knees, pulling the crisp morning air into my lungs.

"First day back is always the worst," Owen commented.

"You saying I'm slow?" I panted.

He shook his head. "No, I'm saying you haven't run in more than ten days and you're winded."

"Am not."

Owen glared at me. "You are grabbing your knees and cannot say more than three words without taking a breath."

I shook my head. "It's the magic." I tried to inhale through my nose quietly. "You know, my all-consuming power." That was six words. Another breath. "Makes it harder to run."

Owen rolled his eyes. "Wow." He took off his backpack and unzipped it to get out the wooden swords he'd packed. This morning Owen had decided it was time to get back to my training. Both physically, with running and wooden swords, and also my magic. Fortunately, we split the time between those three things, but I felt as if I was going to be training with Owen day in and day out.

It wasn't that I disliked Owen or his company. It was that I disliked Owen barking orders at me all the damn time.

"Come on, Your Highness," Owen said as he gestured with his wooden sword. "Let's see what you've forgotten."

Remembering what felt like a thousand times he had told me to tighten my core, I did such, and automatically shifted my weight onto the balls of my feet, making sure I was ready to move.

And move we did. Owen barely let me take a breath in between his advances. Unlike with the running, I hadn't lost as much with the sword as I had in being in physical shape. Soon the only sounds heard in the forest were the clacks of our wooden swords and the crunch of the leaves under our feet as we danced around one another.

I thought back to Krew telling me my magic was a built-in defense mechanism. I was able to keep my magic down easier now, but I was also a second or two quicker at suspecting what Owen was going to do before he did it.

Soon instead of stepping away to block his advances, I was stepping into them instead.

Owen grinned. "She gets it."

I spun away, knowing he was going to go for a side shot and

smacked his sword. He squinted. I wondered if I should not have poked the bear.

"You want to dance, Your Highness?"

Seeing my one and only opportunity to put in an advance until I was sure to be defending my very life, I spun around him and went in high like I would hit at his shoulders, before dipping the shoulder that held the sword at the last moment, smacking him in the calf.

Owen glared at me. Just stood there and glared.

I gave him a bow dipped in mockery. "That was a yes, Owen."

With a yelp I jumped back, feeling the very tip of the sword graze my stomach.

"I feel," Owen said as he lurched forward and swung at my neck, "as if I have trained you too well." Having blocked his shot there, he swung down for my legs, which forced me to jump back. "It is giving you a bit of a false sense of confidence."

I blocked and shoved his next shot at my stomach. "You know, you could just say I've improved."

He wrinkled his nose and spun around me, dropping down to go for my feet. "But then we'd have to worry about your ego, Your Highness."

I blocked him at my knees. "And yours, since you are such a great teacher."

He snorted and increased his speed. Toward the end, I was again panting, and it had been clear in the beginning he'd been going easier on me. But the extra second of reaction time I had to defend his advances was making a huge difference. If Owen would have gone that hard at me before I had magic, I would have been riddled with bruises. As such, I only had one graze and one spot where he'd managed to hit me. Knowing how good of a swordsman he was, I was going to call that a win.

Owen was at least also breathing heavily. Though I was tired enough I didn't want to anger him by pointing it out verbally. I knew he'd exerted himself harder than usual and that was all that mattered.

"I have a deal for you," Owen offered as he took my wooden sword and put it in his backpack.

I squinted. "What kind of a deal?"

"Practice defending my advances with your magic, and then I will let you heal two more trees."

I gave my head a shake, surprised with every little word of that. "What?"

"Krew said that because of the other night, the whole Renna thing, we can sell the fact that you were upset and crying in the forest again." Owen held up a hand as he dropped the bag. "And I know. My magic won't work on you. But I'll still throw it at you anyway, wrapped around objects until they almost reach you, just to get you used to the feeling as you figure out what to throw back at me." He paused. "I know you don't like using your magic on people, Jorah. I get it. But if you can't learn to trust your magic, at the very least, you need to learn how to react and use it without hesitation. If you hesitate for even a moment with the king, it could very well mean the difference between life and death."

I inhaled deeply. I didn't know how to explain to Owen that since my magic helped me the other night, I seemed to have some sort of weird agreement with it. It had wanted to protect me just as much as it did Krew. Up until that moment, it had felt like Krew's magic that was just living in my body. But when it had been fighting to the surface, wanting me to use it to protect myself from everyone else, Krew included, I realized that it was also *mine*. "Okay."

Owen stood there a second just looking at me.

"What?"

He shrugged. "I expected more of a fight is all."

"Well, I get to heal two trees, right?"

He nodded. "Yes. Depending on how quickly we finish, maybe even before we go feed the wolves."

I gestured with a hand. "Well, shall we?" I gave a shrug. "Seems like it will be fun for me but not you, since your magic will not work on me."

Magic flew out of Owen's hand and wrapped around a stick, that he sent rolling around the ground in the direction of my feet.

For a moment I almost didn't move. Magic couldn't work on me. But then I remembered the caveat to that. Like when Owen had first warmed a blanket for me, magic could still work on my surroundings, just not my person.

With a shove of my hand, I blew the stick away only to find more. Numerous smaller sticks and one very large log were rolling my way. Depending on if Owen sent them all at the same speed or not, it was going to be difficult to avoid them all.

"Great," I muttered. I noticed the hum and burn of magic in my veins and for once it felt welcome and not a burden. With one pulse of magic out of my hand, I froze all of them.

I smiled triumphantly only to find sticks and pebbles flying my direction. So many they were about to be raining on me.

When I woke up today, I hadn't really considered a morning stoning to be on my schedule.

Before Owen dropped them on me, I reacted, my silver magic rushing in and replacing all Owen's green. I froze them all in the air.

While I understood what Owen was doing, preparing me for the one way other Enchanted could use their magic against me, I was still annoyed with him for it all the same. In one push, I sent the sticks and rocks all back toward him. Except I imagined there to be a hundred little domes of magic around them, protecting them against his magic while I sent them all hurtling his way.

Having not expected me to do that, with a curse, Owen was

soon jumping and moving, doing his best to not get waylaid by my literal onslaught of sticks and stones.

As one decent sized pebble struck him in the shoulder when he jumped over a log, I couldn't help but snicker.

On and on we went. Owen finding random objects in the forest to throw at me. At one point he was moving so quickly that I didn't have time to send everything back to him or put the domes on them to keep them under my control.

By the time we stopped, my skin was buzzing and I was feeling the adrenaline high of having used magic.

Owen seemed more out of breath than I was. It might make me twisted with the amount of joy that brought me.

"Are we done?" I asked.

"Yes, Your Highne—"

Unable to resist, I sent magic to blow him backward, and then suspended him in the air. Upside down by a rope made of my silver magic.

Having been tired from using so much magic and being completely unsuspecting, Owen was now suspended in the air, his head level with mine as he dangled in front of me. "What was that you were saying about my hiney?"

Seeing him try to glare at me upside down was just too much to resist. A laugh erupted out of my throat, followed by an entire fit of giggles.

Owen may kick my butt on the daily in swordplay, but thanks to Krew I was strong enough with magic to mess with him a little. And it was the *best*. Possibly the best damn thing that had happened to me since becoming bonded to Krew.

"You don't think I can get myself down?" Owen challenged.

I shook my head. "I do, but don't. You'll break your neck—"

Owen's green magic sliced through my silver magic holding him upside down, and he began to fall.

I immediately released my own magic to catch him, envisioning a hundred pillows for him to land on. Owen fell into my magic, and then bounced up to his feet. He could have possibly done the same with his own magic, made it somehow catch him, but he hadn't. Only my silver magic broke his fall.

"You ass!"

He gave me a shrug. "I trusted you to save me."

"You could've died," I argued. "Not exactly a good trust exercise."

He grinned. "Maybe not, but a decent one at seeing if you'd hesitate with your magic or not."

I tipped my head back and groaned. "Can we go heal some trees now?"

Owen held up a finger. "Stretch first. Then trees."

"Fine."

I was still shocked Owen had trusted my magic enough to have caught him, but it'd been such a great morning that I wasn't going to let Owen's poor decisions ruin this day.

Minutes later as we walked in the direction of The Dead Lake, Owen asked, "Do you want to train early mornings or late nights? Doing both is hell on both of us and you use enough magic now that there is no need for both. So I'll let you pick."

I thought that over. "If we train early morning, Krew and Keir will be done with their usual training sooner?" I hated mornings. Loathed them entirely, but I also enjoyed being able to spend my nights with Krew. If he had to practice with Keir and then with me every night, we were up entirely too late every night. Though maybe that was safest to keep from the king, I selfishly wanted those nights with my husband.

"Yes."

I wanted to stomp. I couldn't believe I was actually signing up for this. I knew I needed to practice combining my magic with Krew. And then we needed to see if Keir's magic would combine with Krew's once his combined with mine, but I also preferred training with just Owen. He wasn't my husband. He was a safe place I could use my magic without the added emotions of having the princes around. "Mornings."

"You do know we will have to be up at dawn to train every morning before the king awakes?"

I sighed. "I do."

Owen grinned but then threw out, "You know I'm not going to go easy on you, right honey?"

"You know I'm going to be belligerent every morning, right honey?"

As soon as we made it in view of the lake, still black unfortunately, I looked at the two healthy and growing trees I'd already healed. I had wanted to heal one or two a day and turn them all to green, but Krew and Keir had been adamant about it being a slow process. Doing too much too fast would be a clear sign to the king that something drastic had changed.

Like me being given magic.

"Can I do that huge one over there?" I asked. "Its roots touch the lake." Drawing my magic into my fingers, I shot it into a sound barrier and magic barrier around us, making it thick enough to block out anyone who would happen upon us. I'd rather them see a random dome of silver magic than see magic flowing from my palms.

Owen was eyeballing my magic when I turned to look at him. "Sure."

In a few short minutes, I had healed the large tree with the roots in the lake and one other small tree next to it.

I smiled triumphantly as I walked back to where Owen stood. "Let's go feed the wolves now."

"Race you back to the kitchen?"

He didn't give me the opportunity to answer, he just took off.

"That's cheating," I called as I took off after him.

As we wove our way back to the meadow, feet pounding into the ground as we ran, I felt and heard footsteps near to us.

Slowing slightly, I saw a gray and black blur through the trees running alongside us.

Rafe. Rafe and his second were running with Owen and me.

We slowed to a walk as we hit the meadow.

"I'll go get the food," Owen offered. "Don't piss off the wolves while I'm gone."

I sat down in the grass right on the edge of the meadow while I waited for him to return with the food.

"Hi, Rafe," I called out nicely to where they had also stopped running and now stood watching me. "Who is your friend?"

I looked to the other wolf, the scar running across his nose.

"He's beautiful. I don't know where he got that scar, but I am glad he is still here."

As if understanding my every word, the two wolves came forward a few steps.

I kept my voice soft. "Owen is going to grab the food, then you two can eat."

Rafe stepped forward, sniffing along the ground as he approached me. Remembering how all the wolves had showed up the night of our wedding, probably having felt the shockwave of magic from the actual bonding, I felt nothing but respect and awe for these creatures.

I loved these wolves. I wanted the forest healed and fixed for many reasons, but I also wanted to see their pack healthy, too.

The black wolf followed behind Rafe, far more tentative, stopping to look me in the eyes every few inches.

"It's okay, buddy," I offered. "I do not wish to harm you."

Rafe, having reached me, sniffed my hand and then nudged it with his nose. I gently ran my fingers along his nose like I knew he liked.

"We have come a long way haven't we, Rafe?"

The other wolf slowly approached. Though the black wolf never touched me, he did get almost a foot away, sniffing in my direction the entire time. Once he got as far as he felt comfortable coming, he wagged his tail gently.

"Nice to meet you too," I smiled. "We are going to need a name for you, aren't we?"

Both wolves snapped their heads up in the direction of the back hedge and I knew that Owen must be returning with the food.

"Ready for breakfast?" I asked them.

The wolves backed up into the trees by the time Owen made it back over.

I was smiling ear to ear as we walked back across the meadow to the castle. I needed a shower and a nap. Particularly if I was going to have to switch my days back to normal hours now. But it had been a good morning.

* * *

I READ one of the queen's journals as I waited for Krew to return from dinner. We'd long since finished checking every page for any more secret messages, but now I just read them for entertainment. To get to know the mother-in-law I should have met but never would. A woman I think I would have really loved.

I was exhausted. It had been a great day, but I was ready for bed. I yearned for the days when we could train in daylight hours, not having to hide it from the king with either late nights or early mornings.

Furthermore, I yearned for the day we all didn't spend multiple hours a day training to kill the king. It'd be nice to be able to train for *ourselves*. Or find some other less violent hobbies. I wasn't sure when the last time Owen just sat down to read a book was, but his neck muscles told me it'd been a while.

Some day. Some day, Keir and either Gwen or Molly could run the country, king and queen, and Krew and I could raise Warrick and our own family in some random wing of the castle. Krew would have to keep the disloyal at bay and continue his work with The Six, and I'm sure also help his brother in numerous ways with the weight of the crown. And Owen would be there too, not needing to be my personal guard any longer, but back to helping Krew and being his shadow. But we would all be free. Free to not only live our lives, but also free to finally fix the issues that plagued Wylan.

Of course, there was also the chance that Krew was the true heir to Wylan and we would be the ones ruling the country. And though that thought had long ago plagued me, I also knew Krew would, unlike his father, be a just king. The truth was that it didn't really matter which brother became king. The day Theon was off the throne was the day the healing in Wylan would begin.

Krew came in the door shortly after and I realized that I'd been daydreaming and not reading any more pages of the journal for multiple minutes now.

"I am not training with Keir tonight," Krew informed me.

I smiled. "I am not training with Owen tonight."

As he began taking off his tailcoat he added, "I heard the two of you will be switching to mornings." He threw his tailcoat at the foot of the bed. "And Keir and I will probably only practice a few nights a week now. We need to keep our focus on finding the object which holds our mother's magic, which can fortunately be done in the daylight."

"No word about the ring yet?"

Krew shook his head. "No. No good news anyway. It appears it may be just that, a ring."

I sighed. After all Nara had done and the lengths they had gone to in order to get the ring, it still might not be the object with the queen's magic. And they'd already stolen the king's dagger to have it tested also. What other object could it be? Was it possible it was a small coin or something that we had never even seen? Something so small it could go on his person unnoticed? Or was it the crown itself? There were still too many possibilities to narrow it down confidently.

I groaned as I moved to the edge of the chair to stand up.

Krew gave me a confused look.

"We started back up running today," I explained. "I am sore."

"Owen said you had a good day of training though."

I grinned, still unable to get the image of Owen dangling upside down in front of me out of my mind. "It was." I looked at Krew and paused for a moment. "I didn't know how to explain this to Owen, but until the other night, I always considered my magic *your* magic just trapped in my body." I took the hand Krew held out for me to help me up out of the chair. "It wasn't until it wanted to protect me and help me, even from you, that I realized it was mine too. So maybe there is one good thing that came from that night."

Krew helped me to my feet and ran his fingers through my hair. "Of course it's yours." He brushed a gentle kiss to my lips. "It was a gift. To you. I knew when I gave it to you it would no longer be mine. But I also know you struggle with it at times. Owen and I see that, but we also see the potential. Not of what you can do for us, for the cause, but of what you will be able to do *for yourself*. I hope there soon comes a night where you sleep well because you know you are not helpless nor will ever be defenseless again."

I knew we were both exhausted and still recovering from the night of the ball, but there was only one thing I wanted right now. Krew had still somewhat kept his distance from me since our argument. I remembered his words from the morning when I woke up with the dome around me. *I will not touch you until you wish me to.* He needed sleep last night, but tonight more than I wanted him, I needed him.

I needed to forget all about the king, about which object held the queen's magic, and about how we could ever attempt the impossible of getting his father off that throne. I just needed *him*. To feel with my own fingertips how alive he was. To finish exploring his body in a way that ensured I'd live a thousand lifetimes and never forget it.

Krew?

Yes, love?

I was sure to regret this decision when Owen would roll me out of bed long before dawn, but I couldn't find it in me to care. *I need you to touch me.*

Without another word, Krew made all space between us vanish and kissed me with the kind of thoroughness that made me feel as if it'd never be enough. No matter how much time we had left together, it'd never be enough.

CHAPTER 16

"I am numb."

We'd just been in a meeting for the tour of the kingdom, which had taken hours. The Assemblages were officially down to six women. Krew's Assemblage consisted of Renna, Isla, and me. Keir's held Gwen, Delaney, and fortunately for Renna and me, Molly. Of the six of us, only Gwen and I were from the lower levels of the kingdom. But I also knew from getting to know Molly, she was somewhat considered a lower level of the kingdom because her family line of magic was weaker. So though she was Savaryn-born, she was treated as if she was from Rallis.

Still, this was going to be quite the adventure for the Savaryn women who had never seen anything other than Savaryn. Molly seemed to be the only one who was overjoyed with the concept of visiting the other levels of the kingdom. It felt as if the others viewed it as if it were an inconvenience.

I smiled at Renna. "Silvia had told me the meetings with the Assemblage advisor were boring, but until I experienced one myself, I just didn't quite understand."

Molly slipped her hand into my arm on the other side. "Are you excited to be going on a tour of the kingdom?"

I gave her a look. "Yes and no. Since I can't fully explain here, we will go with yes." I was honestly terrified. I would have to keep my magic reigned in all day, plus I hadn't been back to Nerede since the fires. I only hoped the disloyal wouldn't use this as an opportunity for another ill-advised plan.

Feeling a trace of magic travel in my palms, I squeezed my hand and willed my magic down. "I am happy to see my mother and see how fast the king has been rebuilding the bakery, even if I know it will only be for a short amount of time."

"It sounds as if we are taking half of Savaryn with us," Renna stated.

I knew what she wasn't saying. The king was making a show of sending numerous commanders and their men, ensuring there would not be a disloyal attack on the way. I hoped with Gwen and I still in the Assemblages, the king was right. The people of Nerede had given me their word; the people of Rallis, however, I had no connection with.

I was a little surprised we were doing this tour to begin with. Parliament had suggested it to the king as a way to rally support behind the princes as the Assemblages ended, and the king must have decided it was worth the risk. Either that or he was hoping something happened, just so he could deal with it.

"I'm heading down to the gardens for fresh air," Molly declared. "You two want to come with me?"

I had already trained with Owen today, so other than a nap, I was free for the rest of the day. Fresh air sounded fantastic. Particularly since I wouldn't have to run or train in it. I could just walk the scenery with Renna and Molly. "Sure."

We let our guards know and headed with them down the stairs in the direction of the gardens. We would have invited Gwen too, but she had been avoiding all of us since the argument we had while playing cards.

"Don't worry though," I told Molly. "If Keir shows up while we are down there, Renna and I will mysteriously have other responsibilities to attend to."

Molly rolled her eyes. "So subtle."

"Emergencies do happen," Renna added.

Molly glared. "What kind of emergency would occur while in the gardens, pray tell?"

"An unexpected . . ." Renna began but stumbled as she thought for more words.

"Bosom . . . happening?" I added.

Molly's eyes looked ready to leave her head entirely. "An unexpected bosom happening? *That* is the very best you can do?"

Renna swatted at the air. "Like these men know anything about bosoms. We could probably say we had a leaky bosom because of our cycle, and they'd likely just agree and get rid of us as fast as possible. They know nothing about the inner workings of a woman."

"A leaky bosom?!" Molly wheezed. "None of us have children yet. As if we are all just walking around ready to spring a leak at any given moment."

"Some of us more so than others," Renna deadpanned while looking directly at Molly.

We laughed as we rounded the corner outside, Molly having to grab the side of the doorframe for air.

"I hope," Molly laughed, "the two of you never have to concoct a story on the fly. Your plotting skills are left wanting."

I saw some blonde hair in the distance as someone turned the corner.

Knowing we were the only consorts down here and there was likely only one non-consort person it could be, I grabbed my skirts and followed.

"Jorah?" Renna asked, amusement still on her voice as she finished laughing.

"Nara," I whispered.

The three of us sobered immediately and hurried to catch her.

But she was also picking up speed, so though we could see her back, we found we were not gaining on her at all.

"Nara," I called out lightly. I didn't want to make a scene. But I did want to see her with my own two eyes to see that she was well.

She hesitated but didn't turn around.

Molly whispered, "Distract her, I'll cut her off."

Her words barely registered before she abandoned the walkway to hop over some bushes. And fell.

"Umph."

I pressed my lips together to keep from laughing as Molly popped right back up and cut across the starting-to-green grass to intercept Nara. There were enough thick trees lining the spot where Nara stood that if Molly crouched down, she would likely be successful.

She was right. Her plotting skills were way better than ours.

"We just want to make sure you're okay," I said to Nara's back. "That's all, promise."

Nara took one small step forward.

"And we miss you," Renna added. "Gwen and Molly had a falling out. We are short two card players."

That had Nara turning slightly, lines in her forehead as if she wondered what had happened.

"It gets exhausting besting these two in cards every time," Renna added. "You are welcome to come play again."

Now Nara turned the rest of the way around. "And now I know you're lying."

I smiled triumphantly. "Only the last part was embellished." Renna and I began taking slow and small steps toward Nara. "Molly and Gwen really did have a falling out. That part was true."

"Over Prince Keiran?" Nara asked, crossing her arms.

Molly popped back out of the trees and onto the walkway, effectively trapping Nara between us. "Of course."

Nara spun in the direction of Molly. "You have a twig. In your hair."

I tried to trap the laugh in my throat but seeing Molly standing there in such a lovely gown with a twig coming out of her hair was just too much given our already silly conversations earlier.

And then we were all laughing, even Nara.

"Are you okay?" I asked Nara as soon as the laughter died down. "We truly just wanted to know you were okay."

She looked from Renna to me and then to Molly. "You guys know? That I'm—"

"Spending time with the king?" Molly offered wisely. "Yes, we know."

"How—" Nara shook her head. "Never mind. That question has an obvious answer. The princes."

"To be fair," I explained, "only Renna found out at first. Then because she was worried about you, she told Molly and me."

"Oh. That makes sense, I suppose," Nara said with a tight smile.

She looked okay. A little tired with the dark circles under her eyes, but she also didn't look bruised and battered. So there was that. I kept scanning her arms, wanting to look at her wrists for bruises that matched the ones I'd been given by the king, but from what I could see of her skin from around her navy gown, she was fine.

"So are you?" Molly asked gently in that way that only Molly could.

"Am I spending time with the king?" Nara asked. "Yes."

Molly shook her head. "No. *Are you okay?*"

Nara took a deep breath. "Yes. I'm okay. Not . . ." She trailed off. "I thought being the king's mistress would be far more . . . glamorous? He is kind to me though. And I'm not in Rallis."

He was kind to her likely because she was giving him something he wanted. I swallowed down how repulsive that thought was. Even if Nara was blind to it right now, she still needed to be saved from this man.

"Well, if you are ever not okay," I added at a whisper. "Please let someone know?"

Nara bounced her shoulders in a shrug. "I think sometimes even he just gets lonely. And for the most part he is easily . . . satiated."

I tried not to lose my lunch on the spot.

"He can be charming when he wants to be and is quite handsome for his age," Nara finished.

Molly also looked like she wanted to gag. "So, are you happy?" she asked.

Nara cocked her head. "No. I wouldn't say that I am happy. But I also wouldn't say that I am unhappy. I am out of Rallis. So for now, that is enough."

I took a deep inhale, trying to bite my tongue. If she wasn't happy with the king, then what did she think she was doing sleeping with a man who tortured people that merely irked him? Did she truly have no idea what kind of volatile situation she had just planted herself into? I'd always taken Nara to be shy but observant, not oblivious. Then I thought of her curiosity with the Hallow's Eve outfits. Maybe there was a lure to being the king's mistress. While it sounded like the makings of a grand love story, instead she'd planted herself in the middle of a tragedy.

I pushed my magic down and decided that to get Nara to see the light, tough love would not be getting us anywhere. We were going to have to kill her with kindness. Maybe there was a reason she didn't want to return to Rallis. Or maybe there wasn't. Either way, we needed to get to the bottom of this.

"Will he allow you to play cards with us?" I asked nicely. "Or see us, I suppose, since he doesn't know we play cards."

"Oh, he knows," Nara said with a smirk. "He just doesn't care."

"Well he used to," I snapped, unable to say it nicely. He'd left bruises on my wrist for that very reason.

"I will ask," Nara said, unaffected by my harsh tone. "He feared his sons' reaction to our . . . *relationship,* so there for a while I was sequestered away." She paused. "Now that the princes know and the cat is out of the bag, so to speak, he may allow it. Just as he allows my trips down here for fresh air."

Until this moment, I hadn't realized how docile Nara was. Of course the king would have picked her. The king's most glaring flaw was his constant need for control. And Nara was what he believed pliable. Easily controlled.

I had a sinking feeling in my gut. If Nara was truly just after an escape from Rallis, that was one thing. But if she was after a crown, the princes had severely underestimated her. How they had convinced her to take the king's ring was beyond me. Having seen her in person made me even more terrified for her.

And trust her even less.

* * *

I WAS in a hurry to get back upstairs and explain to Owen everything that had happened downstairs with a thick sound barrier up. He'd of course been in the gardens with me, but with the other guards, he had kept a respectable distance. He'd heard nothing of our conversation, but I just knew from the tilt of his jaw he was dying to know what had transpired.

Not that a lot had happened, but I still wanted to know his opinion on how trustworthy Nara really could be now that she was sleeping with the king.

As soon as we were in the room, I slipped out of my heels and moved to put up a sound barrier. Just as I was about to release my magic, I stilled.

There had been a blanket on the bench at the foot of the bed that was now on the couch. It was a blanket I adored but Krew loathed because it made him too hot. He never would have grabbed it and put it there.

My eyes went to the fireplace and saw one of the queen's journals knocked onto the floor from the footrest.

I always left the journal I was reading on the footrest. And knowing the message his mother had sent to us in those journals, I never would have been so careless to leave it upon the floor.

"What is it?" Owen asked, his own green magic making the sound barrier I'd been about to create.

"Someone has been in here," I explained. "And Silvia doesn't normally move our things around."

"Krew has been busy all day, I thought," Owen added.

I gave him a nod and moved to look in the next room over. Nothing looked out of place except the dresser where Krew kept his bottles of liquor had a drawer slightly ajar.

I felt my magic crawl up my arms and down my spine. Someone had been in here.

Love? Everything okay?

He must have felt my surprise down the bond. *I don't know. Someone has been in your wing.*

As in someone other than Silvia or Owen?

Yes. There are only three things out of place, but I know Silvia would not have messed around near your liquor bottles.

Krew was quiet a moment, likely talking to someone wherever he was. *I'll be up within the hour.*

Owen joined me and began looking around. "Anything?"

"A drawer ajar. Whoever was in here was looking very carefully and doing their best to make it seem that they hadn't been here at all."

Owen's forehead wrinkled.

"The Six?"

Owen shook his head. "No. Though they have access to his wing, Krew has rules for when they can come. Showing up unannounced would majorly piss off Krew and they all know that."

I had been trying to block him out of my memory entirely and I hated that I hadn't asked or given him much thought these past few weeks with everything going on. "Easton?" My skin hummed, as my magic seemed to loathe him just as much as I did. The man who killed my father.

Owen gave his head a shake. "He is still in the mountain. Kind of. It's a comfortable sort of jail. Not like the part of the mountain where the king likes to inflict pain. He will be there until the Assemblages are done and Krew has calmed down enough to deal with him."

I rubbed my head. "Who would have been in here, then?"

Owen gave a shrug. "The king or one of his minions, likely."

"Looking for the ring," I added.

Owen gave a nod.

The door opened and Krew came in, finding us still looking at the drawer partly ajar.

Krew moved to replace the sound barrier he had broken through at almost the same time I did. Our magic combined as it hit the main door to Krew's room, and instead of looking like a webbing of magic, it seemed to form a brick wall.

I'd been so busy training with Owen lately that I had done very little combining magic with Krew yet. We'd been too busy waiting around for Krew's magic to vanish, except it never had.

"Wow," Owen commented.

I gave my head a shake. "Was it because I'm feeling anxious and paranoid? I did not send *that* much magic."

Owen just kept staring at the sound barrier with his head cocked, the weirdest expression on his face.

"I might just be being paranoid," I offered as I spun toward Krew. "But the blanket was moved from the bench to the couch, one of your mother's journals knocked on the ground carelessly, which Silvia or I would never do." I pointed. "And that drawer is now ajar."

Krew was immediately next to me, his hand on my lower back. "No. You are not paranoid. I have no doubt my father sent someone digging."

"Don't you have a guard outside the door at all times or something?"

"Yes and no. When either of us are here, there are guards there, yes. Three when both of us are here. But during the day there are occasions of shift changes when it can go unguarded for a few minutes. Everyone knows better than to dare come near my wing." He paused. "I will remedy that immediately. It just hasn't been an issue in years. And it is only unguarded for at most ten minutes while the guards check in with me wherever I am located."

I thought back to how Krew had been when we'd first met. I was pretty sure he made it clear to everyone that he was not someone you just stopped in on. He had a point. Still, with all the secret meetings he had with The Six and such, it was probably a good idea to keep his wing locked up tight.

Krew rubbed his hand up and down my back. "I am sure it was just my father or one of my father's men. Looking for the ring." He paused. "Which they will not find."

I nodded. "Okay. That's kind of what Owen and I assumed." I would have also maybe suspected Nara, but since we had just been in the gardens with her, she was officially off the hook.

Krew looked out the window a moment as if looking for the ring.

"What?" I asked.

Krew gave his head a shake. "With the tests they are running, the ring thus far has been acting like only a ring, not an object siphoned with magic." He paused. "I can't help but wonder, if the ring truly contained my mother's magic, would my father have cared about making it look like he hadn't been here? He'd have just tossed the entire wing."

I sighed. "So you don't think the ring is it?"

Krew shook his head. "No. I don't."

"Then why still look for the ring?"

"I have no idea. With as much as my father likes shiny objects, and as often as he wore it, he probably just misses the damn thing."

I rubbed a hand at my temples. "But do we need to be concerned that he thought to search here? Given that Nara was his only initial suspect?"

Owen snorted. "Not really. If anything goes missing, or if anything goes wrong for that matter, the princes are usually the first to be blamed."

Krew rolled his eyes. "That's definitely true, but he could just ask me. I wish he would so I could try to get a read on him."

My eyes went back to that drawer ajar. I wanted to walk the entire wing and check all the closets. Also under the bed since I knew personally what a good hiding spot that could be. It was just strange to consider that one of the king's men had been here. My safe place.

"Are you all right?" Krew asked gently.

I popped my shoulders up into a shrug. "I don't know. I don't like the thought of your father or one of his men in your wing."

"Our wing," Krew corrected.

"Our wing," I agreed.

Owen pointed at the door. "I don't think you are going to need to worry about it happening again if your magic can do that when combined."

He had a point. Other than the silver magic that we wouldn't want one of the king's men to find. "Maybe it was a fluke?" I offered. "Because I was stressed out thinking that someone was up here? In my safe place?"

Owen glared at me and crossed his arms. "Nothing is ever a

fluke with you, Jorah. Not your magic. Not the damn wolves in the forest. None of it."

The wolves had started running with us in the forest in the mornings. It was making getting out of bed in the morning a little easier. I fought the smile tugging on my lips.

"Do it again," Owen challenged. "Take it down and put it back up if you don't believe me."

I creased my forehead thinking of all the nights I had trained with Krew and Keir both. "Why haven't we gotten around to combining our magic more yet?"

Owen snorted. "Because you've been too busy combining . . ." he paused to bring his hands together, interweaving his fingers, "yourselves."

I should have been surprised with his crassness, and yet I wasn't. It was just how Owen was.

Krew shot me a grin that had me catching my breath. "We have been *rather* busy. Also *rather* thorough."

"Stop." I rolled my eyes. "Owen isn't going to let this go until we do a barrier again, so get your thoughts out of the gutter."

Krew trailed his hand down my back. "Likely not."

With a flick of my fingers, the barrier fell, and I sent another one back to replace it. This time taking extra care to envision only the smallest amount of magic.

But the moment Krew's navy magic joined with mine, the same thing happened, both strands of magic becoming significantly thicker. Rather than becoming a light blue color, it just looked like a significant amount of silver magic outlined in navy, his magic wrapping around mine to further protect it. I wondered if he was the first one to send out the magic, if my silver would outline his. And could Keir's combine to his, strengthening it even more?

Owen was shaking his head as he rocked back on his heels. "Well, will you look at that."

I closed my eyes a moment, trying not to get too far ahead of ourselves. "Can we just go back to the fact that one of the king's spies could still be hiding in *our* closet right now?"

Owen cocked his head at me. "Ah no, honey. I swept the entire wing as soon as you suspected someone had been in here." He squinted. "I'm a little wounded you would assume I didn't."

"Hey Raikes," Krew began.

"What?"

"How about you take the rest of the night off? I just cleared my schedule to come deal with this, so I'll stay with Jorah until dinner."

Owen crossed his arms. "You two are just *a lot*, you know that? We need to be doing some more combining of another sort soon, all right?"

"Agreed." As Krew laughed, Owen headed for the door, breaking the sound barrier as he went.

I spun to look at Krew, grateful for the extra time with him since he would be training with Keir tonight, but surprised with it all the same. I didn't say anything, I just looked at him.

He put his hands on my waist and then pulled me in closer. "What?"

"You just got rid of Owen because—"

"Because he pulls extremely long hours," he leaned down to brush a light kiss on my collar bone, "protecting one of the two people I love most in the entire realm."

I felt the smile playing at the corners of my mouth. "Is that the only reason?"

"No." He switched to the other side of my collar bone. "I found seeing our magic combine *extremely attractive*."

As soon as he brought his head up to meet my eyes, I whispered, "You fiend."

He brushed a gentle kiss to my lips. "I don't think you realize all the times I wished to touch you and couldn't. Either because I was supposed to be only faking a relationship with you or because you needed time and space to heal from my brother." Another kiss. "You were always just out of reach. Sometimes this doesn't all feel real."

I laughed as he scooped me into his arms. "I know *exactly* what you mean."

CHAPTER 17

As we loaded into open-topped carriages for the tour of the townships, I was relieved for the weather. It was still quite chilly this morning, but the sun was shining, and we were sure to have a warmer day than it had been the past week.

I longed for spring. I longed for the days the sea started to warm and breezy walks on the beach were welcomed and not chilling. But for today, I would take it. I had a blanket across my lap for now, but by the time we returned to the castle, I shouldn't need it.

Krew and his Assemblage had one carriage, Keir's another. The horses were commanded to begin walking, and we were off. We were told it was going to be like a five-hour parade. The people of every level in the kingdom would wave and line the streets as we came by. So though I was used to this trip at this point, I was not used to being made a spectacle of in front of every level of the kingdom. All in a day's work.

I was on one side of Krew, Isla on the other, Renna sitting across from us. Were it not for Isla in the carriage with us, I would be able to use my magic out of view at our feet. As such, with Isla sitting right next to Krew, and the king's guards all around us, I was just going to have to suppress my magic all day.

I hadn't gone so long without using magic since the first days after I received it. I wasn't sure how this would go. And losing control over my magic in a street full of people seemed like a bad idea.

Owen and I had trained hard that morning in anticipation of the tour and I felt fine for now. This trip took us between three and four hours when Owen and I normally traveled, but because of how slow we would have to drive through the groups of people, it would likely take five there and four back. We would stop in Nerede long enough to swap out the horses and then would head back.

It was going to be a long day.

I glanced over at Owen, riding horseback right next to my side of the carriage and he gave me a smile like he was channeling me luck.

I didn't need luck, I just needed to not use my magic in front of a large amount of people today. Granted the king was going to figure it all out eventually, I just hoped it was going to be closer to his date with death than today was.

The first wall creaked open and I saw lines of Savaryn people, waving and cheering. Keir's carriage was in front, and as soon as we slowly started forward, I saw Molly, Gwen, and Delaney wave at the crowd. People lined the road for as far as I could see.

It felt odd watching the Savaryn people cheer and be so *frivolous*. These were the most powerful people in the kingdom. The Enchanted. The king's army. And here they were, all smiling and cheering and having a good time. I'd seen these people at the balls often, but I'd never seen them like this. They looked so . . . *normal.* Because we were of course in Savaryn and not one of the lower levels, the Savaryn people had brought flowers with them, throwing them at the carriages as we maintained our slow speed.

Normally I would judge them for being so wasteful, but they all looked like they were having such a great time, I couldn't find it in me to be mad. I just knew in Rallis and Nerede we would not be getting any flowers.

"No one dare drop their smile," Renna said through clenched teeth. "You know how Savaryn people love to talk."

Isla snorted a laugh of agreement. I think that applied to all levels of the kingdom. And I was pretty sure my face would be sore by the end of this if I was expected to smile and wave for all of it.

Fortunately, though, after the first two miles or so, the lineup of people started to thin. The majority of people had lined up near the wall for the parade.

I saw Leon and Kallon Givicci standing in a clump of people. "Renna," I offered. "On this side."

Krew made the sign to the guards and carriages to stop, and the carriage had not even stalled before Renna was out of the carriage and hiking up her skirts to race to her family. They met her in a huge hug of smiles and limbs.

Guilt washed over me watching all of them in what appeared to be the front lawn of their home. Renna should be back here with her family by now. She and Jo both. But they were stuck at the castle for at least another few weeks, if not another few months.

But seeing their big family, and how genuinely happy her siblings all seemed to see her, it made me happy. I didn't have siblings, but I always imagined if my parents had been able to have more children, we would have had a close-knit family like Renna's.

Are you all right, love?

I looked at him where he was moving to get out of the carriage also and smiled through watery eyes. *I just love her family. That's all.* I didn't want to add that I hoped we could someday have a family like that. It felt like I was supposed to be accepting eventually becoming a widow, not dreaming of any futures.

"Jorah!" I spun to see Renna's dad Leon walking over to the carriage. "Get your butt down here!"

Out loud, I asked Krew, "Do you mind, My Prince?"

He shook his head. "Of course not, love."

He helped me down from the carriage, shook Leon's hand, and then Leon was hugging me, twirling me around as he did so. Summer, Renna's mom, was right behind him. And Renna's sisters and brother.

"You are causing a scene," I whispered to Summer as she, too, hugged me.

"Who cares!" Kallon boomed as he wrapped his arms around Summer and I both.

Krew got plenty of hugs too, and Leon even somehow snagged a hug from Molly.

The guards grew snippy five minutes later, so we all loaded back up to head further on the trail. Renna and I swapped positions, as to keep it fair for Isla. We were told to take turns sitting by the princes in our long meeting with the Assemblage advisor. Krew stretched his long legs out before him though, his ankles brushing up against mine. He was somehow keeping me within reach.

Ten minutes later, we pulled up outside Delaney's house, and she took her turn with her family. Both she and Keir exited the carriage to greet her family.

When we stop for Isla's family, try to use some magic to move your shoe.

That was a good idea. If I could do that now, somehow find a way to use it once and once later, I might just make it through the day. *Okay.*

We were stopped for what felt like a shorter time than we stopped for Renna's family, and then both carriages were in motion again. The guards looked annoyed, as this was turning out to be the slowest trip through Savaryn ever, but the good news was that after Isla and Molly, there was only one woman in each of the lower levels of the kingdom. So we should be able to pick up speed after Savaryn.

I believe we will have one lavatory stop as well at the wall so be sure to use your magic then too.

Okay.

You are tense, love. Please try to relax.

I glared at him. *It's so very easy to do that when you merely command it out of me.*

Renna elbowed Krew so fortunately I didn't have to hear Krew's witty comeback. I looked away and at the scenery, hoping it wasn't too obvious we were having an entire conversation without words.

Onward the horse's hooves clacked. I tried to take some deep breaths and focus on the sun shining and the full view of the scenery, but there were so many horses' hooves, because of all the guards, that it was quite loud and annoying. We were barely able to hold conversations out loud at all until the road widened halfway through Savaryn and the guards were able to spread out.

Deciding not to carry on in awkward silence the entire trip, I turned slightly toward Krew. "Where in Nerede are we swapping horses?"

He rattled off the location of a farmer who'd stalled the royal horses for the past few days for this very reason.

I smirked.

"What?"

"What are the odds you will let us have twenty minutes so I can take Molly to see the sea? She's always wanted to."

Krew cocked his head. "I'm sure all of us, guards included, will be ready for a break by then."

There was a gasp. "Really?" Isla asked.

Krew gave her a tight smile. "Why not?"

Isla beamed at me. "I've always kind of wanted to see it too."

"Well don't get too excited, the water will still be absolutely frigid," I warned her. "But the beauty will be the same."

I felt awful for this newfound friendliness I had going with Isla. She assumed it was because we were the other women, and Renna was for sure marrying Krew at the end of this. Little did she know, I'd already won.

I didn't want her to hate me, but I feared it'd happen anyway when it came down to it. But for Renna's sake, I almost wished Krew would take Isla and me into the final two, so Renna could finally leave the castle.

"It's just around the next bend," Isla whispered excitedly, eyes on the road before us, seeking out a glimpse of her family's estate.

As the horses began slowing, my magic slightly buzzed. I pushed it down, willing it not to be seen on my skin.

I was fairly certain I'd be fighting my magic down today, but I hadn't really thought it would happen this fast. That was why Owen and I had trained so hard this morning. I wasn't even out of Savaryn and my magic was already flaring? How would I be expected to last the entire day if I couldn't even make it out of Savaryn without issue?

While Krew helped let Isla down, I took a moment, shutting my eyes and trying to calm my magic.

As soon as Isla was walking toward her family, her back to us, I immediately kicked off a shoe and used my magic to move it back and forth, keeping my hand and shoe both underneath the blanket draped across my lap, as not to draw the attention of any guards.

My shoulders went back as my magic flared yet again. Despite using magic to move my shoe, I felt the hum of my power hit me in a wave, my magic wanting *out*.

"Jorah?" Renna asked, sounding fuzzy because my magic was increasing in intensity.

I looked at my free hand, astonished it was not crawling with silver with how I felt. Any minute now I would feel that pulsing sensation and my veins would begin glowing.

"Jorah," Krew asked more urgently from where he stood just outside our carriage, "what is it?"

Why was he still here? Shouldn't he be greeting Isla's family? My panic was rising. There was no way I was going to be able to contain this. It was going to overtake me. The pressure of it was so great I thought it might snap my spine in half.

Owen was off the horse and beside me in seconds, trying to ask me to take some deep breaths before anyone noticed.

That was when I noticed Krew's magic also flaring. I vaguely remembered his word choice from weeks ago. A built-in defense mechanism.

But then I felt it. I felt the threat. I opened my eyes to look over Krew's right shoulder and saw her.

Aiyana.

CHAPTER 18

I hadn't thought of her in weeks. Her father had attacked me on Hallows' eve and as a result, Michael Noyer was in the mountain being held by the king until the Assemblages were over. Aiyana had also been kicked out of the Assemblages because of it. There'd been no goodbyes, no time for me to dwell on the fact that she had finally gotten what she deserved.

Krew said that they'd watch Aiyana in Savaryn, make sure that she left the Assemblages and me well enough alone. And she had. Though she hadn't been invited to any of the balls since. So maybe she had just been waiting. Waiting for an occasion such as this.

"Krew," I gasped.

But then Aiyana, eyes on me, lifted her hands and shoved outward, her pink-colored magic barreling straight toward me.

Unable to contain it any longer, having only thought of what I would do if I was with Owen in the forest and not around people, my silver magic flew from me, out from under my blanket. But Krew's navy magic was also in the air. And Owen's green. There were so many colors of magic flying to meet the pink that I lost count. I was fairly certain I saw two hues of blue, Renna's red magic, and a mess of different colors of the guard's magic too. One orange, a lot of yellow, a few green. The one color which I was sure I didn't mistake was Molly's teal magic.

My silver magic got there a half a second faster than the rest, disintegrating whatever Aiyana had attempted to do into what looked like a thousand dust particles that fell. The explosion of all the different colors of magic around it caused all of us to shield our eyes from the brightness of it.

Keir's magic, however, raced along the ground past the rest of ours, and wound around Aiyana, like a rope, starting at her hands and then traveling upward until it wrapped all the way around her.

Guards were off their horses, wasting no time moving toward her while Keir maintained a steady stream of magic aimed right at Aiyana.

"Why is she even here?" I whispered.

"She lives in this part of Savaryn now," Renna explained quietly and quickly. "The king demoted the Noyers. While they used to live just outside the wall to Kavan Keep, they no longer do."

I looked up to see Krew vibrating and glowing with magic. "Stay with Jorah," he bit out to Owen. He and Keir were heading toward Aiyana.

Please don't kill her.

He looked over his shoulder, his eyes meeting mine for the briefest of moments. *I won't, but her days of being allowed near you are over.*

I turned toward Isla's family, all of them standing there in shock at the attack. Isla's guard was by her side, making sure to protect her too.

"Think anyone noticed?" I whispered to Owen.

He gave his head one shake. "With all the magic in the air, not a chance. It all happened too quickly."

Isla would have been the only one positioned to see the silver strands of magic leave our carriage, her and maybe a guard or two, but I was hoping that Isla had been busy with her family, and the guards had been busy scanning our surroundings and not looking directly at me or my blanket in that moment. Aiyana might have noticed the silver also, but even she wouldn't have been able to see my hand to see that it came from me.

"Are you okay?" Owen asked softly.

I knew what he was trying to ask but couldn't. He needed to know if I needed to use any more magic.

"I'm okay," I nodded. I was feeling much better now. The tension felt like it had all left my body. Granted I'd felt tense before practicing with Owen, with my magic fighting to defend me, but I'd never really understood just how fast my magic would rush to the surface if a threat was near. It was like it had been trying to warn me.

I had no idea why it didn't do that whenever I was in the presence of the king. But then again, since the king didn't want me dead anymore, maybe that was why. He'd yet to try to use magic on me.

Aiyana was screaming and crying, drawing my attention back to her. She was far enough away that I couldn't hear every word, but I got the gist of her trying to tell Keir that I had ruined her life. That I deserved it.

I didn't know what was said, but Keir stepped forward and said some words that had Aiyana paling, and Krew grabbed Keir, I think in an attempt to calm him down.

Four guards were assigned to stay with Aiyana, and one rider was sent to the wall to send for a carriage. Aiyana wasn't going back to the castle. She was apparently going to be reunited with her father. In the mountain.

Isla got a little extra time with her family, and Krew walked over to them to personally apologize for the interruption.

It felt like hours before we were all loaded and in motion again, but it was likely only about an hour. Krew had me sit by him, somehow understanding I needed to be near him after all that, and Renna again took the spot across from us. Krew reached his arms around both Isla and me, but he kept his hand wrapped around my shoulder, his thumb rubbing a slow track along my skin, trying to calm me. Or maybe himself.

"Huh," Isla commented. "Already drama and from Savaryn." She sighed. "And I would have thought with that much magic, the blast of color would've been brown. Not white."

I was glad I wasn't facing Isla in that moment. The blast hadn't been white. My silver magic had just been most of it.

"I've never seen that much magic all together at once," Renna admitted.

"Me neither," Isla agreed.

"Nor I."

Isla peeked around Krew to look at me. "She has always had it out for you, Jorah. I'm sorry that happened."

Thanks to Aiyana, all of Savaryn almost found out I had magic. I gave her a winced smile. "Me too."

* * *

THE PEOPLE of Rallis had made signs. I was shocked to see that a few of them even had my name on it. Most said "Prince Keiran + Gwen" but a few had "Prince Krewan + Jorah."

So they didn't throw flowers at our feet, they made signs supporting the women of the lower levels of the kingdom. My heart warmed at the thought of the time and effort they'd put into making those signs. Despite knowing that they'd likely anger the other women, they'd done it anyway. In a show of support.

Of course, more than half of those people would likely be more suspicious of me if they knew I was Enchanted now too, but they also all knew whoever won each Assemblage was to be given a drop of magic anyway. It was the notion that someone from the lower levels of the kingdom could be good enough for the highest level.

If the Savaryn people were acting cheerful and frivolous, the Rallis people took it a step further. We passed a barrel of what I assumed was wine, and people were passing around cups.

They weren't just cheering, they were *celebrating* one of their own making it to the final three options.

We passed a clump of people, cups in hands, arms around each other as they sang some sort of song.

"They are crazy," Isla said, speaking loud enough for us to hear her over the crowd.

A man spoke to a guard and then handed Renna up a cup of wine over the side of our carriage. She laughed. "And completely endearing."

"That could be poisoned you know," Isla said, clutching her chest.

Renna gave her a shrug and took a sip. "I don't think they're that foolish. They want Gwen to win, poisoning one of us would jeopardize that."

Twenty minutes later as the carriage slowed for Gwen to greet her family, I looked at Renna in the eyes, then Krew.

I sent down the bond to Krew, *How many disloyal are there right now just standing around?*

Krew looked around, gray eyes scanning the area. *Between ten and twenty. But word has traveled from Nerede to Rallis that the crown princes may be on their side. I suspect they are here for Gwen's safety and a show of support, not for harm.*

Says the prince who got shot with an iron laced arrow.

Krew smirked. *Still mad about that?*

Yes.

Me too.

My magic was much easier to contain since I had used it back in Savaryn at Aiyana. I wanted to feel bad for what was sure to happen to her. I wasn't sure she deserved to be tortured or beaten by the king, but she had also chosen this violent road.

So I wasn't going to let thoughts of her ruin a moment more of our day. I was sure Krew and Keir would have to deal with her plenty once we got back to the castle.

Owen's horse weaved over closer to our carriage as Gwen loaded back up. "Ready for Nerede, Jorah?"

I grinned. The last few times I had been to visit, there was chaos. The attack. The fire. Hopefully this time there wouldn't be any. I thought back to Krew's and my trip for the harvest festival and how much fun we'd had with the people of Nerede. "Yes."

As soon as the wall was in view, my heart stuttered. This was the very wall my father had worked on. His noble decision on this wall being the reason for his death.

But beyond that wall had been the only life I'd ever known. And in a few short months I had gone from loathing the other levels of the kingdom and all Enchanted, to becoming one of them. I didn't belong in Nerede any longer, yet somehow, I did. It was a juxtaposition I just didn't know what to do with.

As the wall creaked open, Molly spun around from where she sat in Keir's carriage and sent me a thumbs up.

I was home.

It was no longer the clomping of all the hooves that made it impossible to hear any of the others, as the horses were now on the dirt roads of Nerede, but instead it was the crowd cheering. Like Rallis, there were signs. There were also paper streamers being waved within the crowd by little kids.

These . . . these were the faces I knew. The faces I had passed by on my way to the bakery. The faces I had worked alongside of for so many years. The faces who had erased the words Iron Will from their vocabularies in an effort to protect their own.

I wiped at a tear, unable to help the level of emotion I felt rolling through me. And yes, they were cheering because it was a parade of sorts.

But also *for me.*

Who was I to deserve this level of support?

In that very moment I decided should Krew actually be the rightful heir to the Wylan throne after all and survive long enough to become king, that for these people I would become the best damn queen I could be. I'd not only do it but do so tenaciously. *For them.* If for no other reason than because they deserved someone who would fight for and protect them just as they had done for each other all these years.

As the king so often liked to remind me, I was Jorah *of Nerede.*

Maybe Krew being crowned king wouldn't be such a curse after all. If we could fight together for a better Wylan. If we could stop the deep divisions of this country on the basis of magic and create a better country for all her citizens.

Maybe we could help.

Krew reached over and brushed another tear off my face before giving my hand a squeeze. *I love you. Welcome home.*

And I love you.

As soon as I had myself together, willing my tears to stop, I looked around, trying to see what the people had been able to rebuild from the fires, or what was still in ruins. The last time I'd been here, a lot of it had been smoking and charred. It was nice to see people smiling and laughing rather than running in fear.

I couldn't see much around the crowds, but I knew the damage was still there. Between working long hours for their living, it would take more than a month to rebuild everything that had burned.

As we turned down a road with more damage, Renna put a hand up over her mouth. Blackened posts and remnants of homes stood there like a flashing warning sign to anyone who dared to cross the king. While some houses looked devastated, others were only half gone. Either way, there was no way these people could sleep in those homes. They'd been without homes, likely cramming in to live with another family, for the better part of a month. Though it looked like they had cleaned up the area, it also looked like they were months away from having their homes back. They needed the better weather spring brought to help a little in that endeavor too.

I fought the tears swelling back to my eyes as we finally made it through the cheering crowds toward the market street. I knew what I was going to find. Charred ruins of most of the businesses. I knew from Owen that Mother had been baking from our home with the help of a few of Hattie's kids while the king had her bakery rebuilt.

But she was one of the lucky ones because the king was rebuilding it for her. None of the other businesses had that luxury.

Isla gasped. "This was all from the night of the ball?"

I gave her a tight smile. "Yes."

She shook her head. "I had just assumed it was a small fire. Of some sort of important structure." She paused. "Not this."

I went to respond but then I saw the bakery. The last time I'd been there, I'd been clutching my mother's pink scarf and standing in the ashes of the bakery. While the rest of the street was definitely in varying degrees of repair, Mother's shop had boards up, a shingleless roof, and a huge brand-new picture window at the front, in place of the smaller old one. The bakery wasn't done by any means, but it was much farther along than the other businesses were.

That progress wasn't what warmed my heart, it was the people standing before it.

My mother. And Flora. And Hattie. And the orphans. Each of

the kids had paper streamers and chains and were waving them in the air and jumping up and down as soon as they saw the horses.

Without a word to Krew, I hoisted myself down from the carriage, beating both carriages to the kids as I ran for them.

"Jorah!"

Gavin caught me first, hugging me hard, as I went down the line to hug the rest of them. I grabbed Alani and carried her with me, making sure to give each and every kid a hug. I didn't know when I'd see them all next. And I missed them. I missed them so terribly much.

When I got to Warrick, I made sure to lean down to his level. "Hi, Warrick. How are you?"

"Jorah!" He hugged me hard. "I'm so much better now that you're here. And you brought Prince Krewan too!"

I had to close my eyes and will my magic down. I wanted to scoop him up, load him into the carriage with us, and smuggle him into the castle. I wanted him at the castle with us every day. I wanted a lot of things, and right now I could do none of them. I didn't know how Krew had done this for the past seven years.

"Jorah," Hattie greeted, hugging me hard. "We miss you, dear girl."

"I miss you too," I choked out.

"Come visit us," she paused and gave me a wink, "just not too soon."

I laughed. I was heartbroken my mother and these people who had become like a second family to me couldn't have been there for our wedding.

It wasn't fair. They should have been there. *Warrick* should have been there.

"Flora," I greeted. "Balls at the castle just aren't the same without your skill."

She swatted at me. "Oh, stop it."

"Mother," I grinned as I hugged her next. "I see the bakery is well on the way to being rebuilt."

She turned me so we could look at it, leaning her head on mine. "What do you think?"

I gave her a tight smile and swallowed hard. "I think even if the king made it out of pure gold, nothing would ever top the old one."

She nodded and sniffed. "I know."

"Please let me know if there is anything I can do to help any of you," I whispered.

She patted my hand and whispered, "Your prince has already been helping. He has been sending food to Hattie's as well as extra for the families displaced."

I hadn't even known that. I vaguely remembered Krew barking orders the night of the fire, but I'd been in a bit of shock and hadn't paid attention to every detail. Smiling, I sent down the bond, *I am thinking of numerous things I'd like to do when we get home.*

I felt his amusement. *Looking forward to it.*

Then Krew was there, a hand on my lower back. "Mrs. Demir."

She beamed at him, bowing quickly before giving him a side hug.

I laughed. He had barely left the carriage for Isla's family, and here my mother, Eleanor Demir of Nerede, had managed to sneak in a hug.

"Don't say it," I groaned, seeing the look on Krew's face.

"I am fetching you as we are to head to the stables to swap out horses momentarily."

I looked up at the fluffy clouds in the sky and sighed. "But we just got here."

He smirked. "I know, but we will be back. Hopefully without a four-hour long parade to get here."

Hattie smirked. "Not one for parades, Your Grace?"

He sent her a look. "I think you already know the answer to that, Hattie."

Warrick and a few other children swarmed Krew. He put his hand over his chest like they were truly wounding him, and I tipped my head back to laugh. Our visit might have only been five minutes or less, but it had been worth every minute of this exhausting day.

* * *

"PLEASE," I begged the princes as we all got down from the carriages. "It's walking distance, I promise. It'll take us ten minutes there and ten minutes back."

Krew rolled his eyes. "Fine."

Molly looked at Krew with wide eyes before popping me in the shoulder. "Well done. Now let's go!"

The whole group of us began walking along the road which I knew would bring us to the shore. We had to take no fewer than ten guards who were very displeased with this outing. They wanted us to get back in the carriages and back to the castle as soon as possible.

But I had promised Molly I'd show her the sea. So we were going to see the damn sea.

Molly looped her arm in mine, and I grabbed Isla's next to me the same way.

"Will we see some sort of sea creature?" Molly asked.

I giggled. "In shallow water, Molls? You've been reading too many books."

Isla snorted a laugh.

"True," Molly deadpanned.

Five minutes later, Molly's breath caught and her feet stilled. She was taking in the vast blue expanse for the first time of her life. She'd only seen it from afar, never like this. Close enough to feel the breeze whisper across her skin and hear the constant lapping of waves at the shore.

She sniffed loudly. "It's lovely. Positively lovely."

I tugged her arm and gestured with my head. "Well, we should get you a little closer view, don't you think?"

She didn't have words, she just nodded and we were moving toward the shore.

Finally making it to the beach, we all stood there in the sand, taking in the sea.

"It is beautiful," Isla admitted.

"Sometimes I forget how small Wylan really is in the grand scheme of things," Gwen added, her arm in Keir's.

"To hell with it!"

I spun to see Molly chuck her shoes over her shoulder, pick up her skirts, and sprint for the water.

"It's going to be cold!" I hollered after her.

"I don't think she even remotely cares," Renna commented.

"Come on, Jorah!" she yelled over her shoulder.

I stomped a foot down. "You know I hate being cold!" I kicked off my shoes none too gently. I knew she was excited, but now we were going to be cold the entire trip home. This was not the best plan we'd ever had. Molly was supposed to be a better plotter than we were.

I tugged on Renna and Isla's arms. "If I'm going in after her, you are too."

Isla surprised me by immediately kicking off her shoes.

"I'll warm these while you are all gone," Krew offered, knowing how very annoyed I was by all of this.

"That's actually quite nice of you," Isla blurted out.

I choked on a laugh, trying to contain it in my throat.

Krew glared at me.

With one more smile, Isla and I raced after Molly.

Renna grabbed Delaney too, but Gwen had apparently opted to stay with Keir. I wasn't sure if it was the ongoing tiff with Molly or what, but I didn't care.

Molly was squawking and laughing, her hair blowing around her wildly. She had her arms out and was twirling in the water. "You were right!" she laughed. "It's freezing."

Isla let out a yelp and I gasped as soon as the cold water hit my toes.

Delaney and Renna were also shocked seconds later as they made it in. None of us, besides Molly, were brave enough to go in past our ankles. We walked in a line, Molly on the deepest end, along the shore with our skirts hiked.

I was sure the Nerede shore had never seen anything like this before. Five women. Dressed in the most elaborate gowns, frolicking in the water like a bunch of young girls.

We only got so far before a guard snapped at us to turn around. We obeyed, our teeth already chattering with how cold we were.

As we made our way back over to our shoes, laughing as we tried and failed to shake all the sand off us, Krew's magic hit the bottom of each woman's dress, immediately drying it.

"Dammit," I muttered. I could dry mine myself, but not with everyone standing there.

"Oh no," Isla commented. "Jorah's cannot dry?"

"Not while she's in it," Krew admitted.

This time it was Keir choking on a laugh. I pressed my lips together in an effort to keep from joining him.

Krew glared at his brother. "I didn't mean it like that. I mean we will have to see if the kind farmer who has stabled the horses will allow her to change out of it and hand it to me, in which case then I can dry it, yes. Just not while it is on her person."

"Oh sure, Prince Krewan," Molly joked. "You just want to see her naked. Or in the very least, wearing *significantly* less."

Always, Krew sent down the bond to me while glaring at Molly.

Unable to keep it in any longer, I grabbed at my knees, laughing hard. But we all were, so it wasn't any more awkward than Molly had already made it.

Krew threw up his hands. "Let's get going, before Jorah freezes to death."

Renna grabbed my arm as we began walking. "He's just in a hurry to see you in your skivvies."

Giggling, I made it a point to reach for Gwen's arm with my free hand as we began the walk back to the stables.

For the longest time I had refused to befriend these women, knowing that we'd only know each other for a short time, but in this moment, I could not be happier for each of them. And as the Assemblages eventually ended and we all returned home, I was determined to keep these friendships I had been so against.

CHAPTER 19

My feet pounded in the forest, and my shadows followed, running alongside me, one on either side. They were more graceful and quieter than me despite having double the legs, and they had no path to make a way for them either.

Every morning Rafe and the black wolf ran with me. The first morning it had happened, I'd been overjoyed. I had never expected them to keep coming back. Yet they ran with me now every morning, and then ate breakfast while Owen and I trained. It was becoming our new routine.

I didn't even mind getting out of bed this early anymore. I got to run with the wolves. It was my favorite part of the day, though I wasn't about to admit it to Owen.

My hand hit the rough bark of the tree we always ran to, and I grabbed my knees. "Ready guys? Just the trip back now."

Rafe's tail gave a low swing and he put his head down, ready and waiting for me.

I wasn't sure because I couldn't speak wolf, but I thought the wolves enjoyed this even more than I did. And I had no idea why.

"Let's go!"

We took off, and I grinned, going even faster paced than we had the way there. Owen stayed near the meadow, knowing that with the wolves with me, I was well enough protected. That and my own magic.

My lungs were burning and I wasn't sure how my legs were even still attached by the time we made it back to the meadow. I wasn't sure I'd ever enjoy running, but I did enjoy how happy it made the wolves, so I at least hated it less now.

Where Owen normally stood in the meadow, there were now two men. And I knew from the bond exactly who they were.

Seeing Krew there, the black wolf pulled to a stop and let out a low growl.

I slowed to a walk, turning to look at him. "It's okay, that's just Krew."

He let out another low growl.

Rafe was halfway between me and Owen, not growling or seeming mad.

I put out my hand to him and let him sniff it before rubbing his nose, our usual way of saying goodbye to one another.

Krew was leaning up against a tree, his arms crossed while he chatted with Owen. Something about his relaxed body language just did it for me.

"Morning," I offered.

Krew didn't move. "Morning, love."

"At least Rafe isn't growling at you," Owen offered to Krew.

"No, but the other one is. Apparently not all has been forgiven and forgotten."

I looked back toward the black wolf, who was watching Krew cautiously. I smiled at Krew, knowing that what he'd had to do to Rafe in releasing him in the forest had killed him. "I thought you had a meeting with your father this morning."

"I do. I just wanted to see the wolves training with you for myself."

Owen and Krew exchanged a glance as if they were the ones able to speak telepathically.

"What?" I asked, grabbing my knees for a moment and trying not to outright pant. My lungs felt no longer in my body as I couldn't seem to find any air.

"Nothing," Krew said with a smirk. "Owen and I just think the wolves understand who feeds them."

I got the feeling there was something they weren't saying, but then Krew was giving me a kiss on the temple and leaving back toward the castle for his meeting.

Owen flicked a finger at the food dishes. Rafe and the black wolf usually only ate out of the one dish, leaving the other for the rest of the wolves who we assumed came by to eat later.

We quickly made our way to our new spot in the forest for training. With the lake area getting lots of traffic from the king's guards checking on the healed trees, we decided it best we find a new area. It was only about a half-mile walk from the meadow and in the opposite direction as the lake.

I'd barely even stopped walking when I felt my skin buzzing and threw out some magic to block off whatever object Owen was chucking at me that time.

"Rude," I told him. "I wasn't even ready yet and that wasn't exactly a small stick."

"I trusted you to stop it," Owen offered.

I glared at him while I sent a breeze to knock him backward. "You know my husband doesn't like me to be covered in scratches."

Owen let out a laugh and kicked up a series of rocks my way. "How you didn't figure out he wanted you way back then is beyond me."

I thought back to how Krew acted after the attack in the forest by the men Michael Noyer had hired. At the time I thought it was just because he was feeling protective over all the consorts.

And then Owen picked up speed and intensity with what he was throwing at me, causing me to stop talking and concentrate. What no one had really told me before I had magic was how much concentration it took when you were first learning how to use it. It was very hard to keep your focus on your magic, to will it to do different things, and simultaneously do something as mundane as carrying on a conversation.

I was in awe of Keir and Krew every day.

At one point, I was able to take control of a large log Owen had sent rolling toward me and send it back at him. Just when he jumped to avoid it, I hit him with a breeze that had him rolling on the ground.

I couldn't help the laughter that spilled out of me.

But then he sent my wooden sword flying at my throat. I had to stop it, take control of it, and then grab it, all while Owen was sprinting at me full speed with his own wooden sword ready to take my head off.

I narrowly managed to escape, jumping back and then swinging around because instinct told me the second hit would be right on the heels of the first.

On and on we went, my magic training mixing with my physical training. But what Owen had just done did give me an idea.

I continued deflecting Owen's advances, moving this way and that, trying to back my way near a bigger tree. I tried to do so without eyeing the tree or focusing on it, for fear Owen would catch onto my plan. But I must have been a little distracted because Owen did pop me in the arm once.

"Sorry," he offered, and lightened up a bit on his attacks.

Deciding I would play off his sympathy, I released my magic into a rope, wrapping it around one of the low, thick branches, and grabbed onto it with one hand. I used that rope and the help of my magic to swing myself around the tree. As I came around the other side of the tree, I brought my legs up and kicked outward hard with my feet at Owen's chest, effectively knocking him to the ground.

And then just as he'd taught me, I had a foot on his chest and my wooden sword pointed at his neck.

Owen's mouth fell open and I tried not to evil-laugh my victory.

"That was . . . brilliant."

I switched my sword to my left hand and offered my right one to help Owen up. He took it, mostly hoisting himself up.

As soon as he was standing, I handed him my sword. "Let me guess, stretch time?"

Owen smirked as I leaned over to stretch the backs of my legs.

"Why is it, Jorah, that you can do something like *that* when you train with me, but then with the princes you hesitate and are more timid with your magic? I just don't get it."

I sighed as I looked at the leaves on the ground and swayed slightly, making sure my legs were getting good and stretched out. If I'd learned anything in all my trainings with Owen, it was that if I didn't stretch my legs out well, I'd pay for it later.

"I'm serious, Jorah," he continued. "When it is just the two of us, you are amazing. Not for a woman, but for an *Enchanted*. Man or woman."

I stood up and extended my back, trying my best to do my stretches diligently.

He reached out a hand to stop me. "Jorah."

I inhaled deeply, my eyes traveling the direction of the castle, the direction I knew Krew was in. "I don't want to answer this."

"I noticed. I've never seen you stretch so attentively."

I rolled my eyes.

He nudged me with his elbow. "Talk to me. You know you can tell me anything."

I groaned and stared up at the trees. "It's just that Krew is my husband? I don't know. I don't want to look like a fool around him. If he were here, I wouldn't have tried what I just did on you because I wouldn't want him to see me fall on my butt." I paused. "No offense to you, but it's just that you are a safe place for me. Krew gave me almost all of his magic. Well kind of. He was supposed to have only a drop now but somehow, he still has his. But all the same, I feel pressure to not disappoint him with the gift he's given me."

Owen tipped his head to his shoulder while considering what I said.

"And if that's not enough," I added, "the times I have seen Krew use his magic, he is an artist with it, tossing it this way and that while in total control. He makes it all look so easy, though now I realize how extremely not easy it is." I shook my head. "And it's all so very . . ." A shiver traveled up my spine as I remembered Krew's words from when our sound barrier combined, "*attractive.* It is entirely easier to focus around you than it is around him. Again, no offense."

Owen pressed his lips together a moment. "So in other words, I don't turn you on?"

"I—" It was a lot more than that, wasn't it? I didn't even know any more. "Yes? But also the disappointment thing too."

Owen shrugged. "You do know he didn't give you all that magic to see what you could do to his father with it, right? He did it only so that you could protect yourself."

I shrugged as I turned to head back to the castle. "Yes, but I still want to feel worthy of it."

Owen pointed to the tree I had used to swing around and kick him. Where my magical rope had swung me, the branch now held leaves, and the exact imprints from the rope left moss on the bark.

"Oops."

Owen squinted at me. "Did you do that on purpose?"

I shook my head. "No, but I can't say I'm really sorry about it either. My magic and I just seem to agree about the forest needing healing. It's like my magic recognizes what I subconsciously want." And I had specified when I was willing my magic to make the rope for it not to hurt the tree or branch; I hadn't told it to heal it though.

Owen rolled his eyes. "You and this damn forest."

* * *

"I THINK," Owen said later that evening as we headed back to Krew's wing, a moving green sound barrier around us, "you should begin practicing with Krew more. Maybe once or twice a week. Ease into it."

I had just walked the gardens with Molly and Renna and was feeling starved. I didn't want to talk about magic right now, I needed food. Now. Before I withered away into nothing.

"I don't want to mess with the progress we've been making," Owen continued. "Not at all. You are learning and catching onto things fast with me." He paused. "Way faster than I ever would've thought for someone not raised around magic. No offense."

"None taken," I provided.

"But you are going to have to get used to using your magic around Krew and get used to seeing him use it too." Owen shot me a grin. "When it is time to make a move on the king, we can't have you sitting all wanton over in the corner unable to form a coherent thought."

"I—"

Owen turned to me. "Get it out of your system. Just like sleeping next to him, you'll get used to it eventually. You just haven't seen him use his magic enough yet."

He did have a point. But I was also doing a whole lot more than just sleeping beside Krew these days. I wasn't going to say that though.

Feeling Krew down the bond, I realized he was in his wing also. "Krew is back," I told Owen.

His forehead wrinkled. "But they are preparing for another parliament session."

I shrugged. I also hadn't thought I would see him until after dinner, which was why I was in no hurry to leave Molly and Renna. I could feel that Krew was not happy about something and immediately wondered what the king had done now.

As we entered Krew's wing, I found him sitting with a whiskey at his usual spot at the table.

"Rough day?" I asked as Owen and I turned the corner, me sitting down on the couch and Owen naturally flopping down next to me.

Krew kept his attention looking out the window. I knew he was angry. I could see it on his face, not to mention what I felt down the bond. Like I knew the sky was blue, I knew he was bothered. I just didn't know if the reason was his father, or dealing with Aiyana, or what had him upset.

"He's pissed," I whispered to Owen.

Krew turned to glare at me. The first time he'd looked at me since we entered the room.

Owen ignored him and looked over at me. "Noticed that."

Krew switched his glare to Owen. "I am not pissed, I am merely . . ." he paused and looked at his whiskey as if he wanted to down it in one gulp, *"displeased."*

Owen gave me a look. "Yep, totally pissed."

I snorted a laugh. Now was not the time to laugh, but it was a little funny. "I am sorry, My Prince. Whatever has you so *displeased?"*

Krew ran a hand down his face. "Never in a million years did I think I would find my soul mate. And never in a million years after that would I have thought that *my* best friend would actually prefer her to me and always take her side on things."

Owen gave me a guilty shrug that had me failing to shut down my laughter.

Krew shook his head. "I hate it when the two of you gang up on me." He flicked his finger, and a navy sound barrier was at the door faster than a blink.

Owen held up a finger. "On that note. If it makes you feel any better, I was able to determine today that the reason why Jorah isn't as confident with her magic around you like she is around me is because she gets turned on when you're using your magic."

"Owen!" I hissed.

Krew's lips turned upward for the briefest of seconds.

Owen's nose wrinkled as he turned to me. "I might like you better, but I knew him first."

"Traitor," I muttered as I turned to reach for the blanket draped across the back of the couch.

"And what is *that*?" Krew snapped.

Faster than I could respond, he was crouching before me, looking at the spot on my arm where Owen's sword had grazed me earlier. I'd put the healing salve on it right away after my shower, worried Krew would notice.

"That was my fault," Owen offered. "Training accident."

Krew's magic flared along his jawbone. *"What?"*

I reached out to turn Krew's face toward me. "I deserved it, really. Shortly after, I kicked him in the chest."

Krew looked at me and then back at Owen, his magic flaring in his wrists as he pinched his nose. "You two and your training."

"Is there a problem?" Owen asked. "I know you don't want me to hurt her, but very rarely do I nick her skin at all."

Krew tipped his head back to the ceiling and stood only to begin pacing. And if he was pacing then he was far more pissed than he let on.

"You apparently healed part of a tree today," Krew stated.

"I did," I admitted, feeling like Owen and I were about to get a scolding and I had no idea why.

"My father's men found it today," he continued. "Because they scan the forest every day now for more improvements."

If they found the spot from today, they must have scanned quite the area because it was in the new site, not anywhere near the lake.

"At this point, doing any training at all in that forest seems reckless. At some point they will find out."

I stole a glance at Owen and quieted.

"Yet the wolves are running protection for you and the forest keeps healing. So how can I be the fool who asks you to stay away from the forest?" He ran a hand down his face. "Everything in me says that I should demand the two of you stop healing so much as a blade of grass in the forest, but I know that to do so will only hurt Jorah."

He wasn't just bothered, it was that he was being torn in two different directions and *that* was why he was pissed. Not necessarily at us, but because he was put in a position where to do the right thing, I would be hurt. But if he allowed us to continue on, I could still get hurt, this time from his father. His father would find out I had magic and there would be hell to pay.

I let out a sigh. "Well as for today, you should tell him that I got hurt over by that tree, because it is not far from the truth. And I have learned from the best in that to tell a spectacular lie, you need to have it run as close to the truth as possible. The scratch on my arm should only help prove that story to be accurate."

Krew stopped and crossed his arms. "Tell me what to do, love. I want to tell you to stop healing the forest. To protect both you and your magic." He paused. "But now Father almost expects something to be healed weekly."

"So we do both," Owen offered. "We will cut back to a few

mornings a week training in the forest, allowing Jorah to heal only the bare minimum. The rest of the time we can practice in the castle."

I closed my eyes, feeling frustrated. What was the point of all this power if I couldn't use it to help? "He's going to find out eventually, you know," I offered at a whisper.

"I know."

I opened my eyes, blinking fast. "I almost wish it'd just happen already. So I can use this power for the one thing I enjoy using it for."

"The Assemblages are supposed to run until summer," Krew offered. "We are months away from the public wedding, which will be required."

My eyes went wide. "You wish for me to stay out of the forest for *months*?!"

"No." He shook his head. "That is not what I wish. But you may have to stop healing the forest for a while."

I looked at Owen. "I don't know if that is possible."

Krew was looking at me with concern etched all over his face. "Why?"

I gave him a shrug. "The night I used my magic to make the dome, after I saw you and Renna, I had a fleeting thought about how cold I was. But my magic knew I was cold and knew I wanted to be warmed. Likewise, today, I didn't will my rope to heal the tree, only that I didn't want to *harm* it, but my magic seems to understand how badly I want the forest healed. Both of those times I didn't actively will it to happen in the moment, though they were both things I did want."

Krew rubbed his hand over his lips. "It's your will. Your magic is reacting to your will. It feeds off it in a sense."

I gave him a winced smile. "Well, if you want me to stop healing the forest, you are going to have to keep me from using magic in it at all."

"There has to be some sort of balance we can find," Owen offered. "Jorah can't just keep being the one to give up everything in order to keep her safe."

"I know that," Krew snapped.

"So I have this power. I finally have a way to fix the forest, and I am just supposed to sit here and do nothing?" It had already been more than a week since the last time I had tried to fix the lake and I felt awful about it.

"I don't know," Krew offered. "I just want you safe, but I have no idea how to navigate this. I don't wish to cage you, or the power I've given you."

I clenched my fists in frustration. We'd just gotten into a routine with the wolves. I didn't want to change it. Owen and I had both been feeling relatively good about my progress too. "You can demand I stop healing that forest, but I will still show up every day and run with those wolves. They show up for me, and so I'm going to keep showing up for them."

Unable to take this conversation any longer, I spun on my heel and headed out onto the balcony, ignoring the fact that I was starved and going to be cold now too.

Minutes later, I felt Krew approach from behind me, wrapping his arm around my waist. "Owen left for the night. And I'd like to apologize. I'm sorry, Jorah. I don't know what to do. I don't want to keep hurting you to keep you safe, I just know we need to be careful."

I watched as the sun finished painting the sky orange. "I'm so tired of being stuck."

Krew put up a sound barrier around us. "Care to explain?"

I gave a shrug, not bothering to face him yet. "I can't go to the kitchens because your father doesn't like the company I keep. I can hang out with Renna and Molly, but only if we do activities your father would approve of, walking in the garden like the pretty flowers we are meant to be. I can use my magic but never around your father or anyone other than Owen. I couldn't even tell one of my best friends we got married and bonded because it put her at risk. Not to mention every time I so much as see Warrick, I want to load him up and bring him with us."

I stopped only momentarily, chest heaving. "And the worst. The worst part is that I want to imagine a life with you. Part of the reason I got so choked up watching Renna's family was that I was imagining that for us. A family that just truly loved one another." My voice cracked. "But I am just supposed to be accepting what little time we have together without making those plans. Making those dreams. I'm not allowed to think of the future, and I'm not allowed to fully enjoy the present. So what do I have then?"

"Jorah."

"I don't want to be a widow, Krew. If I have made all these sacrifices just to become a widow at the end of the day, *none* of this was worth it. None of it."

He spun me, wrapping his hand around the back of my neck. His other hand remaining at my waist. "I want that too. All of it. That is why I pushed for the plan with Nara. Why I am obsessed with figuring out which object holds my mother's magic. Because if we have that, love, we win."

I knew he was right, but it didn't help my current level of dreariness. We were no closer to figuring it out now than we had been when we first read his mother's journals.

With a sigh, I whispered, "Just feed me and then take me to bed."

"You haven't eaten?"

"No. I went for a walk in the gardens with Renna and Molly. So of course we didn't get up here at the usual time."

"Why didn't you say so?" He immediately strode for the door to send for food.

"Because I'm currently too busy wallowing in self-doubt and self-pity."

"And food will help?"

I gave him a nod, feeling my lips smirk. "Among other things."

He gave me a slow smile full of promise before opening the door only long enough to bark some orders at the nearest guard.

He skipped the dinner with the royal family and stayed with me the entire night. We didn't have the answers. We didn't have a plan. And the thought of being stuck like this for months on end sounded disastrous.

Eventually, something was going to have to give.

CHAPTER 20

"So," Owen began as we walked back in from my run with the wolves.

"So?"

"Since parliament is in session at the castle for the next three days, why don't you shower and then we can spend some time in the kitchens this morning?"

My steps faltered. After our conversation with Krew, and to obviously make sure the king didn't catch on to the fact I now wielded magic, Owen and I were back to practicing all hours of the day. Every three days Owen would decide when we were training and what time. There was no rhyme or reason. Sometimes he rolled me out of bed during the dead of the night. Sometimes we did early mornings, as was our old routine. Sometimes late nights but separate from the princes. Sometimes we were inside at our old training room, sometimes we were in the forest. And thus far, I'd only accidentally healed one small tree.

I was calling that a win.

We were trying to make our training pattern as unpredictable as possible. I didn't know what a full night's rest even looked like anymore, but true to my word, I kept my routine of running with the wolves in the morning. And most afternoons, I took a two- or three-hour nap out of sheer necessity.

"Won't one of the king's spies find out or something?" I asked Owen. I'd love to spend some time in the kitchens, but I also didn't want Maurice and the rest of the kitchen at risk.

"They'll be too busy today. The kitchens will be also, so we might not be able to stay long. But by the time we make it there, they might be almost done with lunch."

He had a point. Maurice was likely in charge of feeding all of parliament for the day if they were meeting at the castle.

Owen gave me a shrug. "Better than nothing? I'll be sure to watch the hallways. If anyone shows up who we don't trust, stand up and head for the door, acting like you were just passing through."

I knew Owen was only trying to help, but I also knew that freedom was only a mirage until the king was gone. Or until it was known I had magic. It all felt futile. With a combination of my magic and my training, I was now the safest I had been at the castle. But I still had to act like I was one of the most vulnerable in Kavan Keep.

I let out a sigh. "Maybe for just twenty minutes?"

Owen nodded. "Of course."

After a quick shower, I found there were more bodies in the kitchen than we were used to. Maurice had apparently called in extra help for feeding the parliament members.

"Rinaldi!" I found myself smiling ear to ear in seeing my favorite server.

He gave me a little bow. "Well hello, Miss Demir."

"Are you serving today?"

He gave me a nod. "Yes. Me and three others." He paused to smile. "Non-poisoned drinks, of course."

Knowing how stuffy some of the parliament members could be, I offered, "Good luck."

"He does not need luck, Tiny," Maurice's voice boomed. "Not when he delivers my cooking."

I rolled my eyes. "Your ego is still overly inflated I see."

Maurice winked. "Would my kitchen hold such a reputation if I did not, in fact, exude excellence?"

Jakob gave me a look from around Maurice's back which had me fighting off a laugh. "Well your overly inflated ego aside, I came to see if I could reward all of your hard work with some cookies. I don't mean to be in the way, I merely wondered when would be a good time?"

Multiple sets of eyes darted to Maurice, waiting for his answer.

"You heard the woman!" he barked. "Ten more minutes, then cookies!"

I turned to Rinaldi and another of the servers I recognized. "I will make extra and leave some for those of you busy serving the food." I spun back toward Maurice, knowing how much of a bother it must be for me to show up right at the end of a massive meal prep. "I can go start the dough upstairs and be out of your way. Then I can return shortly to bake them. Deal?"

Maurice shook his head. "No. No deal. Sit your tush on a stool. We are finishing the presentation on the dishes now and they are gone."

"And the dessert?" I asked.

Tilly put a hand on her hip and looked at me from over the top of her glasses. "Cheesecakes, which were all made last week and frozen."

Maurice pointed. "Stool, Tiny. I demand it."

Sparing Owen a glance, I did as I was told.

The last dishes on the counter were drizzled around the rims with a brilliant red sauce; raspberry, if I had to guess based on the color. In the center of each plate was a serving of mouthwatering roast and creamy potato mash. Then those dishes were loaded onto the carts and rolled out of the kitchen. The salads must have already gone out, then. And I noted the dessert carts were already loaded and waiting in the walk-in fridge, ready to go as well.

As soon as the last server left, Maurice began clapping, the others chiming in. There were pats on the back, hugs, and laughter all around.

These people reminded me so much of Nerede. Of a family that wasn't blood, but chosen. Maurice didn't just run a kitchen; he ran the family.

"Miss Demir," George began. "Would you like your food down here?"

I shook my head. "Absolutely not. I'll have whatever you are all having."

Maurice glared at me and took the handful of food trays left, six for the six consorts, and slid one across the counter at me. "Eat. And then it's time for the cookies."

I was rather starved, so I didn't argue. Maurice had enough extra meat that he made small sandwiches for the rest of them. Someone started playing music from a speaker. This was one of the busier days in the castle, yet they were laughing and soon dancing around in the kitchen. The dishwashers were a room over, ready and waiting for the salad plates to return, but the kitchen staff was done with their portion. Done until the evening meal, which unless certain parliament members decided to stay, would be decidedly easier.

I felt awful sitting and eating a plate of their hard work while they merely got the leftovers. But I knew better than to argue with Maurice. If I hurried up and ate, then I could treat them to cookies.

The food was delicious, and I was sure to tell them all so. I hadn't realized how hungry I was until the first bite hit my lips. The mash was a sweet potato of sorts, the roast seared to perfection, and the fruity sauce with it was above and beyond. My taste-buds were going to burst. It was all so mouthwatering.

As I ate the last bite and wiped my mouth with my napkin, I shook my head. "Cookies after all that is going to feel inadequate."

"Nonsense!" George called. "Not your cookies. Never your cookies."

I looked to Owen and laughed.

"I'm with George," he muttered from where he leaned against the doorway.

As I walked to one of the sinks to wash my hands, a thought struck me. *Krew?*

Yes, love?

I am in the main kitchens making cookies for the staff. Could you let me know when the session with parliament is wrapping up? That way I can make my exit here with plenty of time to spare.

Only if you save some for me.

Of course.

I hope you have a better afternoon than I am likely to have.

Poor, spoiled Prince.

I felt his amusement before he answered. *Stop being facetious. I about spit out my drink.*

With a smile on my face, I grabbed the butter and got to work. Deciding to quadruple the batch instead of double it, I was soon stirring and measuring.

Though the others had to be tired, every single one stayed. I wondered if things would change once they all knew I was a crown princess. I hoped not, but I knew better.

Once I was found out, everything would change.

* * *

AFTER STAYING in the kitchens for a few hours, Owen and I decided to go for a walk in the forest. I was mostly just curious if I would find any of the king's spies out there. We were bound to run into them eventually.

"I need a nap," Owen groaned as the matted down grass of the meadow swished at our boots.

"You could've stopped after three cookies and you probably wouldn't feel that way," I offered.

"But where is the fun in that!"

As we came into view of The Dead Lake, my magic stirred. I wanted to heal that lake and my magic, as an extension of me, knew it. And if it took me every day for a year standing in that nasty water and pouring my magic into it, then that was exactly what I'd do.

It was back to being a cold day, but with spring approaching, I was hoping the cold days were getting fewer and fewer. Though the more the weather turned to spring and the more I had to stand back and watch it, knowing I had the power to turn the forest green but couldn't use it, I was going to struggle.

Time was somehow taking an eternity and also passing in the blink of an eye.

Feeling disheartened we hadn't run into either the wolves or the king's spies, I went over to one of the trees I had healed and sat on the ground a moment, looking up at all the leaves. The healed trees stuck out in stark contrast against the brown and black of all the others. And a grassy area circled the bottom of each tree I'd healed.

I wanted to send magic all around the ground trying to heal all the grass, creating a bed of green around The Black Lake. It pained me to not even try. But the priority right now was the king. Once the king was gone, I could be out here healing anything I wanted. Day after day after day.

I put my hand to the ground and promised, "Hang on, forest. First things first."

Owen was a wise man and did not comment on my talking to the forest.

Feeling something on my hand, I gasped, pulling my hand back quickly. It'd felt like . . . like a spider. Like a tiny leg had just tickled my smallest finger.

Looking down at the grass and squinting, I saw that it was a small orange caterpillar, not a spider.

"Owen!" I hissed. "Look!"

I wasn't that enthralled with insects, but I had also never seen a single bug in all the time I'd spent in this forest. So I scooped up the little guy and placed him in the palm of my hand.

Sure enough, the fuzzy little creature was alive and well, scooting along my hand. He went blurry before me as my eyes burned with tears.

This was . . . *everything.*

I'd helped heal these trees and slowly but surely, the forest was coming back to life.

Everything okay? Krew sent me.

I wiped my eye with my free hand. *Yes. I just found a caterpillar in the forest.*

I felt nothing but pride down the bond. And the weight of it almost sent me to my knees.

I'm in the throne room trying to disguise the fact that I am smiling like a fool. Meanwhile the others are talking taxes. I'd rather be with you and the caterpillar.

I've had a great day. Wish you could've been a part of it.

Some day, love. Some day.

I passed the caterpillar off to Owen, the feel of the tiny legs on my palm a bit too much for me. He gladly took it over, bringing it close and examining it right in front of his face.

"Unbelievable!" Owen exclaimed. "I almost want to take it for the princes to see, but I don't want him to die."

I laughed. "Is it ridiculous that I'm crying over a silly caterpillar?"

"No." Owen shook his head. "Not when your hard work is why he's here."

"How do you know it's a he?"

Owen squinted even harder at the caterpillar, and I burst into giggles.

While Owen continued to play with the caterpillar, I closed my eyes and thought of a day where the forest would be green, teeming with birds and bugs. It might not be this spring, but hopefully by next spring.

"Owen?"

"Yeah?"

"Can we go train?"

His head snapped back. "Now? Why?" He paused. "Wait. Because you know I'm full of cookies and likely to be slow right now?"

I smirked. "No. Just because I feel like it."

His eyebrows shot up. "Well this is new."

"I want to heal this forest, but I can't until the king is gone. So first things first."

Owen put the caterpillar on the ground so gently it made me smile and then moved to cross his arms. "First thing first is actually the object with the queen's magic. Or did you forget about that part?"

I shook my head. "No. But that I cannot control. My magic, I can, however."

Owen was grinning ear to ear.

"What?"

He cocked his head. "Correct me if I'm wrong, but I think you trust it now." He held up his thumb and pointer finger with barely any space between them. "Just a little."

I squinted. "Fine. A little."

And then he was hugging me, spinning me around.

As he put my feet back on the ground and we started walking toward the castle, he said, "Fine. We train. But I do need to remind you that if the princes can avoid your help in this, then they will. It is not as if you have to take on the king alone."

I stopped walking and looked at his back. "Do you really think I'm naïve enough not to notice that magic not being able to be used on me or whatever I'm touching doesn't give us a rather hefty and distinct advantage?"

Owen stilled and turned toward me. "But Krew doesn't—"

"Krew," I interrupted, "can be mad at me all he likes for taking an active role in taking down his father, but as long as he is living and still here to be mad at me, do we honestly care?"

Owen smirked. "Fine."

I grinned. "Fine."

So we trained. And we'd keep training. So that when the moment came for the princes to take down their father, I'd be anything but a useless princess.

CHAPTER 21

Two days later, Owen woke me from a well-deserved nap to inform me the consorts were being beckoned to sit in on the closing session with parliament. The eventual queen would sit in on all those meetings once crowned, so now that the Assemblages were down in numbers, the king deemed it necessary we attend to observe.

I groaned, so not in the mood for anything other than sleep after a hard training session with Owen. But Silvia came in right behind Owen, preparing to get me ready.

I just wasn't in the mood for a fancy gown and parading in front of a bunch of old men who were supposed to be bettering Wylan, when very few actually did.

Really? I sent Krew while Silvia applied my makeup. *We have to come sit in on parliament?*

You don't want to spend more time with your husband?

I would love to spend more time with you. In a variety of different ways. But in the throne room with parliament is not one of them.

I'm listening.

I pressed my lips together to keep from laughing. Within thirty minutes, I had my hair and makeup done, and was wearing a consort appropriate dress.

By the time we made it down the stairs, I had found Renna.

"Ready for this?" Renna asked.

I shrugged. "Does it matter? Ready or not."

Renna wrinkled her nose. "My father used to serve on parliament. From everything he has told me, it's very boring, sorry to say. Not looking forward to it."

The consorts were all lead up to one of the balconies. The throne room looked less like a throne room than I had ever seen it. Parliament sat in two sets of seats facing one another with the king and princes up at the dais in their extravagant chairs.

I tried to pay attention as I sat down. My heart entirely skipped a beat when I heard something about a shopkeeper smuggling goods, thinking of the bakery and the agreement among shopkeepers in Nerede, but it turned out they were talking about a shopkeeper in Rallis who had been forging documents to keep more of the profits himself.

Then they moved on to discuss a tax increase. It seemed half of the room was for it, and half against.

I could think of three or four small businesses in Nerede which would crumble if faced with having to give away more of their rations. Most of Nerede needed what little ration we were given to make ends meet. I knew for a fact most spent it on food.

And if they intended to increase the taxes, thus reducing the ration allotment, with the intention to better things in the lower levels of the kingdom, that would be one thing. The tax increase might cancel out the reduced ration if it truly helped the people of Nerede in terms of something like bettering our roads or fixing our roofs. But from what I was hearing, they were only increasing taxes to pay for some new homes in Savaryn, and an entire section of existing Savaryn homes getting updated.

And by homes they meant mansions.

They needed more money to make the already nice homes nicer? Nerede wouldn't see a single improvement from that tax increase. The roofs of Savaryn might as well be made from gold while Nerede would always be forced to fix ours from our own pockets.

I looked over at Krew. He was leaning against an arm of his throne chair and looking bored. *I loathe this already.*

I know, love. Just know that when either Keir or I rule next, there will be no more increased taxes.

Isn't that up to parliament and not you?

Krew's eyes found mine up top. *No. The king chooses the parliament members. They argue and bicker and then vote on issues. Father holds the ultimate power though, particularly now with my mother gone. He can ignore their vote, even on the rare chances they are all in agreement, if he decides to. His is the only vote which matters.*

So what is the point of parliament then?

There is none. It is merely there to appear that Wylan cares about anyone in her lower levels of the kingdom.

I made sure my magic was pushed down. It was a good thing I'd trained with Owen so hard this morning, or I'd likely feel it humming beneath my skin already. As it was, I felt fine. In control. It was also like the more I got used to having magic, the more my power knew to behave in certain situations. Particularly in the presence of the king. Though I was not ready to experience another one-on-one conversation with him any time soon.

My mother also held a vote as the queen, though. Either my mother and father had to agree on whatever it was, or it got tabled for another session. Now that she's gone, only his vote matters.

I considered Krew's words for a few moments.

If you become queen, you will never be forced to vote my way of thinking either. You will be my equal. Every step of the way. Your vote will matter just as much as my own and I will not intimidate or scare you into voting similar to me.

I didn't know if I wanted all that power. Not because I was scared of it, but because I didn't know if I would be any good with it. Gwen would be outstanding. Renna as well. Even Molly would be a just and caring queen. But me? I just wanted to heal the forest.

I tried to think about the forest for a while, totally ignoring the conversation before me. It was best to not listen to them bicker about improvements to the already nicest level in the kingdom.

Renna was wiggling her foot, and at one point Isla, next to me, jerked once, likely falling asleep as the parliament members below us continued to argue back and forth about taxes and how much of an increase was needed.

I was under the impression we were only to be in for the last hour or so of parliament, but their bickering soon turned one hour into two hours.

The king called for a final argument from both sides. An older man wearing glasses who had not said much thus far, stood. Or attempted to. It was an arduous process as he was quite frail, his cane the only thing that accomplished the feat for him. He had a white beard and was mostly bald but for a few long white whisps of hair swiped across his head.

"Your Grace," the man began. For as frail as his body seemed, his voice was sure and strong. "I strongly implore you and humbly request that you do not do this. Even a small increase in taxes will be detrimental to the people of Nerede. Particularly after the recent fires." He paused and sent the king a pointed look.

A cold shiver traveled along my arms. I stole a glance at them to find little bumps all along my skin. It wasn't my magic. It was a parliament member making a stand against our king for my people. I couldn't help but lean in to better listen.

"However warranted or unwarranted the fires may have been, reduced ration allotments during a rebuild will be detrimental. And while some of us have gotten quite cozy up here on the mountain, I request we all remember where we grow our food and why it is we live so comfortably."

The frail man took down his glasses. "Though a ration decrease to those of us with a bigger ration allotment seems minor, affecting none of us in Savaryn, to the workforce of our country it is not. And you do not cripple the workforce. You keep them happy. You keep them working. You keep them distracted." He paused. "If you increase their taxes after the stunt you pulled last month, they will grab their torches. And likely wind up murdered." The entire room seemed to gasp with the man's audacity. "And if the workforce is all dead, who will be putting your food on the table, Your Grace?"

I wanted to stand and clap. I wanted to hug the man. He got it. He got what so very few up here on this mountain did.

"Excuse me?" the king snapped. "The stunt *I* pulled?"

The old man didn't even flinch under the king's harsh tone. "Did you or did you not intend to punish them and reassert your dominance? Both of those things you did." He squeezed his cane harder. "To give them a tax increase now is to fan the flames of rebellion. A rebellion already barely contained as it is."

"Do you not remember, Martese, they attacked my son?" the king asked, and I knew from the look on his face that this old man was at risk of a lashing. I wasn't sure as frail as he was if he could even survive it. Even just thinking of the word lashing made me shove all my magic down and bury it deep. I was still not over my own run in with the king.

"A failed attempt," the man evidently named Martese responded. "As he is alive and well. They failed. And then not only did they fail, but they paid for it dearly. Some with their lives. But you forget, Your Grace, that their efforts are what makes the country run so smoothly. Not to mention you leave them on the shore to their own devices, falsely assuming they are idiot enough to never hop on a boat and simply leave." The man paused. "If you do not smooth this over, we could lose Nerede. And if we lose Nerede, if we lose our workforce, Wylan will fall."

There were gasps heard throughout the room.

The king took two steps toward the man and my stomach dropped. I'd never immediately adored a person like I did this frail man.

"Death may knock at my door at any moment now," the man said, stilling the king's boots. "So you, Your Grace, do not scare me. You are nothing but a power-hungry fool dressed up with a crown. A true king would put in the work to smooth things over to squash the rebellion."

The king's magic was in motion though his feet remained rooted to the ground. My magic burned in my palms, but I willed it down. I wanted to help the man, but I could not. Not here. Not now. Not with so many watchful eyes.

He was Enchanted. He had magic. Would he be able to help himself?

Just as I was regretting my hesitation, in a blur of crackling energy, blue magic was intercepting the black. It was navy, but also a brighter blue. And though only those who knew each brother's magic color would notice, as they neared Martese, their magic combined, blowing the king's magic away.

The king ignored the obvious slight by his sons. "No. A true king would just squash the rebellion. Like I have already done and will continue doing, unafraid to dirty my hands to accomplish it." He spun back to walk to his throne. "Parliament dismissed. Get out of my sight. All of you."

As the king leveled his stare on the princes, my breath caught.

He knew.

He knew the princes were bonded.

* * *

ALL THE CONSORTS were to dine with the royal family that night. Given time to freshen up, the consorts were escorted back to their rooms. I immediately put up a sound barrier, started the fire, and began moving objects around the room. If I was going to have to survive a meal in the presence of the king after all of *that*, I needed to use the power humming in my veins.

Feeling Krew nearing his wing in the castle, I was confused. I was sure the king would have cornered Keir and Krew.

The door swung open and there he was, walking toward my sound barrier and adding his own magic to it. My dark prince. Who had come to the defense of an innocent man today for no other reason than it was the right thing to do.

"He knows," I said out loud, wondering why I was the only one panicking about this.

Krew walked right past Owen by the couch, as if not even noticing he was there, placed his hand around the back of my neck, and pulled me in to kiss me hard.

"Right. I'm going to disappear now," Owen said, humor in his tone. As he got to the door he added, "Uhhh, Jorah, could you stop moving the books before you get excited and fling them too hard?"

Krew paused, smiling, and I dropped my magic, knowing Owen was right. As soon as he was gone, I put a sound barrier back up.

Not understanding why Krew just kissed me with such intensity, I said quietly, "Your father knows the two of you are kin bonded now."

"Yes," he agreed, never taking his eyes from mine.

"And he is likely pissed about you standing up for that man."

"Yes."

"So now seems like a great time to randomly kiss the hell out of me?"

"Yes."

My lips twitched.

He kissed me again. "*You.* I was bored out of my mind, so I just paid attention to our bond instead. I felt your emotions the entire time. Your concern for Nerede. Your pride for your people. And how happy it made you that he would stand up for your people. And then I felt your panic. I was just sure you were going to save the man yourself, which is why I didn't hesitate to use mine. Actually, Keir said he considered the same thing. That's part of the reason why we both acted the way we did."

They'd both thought I would use my magic to protect that man and the secret about my magic would be out?

"But I do not regret standing up for Martese for even a moment. Had you not been in the room, we would've done it anyway. And standing up against my father like that might irk him, yes. But showing that Keir and I are united in front of parliament is worth his wrath. He was going to find out about the kin bond eventually. We can explain that it is to protect one another, and he will likely approve of it. He will be irritated he didn't know about it before now, but he will not be mad we are bonded."

He was explaining things so fast while looking at me so intently that I was struggling to keep up with it all.

"But out of everything that just occurred, the thing that shocks me, is that you kept calm and were able to keep your magic from flaring. I felt how badly you wanted to use it. And I cannot wait until the day where you can defend whomever you choose."

He placed his hand over my chest, his fingers dipping under the material at my shoulders. "This heart of yours, love, is pure. In a castle cast into the shadows of my father's ways, you are the glimmers of sunlight finding a way to infiltrate the smallest of spaces. I *loathe* that you had to contain your magic today. I am sorry. And I cannot wait for the day we unleash you upon the realm."

CHAPTER 22

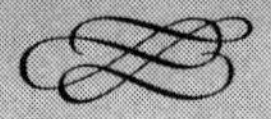

"So this is awful," I stomped as we made our way through the forest.

"But tomorrow we go to Nerede," Krew offered from next to me. "We are up late tonight, and tomorrow we are free to see your mother. With my father's blessing, even."

"Only because he thinks I'll deliver more disloyal news." I squinted at him. "Manipulative much?"

He grinned. "I wouldn't dare manipulate *you,* love. But you do need to stop avoiding this."

I hated how right he was. I was getting better with my magic every day. More than a week had passed since I'd found the caterpillar in the forest. Just as Krew had suspected, the king hadn't really been that mad about their kin bond, just pouty they hadn't told him. We'd all even managed to survive another ball around everything else going on.

And though I was still using my magic and training with Owen daily, the area I had been avoiding was combining my magic with Krew's. So Owen had arranged a training session for just me and Krew.

Krew turned to me and took my palm, lifting it to brush a kiss across it. "Owen may have let it slip you are afraid to disappoint me while you figure out how to wield your magic." He paused. "It's not possible for you to disappoint me, Jorah. It took me years to be able to control my magic, and then years to strengthen it. You are already leaps and bounds ahead of where I was after my magic settled."

I closed my eyes for a moment. "I know, but I also just want to feel worthy of this power. I don't want to merely walk around with the knowledge that I can protect myself, I want to heal the forest. And when it comes down to it, if touching me keeps your father from being able to use his magic on you, then I want to be there when you face him."

"Okay."

I squinted again. "Okay? That's it, just *okay*?" Under my breath, I added, "I was expecting way more of a fight."

"Okay," he repeated. "I wouldn't want you to face him alone either. I get it. I don't *like* it, but I get it. And I cannot deny what you can provide for us in being immune to magic both on your person and with your touch." He paused. "But if you are going to help me take him down, we need to practice combining our magic."

I tipped my head back to look at the stars, knowing he was right.

"If you are going to be there, I am going to need to keep my wits and not panic when he goes anywhere near you. Once he learns we are bonded, I fear you'll likely be there whether I want you there or not. Practicing with me like you do with Owen, holding nothing back, will help with that. Seeing what our magic can do, the different ways we combine it, will help with that."

I let out a sigh. "Fine. Let's get started."

"Owen says he always starts out with chucking random objects at you. Let's start there and then work on the combining."

"Fine."

Before I even had time to think, a branch was headed for me. But because Krew was nicer than Owen was, at least it wasn't coming directly at my head.

I flicked it away with a breeze, and then picked up a rock to send at him.

We were timid at first, throwing a small twig, a rock here and there, but then somewhere in the middle, we both got slightly competitive, and things picked up.

Krew stopped flirting with me to concentrate and that's when I truly understood how strong and disciplined Krew was with his magic. How quick he could envision things and make them happen.

As I ducked from another branch, just to blow away more rocks, I considered that Krew might not have ever done this against someone who was his full equal before. I knew he was more disciplined, but was Krew truly stronger than Keir? I might be stronger than Keir now too for that matter, but I didn't think for even half a moment I was nearly as fast.

So I moved toward him, just like I had with Owen and the wooden swords, making it seem like I was barely keeping up.

As soon as I was close enough and Krew was facing the correct direction, I released my magic into a rope and swung around it to land behind him.

He must have felt my change in direction through the bond because he somehow knew and spun around.

I hadn't really wanted to kick him like I did with Owen, I'd just wanted to land behind him for a surprise attack, but now I was committed.

But instead of letting me kick him, in a move faster than humanly possible, Krew stepped toward me, caught me, and physically lifted me from the rope. I was now straddling him, in his arms, and definitely not behind him. My feet were also nowhere near the ground. This was the worst surprise attack in the history of surprise attacks.

Krew smirked as he made no effort to put me down. "Was this what you were going for, love?"

I gave my head a shake. "No. I was able to kick Owen to the ground when I did it to him." I smirked. "But he also can't feel if I change directions."

"I'm curious how you're going to get out of this one."

He turned and moved so my back was to the tree and began slowly letting me down. Seeing his skin with a slight glow to it, the gentle care he took with me, the way he had just been walking while carrying me, it was all entirely enticing.

"Jorah," Krew warned.

"What?"

"Stop feeling what you're feeling right now. We're supposed to be practicing magic."

I brushed my hands off. "Right, right. Can we hurry up and get to the combining magic though? Because you know. Feelings."

Krew tipped his head back to laugh, then kissed my temple as he offered me a hand to pull me away from the tree. "We are going to need Owen on these trips just to keep us focused, I'm afraid."

I considered that. "Maybe a few times of just us and then we should totally try ganging up on him. Could be fun."

For the next fifteen minutes we combined our magic to move objects. It took a little getting used to. The first few objects we had entirely too strong of magic, so they went flying.

"Interesting," Krew muttered. "I need to send like a quarter of what I would for an object that size."

I nodded my agreement as we moved to an even bigger log. But despite sending far less magic than we would've if using magic separately, we were still able to move the log and keep it moving in a pattern.

"What does that mean?" I offered as he gestured to a fallen tree. "Wait. You want to move *an entire tree?*"

"Use the same amount as last time. Just humor me?"

With a shrug, I sent my magic out, doing as he asked. The tree was massive, the roots bent and broken at least three feet in the air from where it had fallen. It would've taken more than ten men to even budge it. Yet here we were, trying to use our magic to do just that.

Krew's navy magic weaved together with mine before it even reached the tree. There was an eerie creaking noise from the tree, and then sure enough, it started slowly sliding.

"Let's try to lift it," Krew offered. "Just a little."

I shook my head, thinking he had lost his mind, but did send more magic to help his. I found I didn't even need to know specifically what he was willing the magic to do, I could just will my own to help his and that was enough.

Our magic again wrapped around the tree, and it began pulling upwards. The creaking noise was much louder this time. Instead of our magic just lifting the tree in the middle, it wrapped around the trunk, and it also traveled up the branches and down to the roots. It wasn't being lifted from one point, but from all the points of the tree.

I gasped when the tree was fully off the ground a few inches. Part of the branches were still brushing the ground though, so we sent a little more magic to finish lifting it.

We had to lift it about four feet into the air before the branches were fully off the ground. But our magic was lifting an entire tree. Without either of us using a significant amount of power.

If I would've tried to do this on my own, given the size and weight of the tree and all the magic I had already used today, I was certain there would be blood trailing from my nose already. "What does this mean?" I repeated.

"It means," Krew said as he began walking for me while the tree still hung in the air, "that similar to the other day with the sound barrier, together our magic is more potent." I began backing up, recognizing that look in his eyes. "It means," he continued, "that while we might be powerful apart, we are more so together." His hands were now on me, one on my waist, one cupping my cheek as he yanked me into him.

"Krewww," I warned. "Stop feeling what you're feeling right now. We're supposed to be practicing magic."

He brushed a hard kiss to my lips. "That is not likely. I have *feelings* about you all day long." He moved back in to kiss me again but instead said, "You haunt my every dream. And even in my waking moments, you somehow command those thoughts as well."

As he trailed a line of kisses down my neck, I managed to form words enough to get out, "Krew. The tree?"

"What about it?" he asked without moving, his breath on my neck.

"It's still in the air. We can't just leave it up there all night."

He still didn't move. Nor stop his pursuit, his hands trailing just shy of the areas he knew would drive me to madness. "Could you? I'm *quite* busy."

With a snort of a laugh, I reached out to stop our magic. Owen had taught me the method which he had compared to being as simple as blowing out a candle. I'd done it enough times by now that all I had to do was visualize our magic being snuffed out and simply close my palm.

The tree crashed to the forest floor loudly. I had been a bit too distracted to soften the landing.

"Whoops," I offered. "Should have sent my magic out to catch it."

Krew finally stopped, but only to lift me into his arms. "Best not let my father's spies find us out here then. Shall we?"

"We can walk. You know how I feel about this."

Krew grinned at me. "Yes, but I have lots of *feelings,* love. So many in fact that we may be up a while."

I held onto his neck for dear life as he shot us into the sky.

* * *

IT FELT odd to meet my mother at our house. I was so used to meeting her at the bakery. We spent far more time there than we'd ever had at our house anyway.

Still, she poured the tea as we crammed into our little townhome. Krew put a sound barrier around the four of us, extra guards standing outside the home just in case while Owen was with me as usual.

"So," I offered as soon as the tea was all taken care of. "I didn't get a chance to mention this while on the tour . . ."

She looked up at me and smiled.

Don't torture the woman, just tell her already.

Rather than outright tell her, I held my palm out, letting my magic blow a slight breeze around her hair and then dissipate.

She gasped.

"You—You're," she paused, her eyes bulging. "I don't believe it."

"Surprise?" I offered.

Her eyes were still attempting to leave her head. "Were you already bonded when I saw you last?"

I gave her a nod. "Yes."

"And I didn't even notice?!" she asked, her voice going up an octave.

"Apparently not."

"I am your mother," she explained. "I thought I would have noticed."

I took a tentative sip of my tea. "Well, as it turns out, I am still me."

Krew reached over and took my hand, bringing it up to brush a kiss to it.

"Did the two of you get *married*?!"

Krew's smile could be categorized as nothing but cocky. "Mrs. Demir, Jorah is horrible at explaining things as it turns out. Please allow me."

She pressed her lips together as if to keep from laughing and gave him a nod.

And for the next twenty minutes, my moody and dark prince explained to my mother that yes, we were married. How sorry and apologetic he was that she couldn't be there, but that we had moved things up after the fires in Nerede so that I wouldn't have to feel helpless ever again. And that when we had our public wedding in front of Wylan, he promised she would not only be there, but be pampered and taken care of right alongside me. And then he even explained that we were soul bonded, not heart bonded. My mother almost fell out of her chair at that moment, but I was too caught in the moment of watching him carefully explain everything to my mother to laugh.

"So, Mrs. Demir," he ended. "Your daughter and I are married. We are soul mates. And when we are not attempting to figure out how to remove my father from the throne, we are deliriously happy."

"Well." My mother put down her teacup calmly. But then she was moving, wrapping her arms around Krew and hugging him hard. "I am so happy for you both." She moved from him to me. "Don't you worry about me not being there. Your wedding ceremony is about the two of you, not anyone else."

I wiped at my eyes, knowing she was right, but wishing she still could have been there all the same.

Krew must have felt what I had been thinking because he added, *As soon as my father is gone, she will be at the castle with us.*

"Oh, and Krew and I can sometimes feel one another's thoughts and emotions," I offered.

She sat back down, looking from one of us to the other.

"They talk telepathically too," Owen offered from the window. "It is equal parts amazing and odd."

"I—" she closed her mouth before opening it again. "I know nothing about soul bound couples, apparently."

"Nor did I truly until I became half of one," Krew provided.

We were halfway through Krew explaining that the king didn't yet know I had magic and why we were trying to keep it a secret for as long as possible when there was a knock on the door.

Owen looked to Krew and Krew shook his head.

"I will answer it," Owen said nicely to my mother. And then he gave me a look as if he expected it to be Will or something. As soon as he hit Krew's sound barrier, it fell.

Owen opened the door and from where I was sitting, I saw Beau Jones, Theodore's father, standing with one of Krew's guards. I wasn't sure if he was the outright leader of the disloyals in Nerede, but I assumed he was. Either the leader or near the top.

Owen turned toward Krew. "Your Grace, it is Beau Jones."

Krew gestured with a hand for Owen to bring him forward. My mother got up to move to the kitchen, offering him her seat and leaving to grab another place setting. Krew put up another sound barrier at the door.

After looking bewildered at the magic covering the walls of my mother's townhome for a moment, he turned to me. "I am so sorry to interrupt on your time with your mother." He bowed his head toward Krew. "Your Grace, the disloyals in Nerede are becoming more and more restless. I have urged for them to wait, but there is a plan in the works that is nothing short of reckless. I fear more Nerede blood will be spilled—"

"So you've come to let us know?" Krew said, not unkindly.

"Yes," he again nodded at Krew. "I am still feeling the weight of the responsibility for the attack on you, Your Grace. I don't wish for what happened that day to happen again. I've come to warn you, and to also ask for your help."

For the next ten minutes, Beau filled us in on how there were a group of Nerede men who wanted to overtake one of the carriages sent for goods, hide among the supplies, and ride it back up to the castle into Kavan Keep. They even had a specific carriage rider in mind who they thought was a disloyal sympathizer.

"And if they manage to pull it off and ride it all the way up the mountain?" Krew asked.

"Find a way to get to the king, obviously," Beau added.

I brought a hand up to my temples. "So while we are proactively trying to keep the king from raising taxes yet again, you all are scheming another reckless plan."

Krew shot me a smile. "This one, at least, is a little better thought out."

"The king wants to raise taxes again?" Beau's head went back. "That will crush us. After the fires that will absolutely—"

"I know," I told him. "I know."

"We have three weeks until the next joint parliament session with my father, so we need for there to not be any other reasons for him to punish you right now," Krew explained.

Beau put up a hand. "I hear you, Your Grace. Even just the knowledge that there is a tax raise in play might calm everyone down."

"Or send them over the edge," Owen offered from his position at the window where he was now leaning, arms crossed over one another.

"The idea of having more disloyal in Kavan Keep itself is alluring though," Krew offered. "I need for you to pick three or four men. Men that can handle themselves well enough to keep their cool. Men who know if they get found, it will likely result in death. And if they still wish to come, I can get them servant jobs in the stables or barracks. No smuggling in, they can just walk right in."

I was looking from one to the other. "That's dangerous."

Krew gave me a look. "I know, love. But if they are reckless enough to try to ride up the mountain to Kavan Keep, they're already playing at a dangerous game. This will give them a way in, though I will request no one move until I say so."

Beau's eyebrows were up. "That is—I am sure that at least two of the men would jump for that opportunity."

Krew leaned in. "But do you trust them enough to listen to me and wait until the time is right? Because if they get impatient and start making their own plans, they are signing their own death certificates."

Beau started nodded as he was thinking. "I will personally vet them out. Even just this alternate plan should delay things a few more weeks. Hopefully three."

"I appreciate your cooperation," Krew said. He looked at me and then I felt him say through the bond, *Show him what you can do.*

I looked to him shocked. *What?*

Nerede needs hope right now, love. They need something to hold on to after the tragedy of the past few months. Show him.

You trust them enough to keep it quiet?

I do. My father hasn't found out I'm a disloyal yet.

My mother muttered to Owen, "Oh, I see what you mean now."

Out loud, Krew said to Beau, who was looking from one of us to the other, confused, "There has also been a new development up at the castle. One I am going to need for you to approach with an abundance of caution and care. Very few people at the castle know about this. Can I trust you with it? Trust that you will keep this knowledge safe with whom you tell?"

Beau was nodding so aggressively I thought his head might roll off. "Of course, Your Grace."

Krew gave me a nod.

I opened up my palm, allowing my magic to increase in intensity and buzz before I released any of it.

Beau gasped and scooted backward, which I was not offended by. A few months ago, I would've likely done the same.

I curled my fingertips in and then shot them all outward, and a hundred tiny orbs of silver magic appeared in the air. I left them there for a few seconds before closing my fingertips, sending the orbs into a breeze that swept across the room as my magic dissipated.

Beau's mouth was slightly ajar.

"Surprise?" I offered again.

"H—" his voice squeaked. "How?"

"Jorah and I are bonded. She is now Enchanted," Krew offered.

"Does this mean that sh—" he gave his head a shake. "Does this mean that you choose her? Does this mean that she may become queen?"

Krew looked into my eyes as he said, "She already is a princess. Queen or princess is not up to me, but I do rather think she'd make an exceptional queen someday." He looked back to Beau. "And there's more."

His eyes tried to leave his head. "There's more?"

"I didn't give her merely a drop of my magic. She is . . . quite strong," Krew explained vaguely.

I took pity on the poor man, adding, "Krew is no longer the only Enchanted who can kill his father." I paused. "And because of our bond, our magic can combine. Separately, right now either one of us may be strong enough to remove the king. Together?" I stole a glance at Krew, my eyes locked on his. "Well together, we will *not* fail."

Beau clutched at his chest while my mother just looked worried.

I am absolutely going to ravish you later, Krew promised.

I pressed my lips together to keep from laughing.

Beau sat there stunned for a moment and then he was kneeling at my feet, grabbing my hand. "Thank you. Thank you." He shook his head and I thought I might have seen tears sitting there. "I don't envy the burden you carry in having to take down the king, the risks you take in living under the same roof as him, but dear girl, thank you."

"My point is," Krew added, "that things are in play, Mr. Jones. Though it may not feel like it here in Nerede, particularly after the past few months, I can assure you, major things are in play. My father has an object in his possession which is increasing his power. We need to figure out what that object is. As soon as we know, we will remove it from his person and remove him from the throne."

Krew switched his attention to my mother. "And it is not up to only Jorah and me. My brother is ready when the moment comes. Officer Raikes here is ready when the moment comes." He paused and looked back to Beau. "I understand the people of Nerede need hope right now, Mr. Jones, and Jorah is that hope. She is the greatest hope for us all."

CHAPTER 23

"Nice try."

Owen threw a large rock at me, while at the same time throwing a breeze out at Krew.

With a manic laugh, I wrapped my own magic around the rock, and sent it hurtling back at him at the same time I sent a breeze at him, knocking him backward, losing his focus on whatever he'd been about to do to Krew.

Krew sent his own magic slithering along the ground. It wrapped around Owen's ankles while he was still being blasted with my wind, and he let out a curse word. Krew's magic was traveling upward. It only looked like a few vines of navy magic, but I knew better. I'd seen Krew's magic do the same thing to Michael Noyer and render him paralyzed, as if the magic were some sort of cement.

But then out of nowhere, a blast of magic stopped Krew's. It hadn't been green either.

"How about we make this a fair fight?" Keir asked from where he casually stood watching.

Krew, Owen, and I had been practicing what we had thought

had been alone. Krew had been wanting to get a feel for how we could combine our magic against another Enchanted. Owen, of course, had been our test subject.

Keir knew we had been practicing together, but we hadn't expected him to just show up and join us either.

"So you want to be on Jorah's side then?" Krew asked with a glance at me.

I smirked. He was implying that he and I were the strongest, not he and Keir.

"Nope. I'll take Owen."

Owen bowed. "I am honored, Your Princeness. Let's take these two down a peg or two, shall we?"

"Delighted to," Keir provided before releasing his magic, the night sky turning bright blue as he and Krew's magic clashed together.

They'd practiced together often, so it was almost a dance for them to attack one another. The same with Owen and me.

As I turned my attention on Owen, a stick wrapped in bright blue came flying at me. I easily batted it away. Using Krew's magic as inspiration, I was about to send out my magic like a vine, running along the ground, to pull Owen down. "And here I thought we'd play fair."

"Never!" Owen yelled.

I knocked away another rock, not even taking the care to notice which color of magic held it as I focused on my magic.

I opened my hand, palm down and released my magic.

Seeing my magic slither along the ground and then thicken as I sent more magic outward had me smiling. Sure enough, while Krew was distracting both of them, my magic wrapped around Owen's right foot, then the other. Seconds later, as soon as Owen was wrapped up, my magic had also reached Keir, doing the same.

I waited for a moment, sending a steady stream of magic outward, and then when I was satisfied with the strength of my vines, I reached out and tugged on my magic. It was something I'd seen Krew do only once before. Sure enough, my vines of magic pulled Owen and Keir's legs out from under them. They grunted as they both fell to the ground.

But having anticipated that, I'd also sent out magic to make a soft landing under their heads. I wanted to learn how to wield my magic and help take down the king, but I also didn't want anyone to get seriously hurt. I didn't want to almost kill Keir a second time.

"Well that was unexpected," Keir muttered from the ground. "Wait, did she cushion our fall?"

Owen leaned up on an elbow. "Welcome to fighting Jorah. She kicks your ass while ensuring you don't break it."

Keir laughed.

I stole a glance at Krew to find him looking at me with pride. *Stop with the feelings,* I reminded him.

I'll have plenty of feelings. Later.

It's already late and we have a ball tomorrow for a certain two spoiled heirs of Wylan having birthdays.

Well technically it is already my birthday. All the more reason—

He cut off because Owen hit him with magic, sending him sliding off. I sent my own magic off to intercept the green magic, having barely had to think about it.

"I've learned," Owen said where he now stood. "To wait until they are in each other's heads. They distract each other every time."

And then we were off again. Instead of using magic on either Keir or Owen, I tried to focus and send out whatever I was imagining to both at the same time. But it took entirely more concentration than I was used to, and ten minutes later, I felt the sheen of sweat on my forehead.

"Love," Krew called out loud.

"Yes?"

"Let's not push too far tonight given that we were already practicing before this. End this, would you?"

Knowing exactly what he wanted, I sent my magic out into a dome, surrounding both Owen and Keir. Every night we practiced with Owen, this was how we wrapped things up. I set up the dome, Krew fortified it, and Owen played around with seeing if he could get himself out of it in only a few minutes.

Thus far he'd only succeeded in taking down one of the domes with our combined magic.

"Wow," Keir muttered. "Impressive."

I'd purposefully left the sound barrier aspect out this time, wanting to hear their banter.

Feeling my skin humming with that adrenaline high, I walked over to Krew, who wrapped an arm around me and waited with me.

Through the few gaps in the dome, I saw some flashes of magic. I didn't know what Keir was trying, but it obviously wasn't working.

"I won't be much help, I'm afraid. Had my hands full with Jorah. She's becoming a real pain in the ass, though I won't ever admit that to her."

Krew and I both laughed.

"This one isn't a sound barrier, is it?" he called loudly.

"No. It isn't," I confirmed.

"Dammit."

I laughed. It was late. Far later than we ever should have been up. But we were finally getting somewhere with training together. Though I still found Krew using his magic entirely attractive, I was able to set it aside and make it through these sessions while containing myself. Owen still, of course, teased me as if I couldn't.

Owen had been the one who wanted to experiment with my domes of magic, and we found that mine, maybe just because of the way I envisioned them or willed them, were stronger than even

Krew's. But if I sent the magic out first and Krew added to it, they were even more so.

It had taken multiple nights to figure all of that out, and I was still frustrated my nights were spent working on domes of magic and not healing the lake, but I kept reminding myself that once the king was gone, I could heal the lake all I wanted. All in due time.

Keir kept sending out his magic into the dome, but still the dome stood.

"Ready to call it?" Krew asked them.

"No. Give me a few more minutes," Keir offered. "I was late to the party."

Yet five minutes later, the dome still stood, and Krew was scolding Keir on not pushing himself too hard to the brink of exhaustion.

Without prompting, I brought my fingertips into my palm, as if hiding something in my hand, and the dome fell.

Keir was grabbing his knees while Owen slowly brought himself back up to standing.

"Let's go, Your Highnesses," I offered. "We have birthday celebrations tomorrow to attend."

"Who—" Keir breathed heavily, "the hell cares?"

I smirked. "I am fairly certain only all of Wylan."

He shook his head and held out a hand in gesture. "No. *That.* Krew said you'd been working on it, but I had no idea. No idea your magic is that strong together." He paused, shaking his head. "I mean our magic strengthens slightly when we combine it, but that . . . that was *different.*"

"It's gotten better in the last week since they've started toying with it," Owen explained. "I've only been able to break out of it once."

"Then why in the hell haven't we used this on our father?" Keir snapped.

Krew let out a sigh. "Because we don't know which obj—"

"To hell with the object!" Keir gestured with both hands now to where the dome had just been. "Together your magic is more powerful than the two of ours together. Together your magic has to be stronger than his. Even if he does have Mum's magic, they were heart bound. Not soul bound."

Krew added, "You don't think I realize that? You don't think I want to storm into that castle and end this once and for all? Jorah has been Enchanted all of a month and a half. We will continue to practice and bide our time."

"But—"

"But," Krew snapped, "we will not make our move until we know we will succeed." He paused. "He will kill one or both of us if we do not succeed, so there is absolutely no room for error this time."

CHAPTER 24

I was re-wearing a gown. It was the navy one for the very first ball I attended as part of Krew's Assemblage. Krew mentioned that dress the other day in passing, so Silvia and I decided I could re-wear it for their birthday celebration. That was usually frowned upon for the consorts, so Silvia had to get it approved. And then the Assemblage advisor had asked Krew. And Krew had told her if I didn't wear that dress, he'd be upset.

I'd tried to surprise him with it. It was just something small I had tried to do to make his birthday special, but he'd found out anyway. He was impossible to surprise.

So I didn't know what to do for his birthday. What did you give one of the crown princes of Wylan as a birthday gift? In Nerede, we usually just made some sort of sweet dessert and that was all. Because that was usually all we had the time or energy for.

I knew from the queen's journals that jewels were far more common in Savaryn and Kavan Keep. Also on the princes sixth birthdays, they were gifted their first swords.

Swords and jewels. Rewearing a dress. It all seemed rather

inadequate ways of trying to make Krew's day special. A day he also shared with Keir.

Krew had been busy with Keir and his father all day, so I was to meet him downstairs. Ready to get the fancy portion of the night over with, Owen and I headed down. I was feeling irked I didn't get to spend hardly any time with Krew at all. I was in an odd mood, still feeling exhausted from being up late the night before and then dealing with Keir's belief that Krew and I were stronger than the king and whatever object he wore.

But as the cool air hit my bare shoulder, I couldn't help but smile.

The weather had been acting more like spring than winter for once, so the birthday ball had been moved to the gardens. There would be minimal dancing. And this ball was supposed to be more about the princes and less about the pomposity, more of a party.

Hanging from tree branches were tons of strings of lights in circular bulbs. The result was a maze of lights weaving throughout the garden and casting everything in a romantic glow. It was rapidly getting darker out, but the lights helped. And not only were they functional, they were also just beautiful.

We walked one of the pathways I was familiar with, before turning to find the servers and snacks. The servers were carrying around black trays and even they looked happy in the change of scenery.

I found Gwen by the truffles, of course, and went over to talk to her while we waited for everyone else to filter in.

The king was the last to arrive and he arrived with Nara on his arm. I pushed my magic down and tried not to be annoyed. Tonight was about his sons, but the king couldn't handle the attention on anyone but himself for even one night. He'd made his first public appearance with his new mistress instead.

"What is he doing?" Gwen whispered from behind her champagne glass.

I smiled at her so no one listening in would be any the wiser. "My guess is that with only half as many guests as normal, he thought this would be the perfect time to bring Nara around."

Gwen rolled her eyes and I fought off a laugh.

"Have you spoken with her since?" Gwen asked.

I gave her a nod. "Just once. Found her walking these gardens, actually."

Gwen spun so her back was to the king and Nara. "I cannot stomach being near her. While I can understand the need to get out of Rallis, I cannot understand why she'd do this."

We gave each other a look and I knew what she was trying to say. That she didn't trust her. And neither did I. Though Gwen and I had issues of our own which were not likely to just disappear, there was one area we had found common ground. We both understood the king needed off that throne. And sooner rather than later.

For an hour we chatted and grabbed drinks. Then the princes arrived together, the entire room clapping and singing.

I've missed you today, Krew sent to me even as he held a conversation with one of his father's commanders.

I missed you.

Before either prince even got a chance to grab a drink or check in with their consorts, the king stood on a balcony overlooking the gardens, Nara behind him and off to the side, and sent out his black magic into fireworks to get everyone's attention.

"Tonight we celebrate my sons, your heirs to Wylan. Another year has come and gone, another year readying them for the future. So let tonight be about them. They are the greatest things I have ever done for Wylan. Happy birthday, my sons!" He gestured with a hand toward an open lawn where a group was gathered.

Judging by the ladders and bars, it was going to be similar to the other acrobat show we'd seen. Except outside. With minimal lighting.

But was this even a good idea? Would the athletes be okay performing in the dark?

Two chairs were set up front on the lawn, obviously for Keir and Krew, with rows of chairs behind the first two sets. Meanwhile the king took a seat in his balcony, overviewing everything. Nara got to sit up there too, but in a chair scooted back so far I wasn't sure she could see a thing.

For what had to be the thousandth time, I wondered what in the realm she thought she was doing. Did she assume she would just cuddle up to the king and wind up the queen of Wylan? Just like that?

We were ushered over to the other seats. Krew and Keir's chairs were more elaborate, though still white, and I wondered how many throne-looking chairs the castle possessed. I, of course, sat next to Renna and Molly. Gwen was on the other side of Renna, still staying clear of Molly altogether.

As the acrobats began their art of swinging through the air and launching themselves, I realized I had no reason to worry. Though it was dark, they had some tall lights added to the area to help.

The acrobats, men and women alike, all wore sequined outfits that played off the added light and made them glitter through the night sky.

It was beautiful.

A second song played as the two women took to the bars, swinging and catching one another. They were wearing a sheer material that left little to the imagination, but I was still impressed with how they could use their bodies to form such poses that looked so easy, when I knew from the little training I had with Owen, they truly were not. I knew it pulled and strained at their well-toned legs and arms, and yet they smiled through it. As if they were unbothered at all.

Molly leaned in toward me. "I still have bosom questions."

I snorted a laugh. "When don't you, Molls?"

As the two women ended their piece, they landed side by side, joining hands and giving a bow. They were also twins, I realized. Or else their makeup made it very much look like they were.

They sauntered forward, and then much to everyone's surprise, each woman perched on the arm of a prince's chair.

As if a practiced routine, they draped their arms over the back of the chairs, looking quite cozy with their princes.

I shoved my magic down, forcing it to vanish. There was no possible way Krew could have known this was going to happen. No possible way.

Krew leaned in to whisper something to the woman on the arm of his chair and I fought like hell to keep my magic shoved deep down beneath the surface of my skin. I grabbed for the bond, and judging by his emotions I felt, he was also angry this was happening. So I knew that this was not something he approved of.

Why did this have to keep happening to me? Was this just the future I had being married to one of the crown princes? It seemed highly unlikely that women would stop falling over themselves to get to the princes any time soon. Not that I could really blame them because both princes were quite handsome. But like it or loathe it, this was just something I was going to have to get used to. Without unleashing my magic upon the realm. I was going to have to trust Krew and deal with it.

I slammed my eyes shut and took a deep breath as Renna grabbed onto my wrist in support. I felt a hand on my other wrist and realized Molly must have mimicked what Renna had done on the other side. "Just tell me when it's over," I whispered as I focused on the direction of my shoes while taking deep breaths and making sure my magic wasn't crawling along my skin. The king was watching from his perch. I couldn't lose it now. Not when I was this close to figuring out how strong Krew and I's magic combined could be. Another two deep breaths, and I felt okay, magic still contained.

"Well, I believe it is pretty much over," Renna said at the softest of a whisper.

I willed my eyes to look at her, not at Krew.

"They sent them away."

My eyebrows slammed together as I turned my eyes back to where the princes sat, to see both the woman acrobats walking back toward the side of the makeshift stage where they had originally come out of.

"How about that?" Molly whispered.

"I am sure we all know who arranged it anyway," Renna added. "The only thing truly shocking is that the king wasn't down there with them, a woman on either arm of his chair."

I am so going to ravish you later, I told Krew.

His head snapped sideways in my direction, and I could see the grin on half his face. *There is only one woman I wish to be on my lap. Today or any other day.*

By the time the acrobats wrapped things up, I was back to just enjoying the show. They were so very talented. Despite one of them trying to make a move on my husband, I still clapped and had genuinely enjoyed the show.

Molly, Renna, Gwen, and I headed for snacks while everyone moved back to the walkways of the gardens.

I felt a hand on the small of my back and knew exactly who was there. "May I borrow you for a moment, love?"

I gave him a bow and a nod and excused myself from the other women.

Krew took my hand and led me around the corner and along some bushes. We were on grass and not cement, but still on a trail of sorts.

"I had no idea," he whispered. "None. I am so sorry."

"I felt your anger," I offered. "I was wise enough to check through the bond to feel your anger, so I knew."

"My father just wanted to—" he cut off and turned his head to the side. "He must have seen us walk off and is coming this way."

I sighed and rolled my eyes. "Great. Night keeps on getting better."

Krew took a step forward, so much so that I also had to take a step back. And another, and another, until some sort of tree was at my back. It was quite scratchy, but with how my body and Krew's aligned, I wasn't about to complain.

"This trick again?" I whispered as I heard the footsteps coming our way.

As he reached around the back of my neck and kissed me hard, he sent through the bond, *It's an old but efficient one.*

Krew deepened the kiss, as if he didn't know his father was there, and I pulled the lapel of his tailcoat, bringing him in even closer. He didn't stop and neither did I until the king made a noise clearing his throat.

Krew snapped his head that direction but made no move to let go of me. "Bother me tomorrow, Father. It is my birthday, and I am decidedly busy at the moment."

Krew's voice was ice cold.

The king put up a hand. "Well since you didn't like my first gift to you, your tastes having changed, I was only going to let you know that another gift will be delivered in the morning to your room before you disappeared for good."

"Okay. Can *you* disappear now?" Rarely had I heard Krew regard his father so cruelly. Even if he was continuing to trail his lips across my collar bone.

The king, rather than getting angry, smirked. "Happy birthday, my son."

Krew didn't wait for him to leave before his lips were back on mine. As I peeked to make sure the king was really gone, I considered all he'd just said.

"Wait," I gasped, shoving Krew back. "What does he mean your tastes have changed?"

Krew let out a defeated sigh. "Years ago. When I was mourning Cessa . . ."

It all clicked. "You slept with the acrobats?"

He gave me a nod. "Yes."

I wanted to be mad, I wanted to be jealous. It was more than awkward considering the king had just implied the acrobats had been one of Krew's *birthday gifts*, but I also knew I had a past too. Still, I couldn't help but be curious. I could be jealous all I wanted, but I couldn't deny they were beautiful. "Which one?"

Krew winced and took a small step back from me. "Both of them."

He looked like he was preparing for my magic to attack him, his eyes traveling my arms and looking to my palms. Seeing him preparing for my wrath did something funny to my heart. So he had a past with those women. He'd also sent them away immediately and sought me out. He didn't let the acrobat sitting on the arm of his chair stay there for even a half of a song.

Rather than use my magic on him, a giggle escaped out my lips. Then another. "You just looked so concerned I was going to really," I looked around to make sure no one else was with us, "*attack* you."

"Do you blame me? So much feistiness contained in such a small person." Krew's lips curled into a smile. "Let's get to the dismissing portion of the evening, shall we?"

"Let me guess, having feelings again, are you?"

He grabbed me by the hand and pulled me away from the scratchy green tree. "Numerous feelings. Including feelings of making any doubt bouncing around in your cunning head vanish."

Within the hour, we were back in Krew's wing doing exactly that.

* * *

THERE WAS a knock on the door. Realizing my sound barrier was still up from the night before, I brought my fingertips into my palm to drop the barrier before someone saw my color of magic.

If it was Owen coming to wake me for a session, he wouldn't have knocked. And if it was Silvia, Owen would have notified me first.

So whoever it was, wasn't normal.

Realizing I was still very much without clothes, I checked to make sure the sheets and blankets were covering everything adequately.

"What?" Krew snapped from next to me.

The door opened and a man carrying a silver box came in. "A delivery for you, Your Grace."

Without so much as looking toward the bed, the man dropped the package onto the couch and then left as swiftly as he'd come.

"Not more presents," I groaned as soon as he was gone, grabbing my light pink silk robe I kept next to my side of the bed. All I typically slept in anymore was a silk night dress, so I kept the robe close by for better coverage.

Krew grabbed for me, but I was already out of reach, sliding into my robe and slippers.

"Come back to bed," Krew demanded. "That is the only present I need."

I shot him a look while I headed for the box. "Your father sent you acrobats, whom he may or may not have paid to sleep with you, as the first present. You aren't even slightly curious as to what is in this one?" I lifted the box and gave it a shake.

Krew leaned back on an elbow, the covers barely covering anything. "Dreading it quite honestly."

I glared at him.

"Just open it and get it over with."

I pulled the bow off slowly, wondering what kind of horror could be lying inside. It was a fairly large box, bigger than jewels but not long enough for a sword. Felt pretty light too, so unfortunately it wasn't housing the king's dead heart.

I opened the box to find a smaller box residing inside. Of course the king would enjoy even that kind of mind game.

I picked up the smaller blue velvet box and felt nothing but apprehension. It had a hinge like a jewelry box. As soon as I gently opened it, seeing what was laying inside, it slipped out of my hand and fell shut onto the rug with a thud.

My magic was immediately burning in my veins.

Krew had found some pants and evidently thrown them on haphazardly, as he was now dressed before me, but without the buttoning of said pants. "What is it?" he asked as he reached one hand out to me and the other to the floor to pick up the box.

"A ruby ring. Likely for a thumb?"

He went silent as he looked at it for himself. "It's not his. His is still with Hatcher. And will remain with him for a long time."

"So it's a replica then?" I asked calmly as I felt anything but.

He gave me a nod as he closed the box. "Yes."

"Krew, why would your father give you a replica of the ring we just so happened to steal?" I was fairly certain I knew the answer to that, but I needed to hear it out loud.

"Because he knows."

CHAPTER 25

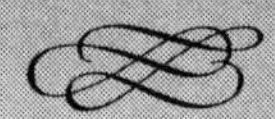

Two weeks had passed since the ring had been gifted to Krew. Since he'd been forced to wear the wretched thing while around his father. The king had merely told the princes he'd lost his so when he sent for another to be made, he'd made both of them matching ones as well.

But every time I saw that red gem on Krew's thumb, it made me uneasy.

I felt like the king was messing with us. He knew we'd taken it from him, and I wasn't sure what the point of all this was, but I was sure that there was some sort of mind game going on.

And that it was very much working.

The good news was that now the Assemblages were down in numbers, the amount of balls were continuing to decrease. So I was personally seeing the king less and less, though the stockpile of my blood we had saved back before the bonding was beginning to dwindle. I couldn't avoid him forever, but the only good thing about Nara being around was that the king was too busy with his own affair to be overly involved in anyone else's. Even the royal family dinners were not as frequent now that the Assemblage numbers were smaller. They were now doing late breakfasts instead, so the king's evenings were free.

I didn't want to think about that too hard.

Though I was still training at random hours of the day with Owen, and sometimes the princes as well, I had been spending more days walking the gardens with Renna and Molly. I was purposefully trying to run into Nara. I wasn't sure she'd divulge much of anything. She was being far too influenced by the king. But I wanted to keep seeing her with my own eyes and checking for bruises.

Though Krew told me she was still alive and well, we hadn't seen her since the princes' birthday celebration. And that made my uneasiness increase ten-fold. She'd been at the last ball, an odd sort of introduction as being the king's mistress. So shouldn't we have been seeing more of her then? Not less?

I was standing on the balcony overlooking the forest after another long day of training. We'd been up from midnight until almost dawn today, and I was shot. But to calm my mind before I dozed off, I was watching the sunset from my balcony. And the best news was that it'd been a gorgeous spring day and I didn't even need to use my magic to warm me. Spring was finally, finally arriving.

"Oh hey, Rafe." My smile was immediate.

I saw the gray blur which was Rafe, a black blur not far behind, and numerous other blips and flashes of fur. How those wolves had survived all this time in a dying forest was beyond me. And I'd only managed to bring a caterpillar back, but hopefully soon the wolves would have more to chase in these woods other than each other.

Like he heard my voice even from this far away, Rafe swung his head in my direction, peeking out from the trees.

Another wolf gave out a yip of a bark, and then he was off again, back in the trees. As fast as they were moving now, I knew they went slow when they ran with me. And even at their slowest speed, I couldn't keep up. But it was still my favorite part of my day.

I felt Krew's nearness before I could see or hear him, and I knew he was likely done for the day too. He'd been busy all day preparing for the next parliament session at the castle. The issue of a tax increase on Nerede was sure to be a topic they argued extensively over.

Grab yourself a whiskey and join me?

I could almost feel Krew smiling through the bond. *Like I would ever turn that down.*

He brushed a kiss to the back of my neck as soon as he joined me, putting up a thin sound barrier around us as to not affect my view of the sunset. "Apologies for being so late tonight, love. Did you eat?"

"I did. Are you all ready for parliament tomorrow?" Hopefully Owen and I would be able to escape to the kitchens. I'd already made up some cookies and thrown them in the freezer for that very reason. While Krew was dreading the day, I was actually looking forward to it.

He rolled his eyes. "I don't know why Father insists on going over the topics with us beforehand. At first, I thought it was part of what he believed was readying us for the throne. But it is likely that of the five topics, four will just be delayed until the next joint session. I'm tired of hearing these same topics and arguments repeatedly."

I spun to look at him. "If you were king, what would you do differently?"

His eyes burned into mine. "All of it. Parliament-wise, I would request that we argue the same topics no more than three times in a row, and then they will be tabled for six months. If we cannot come to an agreement in three sessions, then there is no point. The time spent arguing those same issues could be spent making real improvements that do matter."

He paused and took a step closer. "And my queen will be my equal. My mother had a vote, yes, but she was barely allowed to use her voice." He brushed a kiss to my lips. "I will never do that to you. I will never silence you, even when I might disagree with you. *Especially* when I disagree with you."

As my eyes tingled at his love for me, I felt a laugh bubble up.

"You laugh?"

I put up my hand. "I do, but only because when I came here, I always thought I would make a horrible queen. And now it isn't that I truly believe I'd be a good queen, it's just that I believe *you* would make an exemplary king." Krew was moving in to kiss me, and I felt through the bond that things were going to get intense in a hurry. But before he distracted me, I added, "I know it might not ever be you, Krew. Some days I quite selfishly prefer that *for us*. It's not up to us. But for Wylan . . . they need *you*."

I barely had time to catch another breath before we became a frenzied mess of lips and touch, all wrapped up in a whispered promise.

The looming future remained so uncertain, but I wasn't going to allow my fear of it to keep me from loving this man for even a moment.

* * *

WARRICK WAS with us in the meadow. The three of us were having a picnic like we often did. We heard the rustle of the wolves off in the distance as they chased another rabbit. Soon the weather would turn cold, and we'd be stuck indoors far more often, but I was content knowing that in the spring, the forest would still be alive.

The fall breeze sent a chill down me, but I used my magic to warm myself back up. Looking at the autumn colors of the forest felt so odd. I felt like it should be black for some odd reason.

"Can we still picnic inside?" Warrick asked us. "When the winter comes?"

I smiled at him. "Of course."

"And make lots of cookies?"

I laughed. "Of course."

Krew was looking at us with such pride. "I love you."

"I love you."

I had just turned back to Warrick when I felt Krew down our bond.

I love you.

I turned to look at him, feeling his panic within the words, but he wasn't there anymore.

I jolted awake with a start, reaching across the sheets for Krew's side of the bed. It'd been a dream. But as I grabbed for the bond, I knew his panic hadn't been a part of the dream, it'd just been what knocked me out of it.

Krew?

He didn't respond right away.

KREW?

I could feel his hurt. Someone was hurting him. Or hurting . . . his magic?

I'm fine, love. And whatever happens, I love you.

I kept feeling down the bond for him, focusing hard on where I felt him, though the bond felt a bit muddled somehow. It took me longer than normal, but I knew he was in the throne room. He was in the throne room and someone was hurting him.

And he'd been panicked enough a few moments ago to knock me out of a deep sleep. I'd felt many emotions from Krew over the past few months, but not once had I ever felt him panicked.

Without another thought, I threw my silk robe over my night-gown and glowing skin and began running. Was this about the ring? Was this about the princes' bond? So help me if the king took his whip to Krew again, I would lose my mind and kill him on the spot. Or die trying.

Just last night we had been thinking of the future. That was probably why I'd had the dream about Warrick being here at the castle. But I feared that future was dangling by a thread with whatever was going on in the throne room right now.

Krew?

He wasn't responding to me, but I kept feeling his emotions. I still felt that twinge of hurt, but I wasn't sure if it was on him or his magic. And I felt . . . anger. No, that felt watered down compared to all the fury I felt pouring out of Krew.

I opened the door and bolted for the throne room. Something was wrong. Something was very, very wrong.

"Jorah?" Owen asked as he sped after me.

I didn't respond right away, too focused on the bond and Krew. I ran straight for the elevator.

"Jorah?" Owen tried again, reaching for my arm. "Talk to me."

I forcefully pressed the button on the elevator. The doors didn't open right away, so I hit it twice more. I vaguely noted the other guard standing outside Krew's wing had just seen me fly down the hallway with my skin glowing, so he definitely now knew I had magic.

Owen gently took my arms in his hands and turned me toward him. "Hey. What's wrong?"

I shook my head. "I don't know. I felt Krew's panic. And I think he's hurt. Or something is hurting his magic. I don't know what's going on, I just know something is wrong, Owen."

"Okay, let's go find out." Owen nodded, concerned eyes on mine. "But would you like to get dressed first?"

As the door to the elevator dinged open, I looked down to find myself in my light pink night dress with my matching silk robe tied over it. I'd been in such a rush I didn't even bother grabbing my slippers. I was barefoot.

I felt down the bond again, still feeling Krew's panic and anger. "No. There isn't time." As we boarded the elevator, I added. "You don't think he's finally losing his magic or something do you?"

"Would that make him feel panic?" Owen asked calmly. But I knew from his veined neck muscles he was just as tense as I was.

"No."

"But you can still feel him, so he is alive," Owen reminded me. "Where are they? Can you feel where they are?"

"Throne room. But the bond feels . . . strained or something."

"At least it's not the mountain." Owen's forehead creased. "But I thought parliament was coming today."

I gasped as another wave of Krew's mixed worry and anguish hit me. I grabbed onto Owen's arm and squeezed. "We have to help him, Owen. Please."

"We will, but what are you going to do here, Jorah? If you go in there, there is no way you'll be able to keep a handle on your magic if you see the king hurting Krew."

My magic was still glowing and heating beneath my skin. It had been since the moment I'd woke. If anything, it was building. Ready to protect Krew if need be, I felt no inclination at all to shove it down. "If he is hurting Krew, keeping a handle on my magic is the last thing I will do."

The elevator doors slid back open. Owen and I exchanged a glance. We both understood the day we had all been training for, the day the king found out I had magic, had finally arrived.

CHAPTER 26

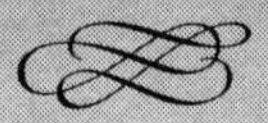

We were almost there; we had just turned the corner and the wooden throne room doors stretching ceiling to floor were in sight.

Be careful, Krew sent to me. *I'd tell you not to do this, but I know better. Father somehow weakened us before putting the gauntlets on Keir and me. We won't be much help. I no longer feel as if he is trying to kill us though, merely teaching us a lesson.*

I gasped, my magic burning brighter and brighter with every step in Krew's direction. Gauntlets? That prick put gauntlets on my husband?

"The princes have gauntlets on," I informed Owen, my voice sounding as full of rage as I felt. "Be prepared for anything."

He grabbed my arm and slowed me for just a moment. "I have trained you well, Jorah. You are ready for this. Do whatever you have to do, and do *not* hesitate for even a moment."

I gave him as much of a smile as I could muster and brought my fingers on one hand up, brushing each fingertip to my thumb as I made the last strides to the doors. I knew what I wanted. I was imagining it before I even hit the doors, giving my magic directions. But I let my magic flare and burn hotter and hotter until it matched the erratic beating of my heart.

And then I *attacked.*

I sent the magic along the floor, blowing the doors wide open at once. Any guards standing by it were blown back by my silver magic.

I kept walking right up the aisle, one hand aimed at the king on his stupid throne, the other at any guards about to make a move on me.

There were numerous gasps as I made my entrance, but I was focused on one person only. My magic headed in droves at the king where he now stood at his throne.

I looked at Krew's gray eyes for the briefest of moments, only to know he was still alive, and then I got *angry.*

Judging by the trail of blood I'd seen on Krew's forearms, he'd fought against the gauntlets. Hard.

The king had made Krew bleed.

Both princes were in their throne chairs behind the king's, wearing gauntlets. In front of all of parliament. Angry didn't even begin to cover how I felt.

The element of surprise worked to my advantage. The king was still looking at me in shock as my magic gripped his hands first, squeezing them into his legs. I cocked my head and sent out another blast of magic, each of his guards and himself further getting trapped with my silver magic. I had a coil of magic around the middle of the king and I was strengthening it with every strand of magic that left my body.

If it crushed him in half, so be it.

The king finally found his voice and tried to say something. "What do you th—"

I sent my magic out to silence him, making him feel pressure around his throat as if I was choking him. His words cut off immediately. "It is my turn to speak, *Your Grace.*"

One guard I hadn't seen, up above in a balcony, sent magic at me to get me to stop.

Before I could react, Owen already had, and he was immediately pinned down with green magic.

I was almost to the dais. I wondered if the parliament members were stunned or shocked as they saw me approach the king, but I wouldn't let anything take my focus off the king. The parliament members were at least not attacking me.

"Where are the keys?" I demanded of the king.

He just stood there, trapped with my magic, his eyes going wide.

I wouldn't stop until I had Krew out of those gauntlets. I had half a mind to just kill him now. I was certain he would only be immobilized for so long, but I had neglected to grab a weapon in my haste to get to the throne room in time. I wasn't even sure I could hold the king long enough to kill him without Krew's magic to join to mine.

"Where?" I repeated.

He tried to speak but couldn't, the pressure I had on his throat too much for words. I let off just a little, only to let him choke out, "On my belt."

I kept my magic in constant motion, fortifying the hold I had on the king's hands as I stepped onto the dais. With every step closer to the king I took, I felt a buzz of magic that was not my own. The king was going to retaliate if I let go of my magic for even a moment. I wanted to put the king and I in a dome as we sorted this out, protected from any guards sure to show up any second and any parliament members who got any ideas, but I also knew I needed to focus, and if I had the king stuck for now, I should move as quickly as possible. For now, parliament was frozen in shock.

"Give her the keys," the king demanded to his guards, his voice sounding strained.

"They can't," I offered. "They're busy. Allow me." I finished closing the distance between us. Who knew how long my magic would hold. But I needed those keys. Krew couldn't help me with his magic, weakened or not, until I freed him from those gauntlets.

As I reached down for the keys, I saw for the first time fear in the king's eyes. He truly believed he might die. And considering the panic he'd given his own sons today, the fear I'd felt from Krew that he might die, I relished in it. I had half a mind to unsheathe his sword next to the keys and drive it into his chest. But would parliament sit back and watch a blatant murder attempt of their king? I had only thus far immobilized the king, I had yet to draw any blood.

Despite an intense feeling of wanting to grab the sword which traveled all the way down my spine, I grabbed hold of the hook of keys instead. Not knowing which key it was, I threw them to Owen as I backed away from this despicable man.

A flash of emotion crossed his face as he closed his eyes a moment. An emotion I had never seen on his face and couldn't figure out. "How?" the king demanded.

Chitchatting with this ass hat was the last thing I wanted to do right now, but I'd do it if it meant those iron gloves got off Krew. "How do you think?"

He tilted his head as he thought about it.

I kept my magic pouring into the king, keeping him immobile. I just needed Keir and Krew. If Krew had enough magic to help me, we might be able to end this, here and now. While I already had the king immobile and distracted. Granted all of parliament being present threw in a ton of variables. There were just too many Enchanted in this room. I had the sneaking suspicion the only reason I still breathed was because I had used the element of surprise to my advantage.

Owen took three tries to get the right key, and then Krew was free. Owen moved right to Keir next.

Please tell me you can use your magic right now, I sent Krew.

Not enough of it. Tell him you were only trying to protect me.

I gave him a slight nod, knowing what that meant. We couldn't end the king today. If I tried to outright kill the king and failed, I would be tried for treason and killed. Likely slowly. I couldn't do this without Krew's magic. But I could talk my way out of this, saying that I was protecting the princes and why.

There was no doubt about it, the king was going to die. But that day was unfortunately not going to be today. And even just the knowledge that I held the king with my power but couldn't kill him yet made me angrier yet, my magic continuing to flare.

I took one step back off the dais but kept my eyes on the king as I began speaking loud enough for all of parliament to hear. "I think we both know this little show today is beyond a call for clemency. You wished today to display your power, reassert your dominance, and remind anyone in parliament second guessing how powerful you are. And after they stood up for a man, following your own rules about magic being used during parliament sessions, you wanted to remind everyone that you can still control your sons." I paused long enough to smile. "I wish to remind you, Your Grace, that they are strong too. Despite you. And that they, either of them, will be twice the king you were today."

"You are Enchanted," the king simply said, not even sounding all that angry after my well delivered soliloquy.

I felt Krew on one side of me. Keir on the other. Owen at my back.

"I did not wish to harm you, Your Majesty. I did not wish to harm anyone. I only wished to protect the heirs of Wylan from whatever traitorous act was hurting them. I did not realize they needed protecting from their own father."

"Release me," he barked. "I would not have truly hurt them."

Do it.

"You already have, Your Grace." I made a show of bringing my fingers in one at a time as I brought my hand into a fist, choking out the magic on the king but not on any of the guards. "I felt it."

My magic may have been gone from the king, but it was still running along my veins, ready for whatever came next. Ready to render him immobile again if need be.

"You are bonded to my son," the king said, as if still working it all over in his head.

Let's get out of here. Before he figures out how weak we are.

"I am. I felt through the bond there was something wrong with Prince Krewan. That he was in pain. So I felt for his location and I reacted to protect."

There was a gasp from behind me, but I didn't dare turn around to see from which parliament member. "But that would mean . . ."

The king's eyes went wide. "Soul bound." He started shaking his head, his forehead creased.

I squinted at the king, "While I'd love to stay and chat, I am not exactly properly dressed for the occasion. I feared Prince Krewan was at risk of losing his life. Now that I can see both heirs to Wylan are, in fact, alive and well from *any and all* threats," I deliberately paused, "we will take our leave and let you all carry on what is sure to be an extremely productive joint parliament session."

The king just kept looking at me. Not murderously like I would have assumed. It must have been the shock. And once the shock wore off, I was sure to be a dead woman walking. Then again, I supposed he couldn't or wouldn't punish any of us right here in front of parliament and that was what was saving us. He was trying to save face by looking unbothered. But I had implied to all of the parliament members that the gauntlets on the princes were an act of treason, so that could be another reason he wasn't using his magic yet.

With a tilt to his head, my magic flared, and I knew he was going to use his magic before I saw it. I placed my hands on either prince's arm while shoving my leg backward to brush against Owen's.

The magic shot from his palms with no notice but dissipated around us. And I couldn't be sure, but I didn't think it was that strong of a blast of magic either.

"We are done here, Father," Keir spat out as he turned and gestured for me to walk out.

I turned, hand still in the crook of Krew's arm as we made our way to the doors.

We were almost free of the throne room when the king spoke out. "Not bad, Jorah of Nerede."

I tensed and slowly turned, only to look him in the eyes. "It is actually Jorah Collette Demir Valanova. Of Wylan."

And because I was still absolutely fuming that we couldn't have just ended his sorry life back there, at the same time I let my hold on the king's guards fall, I used my magic to slam the throne room doors shut behind us.

CHAPTER 27

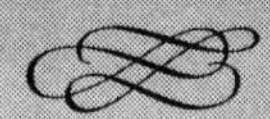

"I didn't realize you had such a flair for the dramatic," Owen said as we rode the elevator back upstairs. "Slamming the doors shut as we went was nice."

I looked him in the eyes. "What can I say, I was angry." I inhaled deeply. "I still am. I am absolutely livid we could not have just killed him back there."

Both princes were quiet and pale beside us.

"What can we do?" I asked more gently.

Krew gave his head a shake. "I think he laced our breakfasts with iron. So we were weak to begin with, then used a dozen guards to force the gauntlets on us."

I felt my magic burn brighter. I was still so obscenely pissed off right now. The king had put gauntlets on *his own sons.* It was a good thing I had just used a lot of magic in the throne room.

Krew moved his arm nearest me to place it around my back. "Calm down, love. You got us out of there." He paused. "I wish you wouldn't have put yourself in danger like that, but if he'd done the same to you, I would've blown the castle apart to get to you. So I get it." Just to me, he added, *Also that was remarkable. I love you.*

As soon as the elevator doors opened, I barked at Owen to have some food brought up for the princes. They needed something not laced with iron in their systems. Possibly a nap. That was what Krew needed most after he'd been shot with the arrow laced with iron, to sleep. I wasn't sure I shouldn't also send for our favorite annoying healer as well. And then there was what to do with Keir, who didn't have as much of a safety net as Krew did with Owen and me there.

"Keir?"

"Yes?"

"Can you stay in Krew's wing until whatever this is wears off? I don't trust your father for even a moment."

Keir gave me a nod. "Of course. I figured I'd be with you guys until at least the end of the day. Father is sure to find us after he tries to save face with parliament."

Owen rang for a server about the food. As soon as the door shut to Krew's wing, I put up a sound barrier and started the fire. We were in our room, Keir in the chair I always read at, Krew on the couch. Owen took post near the balcony door while I paced.

The king was going to find us after the parliament session? To line us up for lashings? Would Keir and Krew have recouped their magic by then? What if this day wasn't entirely over yet?

Keir let out a laugh.

The rest of us turned to him. There couldn't possibly be anything from this morning that could be found even remotely funny.

"I'm sorry," Keir offered as he brought his hand up to his forehead. "I just cannot get the image out of my head of Jorah storming in the throne room in a night gown and giving Father a taste of his own medicine."

"Barefoot even," Krew added.

I looked down at my attire and gave him a little shrug. "Time was of the essence."

That only made Keir laugh harder.

Krew was also laughing as he added, "The first person to have the guts to stand up to Father in a decade, and she does so in a pink nightgown."

"The great seductress, at it again," Owen deadpanned.

I felt my lips smirking even as I stated, "This is *not* funny, Your Graces."

"It's a little funny, Your Highness," Keir argued.

I swallowed hard. Owen had called me that on numerous occasions, but Keir never had.

"And thank you," he added. "For getting us out of there. The weight of those gauntlets . . ." he took a deep breath. "I never want to feel it again. Just thank you."

I gave him a smile. "You're welcome."

"How did you even know?" Krew asked. "I felt down the bond that you were sleeping when it all started to go to hell."

My eyes were on his as I said, "I felt your panic in a dream. Either it or my magic woke me."

"Speaking of panic," Owen began.

I spun to look at him.

"Did you see the king's face when you went for the keys?"

I smiled. "He looked utterly terrified. For his life." It might be weird of me to admit, but I was going to cherish that moment for the rest of my life.

"I wish the two of you could've seen it," Owen added to the princes, who had been behind the king at that juncture. "In all my life, I have never seen him look s—" Owen trailed off, his eyes going big.

"What?" I asked. "What's wrong?"

His eyes went to Krew's then bounced to Keir's. "It's the sword."

"I'll admit I thought about grabbing it instead and shoving it into the king's chest," I provided. "But with all of parliament at my back, I wasn't sure I'd survive long enough to complete the job."

"No." Owen was shaking his head, but his eyes were lit up. "It's *the sword*."

"The object?" Keir asked, moving to stand. "You believe the sword is the object which holds my mother's magic?"

Owen smiled. "I know it is. You didn't see his face when she reached for the keys. That was why he wanted his guards to do it and not Jorah. He was only beginning to understand how powerful she was, but he knew if she had the sword, it was over for him."

My jaw fell open. "You mean to tell me I was that close to it? That close to it and didn't know?" I thought back to the moment I had stepped onto the dais. I had thought I felt the king's magic building to retaliate. What if it hadn't been his magic? What if instead it'd been the sword? The magic of the queen.

I slumped down onto the couch next to Krew. "I didn't realize. I could've ended it had I just gone for the sword. This would all be over." Angry tears filled my eyes. Why couldn't we have figured that out before this morning? We were an hour too late.

I'd been so close to being able to end it all. So close. And now in the days to come we'd have to wait for the king's punishments, in whatever mind game he deemed necessary. It was likely we'd walk on eggshells in these halls until the day the king was gone. I had been mere inches from my dream of picnics in the meadow with Warrick coming true. Of a future with Krew by my side, not as a widow.

And it had all just slipped through my fingers back there in the throne room.

Krew put a hand on my back, rubbing circles. "Do not beat yourself up with the what-ifs. We didn't know. And we still wouldn't know had it not been for what you did today."

Keir was grinning like a lunatic, while I wiped at my eyes. "What now?" I snapped.

He sat down and put up his feet, crossing them at the ankles, looking pleased. "Not only do we have the two most powerful

Enchanted in the realm at our disposal, myself and Owen coming in at a close third and fourth, respectively, but now we also know which object we need to remove from him." Keir looked to each of us. "He can't kill us after what Jorah said down there. And he cannot touch her without parliament turning on him." He again grinned. "His days are numbered." He paused. "Next time, we finish him."

There was one quick knock and the door opened.

Instead of it being George with the food we had ordered to make my sound barrier fall, it instead was the king.

Krew immediately stood and put himself between me and his father. Though he had been somehow weakened, I could still see the navy slithering beneath his skin.

We were all standing, magic flaring, ready for whatever came next.

The king rolled his eyes and flicked his wrist. "I did not come here to harm her. I would've done that in the throne room if that was my intention. So calm down, son."

Krew didn't move. He didn't trust his father at all. None of us did. Owen slowly moved in, likely ready to grab me and jump off the balcony if needed.

"I only came to inform Jorah that she will be needed for all parliament sessions from here on out. Since she is likely the strongest woman in Wylan, based on her earlier stunt, parliament has decided it is time for your mother's proxy. Having just seen what she can do and that she is officially a Valanova, they've of course chosen her and demanded her presence."

What? This day just kept getting weirder and weirder. I was now the queen's proxy?

I also looked down toward the floor as if I was scared, but really I was searching for the stupid sword. It wasn't on him.

I turned over my shoulder to look at Owen, who gave me the barest of nods. He noticed it too. The king knew I'd been so close to figuring it all out and removing the item from his person which was keeping him as the strongest Enchanted in the realm. So he'd taken it off before coming to talk with us. I tried to think of a time I'd seen him without it, but I couldn't think of a single time the sword hadn't been there. Even on the night of the poker game where he'd killed Nico, the man who'd attempted to use magic on Krew, the king had used his dagger, never once unsheathing the sword.

But maybe that was because it wasn't just a sword, now was it? It was amplifying his magic.

"And you are allowing a proxy?" Keir snapped. "*Now?* To what end, Father?"

The king looked at Keir, as if not surprised to see him with the rest of us. "Well parliament has gotten decidedly tedious as of late. She does have disloyal inside information and the added effect of being able to heal the forest. She's helped Kavan Keep in that regard more than most of them have in years. So I am appeasing them. For now." He paused. "But let me be clear, she serves as proxy for a vote with parliament. Not as queen."

I was confused. He had a new mistress, yet I was the one to be serving as the queen's proxy? "Why not have Nara be the proxy then?"

The king smiled at me. "She is not the strongest Enchanted woman in Wylan. Nor is she a Valanova."

It was always about the power with him, wasn't it? I glared at him. "I was neither a few months ago."

"Yes, well, you aren't accepting bribes from my sons to steal things from me either." The king took a step toward me, so I didn't have time to panic over his words. "And about this newest development of your powers, Jorah. Care to enlighten me on how you managed to wed and become bonded to my son, breaking the rules of the Assemblages, without my knowledge?"

Krew's voice was ice cold. "The rules of the Assemblages were to find my wife. I did that. No rules were broken other than your constant interfering." He paused. "And I demanded it after you set fire to Nerede. She was not safe without magic. And we were not safe traveling throughout the kingdom if her touch meant I couldn't utilize my magic."

"And can you now?" the king asked. "Touch her and use your magic at the same time?"

Krew's answer was to move back only a step to wrap a hand around my waist while sending a breeze directly at the king.

He tilted his head. "And the recent healings in the forest?"

"Can be done with my blood, even Enchanted, or my magic," I admitted.

He gave me a nod. "Impressive." He looked from one of us to the other. "You have achieved something very few do. This bonding is a powerful thing. Though I do not appreciate the power play this morning, I do see this can be something that unites Wylan." He paused. "Either Jorah will be a powerful princess or a powerful queen."

"You mean her *power play* to stop yours?" Keir snapped. "And there is no *will be*, she already is a princess, you jackass."

The king groaned. "I understand why you might be frustrated with me over this morning, Keiran, so I will let the name calling go for now. But don't tell me you still pine for her after months of dating your other women. You are smarter than that." His attention switched back to me before Keir could say a word otherwise. "You have contained it well. And are far more powerful than a mere drop of magic should have given you."

I didn't dare even fidget in the silence. I would go to my grave without telling him what Krew had done. That he'd given me far, far more than just a drop. At only a minor cost to his own magic.

The king looked me over slowly. Head to toe. And it was entirely creepy. "It was your will, wasn't it? That stubborn, stubborn Iron Will. Strong enough to deflect magic, equally strong wielding it." He paused, crossing his arms as if deep in thought. "I daresay it has to do with your emotions as well, since your tears also have a healing entity."

He reached a hand out as if wanting to touch my chin or look closer into my eyes. But faster than felt possible, Krew was there, sliding between us and grabbing the king's wrist. "You *will not* touch my wife."

The ferocity in which Krew's voice tore through those words ran a shiver down my spine and had my magic beginning to lighten my veins.

"Fine," the king responded, sounding neither mad nor surprised at Krew's outburst.

And that was when I knew something was horribly wrong. The king should be mad. The king should be irate. I knew from personal experience it was in his nature to punish first and ask questions later. But for whatever messed up reason, he was playing nice.

And I also knew from past experience that was when to worry.

"Oh, and Jorah of Nerede?" the king said with a smile that was likely meant to be kind but just looked twisted instead. "I can appreciate your attempt to protect my sons today, and I do understand that you did not know what the threat was, only that there was one. And I also understand you are new to the power of your magic, but if you *ever* dare use your magic on me again, there will be repercussions. A good princess will remember her place in this castle."

I was still so very furious about the entire morning, I snapped, "Likewise a good king would not put iron gauntlets on his own sons."

The king gave me a nod. "Understood. It was likely a bit too far. I am man enough to admit that."

Keir snorted his disgust.

The king gave me another twisted smile. "But the pink nightgown was nice."

I felt Krew's immediate rage. Just when I was sure he was going to deck him, Owen was somehow there, shoving him back.

"Well. I'm past due for a lunch date. See you all in the morning, bright and early."

"No gauntlets?" I asked.

The king looked me in the eyes. "No gauntlets. So long as you keep healing my forest." He walked for the door but spun back. "Oh, and the royal jeweler will be by later to fit your crown. Your public wedding will be as soon as the staff can organize it. There is no need to continue this sham of an Assemblage any further when parliament already knows the truth." He shook his head. "Believe me, they are not capable of keeping a secret, so Krewan, your Assemblage is officially over." He switched his attention to Keir, "And yours needs to be at the final two by the wedding."

CHAPTER 28

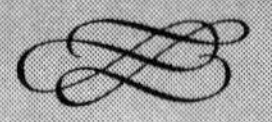

Owen had woken me before dawn. I'd trained with magic with him for an hour. I healed two trees at the lake when we were done, because if the king already knew I had magic, why not? And then I ran with the wolves. By breakfast I had exerted enough energy that hopefully I could survive the first day of posing as the queen's proxy for parliament. Despite all of that, I could feel the tension between my shoulder blades, but my magic was calm for now. Calm and waiting.

Silvia was beside herself with excitement as she readied me for the day. After all, no one had served as the queen's proxy in the ten years since she'd been gone.

I was decidedly less excited. Not because I didn't want to help and pose a check to the king's ultimate vote, but because it was the king we were talking about here.

Silvia had me looking queenly in a light blue gown that looked gorgeous but was sure to be itchy by the end of the long session.

She ran her fingers through my loose waves and then took me by the shoulders. It was something my mother always did too. "You, my dear girl, are still a baker," she began. "You do not need to become anything other than what you are to play the role you've just been handed. You are a baker. You may also be a queen. Both are a part of who you are. Both will help you lead with dignity and grace."

I blinked hard. "Silvia! You are going to mess up all your hard work."

She laughed. "Worth it. Now go rattle up parliament, would you?"

I gave her a smirk. "I'll do my best."

Krew had left early that morning but told me to wait for him to head to the throne room, so I sat on the bench at the end of the bed and took some calming deep breaths.

I didn't have to hide my magic anymore. I didn't have to hide that I was now married to Krew. All I needed to do was get through this first parliament session without irritating the king any further and we'd be fine. As I'd been running in the forest that morning, I had decided that if the king was going to play nice, I was going to play nice right back. I would not let him for even a moment think he was getting to me. Just like the night he sent me that ridiculous dress, I was going to walk in there and play my role flawlessly.

I could do this.

Feeling Krew approaching, I stood. I wasn't ready, just ready to get it over with. But he came in bearing packages.

"Oh no, more gifts?"

He gave his head a shake, smiling. "No. Well, yes, of sorts. Just not from my father anyway."

He held up the first royal blue box. "This is the crown readjusted for you, so it doesn't fall off all day."

Wow. They'd been fast. Just yesterday afternoon I had been fitted for it. I hadn't realized they'd have it ready for me already this morning. I might have actually preferred if they hadn't.

But of course, the king would never allow the proxy to the

queen to sit there without wearing a crown. He was all about appearances.

"And this," Krew grinned, holding a smaller blue box. "This is something I have wanted to give you for a long, long time."

I felt my eyebrows crease. "Well don't tease me. What is it?"

He turned the small box.

If there is a ruby ring for my thumb in that box, I am going to murder you.

"It's not a ruby, love. Calm down."

I laughed.

He opened the box and turned it for me to see, and all the air left my lungs. It was a ring. A wedding ring. Just a ring, but also entirely more. With a round stone which reflected every angle of the light, it had to be one of the most beautiful pieces of jewelry I had ever seen. But the best part was the band that held the massive stone looked like a vine as it wrapped around. The tears I'd been keeping in check were back with a vengeance.

"This was my great-grandmother's. And I knew from the moment I first kissed you that it should be yours. It's of course been added to and adjusted over the years by the royal jewelers, but when I used to only fantasize about you becoming my wife, this was always the ring I imagined on your finger."

I grabbed at my chest, willing my heart not to burst. It was lovely. I'd never seen such perfection in something so small. The vine detail was just . . . *everything*.

Seeing that the band was silver, I held up a hand. "Can I wear it with the original ring too?" I paused. "I love it. I love it with every beat of my heart. I just also loved that ring too."

Krew put up a finger and then pulled my other ring out of his tailcoat. It was usually in the safe, not on his person. "I gave them this ring to ensure the new one would be sized correctly."

He handed it over and I put the plain band on first.

"Allow me."

Krew gently grabbed the other ring and then slid it down my finger. I noticed his band was already on his hand.

I fought off a shiver as it slid perfectly into place. "It fits!"

He turned my hand to kiss my palm. "I am already having a plethora of feelings about you finally being able to wear this."

I looked at the ring on his finger and then up to his eyes. We weren't only about to walk into that throne room as the bonded and powerful Enchanted couple that we were, we were also walking in there as husband and wife. "I completely understand. Let's get this over with first, shall we?"

"Hang on," Krew grinned. "Aren't you forgetting something?"

He reached down and picked up the box holding the crown.

In my awe of the ring, I had completely forgotten all about it.

He reached in and grabbed the crown, gently placing it on my head. "The jeweler will be in next week to discuss a set of crowns that will be made just for you. For now, my aunt's old crown will have to do."

That seemed a bit wasteful, but I was too stunned at what was happening to argue in that moment. It was the same crown I'd tried on yesterday. It was more basic than the one Krew was currently wearing, but I didn't mind. The sentiment remained . . . I was about to wear *a crown*.

I was from Nerede. I was a baker. And here I stood. About to wear a crown. A crown of Wylan.

I took a deep breath as Krew fixed it into proper position, his eyes on mine.

"No matter if you are queen for only this day or queen for the rest of our long lives, you will always be my queen, love. *Always.*"

* * *

TWENTY MINUTES in and I was already bored. Parliament began the session discussing the section of Savaryn estates which would be torn down and built new. I found it entirely wasteful and tried my best to zone them out.

I was next to and slightly behind the king's throne in a chair that matched Krew's and Keir's. Krew was to my left and slightly behind me, and Keir sat on his left. We were dressed like royals. We were all crowned. And it looked as if we'd done this a thousand times.

Yet we hadn't. In ten years there hadn't been a woman on this dais for these joint sessions. I was doing my best not to hyperventilate.

"But the streets will be hard to navigate if more than one house is built at a time. It could affect the supply cart's deliveries from running on time."

House? Mansion is more accurate. Also I'm cold.

The only thing about this day that was getting me by was that Krew and I were carrying on full conversations with each other while parliament bickered. But I had wished I hadn't forgotten the jacket Silvia had laid out for me back in our wing.

"But the families will then be displaced for a longer period of time."

Some of the families for the new estates were apparently going to have to live with other families within Savaryn while their new estates were built. I wanted to feel bad for those families, but the truth was that most of those estates had plenty of room for one or more families. They'd be fine. It wasn't like there had been, oh, say, a fire, and these people had no homes or belongings.

Also the castle was plenty big, but apparently the king did not like extended stays for guests.

"It is more important we get those deliveries on time," someone else argued.

I turned toward the king and he gave me a look like he was also annoyed.

"Are they always this inefficient, Your Majesty?" I asked softly.

"Yes," the king said without hesitation. "Always."

"Why can't they displace one family at a time while they rebuild the estates?" I asked.

The king leaned toward me to say quietly. "The neighboring estates do not want to deal with the noise and toil of ongoing construction right next door."

"That's . . ." I tried to make my face not show the disgust I felt. Surely if they didn't want the inconvenience of the noise of construction, the builders could just go to Nerede instead. The people of Nerede would gladly take the noise of construction if it meant their homes could be rebuilt. I wasn't sure I had a nice thing to say about this. "Do they not even realize how spoiled they are?"

The king let out a guffaw that had some of the members of parliament looking in our direction. "No. No, they do not. You don't know the half of it." The king paused. "I have given my army of Enchanted everything they could ever need as payment for using their gifts to protect Wylan. *Everything* they could ever need." He shook his head. "Yet they continue to want and want and want."

I squinted, wanting to ask a question, but remembering that my goal today was to play nice.

"Say it," the king commanded as we continued to carry on our conversation alongside parliament's. "It is written all over your face you have something to say."

I turned to look at him and gave him a smile before asking, "How much of these meetings are actually dealing with Savaryn's greed versus improvements to the country as a whole?"

"More than half," the king answered honestly.

"A question, Your Grace, before we move on to the next issue!" a parliament member asked. I recognized him as the parliament leader, Mr. Winston.

"Yes?" the king answered, looking just as bored as I felt.

"I meant for Her Grace, Your Grace."

I gave my head a shake. That was going to take some getting

used to. I swallowed and hoped my voice was going to sound double as confident as I actually felt. "Yes?"

"Given the recent healings in the forest, which we understand are from your hard work and care, possibly your magic as well, is there anything we can do to speed up the process? Or assist you in your endeavors in the forest."

I paused. I wasn't sure how much I wanted to say on that matter. "Well, now that everyone knows I'm Enchanted, I assume our king will allow me access to the forest more frequently." I stole him a glance and he gave me a nod. "So I just need the space and time to keep working, keep healing." I paused. "I have attempted to heal the lake on numerous occasions. That is the part that is proving to be most difficult. The lake itself."

Krew added, "But she has at least changed the viscosity of the lake. It is not as thick as it used to be. She is making headway." He paused. "We should set up some rules for when guests at Kavan Keep can enter the forest. I do not want anyone messing with her processes or worse yet, bothering her."

The king gave him a nod. "How about the rest of you stay clear from the forest until midafternoon. That gives Jorah the morning hours to work in the forest?"

The parliament leader gave him a nod. "That is fair."

"And," the king added, "if any of you attempts to interfere with her work in that forest, for whatever reason you believe necessary, you will deal with me personally."

"She is healing the forest," Mr. Winston said with awe. "Why would we want to interfere with that?"

The king glared. "She wears a crown upon her head now, or did you miss that? Not only that, but she is now the queen's proxy. Don't think I don't remember how some of you used to pester my wife in trying to make her see your side of things."

An awkward silence fell upon the room and then we were off to the next topic.

After about twenty minutes of hearing them bicker about disloyal tensions in Rallis, the king turned to me. "I'm jealous."

Of course he would start another conversation with me during the one issue parliament discussed that I wished to listen in on. "Why?"

"Krewan wears your ring today, but not the one I gifted to him."

I looked to the new ruby on the king's thumb and back to his eyes. "And you are surprised by this? Given the backhanded message along with it?"

The king's lips pulled into a smirk for the briefest of moments. "Well, no."

I was torn between listening back in on parliament, or asking a question I just kept coming back to. "Why didn't you send Nara back to Rallis the moment you figured it all out?"

The king thought about it for a moment. "A man has needs, Jorah. I assume you are well acquainted with that fact by now."

I shoved my magic down as I simultaneously felt my skin crawl. It wasn't my magic. Just pure disgust.

Are we done now? I sent Krew. *Also, I'm still cold.*

Krew was moving without another word, taking off his tail-coat, and then reaching it over to me.

The king looked at us quizzically.

"I was cold," I offered before realizing that no one else had heard me say to Krew that I was cold. Not wanting him to connect the dots that we could talk to one another telepathically, something he likely already suspected, I added as I slipped my arms into Krew's warm jacket, "I am always cold. My apologies. Where were we?"

The king leaned toward me again and added quietly, "I believe you were about to tell me why my sons stole my ring."

Be careful, Krew sent to me.

I smiled at the king like I adored him. "But why should I answer a question you already know the answer to?"

The king squinted and looked off in the distance. "I just do not understand how they knew to look for an object of mine." More to himself he mumbled, "I'm not mad they want it. If I had learned such a thing existed, I'd do the same."

I didn't dare look for his sword. I knew it wasn't there today. It'd been one of the first things I checked upon entering the room. "Rather I think the thing you are not understanding here is the power of the love of a mother."

The king gave his head a shake and then shocked me by snorting a laugh. "That woman. Still a pain in my ass even now. Yet I miss her."

I didn't dare say a word, just clenched my teeth together. He likely wouldn't have had to miss her if he wouldn't have siphoned her magic and slowly killed her in doing it. His own greed was to blame for her death.

Parliament was asking the king a question, so fortunately our conversation died. To Krew, I promised, *I wish to drive a stake into his miniscule heart.*

Welcome to parliament sessions, love.

CHAPTER 29

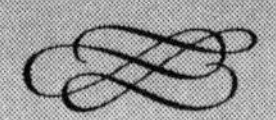

The final vote and parliament session ended up taking every modicum of patience I had. I was able to vote against a raise in taxes, which stopped it from getting approved. For this round. In another month, they would try again.

I wasn't ever voting in favor of something that I knew for a fact would crush Nerede. I hoped they knew that. I might have made an enemy of half of parliament in making my vote, but I'd done it anyway.

Peer pressure would not work on me.

The final votes were all cast, only one issue passing this round. It was a vote on if there should be more patrols in Rallis and Nerede to help curb disloyal unrest. I had voted for it. For no other reason than I felt it didn't matter. The disloyal were out in force, more patrols and guards on the walls were not going to make them disappear, but maybe an influx of patrols would prevent them from making more poor decisions.

Krew had three people from Nerede arriving today to work the stables. One was Theodore Jones, much to my surprise. I truly hoped he hadn't done it in an attempt to get closer to me. I was married now. And also still property of the crown, according to the king.

The other two men arriving were men I did not know personally. Ethan Brogan I had heard of but hadn't met. The same with Roquan Arquise, Jeremy Arquise's brother. Ivy's brother-in-law. Jeremy had died in the showdown with Krew in Nerede. Krew hadn't killed him, the guards who rushed in to help had. But it made me worry. Was Roquan here to avenge his brother? And if he was, did he blame Krew that the plan had gone awry? Or did he blame the guard who'd actually killed his brother? Either way it seemed a little like a disaster waiting to happen.

I was also selfishly thankful Will had not decided to come. I supposed if Beau Jones had told them all I was Enchanted, Will knew I was now forever out of reach. But I still hoped he found happiness back in Nerede. He had helped get me through a dark time in my life. Or maybe just helped numb me to a dark time in my life. Whichever.

"You have done well for the first session as the queen's proxy," the king told me as he stood to dismiss parliament, the rest of the room being forced to stand with him. The king flicked his wrist, and while some people chatted and stayed around, others were ready to be done and seemed to flee from the room.

"Thank you, Your Majesty." I paused. "Unless this is another backhanded compliment."

He let out a laugh. "Not this time."

Sometimes when I said things like that, I thought the king would anger, but I was finding quite often the opposite happened. It appeared the king liked the fight. He liked to see that someone understood his messed-up motives. If no one could see his power plays as such, were they even really power plays at all?

"No, but there is one thing about life in Kavan Keep that you will need to learn," the king offered gently.

"Which is?"

"Only one language has kept peace in this realm for the past twenty years. And it was not the language of fairness. Fairness does not keep peace. Believe me, I tried that. For years. And my efforts fell on deaf ears." He paused. "While your compassion will help you lead and relate to your people, I fear you too will have to learn that fairness doesn't help. It does not keep the peace."

"And what does, Your Majesty?"

"Fear."

I thought about his words. Peace in the realm for the past twenty years. He was not just referring to peace within Wylan herself, he was referring to a time when there were interactions with the other countries. The queen had feared war. Now no one spoke of it because the countries didn't communicate much after the disease which attacked magic almost ten years ago. The disease I believed the king was responsible for. *Fear.* The king had made sure all the countries were living in so much fear, that they had no room to interfere with one another.

I gave my head a shake, trying to make my face not show the disgust, not show the suspicions I held about the king. "That is not the language of peace, that is the language of oppression."

"It is one and the same, dear. Packaged differently, but one and the same."

Careful, Krew warned as he stood talking with Keir, waiting for me to finish with the king.

I squinted at the king. "Fine, so make the other countries in the realm fear Wylan. That is a form of protection, I suppose. What about Wylan's own though? Don't they matter more? Are they not ours?"

The king gave me a nod and turned toward me, as if honestly intrigued by our conversation. "Yes, of course."

My magic faintly hummed with my righteous anger. "Then the backs of the people of Nerede shouldn't be your first line of defense in Wylan. Your army should protect her people. Not her people protecting her army."

The king cocked his head. "But without her army, Wylan falls. Without our Enchanted, Wylan will fall. If I have all of Savaryn at the shore, it leaves Wylan vulnerable."

I raised my eyebrows. "So there is no guard station, not a thing except guards at the first wall? You wonder why Nerede people feel a pull toward the disloyal? You have done nothing to show them they matter. Instead, you've lined them up for slaughter should trouble come lurking. What would happen if another country did come? They'd take over Nerede in a heartbeat and the rest of Wylan would be cut off from the resources we all need. Mainly food. In an effort to protect the Enchanted, you've left us dangerously vulnerable."

The king considered what I said. "A station at the shoreline would give greater and more immediate access to the docks. You think that could help tensions and not worsen them?"

"That depends," I offered.

"On?"

"If you're willing to rebuild their homes first."

The king's head snapped back. "Why should I have to rebuild their homes? The fires were punishment for the attack on Krew. Or do I need to remind yo—"

I allowed my magic to flare because there was no use in hiding it anymore. "You do not need to remind me of *anything*. I remember well, *Your Majesty*. I was the one with Krew every minute he was in the infirmary. Every minute you weren't punishing me for it, that is."

The king went quiet but put out a hand encouraging me to continue.

"The problem is that Nerede has been carrying such a heavy load with little to no respect for too long. If another country came knocking right now, I'm not so sure the people of Nerede, led by the disloyal, wouldn't rush to help them. In your thirst to make them fear, you've lost their loyalty. And no amount of fear you could inflict on them at this point will get that back."

"So I am to help Nerede? You really think they will allow me to be their savior after the fires? They'll just forget it altogether?"

I shook my head. "No. *You* will not be their savior, but I can be. Because I am one of their own. Whether I become the eventual queen or remain a princess will not matter. Either way, I am the bridge."

The king gave his head a shake and then another smirk graced his lips. "You are far more valuable to Wylan than I ever would have imagined, Jorah of Nerede. I was wrong about you." He paused. "I shall make you a deal. Heal the lake and I'll rebuild their homes."

I took a deep breath and looked around. Much to my surprise, ten or more parliament members were still in the room, and doing quite a horrible job of looking like they were not eavesdropping.

A voice from behind us spoke up. Keir. "He offers that only because he thinks you cannot do it."

And he is curious to know if you are powerful enough to do it, Krew added to just me.

"I'm not entirely certain this is a fair deal, Your Majesty," I said on a sigh, suddenly exhausted and ready to be done for the day. "I've been attempting that for weeks."

The king grinned his twisted smile that always made me want to rip it off his face. "Like I said. You need to learn that fairness gets you nowhere. Proper motivations, however . . . ."

How had he taken this entire conversation and turned it into another one of his lessons he loved to bestow upon people?

I am going to kill him, I told Krew.

Not if I beat you to it, he promised.

I looked directly into the king's eyes. "Fine. We have a deal."

* * *

FOR THREE DAYS, I poured magic into the lake. The first day I tried two different times, morning and night. Krew and Owen thought I should back off. The king had told everyone to stay clear of the forest in the mornings, but surely he'd send his spies lurking about to see what I was up to. If I didn't heal the lake, the king would think I was weaker than I truly was. Krew and Owen were wanting to play a mind game right back at the king.

But dammit if he hadn't been right. I was properly motivated. I wanted those homes rebuilt. Those homes that I felt partially responsible for.

I woke from a nap that afternoon and stretched. I was sore. I had been training with Owen as usual, back to our early morning routine, but also had been using far more magic than normal.

I was exhausted.

Love.

Krew?

Now that you're awake, you may want to go check in on Molly. Renna is leaving tomorrow as well. You might want to spend some time with them tonight.

Sitting up, I immediately felt down the bond. Krew was with Keir. In his wing. And if I was checking in with Molly, that meant . . . that meant Molly was out.

What?

It's ugly in here too if that's any consolation.

I threw off the covers and immediately grabbed for a gown, stopping only to inform Owen we were heading to Molly's room.

I ran part of the way, nervous that Molly would already be gone. What if she'd left and I never got to say goodbye? Granted it was just Savaryn. But from what she said, her family wasn't invited to much.

What would I do at all these pretentious events without Molly to ask me about bosoms?

I skidded to a halt at Molly's door, thankful to see her guard still standing outside it.

I knocked.

Renna opened. "Hey."

"Hey."

Molly was packing. Aggressively. "Welcome to the party," she bit out without looking at me.

This wasn't fair. She would have made an excellent queen. She would have been kind and compassionate. And added humor to an otherwise dark castle. "Molls."

She stopped but wouldn't look at me.

"What do you need? Do you need me to pretend like it didn't happen? Do you need me to pretend that I think this is fair?" My voice cracked. "That I don't think you would have made the best damn queen for Wylan?"

I saw the tear track down her face as her turquoise magic ran along her wrist. "No. You don't have to pretend anything with me."

"It's not fair," I whispered. "After everything you were put through in having to switch because I did. Renna has Jo. I have Krew. You were supposed to have Keir. And we were supposed to change this castle for the better."

Molly looked at me through watery eyes. "You still can, Jorah. And we will still be with you. Just not right down the hallway." She paused. "But if you need us, we will be here."

I looked from one to the other. "I don't know how to do this without you both."

Molly cocked her head. "You don't need us, silly. You've never needed us. But thank you for allowing us in. Thank you for working past your feelings about the Enchanted at the beginning and letting us squeeze in."

I wiped at my eyes. "What am I going to do without you?" Renna was leaving. Isla had already left. Molly was leaving.

I was stuck with Gwen and Delaney.

Molly threw a sound barrier at the door. "You are going to get that evil man off the throne and take it. That's what you are going to do. And you are going to ring for us every week or two for cards —I mean tea."

I wiped at my eyes. "You'll come back?"

Molly smiled tightly. "For you, I'll come back. Only for you."

I looked up at the ceiling, blinking hard. "I know I'm being selfish. Renna has wanted out of here for months."

"A little," Molly offered.

I laughed.

Renna came over and wrapped an arm around me and gestured for Molly. "These boys and their crowns will not break us. Not the three of us. Right, Molls?"

Wiping at her eyes, she came over, and the three of us hugged. They were leaving. They were leaving me alone in this damned castle. I should be happy they were going somewhere safer, but all I felt right now was the weight of how much I would miss them. They weren't even gone yet and I already missed them.

"I do know what I need though," Molly offered.

I didn't hesitate. "Name it."

She laughed. "Let's play cards and have some food brought up. For old times' sake."

"You want to play cards?" I asked incredulously. "Now?"

She shrugged. "I cannot possibly feel worse, so why not?"

I cocked my head and pulled back from the two of them. "Wait. Are you hoping to use the fact that I am feeling emotional about your departures from the castle to your advantage here?"

At the same time, they both answered, "Yes!"

* * *

I ROLLED my neck and poured more magic into the lake that sloshed at my boots around my calves. Renna and Molly were gone. Only Gwen and Delaney remained. Nara too, I supposed. But I would likely try to kill her the next time I saw her for telling the king about the plan with the ring.

Gwen and Delaney were fine. It wasn't like I was entirely alone. But they just were not Renna and Molly.

And the stupid lake would not turn back no matter how much magic I sent into it. I sent magic around it like a box. I sent magic within it as if one with the water itself. And I sent magic gliding across it in waves. I'd even tried wrapping my magic around objects and throwing them in the lake.

The lake remained black. As if anything other than a black lake was completely unreasonable.

I was frustrated. My mother was going to arrive sometime relatively soon for wedding preparations. The royal wedding would be in a few weeks. And though I should be happy, as I had always imagined Krew and I would bring my mother to the castle, I also hadn't thought it would be while the king still lived.

It was putting someone I cared about most in the prettiest gilded cage in the kingdom with that beast of a man running loose in it. It was yet another thing to worry about.

And here I was, pouring more magic into the lake because I wanted more than anything for the king to be forced to rebuild those homes in Nerede.

"Dial it back," Owen barked.

I ignored him. I didn't particularly enjoy burnout, but if it helped the lake, if that was what it took, so be it. Also, I was having a pity party that I didn't particularly feel like pulling myself out of.

"Love," Krew called as he made his way over to me.

I'd known he was on the way to grab me for lunch, I just hadn't been willing to give up yet.

"What?"

"I know you are overwhelmed," he offered. "I feel your worry. But please do not take yourself to the edge of burnout again. Not when you already are feeling this stressed. It will only make the crash of burnout that much worse. Believe me, I'd know."

I didn't stop the magic flowing through my hands, but I did decrease the amount. "Why do you have to be so rational about it?"

Owen snorted a laugh.

But then Krew was there, in front of me, placing his hand on my wrist. "I know. Nothing is going as planned. The plans are changing. It's jarring. I get it." He paused. "It might not seem like it right now, but some of the twists to those plans might turn out to become most unexpectedly beautiful." He placed his hand on my cheek. "They might be the things that keep you going on the hard days. The things that give you the audacity to dream again."

With his hand on my cheek, he gathered his own magic to add to mine. Navy magic traveled up his arms and flashed in his eyes.

I understood through our bond he wanted to help. He didn't want me to carry this burden alone. He'd help me in any way he could if only he knew how.

And with his eyes still lit up, he released his magic to join mine.

The navy and silver mixed from where our hands were inches apart, and together they poured into the lake.

I love you. Thank y—

I didn't get to finish my thought. In a blast of magic, we were knocked to the ground.

CHAPTER 30

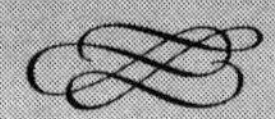

Krew moved my body over his, so he would take the brunt of falling into the nasty water. I landed on his chest near the shore. The top portion of our bodies were out of the water, but the lower halves were in the process of getting soaked.

The blast knocked the air out of me but had also knocked my concentration on my magic too. I had successfully avoided burnout though, as I felt no blood falling from my nose or ears.

But realizing the last time we had been knocked to the ground like that, it had been because of our bonding, I turned for Krew's hand that had been around my back. "Do you still have all your magic? Are you okay?"

"Yes," he said while beaming at me. "Look, love. Look."

That was when I noticed we weren't covered in tar-like water and nasty muck. The water Krew had fallen in wasn't black at all.

It was clear.

The water was clear.

I slowly spun and looked across the lake. Where no light could penetrate before, I now saw the reflections of the tree's branches dancing across the top. I saw logs on the lake bottom that I hadn't ever known were there. And I saw pebbles and stones mixing in that sandy bottom. Even the sea at the shore wasn't this clear.

I scrambled off Krew to stand up. It wasn't just the water at the shore either. It was the water all the way across.

There wasn't a trace of dirt or muck. There was no black at all. It was pure.

I was gasping and kept looking from one side to the other, not expecting it to last. How many times had I tried that? How many times had I wanted to turn the lake but not been able to? But our magic together had done it.

Our bond had done it.

"Unbelievable," Krew said softly as he stood next to me.

"I—" Owen's voice cracked as he gave his head a shake. "I never thought I'd see this day."

Seeing the lake finally fixed, that I had managed to heal it at last, and knowing that the king had only given me this challenge because he thought I couldn't accomplish it . . . it was all too much.

Tears of joy overwhelmed me as I slumped to the ground. "It," I gasped out, "worked."

Krew dropped to the ground with me. "I never doubted you."

That had the tears flowing even faster, trekking downward in record speed.

I looked at Owen, who was still standing there, unable to take his eyes off the lake.

"Owen?"

He looked at me, his green eyes sparkling with moisture.

Without warning, I launched myself at him.

Stunned, he caught me with one arm, hugging me gently.

"You," I gasped out, "were the one who stood here and allowed me to keep trying day after day while protecting me from burnout." I was getting tears and likely a little snot on him, but I didn't really care. "Thank you."

He spun me around and laughed. "You did it, Jorah!"

As he put my boots back down, I looked at Krew, "No. *We* did."

None of us wanting to leave, we walked around the lake, taking in all the different angles and the way the sunlight would bend around the thick branches of the trees and reflect off the water. Then we sat at the shore, Owen on one side of me, Krew on the other, our boots touching the edge of the water. The *clear* water.

The Dead Lake was dead no more.

* * *

I WOKE to the door to Krew's wing slamming open and breaking the sound barrier I'd had up. I reached for the covers, making sure all of my body was covered.

Thankfully it was, because in came the king with two of his personal guards and Owen on their heels.

"You healed the lake."

Krew leaned up lazily. "Get out."

"She healed the lake!" the king repeated.

"She is also not decent. Out!" Krew barked.

The king looked the length of me, seeing me wrapped up in the sheets. He gave an exasperated shrug as he looked out the curtains. "It is not even dinner time. The middle of the day!"

I cocked my head while gripping the sheets tightly. "A man has needs, you know."

The king rolled his eyes. "I will wait in the next room. Get decent. I want to know how you pulled it off."

"Seducing your son?" I asked with raised eyebrows just to be a pest. "I just used my womanly wiles, of course."

The king flicked his wrist in annoyance while he stormed into the neighboring room.

I snickered as I grabbed my robe and threw it on. As I gathered my clothes up off the ground and went to the bathroom to change,

I said to Krew, *How do you want to play this? What should we tell him about the lake?*

We tell him that it took all three of us, Owen, you, and me pouring our magic into the lake to the brink of burnout to work. He cannot know how powerful our magic is together. Later, I'll make sure Owen knows also so our stories all match.

Fully dressed, we made our way into the other room. The king was seated at the chair Krew normally sat at for his meetings with The Six and it didn't feel right at all.

"So?" he said with a hand. "Care to enlighten me?"

"Sure, Your Majesty," I began as I took a seat on the right of him. "But can I have your reassurance that you will in fact rebuild the Nerede homes?"

He again rolled his eyes. "Yes, yes. Now out with it."

"How soon?" Krew asked as he took the chair next to me. "I know how your deals work, Father. You say you'll do it with no direct timeline as to when. She did her part, and she's been battling burnout for a week because of it."

"Why do you care about the forest so?" the king asked.

I shrugged. "I can't explain it. I just loathe that it's stuck. I've always felt drawn to it. It should be creepy, all blackened and dead, but I've never felt unsafe there, I merely find it sad."

"Also she feels guilty for what happened to the homes in Nerede," Krew added. "She's been out there every day because she wants the homes rebuilt before there is more unrest."

The king's head went back. "But you did not set the fires, nor did you tell them to attack Krewan."

I gave the king a shrug. "We were in Nerede to see *my* mother when it happened, were we not?"

"But it was not your fault," the king argued.

"Tell that to your whip," Krew said coolly.

The king put up a hand. "I will send one group of builders to Nerede in two weeks' time. How's that?"

Krew gave me a nod as if that was suitable enough.

"It just took *a great deal* of magic," I offered, wanting the king to leave already. "And I couldn't do it on my own. Krew had to help. As did Owen." I paused. "I think all the previous times I had attempted to heal it played a role also. Since the viscosity of the lake was already slightly thinner."

The king gave his head a shake. "But after the lake first turned, I sent our best Enchanted out there for weeks. I tried it myself. None of us could get it to do a thing." He paused. "For *months* I sent Enchanted to that lake daily. They never were able to change a thing."

"Maybe it is the timing?" Krew asked. "It's been almost a decade since the lake turned. Maybe enough time has passed that the disease has finally lost its hold."

The king looked out the window at the forest, but I caught his leg bouncing beneath the table. Something about the lake being turned back made him terribly nervous. "It cannot be the timing. Brakken's Enchantment is still frozen because of the disease."

"Well maybe we should check with the other countries," offered Krew, "see if there has been any change for any of them. We haven't heard from Brakken in weeks."

The king stood, as if positively beguiled by something. "It has to have been her Iron Will. That has to be the explanation. I will need a sample of her blood. To see if there has been a change."

Krew and I both looked to one another. He wasn't going to find much. We already knew that.

"Tomorrow," Krew threw out. "She has already done enough today."

The king gave a nod. "So be it."

"Why aren't you happy about this?" Krew snapped as he leaned back in his chair. "You told her you wanted her to heal the lake. Against insurmountable odds, she somehow pulled it off. She did what you asked."

The king put up a hand. "I am happy. This will make many people happy to see or even hear the lake is back to being clear." He stood and gave us both a smile that could not have been more fake. "Thank you for your efforts, dear. That lake has been stuck for so long I just cannot believe it. I long for a better explanation only so should it ever happen again, we would know how to reverse it."

I believed he was possibly halfway telling the truth, but I didn't for a second believe that was all of it. I'd been suspecting the king had been responsible for the disease that hit the other countries and that he had poisoned the lake and forest just to make it seem like Wylan wasn't responsible. If that were the case, wouldn't he be happy to see the forest back to its normal state? The "disease" finally eradicated?

But something about the lake being healed truly disturbed the king. The question was: why?

And then I remembered what Krew had told me long ago . . . that if the forest had magic, it didn't play by the rules of the Enchanted.

Maybe the better question was: what were the rules of the forest?

CHAPTER 31

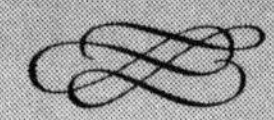

"No wonder you kept her from us." Emric was grinning at his regular place at the table.

That part was true. Krew had been keeping me from them while my magic settled. But even before our bonding, other than popping in to greet them, Owen and I had missed many meetings these past weeks. I'd made myself scarce around The Six. Intentionally.

I'd done so since Easton's betrayal. I knew Krew trusted the majority of these people. I knew I had no logical reason not to. But other than Keir and Owen, and possibly Hatcher, I didn't fully trust them. And I wasn't sure if I ever would. Easton had soured The Six for me. Likely permanently.

The bookshelf remained slid open to the secret passageway for the rest of The Six to filter in. I'd been adamant about not becoming the seventh member of this little group of original disloyals working with the princes, but with Easton no longer a part of it, I'd officially gotten my wish. I was replacing Easton in this group. Our numbers remained at six disloyal commoners and two disloyal princes. Though with the crown I wore on my head anytime I left Krew's wing now, I supposed it was five disloyal commoners, two princes, and one stubborn princess.

"The lake," Emeric continued with a shake to his head. "I haven't seen it that clear in so long I had begun to lose all hope."

"Equally shocking," Hatcher added, "is that you are on time for once, Emric."

Emric gestured with a hand behind him. "I had to leave early enough to see *the lake*."

Hatcher's eyes found mine as he smiled and sat down at his place. He was far more vocal in this room than he was in parliament sessions. It seemed he had vastly different roles within his various masks.

Anderson and Apollo were the last to filter in, and by the flushed looks on their faces, they too had taken the long route and meandered toward the lake.

I knew the only reason we were meeting today was because the king was busy with his commanders so there was a lot of traffic from Savaryn into Kavan Keep today. Owen and I had trained indoors today despite the nice weather, knowing the lake and forest were going to be busy.

Once everyone had a drink and their seats, we were ready to begin.

Emric kept looking at me with the strangest expression. Like I had a horn protruding right out of my forehead.

"I am not going to turn your water into whiskey, so do not even ask," I said as I crossed my arms.

"I just—" he gave his head a shake. "You look normal. Like you did before. And yet I was at that lake today. I saw with my own two eyes what you did."

"What *we* did," I corrected as I stole a glance at Krew.

Apollo gave his head a shake like he also agreed with Emric, and I noted his beard was much more significant than the last time I'd seen him.

Anderson held up a hand, "I think what Emric is trying to say, but doing an absolute botched job at it, is that you are obviously now Enchanted, but have good control over it."

I stole a glance at Keir as I looked to Anderson. "I didn't at first. So thank you, but there is definitely a learning curve."

"She chucked me at a tree," Keir admitted.

Emric's eyes went wide. "What? And I missed it?"

"Like he weighed no more than a feather," Owen added with a grin.

Keir explained, and the men were laughing. I didn't like to laugh about that night though. I thought I had seriously injured Keir. Killed him even.

"As much as I would love to discuss more about Jorah's becoming Enchanted and all that it means," Krew started. "We've much to discuss today and that isn't our biggest concern."

He reached for my hand, but I was far enough around the table that he had to lean over to reach. Apparently finding that unacceptable, he half stood, only to grip my chair and drag it closer to his, the sound of the chair screeching on the floor.

Better?

He draped his hand across the back of my chair. *You were too far away.*

I smirked. *And you are in the middle of explaining to The Six what our biggest concern is right now. Which I presume you didn't mean was the distance between our chairs.*

Oh right.

We both turned back to the table to find them all looking at us in varying degrees of curiosity.

"Insane, is it not?" Hatcher said to Anderson. "Their ability to speak without words?"

He was shaking his head. "I wasn't quite sure I believed Hatcher until this very moment."

"You all are terribly distracted today," I said with a smile. "I believe Krew was about to say the biggest concern is the king's sword."

Since he had been present along with the rest of parliament, Hatcher replayed for the rest of them what had happened when I'd charged into the throne room that day.

Owen added in how he'd figured out it was the sword, and the discussion of what to do with this knowledge began. Combined with the information about the three disloyal men who arrived from Nerede, and we had quite the debate on our hands.

"We have the eight of us, Maurice, and the three Nerede men. You don't think we could take down the king with the twelve of us?" Apollo asked toward the princes as if insulted.

"Just wait for a day he isn't wearing the damn sword, then make your move." Emric stood and I saw his dark red magic at his wrists. "What the hell are we waiting for, if we know it is the sword?" He paused. "From the sounds of it, Jorah and Krew could probably handle him as is. So why would we wait? Act now before he figures out how strong Jorah really is."

"But what if I'm wrong?" Owen argued. "And it's not the sword?"

I gave my head a shake. He wasn't wrong. As soon as he said he thought it was the sword, everything that had gone on in the throne room had made infinitely more sense. Was there still the possibility he was wrong? Yes. It could still be the crown or some other object on the king. But did I think Owen was wrong? No. Particularly not when the sword had been gone immediately following the throne room. The king had practically confirmed it for us.

"You are all forgetting one small detail," Krew snapped.

Emric, having obviously felt strongly about making a move on the king soon, sat down, though he still seemed to vibrate with energy, as if he wanted to bolt for the king right this moment. "Which is?"

Krew took a slow sip from his whiskey glass. "Which is that we still do not know which of us, Keir or I, will rule once our father is gone."

Hatcher gestured with a hand as if swatting at a bug. "I agree with what Jorah said in the throne room. Either of you will be twice the king your father is."

Krew sighed. "It isn't that. I believe either of us would be an improvement also. It is that while my Assemblage is over and has been for a long time, my brother's is not." He looked at Keir before meeting my eyes, and I saw in his eyes the compassion he felt for his brother. They might not see eye to eye on everything, but Krew would still defend and protect his brother from anyone that dared to threaten him. "Keir needs more time."

Hatcher looked slightly vexed with the look he pinned on Keir. "But you are down to two women, Your Grace. How can you not be even remotely close to choosing a bride at this point?"

I suddenly wanted to vanish. Disappear into thin air. Not only had I once been part of Keir's Assemblage, but so had Molly. And I was still so, so pissed at him for letting her go.

Keir rubbed his neck. "I do not feel ready to marry either one of them. That's kind of the problem. Granted it might not even be me, so this could all be irrelevant."

"It's just another variable though," Krew added. "Find a day the king isn't wearing the sword, and then what, gamble on it being Jorah and me?" Krew paused. "That isn't fair to Keir. He should have the time to figure it out. And killing my father now means that Keir's Assemblage is brought to an abrupt end. He would have to choose likely that very day who would be his queen."

As Krew's words sank in, Emric's posture relaxed.

"As much as I want this to be over," Krew added. "It isn't fair to leave Keir with a rushed decision. The last thing we need is to remove my father just to place a young queen on the throne. One who might do further harm to Wylan." He dipped his head toward Keir. "Intentional or not."

I knew he and I were both thinking of Gwen. She was compassionate and kind for the most part. But she tended to see things in black and white. And in the case of Keir, she tended to go after what she personally wanted, the rest of his Assemblage be damned.

She could be a kind and gracious queen. Or she could be temperamental. And the last thing Wylan needed after Theon Valanova was a temperamental queen. Someone who would tear down others to get what she wanted.

His other option was Delaney. She was Savaryn born. She would be a good queen, probably let Keir lead as much as he wanted while she took a back seat and looked the part. But she would do absolutely nothing to bridge the divides in our country.

And then there was me. I had never wanted to be queen. But more than I believed in my ability to become queen, I believed in Krew's ability to rule as a just and fair king.

My heart hurt as I realized something. I knew that in asking us to wait to make a move on the king, Krew was signing himself up for more time apart from his son. In allowing his brother time to make the right decision for Wylan, he was sacrificing time with a son who didn't even know his father.

Soon, Krew promised me down the bond. *We will bring Warrick home soon.*

I gave him a nod, unable to form words. It was too painful to picture. Warrick running the hallways, bringing joy and laughter to everyone he would meet.

"Just pick one," Emric said to Keir with an exasperated gesture.

"I don't know that I wish to marry either of them," Keir admitted. "Or that I would seriously consider it if I weren't required to date them via the Assemblages."

I tipped my head back to the ceiling. It sure seemed like he cared about Gwen enough. They'd had a connection from the start. Before I'd left. But maybe he saw in Gwen what the rest of us had as well. That she was young and too idealistic. At the very least, Gwen needed time. And we were currently running out of it.

Yet Molly would have been the answer to this entire conversation. She would have been a great queen, her personality not capable of possessing any vindictiveness. We probably could have made our move on the king that very night had Molly and Keir been sitting next to Krew and me. There would be two viable and strong options to take over the throne once Theon was gone.

I let out a sigh and pushed my magic down.

"What?" Keir snapped. "You don't get to incessantly sigh about my Assemblage when you aren't even in it anymore."

"Whoa," Apollo muttered.

Emric leaned in, listening intently.

"No, she isn't," Krew bit out just as harshly. "But she still has the right to feel about it however she pleases."

"You want to know what my problem is?" I asked Keir, none too kindly.

"You and Krew are happy, bonded, and strong as hell. So yes. I'd love to hear what your problem is with *my* Assemblage," Keir responded, frustration laced into every word.

"My problem," I snapped, "is that Molly was the perfect option. She is *kind* and gorgeous and would've been a better queen than any of the remaining women, myself included. You had the perfect queen for Wylan right there and you just let her slip through your fingers."

He cocked his head. "Wouldn't be the first time, now would it?"

I ignored that to unpack later. I felt my magic flare as I hadn't used much of it yet today. "You got to choose from Krew's Assemblage whoever you wanted, Keir. You chose her. And then you dangled her there just to turn around and send her home at the end." I paused. "If we are discussing who would be best to sit on that throne, it isn't any of us sitting here at this table. It was her. Of all the Assemblage women, I would have trusted her in that role the most. And now she's gone."

The table was quiet for a moment, but I had no idea if it was because of the awkward tension or because I was allowing my magic to slither along my veins.

Keir's voice was so quiet I almost didn't catch it. "I miss her too."

I let my magic show a little more, flaring with my immediate anger. "You don't get to hurt her like that and then *miss* her."

"Jorah, love," Krew said gently.

I tore my eyes from Keir's that I was locked in on in anger.

"It isn't as if my Assemblage ran smoothly either. In fact, it barely ran at all. And then it was over before it ever really began."

I opened my mouth to argue, but dammit if Krew didn't have a point. The entire process was . . . *difficult.*

"No offense to anyone at the table," Apollo began, "but waiting around for Keir to fall in love seems like a horrid idea. There will never be a perfect time. Never. But right now we have the element of surprise on our side."

"Yet looking long term, acting now still leaves too many doubts for the next king and queen," Hatcher said quietly. He turned to Keir. "How long do you need?"

Keir's head went back as he shrugged. "I have no idea. None. Right now, in this moment, I wish to marry neither of them."

Owen offered, "Well it isn't as if Jorah will be able to keep hiding away and trying to underplay her powers around the king. We don't have all the time in the realm for you to romance them."

"I understand that," Keir agreed. "I'm not the one asking for more time. I'm just trying to be honest with you all on where I'm at."

"How about a month?" Anderson asked logically. "A month buys you some time. You focus on the women of your Assemblage, while the rest of us focus on a plan to get the sword either in our possession or away from the king. We can track when he has it on his person and when he doesn't." After a long pause, he added, "And Jorah will have to slow down her healing of the forest as to not give away her true strength."

I groaned.

"What?" Anderson asked. "I thought that was rather reasonable."

I rested my head against the back of my chair. "Oh it is, minus the bit about the forest. I just realized if we have to wait for another month, I'll have to be the queen's proxy for another parliament session." I paused. "My favorite."

Hatcher grinned. "I'm going to try to be unoffended by that."

"So a month," Krew began. "Our wedding will be in two weeks. The king will be more than busy with a royal wedding in the mix. And then we make our move."

"Quite the honeymoon," Emric added with a snort. "Newly married and plotting a murder."

That had the laughter cutting away at the tension. Emric was kind of the goof of the group, but I understood by this point that he was extremely adept at being able to read a room. Also thrived on other people's drama, it seemed.

As the group went on debating how exactly that move should be made, whether we attacked the king at night, or lured him into the forest somehow, I listened in but didn't really participate any further.

One month.

Somehow putting a timeframe on it made it all the more terrifying. The king had been a thorn in my side since the moment I walked into this castle. Could we really do it? At times it felt like he was as old as this mountain itself. And equally as difficult to kill.

A month from now would I prove to be a widow, or would the king finally be gone?

As soon as the conversation died down and the men called it a day, I said my goodbyes and excused myself out to the balcony. I'd had enough of people for the day. Unless it was Renna and Molly. I just wanted to curl up with a book and escape to a far less scary world for even a moment.

Krew slid his arms on either side of where I leaned against the railing, resting his head on the back of my own.

"There are so many things I wish to do," I whispered without looking at him, for fear that I would not be brave enough to speak. He already knew how I was feeling anyway, so there was no use in trying to disguise it, but there were still things I wished to voice aloud. "So many things I wish to do and see with you. Things I wish to bake you. Picnics with Warrick in the healed meadow. Memories I wish to create and tuck away to cherish. And—" I stopped, my voice thick with emotion. "And only one more month of your touch will never be enough." A tear spilled out of my eye. "It will never be enough, Krew."

He spun me toward him. "I know. Believe me, I know." He used his thumb to brush away my tears. "I hate putting a time limit on it, but at the same time, I want to get it over with. Because all this time spent torturing ourselves about what will happen is cruel. No matter how it ends, gearing up for it like this . . . it isn't fair." He grabbed my cheek, his fingers buried in my hair. "It isn't fair. I've only just found you. Our bond is new and powerful. I can't believe that it will all come crashing down in a mere month."

I closed my eyes. "Is it cruel to wish that this wouldn't land upon your shoulders? That someone else, Keir, or The Six, *anyone* would do this for us, so we didn't have to fear like this?"

He gave me a smirk. "They likely would volunteer if we asked, yes, but do we trust anyone more than ourselves to see it done?"

I hated the answer to that question in a violent manner. "One month," I whispered, resting my forehead against his.

"One month," he repeated. "And since we are on this topic, I need for you to promise me something, love."

"No."

He leaned back to look me in the eyes. "No?"

I gave my head a shake as the tears in my eyes multiplied. "No, I will not make you any promises as if you will not be here with me in another month. My answer is no. I will make no promises to you about happy endings or finding peace. I will have neither of those *without you."*

He closed his own eyes, needing a moment before he could speak. "Promise me then," he began but had to swallow as emotion caused a crack in his voice. "Promise me that no matter the outcome, the picnics with Warrick will still happen." A tear slipped out of the corner of his eye, and it was simultaneously the most beautiful and horrifying thing I had ever bore witness to. "Promise me that he will come to know, if not right away then eventually, how much I love him."

I wiped away his tear, just as he had done with mine. "You will tell him yourself. I have to believe that you will be able to tell him."

He closed his eyes. "Promise me." He swallowed again, and I saw his magic swirling in his cheek bones. *"Please."*

The way his voice had shattered around the word *please* had me caving. I wrapped myself into his arms, holding on with everything I had. "I promise, Krew. I promise."

Krew had once told me that after he got to know me, he raged against time because he had feelings for me that were at odds with his ultimate goal and plan. I don't think I truly understood those words until The Six stamped a one-month deadline onto that goal.

Now I raged against time. I wanted to bottle every moment and run it to a place where the king didn't exist. Where time itself couldn't reach us.

Fate.

Time.

I loathed them both.

CHAPTER 32

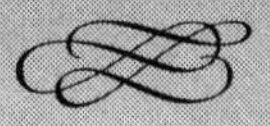

"You have a meeting this morning with your designer for your wedding gown," Owen reminded me as we took the stairs back to Krew's wing after my morning run with the wolves.

"Can't wait." My sarcasm was palpable, doubly so because I was panting. "But I liked the other dress just fine." I had to pause to breathe as I sped up another few stairs. How Owen could just carry on casual conversation while running stairs was beyond me. "Why can't I just wear that one?"

Owen glared at me as we turned to head up another set. "Why are you asking me these questions? You know I wouldn't care. You could wear whatever you wanted to. But royal weddings do not just happen every day around here. So I suppose there is the exorbitant standards of that to live up to."

I groaned and grabbed my knees at the top of the stairs. "Stop talking before I gouge your eyes out."

Owen grinned. "And here I thought running with the wolves had made you less belligerent in the mornings."

I rolled my eyes. "You thought wrong. Do not mistake my fondness for Rafe and the other wolf as fondness for you."

"Can we give him a name?" Owen asked as we headed for Krew's door. "I hate calling him the 'other wolf.'"

My lips twitched.

"What?" Owen asked.

I pressed my lips together. "It's just fitting you would feel drawn to him. The first time I saw them both, the way the scarred wolf protected Rafe, I thought he was Rafe's second. Like you are to Krew. That black wolf is tough and strong. And he may not lead the pack, but he is the one who keeps order. The one who keeps the pack healthy."

Owen snapped his head toward me. "Is that a compliment?"

I laughed as I pulled open the door. "Of course it is, you brute."

"Well, now we really have to name him," Owen muttered as we entered Krew's wing.

I knew Krew was there, sitting at the table in the adjoining room before I could see him. I headed for our bedroom though, knowing I needed to shower before this meeting.

But first things first. "We cannot name him Scar. He should not be labeled for a mere blemish when he is far more." As it turned out, I had a personal vendetta against scars.

"And not Blackie?"

I snorted a laugh. "Gods no. That powerful wolf with a name like Blackie?"

Owen put his hands out in a shrug. "I have never even had a pet before."

I giggled. "Remind me to check in with you before your first child is born."

"That one is easy," he offered. "Owen Junior."

I snorted. "And if it is a girl?"

He paused. "Owe . . . ina?"

"Oweina? This just keeps getting worse." And then I had to sit in the chair as laughter started shaking my entire body.

Krew peeked his head into the room, a steaming cup in his hand, which he handed over to me. "What are you two cackling on about?"

"We are trying to name the other wolf," Owen provided. "And my future children as well."

Krew gave his head a quick shake.

Owen moved his shoulders up in a noncommittal shrug. "It was a natural progression in the conversation, believe it or not."

Krew's lips turned at the corners. "I don't know about you two sometimes."

Oweina hit me all over again and I reached my tea out to Krew to take back before I spilled it all over myself.

"So the black wolf?" Krew asked.

Owen nodded. "We have ruled out Scar and Blackie."

"How about Shadow?" Krew asked.

My laughter stilled. That wasn't half bad. I looked to Owen at the same time he looked to me.

"I want to hate it just on principal, but I can't," Owen admitted.

"I like it too," I admitted. "Of course, we should check with him. See if he answers to it."

Owen's brow furrowed. "You want to check with the wolf?"

I glared at him. "Well yes. It will be *his* name."

"They do run with her in the forest as her guardians," Krew offered as a knock sounded at the door. "Let her do her Wolf-Whisperer thing."

I grinned triumphantly at Owen.

He crossed his arms. "So that would be your designer and you are not even showered yet."

I sat up. "Whoops." Then I paused. "But I only healed one tree? It wasn't as if we were meandering around the forest."

He shrugged. "Actually, they might be early."

I stood and brushed off my pants, feeling bad that I probably smelled awful. "They? There is more than one?"

But then I heard the voices at the door, one voice in particular I very much recognized, right before arms were thrown around Krew at the door.

I knew that voice *and* those arms. In a realm that was chaotic and harsh, often times even unjust, they were my safe place.

Yet my safe place was somehow now in a place that was not safe at all. This castle.

"Jorah, dear!" My mother grinned as she took off her jacket. "There you are!"

I was running to hug her and Flora at the doorway. "You are my designer?"

Flora laughed as she hugged me. "Your prince was adamant it was what you wanted."

I grinned. "It would have been had anyone asked me. I just assumed I was stuck with the stuffy castle designers."

Flora adjusted her red hair into its high bun on her head. "Well, a few are still working with us, but I am the lead designer on your gown, honey."

I thought my mother would be coming sometime next week, not today. I was overjoyed to see them. Also terrified for them to be in this castle and wielded against me as people I cared about.

And Krew? Having known me well enough to bring them here, to bring Flora to design my gown which would be seen throughout the entire kingdom? Sure, it would be seen in person by everyone in Kavan Keep and likely all of Savaryn, but it would also be in a picture which would be on the reports after the wedding. Not to mention the whispers about Flora designing my dress would filter throughout the levels of the kingdom.

I wanted the king gone from this castle. Once he was gone for good, Flora could design as few or many gowns for me as she liked. Mother would be here also. I would feel less terrible about relocating my mother from Nerede and the only life she ever knew if Flora was here with her to keep her company.

I had a suspicion Silvia would be thick as thieves with them too.

Thank you, I sent Krew.

You are more than welcome, love. It was the least I could do.

"Go shower," Owen offered. "I'll ring for Silvia and breakfast. We can all eat and have what I am sure will be a riveting discussion about this gown."

Krew offered to Owen, "Order extra bacon. So you can make it through."

Owen laughed and patted Krew on the back as he headed to do just that.

I headed for the shower feeling entirely happy. If I only had a month or less left of this level of happiness, I would enjoy every second of it.

* * *

"WE NEED to start construction on the updated estates in Savaryn soon," a parliament member explained adamantly. "It is spring now; we are losing precious time for construction."

I internally groaned at Krew.

We were in yet another joint parliament session. My last one before the official wedding to Krew next week. And this one was equally as boring as the last.

I asked only to Krew, *Why don't they just tax only Savaryn for the improvements and then use those funds to fund the said improvements in Savaryn?*

We have brought that up time and time again. But Savaryn feels it isn't fair they are the armed force that protects us and then would have to pay the highest portion of taxes.

Yet it is their greed that is driving all of this. Not necessity.

Correct. And so any time that is thrown out, it is debated, but ultimately it is agreed that taxes for everyone will be increased a small amount across the board rather than adjust them to each level of the kingdom.

But even a small increase crushes the already small allotments the people of Nerede have.

I realize this, love. So do all of us in this room pushing for this not to pass.

The king shifted next to me, leaning toward me with his hand on his chin. "Argue all you want, but two construction crews will be busy for the next few weeks."

"I beg your pardon, Your Grace?" Winston asked.

The king didn't flinch, and in fact, looked rather bored. "You all cannot decide what you want first and when you want it, we cannot even agree on the terms of a tax increase or not, so rather than waste more time while yes, the weather is good for construction, I sent two of the crews to Nerede." He paused. "I made a promise to Jorah if she healed our lake, I would help rebuild some of the homes in Nerede, and so I did. It is not as if you all were going to agree on anything today anyway."

For the first time in my life, I wanted to hug the king.

Maybe just a small hug right before I murdered him. Because priorities.

Parliament looked as dumbfounded as I did. Yes, numerous people had overheard him make that promise to me. But it wasn't as if the king's glowing personality led them to believe he'd actually stay true to his word.

"What?" the king barked. "I don't think a tax increase is really needed for the amount of improvements that truly need to be done. You know Jorah will vote against it as she knows it will further crush Nerede. And she has a point that they are the workforce that keeps us all fed. So in a month, when I pull crews from Nerede, you had all better agree on what improvements are the priority in Savaryn. Ones that can be done without a tax increase. The clock is ticking."

Is he just using me as his scapegoat to avoid another tax increase? I asked Krew.

Likely.

Parliament again was quiet, numerous people exchanging glances and then whispering amongst themselves.

"What now?" the king groaned.

Winston held up a hand. "I think I speak for a lot of us when I ask gently, Your Majesty, if your recent concessions with Princess Jorah are because you are thinking of soon abdicating. It is not like you to change your mind."

A silence blanketed the entire room, sweeping from the parliament members to the guards, and to the very doors themselves. Not a sound was made as everyone waited to hear what the king would say.

The king sat up straight, his body language tense, as if the mere thought of abdicating made his black magic churn beneath his skin. "While one of my son's Assemblages is done, one is not. So no, I do not wish to abdicate at this moment. Once Keiran decides on his princess, I may have her fill in as proxy some as well. While my sons have all but grown up in these meetings, their counterparts have not. Both princesses will be *well prepared* to be queen before they ever so much as touch my wife's crown."

He believes Gwen needs more time too then.

I turned my eyes to Krew's for only a moment. *Agreed, but why is he never without the stupid sword now?*

Krew's eyes were on mine. *I don't know. I felt like the right thing to do was give Keir more time. But since that meeting with The Six, my father has never been without it.*

So why even take it off to begin with then?

Because he knew how close we were to figuring it all out.

I let out a sigh. The sword was always just out of reach, perched on the king's left hip as we sat during these meetings. I had half a mind to just make a move for it and snag it. Just to end this.

The discussion moved again to our upcoming nuptials. We were to host a large banquet following the ceremony at the castle. I had already sat in no fewer than five meetings on all the wedding traditions and customs.

I was exhausted already, and the wedding wasn't for another week.

I answered a few questions and then we were all dismissed for lunch. I spun to Krew only to find Keir on the other side of him looking like he'd swallowed a bug.

"What is it, Your Grace?" I asked Keir properly as I grabbed Krew's elbow.

He gave his head a little shake. "Nothing. For now." The look he gave both of us, his head cocked and his eyes on ours, had both Krew and I understanding that we would all need to chat later.

He should have been wining and dining the remaining two women in his Assemblage, but instead, Keir was up to something.

I FELT Krew before I saw him. Realizing he was just off the balcony, I headed that way. It was a bit too early for the princes to practice, but apparently whatever Keir was up to couldn't wait. That was the only reason I could think of for why Krew would be standing on the ground beneath his balcony.

I'd only just returned from eating dinner with my mother and Flora where they were staying over by the training room Owen and I used. They, of course, also had guards handpicked by Krew.

Owen followed me and we looked over the balcony at the ground where the two princes appeared to be in a heated discussion, by the looks of it. They were both standing within a two-toned blue sound barrier.

"Want to head down to see what they are going on about?" Owen asked gently.

"You were supposed to be off duty an hour ago," I reminded him.

He gave me a shrug. "Like I care. I want to know what those two are bickering about just as much as you do."

I took two steps back from the rail and toward the door before turning around and staring at it. I was a little sore from running today and the training Owen and I had done. I was graduating from a wooden sword to a small real one. My shoulders were sore, but so were my legs from being so tense under my body weight today.

"Jorah?"

Did I really want to walk down all those stairs I had just come up? No. No, I did not.

I gave Owen a slow smile and then I took off. I jumped over the rail and used my magic to glide me back down. And then just before I hit the ground, I had it slow me down, landing me just shy of the ground. I reached my foot down like it was an actual step and not my magic holding me midair.

Owen landed beside me laughing.

With a flick of my fingers, I burst the sound barrier and put up a larger one of my own that encompassed the four of us.

In the nicest voice I could muster, I asked, "What are we whispering about, My Princes?"

Both of them were looking at me like I was some sort of magical creature, which to be fair, I supposed I was.

Krew's mouth was even slightly ajar.

"What even just happened?" Keir asked more to Krew than to me. "Did she ju—"

"Yep," Owen provided while crossing his arms.

"I—" Krew's eyes were on mine as he said, "I have never been more attracted to you in my life."

I smirked. "I will have to admit that it *is* a little fun. I can see why you do that so often." I turned toward Keir with a smile. "Are you all right? You looked as if you had an epiphany earlier today."

Keir gave his head a shake. "No, but yes. I think we should use the wedding distractions and plan a way to get the sword."

"What?!" He couldn't be serious.

Keir looked to Krew and back to me. "He will not expect us to be organized on that day of all days. It has been on his person since just after the throne room. We can hire out a group of men to steal it right off his belt."

"During the wedding?"

Keir gave his head a shake. "No. After. During the rather large banquet at the castle. And hopefully he will be slightly inebriated by the time it happens too."

"He will know it was us," I offered. "He knows we are after an object. There is no way he won't figure that out."

Keir shook his head. "But if we pull it off and have the sword in hand, does it matter? He can try to punish us or get back at us, but between the three of us, we can easily take care of him."

"That gives you less time to make a decision," Krew said gently to his brother. "You have one week to decide what you will do."

Keir gave him a half of a smile. "I already have a fairly good idea of what I'll do."

I wanted to ask, I wanted to demand to know who he was choosing. Not just because I was being nosy, but because whomever he chose may very well be queen within a fortnight.

Owen's eyes flew to mine and then to Krew's. "So we do this? The night of the wedding we create a diversion and make a move after the sword?" He paused and looked to Krew and me. "Knowing that your wedding night could end in blood, one way or another?"

Krew's eyes were on mine as he stated, "I hate how much

potential I see in this plot and how much I wish it never had to occur as well."

"But he will not kill us in front of all of Savaryn," Keir said, grinning as he gestured with his head in the direction of the meadow. "He can't. And not only can't he, but he also won't. He needs this wedding to go off picture perfect right now after the stunt he pulled with the gauntlets. That's why he has been playing nice with Jorah. He knows his approval with the people is at risk."

Owen sucked in a breath. "He has a point."

The rest of the walk to the meadow, the princes discussed if a plan could be made to get the sword off the king the night of our wedding banquet. They would have to hire someone else to then hire a well-known crew of ruffians from Rallis to sneak into Kavan Keep and steal the sword. It would work best if the king was bumped, the sword taken, and then passed around in the crowd and out of sight before the king could pinpoint where it was.

It was madness. It was absolute madness planning something like this within the crowd of Enchanted. And yet the crowd of Enchanted surrounding the king may just be the thing that kept our heads on.

As the night wore on, no magic was being used other than my sound barrier. A plan was hatched instead.

A plan to get the sword. And possibly end the king. On my wedding night.

Though I'd been cherishing every moment that I could, living out every single day like it could be my last, spending my days with the people I loved most and the place I loved most in the forest, all while spending my nights wrapped up in Krew, time had finally caught up with me. I was rapidly running out of it.

I no longer had a month; I had a week.

One week, one royal wedding, and one extremely reckless plan.

CHAPTER 33

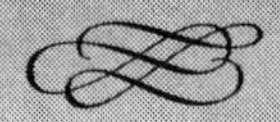

"You look absolutely—" My mother cut off, wiping at an eye.

"Mother!" I scolded. I was getting married the following day. And with everything on the line, with everything I loved dangling by a thread, I needed her to not make me any more emotional than I already was. And she didn't even know yet that Krew had fully intended to give his life for his honorable cause.

"Lovely," she finished. "Positively lovely."

I looked to Flora and grinned. "Flora has really outdone herself this time."

"The dress is magnificent," Silvia added from where she stood next to my mother.

"As magnificent as the wearer," Flora said with a wink while she walked around me, looking for adjustments. I'd already tried it on three times over the past week though, so there wasn't anything to adjust.

The dress itself was simple at the core, but then was adorned with layers of detail and extravagance. The dress was pure white, the top layer woven with lace and sparkles. There were two tiny straps at least, but they were hardly there. I hadn't wanted a poofy dress because of my stature and the firm belief I looked like a troll while wearing them. So this dress was instead form fitting until the waist where it flared out. But since a long train was the traditional wedding attire for a royal wedding, Flora had made a long train of lace and tulle; it just attached at a thin belt around my waist. It was detachable, thankfully, so I didn't have to lug the train around the entire night. I thought Flora might possibly be a genius for having thought of the idea.

"Let's check the train again," Flora added. "Before the prince returns."

I smirked. "Like we haven't been married already."

Silvia shook her finger at me. "No, no. He didn't get the surprise of seeing you in the dress because the two of you just walked out to the meadow last time. This time, let him be surprised."

Surprised yet dreading the ending of the night and what it would bring. "Okay," I relented, "let him be surprised."

For twenty minutes more, they situated the train this way and that. In the morning meeting before the ceremony, I would have one practice round on the stairs I would have to climb in the chapel of the castle.

I hadn't even known there was a chapel, and I'd been living in this castle for months. Yet there was. One I had to climb a set of thirty steps to get into.

"Okay," Flora admitted. "I am finally happy."

That was saying something, because if she had been unhappy with so much as one sparkle or sequin, she demanded the other designers swap it out or fix it. It'd been quite the process to get this gown to its final stage. But I supposed with the entire country watching, Flora had every right to be as picky as she wanted.

"Me too, and just in time," my mother added. "We have lunch with Krew and Jorah in twenty minutes."

Soon enough I was changed back out of my gown, and we were waiting on the food.

"Will you stay and eat with us, Silvia?" I asked.

Her brow furrowed. "Whatever for?"

"Lunch?" I asked gently. "Flora is staying too. So please stay?"

"I—" she cut off and put her hands on her hips. "Are you asking as my princess right now?"

I grinned. "No. No demands. Just asking as your friend who wishes you to stay. Your friend who may have already informed the kitchens that you would stay for lunch."

Silvia swallowed, and I thought I might have seen something resembling tears in her eyes as well. "Well, fine then. Manipulate me into it, why don't you?"

Flora snorted. "Because it was so very hard to do so."

Silvia coughed a laugh and then we were all laughing.

Krew arrived just before the food. "Ladies," he greeted as we sat at the table normally used for The Six.

Granted there were only four of us, but this was my version of The Six. We may not have been trained in subterfuge or killing, but the women next to me were the women I trusted most in the realm. Add Renna and Molly, who had arrived yesterday for the wedding, and I was well on the way to having my own version of The Six.

Krew brushed a kiss to my forehead as he sat down next to me. "They have decided to prep the gardens for overflow room because of the number of people who accepted their invites."

Flora smiled slowly as if glad.

"So I would avoid the gardens, otherwise you all might be put to work," Krew added.

"I adore those gardens," Silvia said as the food cart arrived at the door with a knock. "So I don't mind."

"We should help too," my mother urged. "Now that Flora has the gown ready."

"Please take your guards," I pleaded. The guards who were standing outside the door with Owen as we had lunch.

My mother gave me a nod, though I knew she was annoyed with the guards following her every move.

George brought the food in and took it upon himself to deliver each plate to the table, setting them before us. Sometimes I forgot how young he was, he couldn't have been more than sixteen years old.

"Hi, George," I greeted. "How are things in the kitchens?"

"Hi, Jora—" his eyes went wide. "I mean, Your Grace."

I turned to face him. "It's quite all right George. You knew me as just Jorah first, remember?"

George sat my plate before me and bowed. "You were never just anything, Your Grace. Best cookie baker I have ever known! Worthy of a proper title for that alone."

I snickered.

"As for the kitchens," George said as he grabbed Krew's plate. "They are in full swing with wedding prep. Maurice brought in three Savaryn chefs and is overseeing everything between three kitchens within the castle. Lots of guests means lots of plates per meal. More than our main kitchen can manage."

"So in other words, he's being more difficult than usual?" I fought down a smile.

George placed the plate before Krew. "Absolutely, Your Grace."

I laughed. After being introduced to my mother and Flora, George went on his way. He had no time to kill due to the mad prep work in the kitchens. I almost wanted to make an appearance in the kitchens only to be a pest, but I also respected Maurice. More so than I would enjoy his discomfort.

We ate and chatted about the events of the next day. There were so many details that I lost track of trying to keep it all straight. There was the wedding. Then the banquet and meal following. Honestly, the plan in place for the banquet was what I spent most of my focus on. Making sure that all went as intended would literally save the country, not this elaborate wedding. Plus, the Assemblage advisor was a wedding coordinator of sorts, so she would make sure I stood where I was required to and said all the proper words as I publicly became an official princess of Wylan.

"I do have another request for tomorrow," Krew said gently as he took a drink of his lemonade.

I knew exactly what he was about to ask of them, as we had discussed this the night before.

"Yes, Your Grace?" Flora asked.

Krew looked at my mother and dipped his chin. "I would like for you and Flora, Silvia you as well if you are still there by that time, to retire early from the banquet tomorrow night."

Suspicion crossed my mother's features from the set of her jaw to the way she narrowed her eyes at Krew. Something she had done to me more times than I could count. And though Krew was my dark prince, I also knew he was no match for my mother. "And why is that, Your Grace?" she asked, her tone all business.

"There is something at play tomorrow. And it would be better if you were out of there early," Krew explained. "Just after the meal is served."

"And the less you know, the better," I added with a wince of a smile. "I wish I could say more, but in case anything should not go as planned, it is just better you do not know. Hopefully the morning after we can explain everything."

Silvia glared at Krew. "Will this ploy end up in you or your brother wearing a different crown immediately following?"

Krew didn't even flinch. "It could. I hope not, though. It doesn't have to come to that, but it is always a possibility."

The three older women looked amongst themselves as if they, too, could communicate telepathically.

Flora waved a hand. "We will just say that being from the

lowest level of the kingdom, we were worn out and not comfortable being around all the Enchanted."

"Should be more than believable," my mother added.

My heart swelled at their willingness to help, even if they didn't like it or didn't understand it. "But it ruins your moment, Flora. Your moment to weave around the Enchanted and have them know that of all the artists and designers in the kingdom, your work was what I chose to wear."

Flora gave me a smile. "Don't worry, my dear. My gloating on that front is not limited to tomorrow only."

"We cannot even get through a wedding without whatever this is needing to happen?" Silvia asked on a sigh. "Can't the two of you just have this night to celebrate yourselves?"

"Unfortunately not," Krew admitted, not annoyed at all at her question. "Sometimes the best way to find something that needs finding is within a room full of people."

"You will be careful?" My mother asked sternly. I noticed she was looking at Krew as she asked it, not me.

Krew's eyes briefly touched mine before meeting hers. "Always."

* * *

"Come with me."

I looked at Krew as if he was losing his mind. We'd had a luncheon with my mother, Flora, and Silvia, went directly from there into a meeting with the Assemblage advisor about the wedding the following day, and then we had to come back to shower to go to dinner with the king, Keir, Delaney, and Gwen.

We'd barely had a chance to breathe all day. Neither had Keir for that matter, as he was in charge of making sure the ploy for the sword went off without a hitch tomorrow.

It wasn't that I didn't trust Keir. I did. There was just so much riding on our ability to get that sword from the king.

And here we were, exhausted, and about to have the busiest day of our lives the following day. It was a day for us, but also at the same time, not at all for us. It was a grand show for the entire country; a woman from the lowest level of the kingdom was becoming a princess.

Something I myself had thought impossible. Yet here we were.

So knowing the slew of events the following day, and how early I would have to start prepping with Silvia and Flora, I felt like falling into bed. I wanted to love my husband in every way that a woman could, and then I wanted to fall into a deep sleep. With Keir's plan in place for tomorrow, that was the only way I would be achieving any sleep at all.

"Please," Krew begged. "Humor me, love."

When he looked at me like that with his gray eyes and I felt down the bond how much this man adored me, I couldn't deny him a thing. And he knew it too.

"Okay." I sighed.

Without another word, Krew reached for something, scooped me into his arms, and shot us over the balcony to the ground below.

I hadn't even had time to grab a jacket, or a blanket, or anything, before he'd grabbed me. And though it was spring now, the evenings up on this mountain could get quite chilly.

"Here."

Krew took off his jacket and handed it over, moving the small container in his hands as he maneuvered out of it. Then out of nowhere, he also had a blanket which he handed over to me. He must have grabbed it just before we'd gone off the balcony.

I pulled the tailcoat around me tightly and sighed. The smell of his jackets like this. Rarely did I refuse his jackets. They were always warm and smelled of him.

Not wanting my thoughts to stray to darker thoughts of how I should possibly bottle the smell just in case I was forced to navigate life without the opportunity for a warm jacket, I looked back at the container in his hands. "What's in the basket?"

Krew turned to smile at me as he took my hand in his and started leading me in the direction of the meadow. "Does that cunning mind of yours ever rest?"

"Not recently anyway," I admitted.

"Nor mine," he said on a sigh. "Which is precisely why this is what we should be doing."

"Don't get me wrong, I love this forest. I love healing the forest. But there are *numerous* other things I would like to be doing with you right now."

He sent me that smirk which promised all the best things. "All in due time, love. Just humor me."

"Fine," I relented. "What is it that we are doing?"

He was walking toward an area he must have scoped out ahead of time, stopping and then looking up at the stars. "This was where your tears first bloomed in the meadow." He grabbed the blanket from me and threw it outward onto the ground. He held up the basket. "And this is an array of all your favorite desserts that I requested be made for us and this very occasion."

Tears stung my eyes. "We are having a picnic."

Krew opened the basket to take out a smaller container which held desserts and another small container that held candles. He stuck the candles in the ground next to the blanket, and with a snap to his fingers, the candles flared to life. "We are having a picnic," he agreed.

He sat in the center of the blanket and reached a hand out to me. I took it, settling between his legs, my back to his chest. He handed me the desserts and I could see well enough to see that there were a variety of truffles and some bite-sized chocolate cheesecakes in there. I chose a truffle, smiling over the fact that our first meeting was over a truffle. A truffle that I was trying to figure out if I could drop into my bosom.

"We are having a picnic but also much more," Krew whispered against me as he also grabbed a truffle and popped it into his mouth.

"You're having *feelings* too then?"

"Would you stop rushing me?" I felt his laughter against my back as it shook his body. "It is hard enough to keep my hands off you as is."

"Sorry," I admitted and reached for another truffle. I knew there was nothing else he'd rather do tonight than get lost in each other. "What else was it we were doing?"

"Dreaming," Krew answered simply, his voice going soft. "I don't wish to spend this night lost in the cycle of what ifs about tomorrow. What if we have to try to kill my father? What if we don't get the sword? What if we do? It is all driving me mad, when all I want is an eternity next to you. Moments exactly like this one." He paused and I stilled, listening to his words, feeling his anguish and worry down the bond. "Instead, I'd rather dream. Of picnics right here with Warrick. Of having more children. Of a brighter day for Wylan, one which starts tomorrow as you become an heir of Wylan in your own right."

"Krew."

"So let's take an hour and talk about all those things. All the things we want to do together. Because maybe if we dream of it, it will somehow tether me here to you if the darkness calls."

I spun, throwing my arms around him. "It can't," I choked out. "It isn't time. I will destroy the darkness and whatever stands in my way before I ever let it near you."

A hand of his moved around my body and another settled in my hair. "So dream with me, love. Dream."

Tears were spilling over as I took his cheeks in my hands. "We are going to be married in front of the country tomorrow. We are going to get that sword and your mother's magic away from your father. We will end him, Krew. And then we are going to either take the throne or help guide it. Whichever being absolutely fine, and then we are going to have a long life together." I paused, closing my eyes for a moment. "Warrick will be here at the castle. As will my mother. I will watch you grow old and get gray hair. And likely still be extremely attractive." I took a deep breath. "And together we will chase every whisp of darkness out of that damned castle."

He nodded and rested his forehead on mine as if soaking in my every word.

"You know why I believe all of that? Why I cling to it so?" I whispered.

"Hope?"

I shook my head slightly, our foreheads still touching. "No. Because of you." I moved a hand to place it on his chest. "I believe in this heart of yours, Krew. You have had to endure more than any one person should ever have to. And yet you still strive to right wrongs. You do all of the things no one else is willing to do because you are motivated for your cause." I paused, my inhale shaky. "While hope is a feeling and feelings are fleeting, your heart, how much I trust you, is not. It's as steady and true as the sunrise. It's you, Krew. You have not endured all of this just to have to give yourself in the end." I paused as he wiped away my tears. "And you are not alone."

"No, I am not," he whispered, voice so thick with emotion I suspected he couldn't even speak at a normal volume.

"So we will dream." I somehow managed a smile through my tears. "And then we will fight like hell. Together."

"Together."

"I choose to believe that this is why we are soul bound," I added gently. "That this is why you retained all but a few drops of your magic. Everything has been leading up to the moment we all remove your father from that evil perch of his. So the darkness? It can call all it wants, Krew, but it is no match for this." I closed my eyes. "It is no match *for us.*"

His lips were on mine before I could even take a breath. In between long, mind-numbing kisses and the trailing of fingers over skin, we would send each other down the bond different things we wished to do someday.

Despite the what ifs. Despite the plan for the sword tomorrow. Despite not knowing if Krew was the true heir to the Wylan throne or not. Despite it all.

On this night, we chose to chip away at the impending darkness as we dared to do more than just keep breathing and worrying. Instead, we braved our dreams.

CHAPTER 34

"This hasn't happened in two generations," Silvia said with a hand over her heart as Flora adjusted my veil. "A non-Savaryn born royal. A non-Enchanted to become both royal and Enchanted."

I hadn't wanted the veil over my face and restricting my view, so it would be only in my hair instead. I was actually a little shocked I got to decide at all.

"Since the last woman to wear your ring," Silvia added more to herself than to any of the rest of us.

The ring in question was with Krew, waiting for the ceremony to be placed back onto my finger.

Then her eyes went wide, as if realizing what she said. "Sorry. I should just stop talking now."

I smirked. No matter what Silvia said to me, I was nervous. I was due to make the long walk to the chapel any minute now. It was time.

Though I'd been a princess for the past few months, it was about to be official. Gone were the days of people treating me like a placeholder in Krew's Assemblage. From this day on, I would be referred to as Your Grace or Your Highness.

Molly and Renna were here somewhere among the guests. I'd sent for them early this morning and we'd had tea. I knew I might not even be able to see them much the entire rest of the day.

Royal weddings were intricate and delicate things, it appeared.

I took one more deep breath, looking at my reflection in the mirror. The chapel and two-hour ceremony were honestly the easy part of this day. The meal, banquet, and everything to follow were going to be the hard part.

I turned to my mother. It was normal tradition for the father to walk the bride down the aisle. Since my father was gone, the king had approved my mother to do it.

"Are you ready?" I asked her calmly.

She smiled. "Are you?"

I wasn't about to lie to her. She'd see right through it anyway. "I don't know if I am ready, but it is time. Time to quit hiding in the shadows and step into this role I've only been half living."

Her eyebrows jumped up toward her gray hair piled into an intricate bun. "Then let's go." She paused. "And know that if it were your father walking you down to Krew today, he would be just as proud of you as I am."

I swallowed hard. "I wish he was here. Not to see someone from Nerede wear a crown, but more so just because I miss him."

"Me too," she whispered. "And I have to believe that somehow, he is here. Watching over us today."

I gave her a nod, and somehow the extra moisture swimming in my eyes managed to stay in, as to not ruin my makeup.

Silvia moved forward to open the door to Krew's wing for us. As the door swung open and Owen stood there, I started to lose it all over again. I knew there were no fewer than four guards waiting down the hall to help deliver us to the chapel, but this was Owen. My guard who had protected me and helped me through thick and thin while navigating the dangers of the castle. The closest thing I had to a brother.

"Jorah," he said gently. "It's all going to be okay."

I closed my eyes and gave my head a shake. "It's just you."

"Me?"

I laughed as I opened my eyes. "Yes. I would not be able to get through this day without you. I hope you know that."

He held out his elbow for me to take. "I am right here. And I'll be right here the whole day through."

I gave him a nod and looked into his green eyes. I knew what else he was promising me. Krew and I were not alone. If this plan went to hell, he'd be there every step of the way.

"Shall we, My Princess?"

I took a steadying breath as I grabbed the crook of his arm and then grabbed my mother's arm with my other hand. "We shall."

The castle had never felt so large. While my train was detachable, I had to have it on for this part. We took the elevators, and it still took what felt like an eternity to reach the chapel. It was tucked away in the opposite wing of the castle from Krew's.

By the time we made it to the steps, I felt like grabbing my knees and it had nothing to do with nerves and everything to do with sweat.

"Good thing I am in better shape now," I told Owen as I took a deep breath. "This thing is heavy as hell."

"Just try your best not to trip up these stairs and faceplant in front of your kingdom," Owen jested.

"Not funny," I bit out, looking at the stairs looming before me.

He was grinning as I looked back at him. "A little funny and you know it."

The Assemblage advisor was moving toward us.

Owen looked at her and back to me. "I will be right here in the hall with you until you go in. Then I will be at the main doors the entire time. And when the two of you walk out, I will be right behind you."

I gave him a nod. "Thank you."

"Perfectly on time, everyone! Just as we practiced," the Assemblage advisor beamed as Owen stepped away. I knew from Krew her name was Celine. She hadn't ever been that warm toward me until she was helping with my wedding, and then all of a sudden, she had determined I was more than fine.

I had a sneaking suspicion this wouldn't be the only case of that.

"The guests are all seated, the chapel at maximum capacity. It isn't every day we have a soul bound royal couple, you know. But everything is ready, Your Grace."

I took a steadying breath.

"You will exit out these same doors," she gestured with an arm, "and there are refreshments waiting for you and Prince Krewan in the same side room he got ready in as the two of you wait for the guests to filter out."

I already knew that, from one of the numerous meetings, but the reminder was appreciated. "Thank you."

"You look lovely," she added.

"Thank you."

The next three minutes dragged on for what felt like years. And then finally, with a nod from Celine, I ascended the stairs.

As soon as I reached the top stair, the massive doors creaked open.

My first thought was how much sunlight was in the chapel, stained glass windows providing as much color as the varying gowns before me. I noted the people. More people than I had seen at even the busiest of balls I had attended. Yet somewhere in the mix of pretentious looking gowns and tailcoats were my two best friends. I took a deep breath that somehow wasn't deep enough to fill my lungs, and then my eyes landed on him.

My dark prince. The love of my life. Krew.

I felt Krew's voice down the bond. *I love you.*

I love you.

I took my first step toward my husband. The crowd, the king perched up front with Nara standing behind him, it all just blurred into the background.

I would walk towards him this moment and every moment after.

* * *

HAVING to get through my vows was a feat all by itself. The plan for the sword had made all of this even more emotionally raw than it already was. And whether or not we were successful in that endeavor, whether we confronted the king tonight or another night, I knew it was in the near future either way. So that festering in the back of my mind while I promised again to love Krew all the days of our life had my voice cracking.

"No matter what this cruel realm may throw at us, I stand steady next to you," I repeated from my original vows to him. I left the next part about the darkness never standing a chance because the king was a smart enough man to pick up on that part, but I knew Krew remembered it anyway.

Krew broke the protocol and reached over to brush a tear off my face.

My eyes never strayed from his grayish blue ones. "I vow to love you and protect you, all the days of my life."

I slid the new ring I had picked out for him onto his finger, and then he again broke the rules by bringing my hand up to brush a kiss to it.

But what were they going to do, not allow us to get married?

It was a little late for that. We already were. This was just for pomp and circumstance, for them. Not for us.

"I give you this ring and I gave you my magic both," Krew began as he slid my ring onto the top portion of my finger, "every piece of me that I can give to you, I do freely, none of them in any effort to change you." He paused, his eyes tearing into my soul. "But to protect you."

Knowing the first time he had said those words, moments later he had attempted to hand over all but a drop of his magic to me, the weight of those words hit differently this time around.

Another tear spilled over as he added, "Because getting to love you has been the greatest surprise, but also the greatest *gift* of my life. I am honored to get to love you." His voice cracked and more tears slipped out of my eyes as if in direct response to it. "For as long as my lungs find breath and my veins flow with blood, I vow to love you both fiercely and relentlessly. No matter the distance, from the bottom of the sea to the very peak of this mountain, from the darkest of nights to the lightest of days, I will crawl, fight, and claw my way back to you. Always. I love you. And I vow to love you and protect you, always."

The same sage who originally wed us was there, one of three working the ceremony. Now that the songs were sung, the vows repeated, the rings on fingers, all that remained was for the king to remove my veil and place a crown on my head.

We were almost done.

The king was there as we turned forward and stepped up two steps onto the raised portion where I would be crowned.

"Jorah Collete Demir Valanova," the king's voice boomed. "Daughter of Nerede. Daughter of Wylan. Long may you live, justly may you serve as princess of Wylan." He placed a crown I hadn't seen before on my head. It, of course, fit perfectly. "From this moment forward until your last, Princess Jorah Collete Demir Valanova." He paused. "Long may she reign."

The crowd repeated back in unison, "Long may she reign."

I closed my eyes and felt those words travel all the way down my spine. The king had crowned me. He could take this life from my lungs. He could take Krew from me. But he would never be able to erase this moment, the fact that I, Nerede born, wore a crown.

As the crowd repeated the phrase two more times, the king leaned in and leered at me. “Not bad, Jorah of Nerede.” He gave his head a shake. “Not bad at all.”

The way he said it had my magic crawling. And I was both too emotional and too focused on making it through the ceremony to bother to push it away. The king hadn’t said it in such a way that he was surprised or proud of me, he said it in such a way that he was proud of himself. Like his lessons were the cause for where I now stood, the crown on my head. Neither Krew or I stood here today because of his efforts or upbringing. We stood here, soul bound and strong, despite him. He was not the creditor. He was not the fire which forged our steel. He was very simply just a pest we wished to squash.

Do try not to draw blood during our wedding ceremony, love.

My eyes went to Krew’s as I smirked. *I am doing my very best, but I make no promises.*

The king looked from one of us to the other as if he caught the words said between us. We should likely not speak through our bond less than a foot from him, but I also didn’t care. I was done hiding. And I was done playing nice.

I was Enchanted. I was soul bound. I was a Valanova.

And I would do whatever it took to protect Wylan, come what may.

CHAPTER 35

We were seated and about to start our dessert when Flora and my mother came over with a jacket for me. Though we were inside, as the night wore on and people began leaving, I was sure to get chilled.

Who was I kidding? I was always chilled.

Flora bowed then beckoned to me to join her so she could hand the jacket over. Our entire table also started to stand, as I was now recognized as royalty, but I quickly told them not to, just as I had seen Krew do dozens of times.

A few paces from the table, I frowned as she helped me into the jacket. "This is lacy to match the rest of my gown. I don't feel as if it will keep me all that warm."

But as my arm fully slipped into it, I gasped. It already was warm. The lace, though only a thin material, was somehow heated.

"What is this sorcery?" I whispered.

She grinned. "Your mother and I know how you hate being cold. I had the idea for this long ago, but I could never get my hands on the proper materials to create it. Since I had a team of designers at my disposal, I put one of them on this for you."

"It isn't magic?" If it was merely heated with magic, it was sure to wear off eventually while on my person.

She shook her head no.

I sighed in contentment. "A heated jacket. Your best invention yet."

She beamed.

"Wait," I whispered just as she turned to go. "Will I start glowing at midnight again?"

Her lips twitched. "No. Not this time. Don't tempt me though, Your Grace."

My mother stepped in to hug me. "We will watch your first dance and then disappear right after. I promise."

"Thank you," I whispered. "I need to not be worried about you two tonight."

She smiled at me. "Understood, Your Grace."

"Mother," I scolded. "You don't have to—"

She brushed a piece of my hair back into place. "Of course I do. It isn't every day your only daughter becomes a princess. I've got to live it up."

"Does this mean I am finally off the hook for your constant chastising of my *vulgar* word choices?" Maybe there were more perks to becoming a princess than I originally thought.

She didn't even hesitate. "Absolutely not. You may be a princess, but I will always be your mother."

With final hugs and bows, they were gone. I sat back down next to Krew to try to enjoy our cake.

Keir was not far from us but at another table. I knew within the room was a group of six men who were from Rallis in charge of taking the sword and swindling it out of here.

The king looked to be on his third or fourth drink, so all was going as planned on that front.

"You will have your first dance to start off the dance floor in just a few minutes," Celine told us. "Then you will mingle and greet some of the guests for roughly an hour before your next break."

"And if we never return from said break?" Krew deadpanned.

"Oh, please tell me you are joking, Your Grace," Celine said, eyes wide. "The entire kingdom has shown up to see the two of you."

Krew rolled his eyes. "Only partly. It is not as if we can possibly greet everyone anyway. I also thought it was *my* wedding and I could celebrate it how I chose. *With my wife.*"

"I am sure there will be plenty of time—" Celine's blush went all the way down her neck. "For such things later?"

Stop torturing the poor woman.

Fine.

We took to the dance floor as the entire room stood and applauded us. Krew quickly told everyone to sit and finish eating while we danced. I wasn't sure what was worse, the whole room standing and clapping for us, or all of them sitting and watching us.

I remembered this very room with all the tables set up for eating from my first nights in the Assemblages. But now the tables were so many that there was barely room for dancing at all. I knew as soon as people were done eating, several tables would be moved to make more room.

And judging by the sounds coming in through the doors and windows, there was also quite a meal and party going on outside in the gardens.

It was a celebration, after all.

There wasn't a small orchestra set up like I was used to in the corner, as there had been for the balls, but instead they were up on top of the grand staircase. And I wasn't sure, but just by a glance I thought there were double the musicians as normal.

Krew pulled me in close as the music started flowing downward to us.

A hush settled across the room. I wasn't sure people were even eating at their seats, they just watched.

Which was awkward. It'd be more fun if they joined in and also danced, but this was our first dance as Prince Krewan and Princess Jorah, so I supposed they couldn't.

"Shall we show off a bit?" Krew asked me softly.

"If only to get something on my mind other than the number of eyes watching us," I whispered back.

He smirked and then we were moving.

We used most of the little dance floor we were provided. And knowing I was uncomfortable, Krew kept his eyes on me, so I kept mine on his.

We weren't just secretly married anymore, with parliament and a select few people knowing. We were married before all of Wylan.

And whether or not we would both survive what was sure to be the wrath of the king later in the night, whether or not we would ever become king and queen, we would forever be prince and princess.

Royalty.

"I'm having *feelings* about this new crown of yours," Krew said, his breath on my collar bone as he tipped his head down to whisper in my ear.

The new crown was so light, I had honestly forgotten it was still on my head. "Appropriate feelings I'm sure, My Prince."

"Definitely not."

I laughed.

The song was wrapping up and so he rested his forehead on mine. "I am so ready for this night to be over."

"I agree."

And while the applause signaled the end of our dance, he brushed a chaste kiss upon my lips while promising down our bond that it wouldn't be the last.

Krew took my hand and led me out to the balcony. The same

one Keir had always taken me out on. We stood at the edge and waved at the people below in the gardens and stuck outside the castle, many cheers starting up.

I waved and smiled, unsure if they could even see it or not. I simultaneously decided that my princess wave was going to need some work.

But the people just kept cheering, happy to see us at all. It wasn't lost on me that after our first dance we could have greeted anyone, and this was where Krew had chosen to go first. To the people locked out. The people deemed not good enough to be in the ballroom.

And honestly these people seemed less stuffy, and I wondered why we couldn't just abandon the pretentious people and head down there with them instead. They looked like they were having way more fun.

Krew kept a tight grip on my waist at all times as we headed back inside and began greeting people in the ballroom. We would not be separated for this portion of the evening, evidently.

What had to be more than half an hour in, I was relieved to find Sasha and Juliette Girard. Some people I finally knew.

And I even halfway trusted Sasha. He was the first one to point out to me I might be the counter to the king's power. He'd been wrong because now I was obviously Enchanted myself, but it had been a nice sentiment.

"I am not surprised at all," he whispered to me, "to see you are the last one standing or to hear that you are soul bound."

"Well, I was very surprised at the latter," I laughed. "It knocked the wind out of us. Quite literally."

Juliette grabbed at her chest. "I wish I could have seen it. Our bonding was rather intense too. You'll have to tell me all about it some day soon. Some day when you aren't being passed around a room full of people fighting to meet our new princess."

Her word choice was daunting. "Are you sure you don't wish for me to tell you right now?"

She reached her hand to my wrist and laughed.

My magic flared and I chalked it up to having not used it much due to all the prep work we had for the wedding.

Krew patted Sasha on the shoulder. "Don't be a stranger."

Sasha smiled at the both of us. "Wouldn't dream of it. Wylan has much to be proud of today." He leaned in. "And word has it, there have been parties in the streets of Nerede all day."

I barely had time to process that before my magic flared again. I wasn't sure if it was because of the emotions I felt in hearing Nerede was proud of me, or if again, I needed to use some magic.

Juliette glared at her husband. "Do not make our princess cry on her wedding day!"

I snorted a laugh. "As if I haven't already done enough of that today."

"Congratulations!"

Another couple, having apparently decided we were done talking to the Girards, stepped right up to the space between us and them, effectively cutting them off.

I looked around the smiling woman in front of me, who I had never met, to Juliette, but she just laughed and waved her wrist as if telling us to continue on.

"We are so honored to have a new princess," the woman said with a bow.

I shook my head. "No. I am the one honored today. All I have ever wanted is this man right next to me."

"A true love story," the man said.

But the way he said it had my eyes flicking to his, examining his body language and posture. They were saying all the right things, but were they really going to welcome a princess from Nerede? Bow to a princess from Nerede? I had the hearts of

Nerede and likely Rallis. But some of Savaryn were going to be hard to win over. I had no false notions about that.

"When will—"

The woman's question was cut off as Krew shoved me behind him.

Krew's navy magic was everywhere at once. And mine was causing my skin to glow, begging to join and help him. I had a half a second to decide what to do and knew I couldn't release my magic. Not now. Not here. All of Savaryn would find out just how strong Krew and I were when our magic combined. The king would know how much of a threat we posed to his power.

So I pushed my magic down, though it physically pained me to do so.

And that was when I saw it. Shards of glass had been hurtling toward me. Krew froze them all in the air and then used his magic to travel along the lime-colored magic back to its source.

I caught my breath. I didn't know that could even happen until I was seeing it with my own eyes.

I recognized the man who had apparently sent glass in my direction. He was a parliament member with the last name of Cartier. And he was known to be chummy with the king.

It appeared we weren't the only ones with a ploy going on this night.

CHAPTER 36

A murmur rippled across the room as the lime green magic stopped, but Krew's navy magic was still suspending the glass shards in the air.

People standing between the two men instinctively moved away, creating a pathway between them. The music stopped.

I am going to kill him, Krew promised me.

He took one step forward and without even raising his hand, sent more magic out of his fingertips toward the glass, the glass slowly starting to move back toward Mr. Cartier.

"What is the meaning of this?" the king's voice boomed.

But I knew better. The king had either orchestrated this whole event or in the very least encouraged it.

Mr. Cartier took a step backward, looking to the king as if he wished for help.

Just when I could see the king as he made his way through the crowd, I saw a man bump into him from his left side.

I stilled, knowing this was not supposed to be happening yet. It was far too early in the night.

Unable to look away, I kept my eyes locked on the king. While he turned to likely yell at whoever it was, he bumped into a man on the other side. Faster than humanly possible, the second man must have reached over and unhooked the belt holding the sword and scabbard around the king's waist because the belt and sword clattered to the ground loudly.

The king's eyes filled with rage as he stooped down to pick it up.

But before he could, it was already gone. The first man who had bumped into him and shoved him into the second man had already swiped it off the ground and was gone into the crowd of people. It had all happened so entirely fast. If I had blinked or turned my eyes back to Mr. Cartier for even a moment, I would have missed it all.

And while the king turned to see who had stolen it, the man who had unhooked the belt spun just out of reach of a guard and took off running.

"Thieves!" the king boomed as he turned around, shoving a guard. "Seize them!"

"Seize *him*," Krew spat at the same guards, gesturing toward Mr. Cartier as he neared where the king now stood. His voice was cold and demanding. The guards felt it too, as they hesitated, unsure if they should go after the thieves or the parliament member. "This man has done more than steal; he made an attempt on the princess's life."

"I am your king," Theon Valanova declared to the guards, looking quite bewildered, black magic swirling along his skin.

For now, Krew added.

Though I had only seen them from a distance all night, I felt Renna and Molly as they moved in to flank me.

The guards finally sprang into action to do the king's bidding, and though all of this was a nightmare as far as royal wedding banquets went, I was hoping that Mr. Cartier's feeble attempt provided enough of a distraction and hesitation in the guards that the crew from Rallis could pass off the sword and get out of there before any of the Enchanted in attendance really knew what to do.

"You might want to seize him before I kill him." Krew increased the speed of the glass heading for Mr. Cartier at the same time he sent his magic snaking around his hands, rendering him incapable of retaliating.

Mr. Cartier looked to one hand, then the other, and began moving backward quickly.

"Would one of you, *any of you,* in this room find those men who stole my sword?" The king snapped. "My guards are not the only capable men in here!"

But precious seconds had already passed. By this point the sword should be hidden in the jacket of a man, out of view and on the way to the gardens.

And though the king was right, the room was filled with the Enchanted, the king's army, I knew likely half of them loathed him. Why would they help him? It was just a sword after all. Meanwhile their princess had just been attacked. Should they concern themselves with an object and mere thieves, or an act of treason?

It was all playing into our hands so beautifully we should have thought it up ourselves.

Sasha Girard had made his way across the room, along with two other Enchanted men I didn't recognize, though I knew one was one of the king's commanders.

They each took an arm of Mr. Cartier.

The glass was now hovering in a line around Mr. Cartier's neck. His skin was glowing with his magic sensing the threat, but Krew's magic was like cement all over his hands, making his magic unable to be released.

Krew was still taking casual but purposeful strides toward the man, while the king was motioning in the direction of the thieves and barking orders. Krew made a show of flicking one finger and one shard of glass moved forward, poking Mr. Cartier's neck enough to draw blood.

"Who are you working for?" Krew demanded.

"I don't know what you mean, Your Grace," the man said as more of Krew's magic wrapped further up his arms, helping to immobilize him.

"I think you know exactly what I mean. Someone in this room made a threat on my wife, an heir to Wylan, though a shoddy one at that. Which leads me to believe that someone simply wanted to know if we were powerful enough to defend ourselves." He paused. "Which I can assure you, *we are.*" Another shard of glass started moving toward his neck. "So, who hired you for this little experiment? No matter their rank in this country, they have just committed treason right alongside *you.*"

Gasps traveled throughout the room. It likely didn't take a genius to figure out Krew had just implicated his own father in committing treason against Wylan.

The man's eyes were wide and he looked pale enough to pass out at any moment. I wasn't sure what the original plan was here, but Mr. Cartier did not anticipate having shards of glass being shoved toward his own neck.

"Who hired you!" Krew boomed.

"I—" Mr. Cartier's eyes moved to the king, who was still busy motioning to guards. "I was hired by no one."

But the way his eyes had gone twice now to the king for help was answer enough for me. The king might not have outright commanded this to happen, but he was not innocent in this either.

Krew's head cocked as the second shard of glass pricked the skin of Mr. Cartier's neck.

Wait, I sent down the bond.

Krew's steps stilled as he looked over his shoulder to me.

Don't kill him. Not at our wedding banquet. I do not want that to be the precedent set should we eventually be the ones to rule.

Krew sighed. *I hate how right you are right now.*

I know. But I am okay, you stopped him, and this has played into the plan for the sword quite well.

I wondered how many eyes were bouncing between us as we held a conversation without words.

Krew turned back toward Mr. Cartier and snapped, "Get him out of my sight. Before I kill him. Take him directly into the mountain."

"Just a minute," the king barked.

Krew looked at him, magic still crawling over every inch of his skin. I felt his rage down the bond as he stared at his father and it gave me shivers. He was absolutely irate that anyone would have the nerve to try this at our wedding banquet. That his father would test us like this.

"We should take him to a side room to question him," the king offered, "while the guards check every person in this room for my sword."

"Question him?" Krew snapped. "He just sent glass shards at my wife. I have plenty of questions for him which can be answered while he rots away in the mountain."

"I—"

Krew didn't let him get more than a word out. "*You* have murdered people for far less."

The king held up a hand. "Fine." More to everyone else than to Krew, he added, "My sons and I will be upstairs while we wait for the sword to be located and this man to be delivered elsewhere. The party will resume shortly. As soon as my sword is back in my possession."

* * *

We were in a room I had never been in before, a perfect and pretty fire going in the fireplace, gray couches and chairs beautifully set around a royal blue flowered rug. It was cozy and warm, though none of us were in any sort of mood to appreciate it. Even the guards lining the wall at either side of the doors, Owen being one of them, were rigid and tense.

"I have never been more thoroughly annoyed," the king barked.

"You lost an item," Krew snapped while striding for the king, "while someone tried to harm *my wife*."

Keir shoved Krew back. I had feared that tonight would be the final showdown with the king. And though things with the sword were going somewhat well, I wasn't entirely certain that wasn't still going to happen with all the rage I felt flowing from Krew.

The king gestured with a hand so aggressively I feared the crown might fall right off his head. "She was never going to be killed and you know it. So come off it!"

"So you admit you had a role in this?" Krew's voice went quiet but lethal.

The king cocked his head. "Like I believe for even half a second the two of you didn't have a role in my sword going missing tonight."

Keir's magic was now matching Krew's. "At least our plots don't ruin lives and get people killed."

The king pursed his lips. "I cannot decide if I am more proud of the two of you for this stunt or more annoyed."

My head snapped back. He was proud of them? For conspiring against him? And being somewhat successful for it. Shouldn't he be absolutely fuming right now?

Keir glared at his father. "What can I say, we learned from the best."

Nara stood next to me as if she wished to speak with me. How did she not see by now the lunatic she was sharing a bed with? How many more of these nightmares did she need to see before she believed it?

"I'm sorry," she whispered quietly.

I spun to pin her with a glare. "For the shards of glass or for being the reason my husband was put in gauntlets. Please specify which thing, Nara."

"I—" she looked to the king, who was now watching us, before her eyes briefly met mine again. "Both, I suppose."

My magic flared with all the emotions of the night, plus being able to feel Krew's, and I didn't bother to push it beneath my skin as I promised, "I once considered you a dear friend, Nara, but if you do anything, and I mean *anything*, from this moment on that causes either of the princes harm again, I don't care who's bed you frequent, you will deal with *me*."

I almost felt bad when tears filled her eyes. Knowing the king, she probably had to come clean about the ring or else she would've been hurt herself. I knew that logically. But it didn't change the fact that I was still angry over it. She looked at the king while clutching her stomach as if wishing for him to say something. To defend her.

He gave her the barest of shrugs. "A good princess protects her prince." He turned back to his sons. "We will wait here while they search every damn person that remains on the grounds of Kavan Keep."

"It is our wedding night," Krew seethed. I knew he was trying to get us out of there.

"Oh save it," the king groaned. "We all know this marriage has been more than consummated."

I felt my cheeks heat at his rather rude word choice.

Krew lunged for his father again, but Keir again pushed him back.

"Furthermore," the king added calmly while looking from Krew to me, "the two of you can speak telepathically."

It wasn't a question. It was a statement.

I was still so frustrated with the night's events, that without thinking it through, I blurted out, "Is there a problem with that?"

"I—" the king shook his head. "No. Other than I was not informed."

"It is not *your* concern," Krew snapped. "And if you wanted to know you could've simply asked rather than send shards of glass at her."

The king glared at him. "No one was going to kill her. They wouldn't dare when she is the Enchanted responsible for healing the forest and soul bound to an heir of Wylan."

It was Keir who fired back with, "Just a casual maiming then?"

"Enough!" the king yelled. "Let us get back to waiting for the sword. The only real loss of the night."

The minutes crawled by. I sat in the chair closest to the fire in my white gown, watching the flames and trying to send Krew happy thoughts and observations about the night to calm him down.

It wasn't working. His anger was still rolling off him in waves and it didn't take being bonded to him to feel it.

An hour later, one of the king's guards rushed in, the doors opening abruptly. He hurried over to the king and whispered to him for what felt like minutes before spinning on his heel and hurrying back out.

The king waited a solid minute before he said a word to any of us. Likely just to torture us.

"It appears that when everything went down in the ballroom, most of the guests in the garden fled, not entirely knowing all the details. And the culprits were likely among them so the search for the sword has now moved to the wall."

My eyes briefly went to Keir's, sitting across from me, and I saw an evil smirk quickly cross his features before vanishing.

Keir planted twenty Rallis people among the crowd to start a human stampede, Krew explained to me.

"So now we go back to the banquet and try to salvage this disaster of a night." It wasn't a suggestion; it was a demand from a king to his subjects. “And wait for the sword to be returned to me.”

It won’t be, Krew told me through the bond. *One of the men hid it behind the hedge for Keir. While another has the fake they are running to Rallis with.*

“Go apologize to your people for this ruckus you’ve caused,” the king finished.

“*We’ve* caused, you mean, Father?” Keir asked calmly. “We weren’t the only ones with a scheme tonight.”

The king groaned in disgust. “Just get the hell out of my sight.”

CHAPTER 37

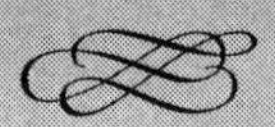

Greeting our guests after they had all been patted down by the king's guards was a somber experience.

Though the orchestra continued to play music softly in the background, no one really felt like dancing or even drinking too much. The Enchanted were all on alert, eyes darting around and constantly scanning the room while they whispered. Likely looking for both a sword and the wrath of their king.

It made my stomach sink. To think of the raw power in this room. The power that was being told to use magic sparingly and only as needed with the attached fear that they could lose their magic if they used it too often. Yet if they were using it more often, this room would be far stronger. There was so much wasted potential in this room and very few people even knew it.

The king hadn't really wanted an army of Enchanted. He wanted a human wall of protection, with no one ever being more powerful than himself.

And it was disgusting. A disgrace to the entire realm. If enemies from the other countries ever did come knocking, we were in trouble. Our Enchanted were weaker with the king on the throne. The throne he had built on a web of bloodied lies.

But then again, if he really was responsible for the disease that had weakened the other countries' magic, he had effectively created himself a bubble in which he was the strongest Enchanted in the entire realm.

"Should we wait for you?" Molly whispered to me.

My eyes went to Keir's where he stood with Gwen and Delaney. "No. You two get out while you can. I'll try to find you tomorrow as soon as I can."

Molly hugged me hard. "Be safe, Jorah. Be safe!"

I turned to hug Renna.

As soon as they left, I felt a deep breath of relief. My mother and Flora were gone. Silvia was gone. Renna and Molly had left. In fact, only a small fraction of people remained.

Maybe we would all survive the night yet.

"So the telepathy," the king said as he sidled up next to me. "Can you do it on demand?"

I turned toward Krew to await his answer, but the king added, "Oh my son is way too furious at me to speak. I'm asking you, Jorah."

"If you wouldn't make a habit out of murdering his lovers, he likely wouldn't be this angry," I commented as if we were discussing the weather.

The king gave me a nod. "Point made. Now answer."

"Yes, we can do it on demand."

He pondered that. "That day in the throne room? When you barged in on the joint parliament session?"

"I can feel his emotions down the bond. I felt he was in pain. I felt his helplessness and the pain of having his magic caged. That is why I did what I did."

The king gave a slow nod. "I used to be able to feel some of

Katarina's stronger emotions, so I assume it is a stronger version of that."

"Before or after you siphoned her magic?" Keir snapped, having arrived with Gwen and Delaney on the other side of Krew. Apparently, I wasn't the only one done playing nice with the king.

The king looked around to see if anyone was eavesdropping. They weren't. The rest of the people were slowly filtering out of the ballroom. Everyone was steering clear of us after the events of the night, and I couldn't say I truly blamed them. I was only here because I had to be.

"Watch it," he threatened.

"What is the point in continuing to pretend like we don't already all know?" Keir continued.

I wasn't sure Gwen had known, judging by the look on her face, but who was I to stop Keir from berating his father?

The king opened his mouth to say something more, but a guard came rushing over. One I recognized as one of the king's favorite guards. The king met him part way, likely not wanting the rest of us to overhear whatever message this was.

The guard whispered something that had the king's lips pulling into a sinister smile.

That small smile took me from feeling somewhat relieved about the events of the night to straight terror.

Did they find the sword in its hiding spot? What was going on?

The king said loudly from where he stood as the guard left the way he came, "Everyone who is not a Valanova or in Keir's Assemblage, get the hell out!"

My eyes went to Owen, standing over at the windows by where I had always looked out. He gave me a look as if telling me to be careful.

I had no idea what the guard told the king, but it looked like our luck for the night was running out. My magic began humming beneath my skin as if sensing it might be needed.

As soon as everyone finished fleeing from the room, the king gave a nod and beckoned to two guards standing at the same side door he had taken me out of to catch Renna and Krew together.

Two more guards came in. Not only was there a sword in one of their hands, but between them they were also carrying Theodore Jones, who looked as if he had already been thoroughly smacked around by the guards.

It has to be the fake, Krew promised me.

We have to help him.

Krew's eyes pierced mine. *We will.*

I felt my magic now brewing at the surface of my skin and let it start to heat me. I was going to need it. The only question remaining was just how much of it.

"These guards," the king began as he walked back over next to Keir and gestured to Theodore, who had been dragged to about thirty feet away, "found this man near the wall as he attempted to pass this off."

Krew took a half a step in front of me, as if to protect me from whatever came next.

"When you came here, we suspected you were working for the disloyal. This only confirms it," the king spat at Theodore.

The guards threw Theodore to the ground and my magic intensified. He could barely open one of his eyes, that entire half of his face red, and he had a cracked and bloodied lip. Though he had to be in immense pain, he immediately brought himself up to his feet.

It took him a few seconds, but he stood tall and looked the king directly in the eyes. His bravery had the tears tickling the backs of my eyes.

The king glanced at one of the guards, the one who held the sword at his side.

Without warning, the guard kicked with his leg at the back of Theodore's knees, who slumped back to the ground.

"Bow before your king," the guard demanded. "Bow and await your punishment."

Theodore brought himself up to his elbow, then ever so slowly moved to his knee, which he pivoted away from the king.

All the air in my lungs vanished as Theodore spun directly toward me, turning his neck and fixing his one opened eye on the king. "I will bow before my princess but never before *you.*"

The king's magic was snaking toward Theodore before he was even done speaking, but Krew and Keir's magic combined midair to blow it away.

"Do not," Keir snapped.

Krew spun toward his father, arms out. "You know we are more so to blame than this man is, so why don't you just take it out on Keir and me. You know that's really what you want anyway."

While my magic increased to throb with the beats of my heart, the king actually had the nerve to hesitate for a moment. As if he were thinking about it.

"As annoyed as I am with you, son, I unfortunately need the both of you." And in that moment, I knew Theodore was screwed.

So without hesitating, I threw a dome around him to protect him, trying to think of bricks laid around it in protecting it.

The king looked at it before he directed his beady eyes at me. A second passed. Two. The king gave one of the guards the slightest of nods and then the king moved faster than would have been possible for someone not Enchanted.

At the same time he released droves of his black magic at my dome, he also reached down and grabbed the dagger from his boot. A replacement dagger for the one we'd already stolen. He tossed it before he had even fully stood back up.

The ground rumbled under the weight of the magic he sent hurtling at my dome.

I held hope my dome would be able to withstand it, but my worst fears were realized as it shattered immediately.

But then Krew's magic was there and snagged the dagger right out of the air, sending it clattering against the wall they had all entered in. While I'd been protecting Theodore, he had been making a move for the dagger. We'd not combined our magic because we'd been too busy moving in different directions to protect Theodore.

"Enough!" Krew demanded.

I took a deep breath, ready to send more magic to protect Theodore, thinking of the weight of the magic being even thicker, and was about to send down the bond for Krew to help, but a sickening wet noise interrupted my focus.

The guard standing next to Theodore had unsheathed the replica of the king's sword and drove it straight through his back.

Theodore fell forward, back arched in pain as he grunted. A lesser man would have screamed in agony.

"You will die a proper thief's death," the guard promised as he still gripped the hilt of the sword. He let go and Theodore fell to the ground.

I sent out magic to soften his fall and wasn't sure if it made it in time or not. But I lost it as Theodore's light brown shirt stained red.

With one finger, I sent enough magic to the guard to surround him. He tried to use his own magic to protect himself, but I was faster. Madder. With my other hand, I chucked the man at the same wall Krew had thrown the dagger to.

There was a smacking thud and then the guard fell limp on the ground.

The king's chin went back. "Did you just kill my guard?"

I wasn't looking at the guard, nor did I really care if I had somehow miraculously killed him with my magic. I was too busy rushing to Theodore, sending my magic at him while thinking healing thoughts like I did in the forest. And then I thought of what it felt like when the quirky doctor had put the pain numbing salve on my lash mark.

Theodore was on his side as I reached him, and I didn't hesitate to lay my hand on his arm, even as it still sent more magic around him.

"Theodore," I gasped. "I'm so sorry."

There was so much blood. Entirely too much blood. I was bound to get it on my pristinely white gown, but I had no other thoughts in that moment other than figuring out how to heal this man. This *innocent* man.

"Help," I yelled to Keir and Krew. "Get that sword out of him while I send more magic into him."

"They—" Theodore said, voice strained, "can't."

Krew was there, his legs hitting my back as he stood protecting the both of us from his father. "He's right. If I take it out now, he will just bleed out even faster."

I shook my head, tears falling down my cheeks as I looked back at Theodore. "No. This isn't your fault. None of this was your fault."

Theodore reached for my hand, and I took his in mine, willing for this to not be happening. He couldn't die. Not when he wasn't responsible for this. I was. Keir was. Krew was. But not Theodore. Not this kind and welcoming man from the lowest level in the kingdom who just simply was brave enough to fight for a better tomorrow.

"Theodore," I begged. "Don't go. This wasn't your fault."

My magic must have finally numbed some of his pain. That or he was too close to the kiss of death to feel pain anymore as his face slackened, the tension in his face and neck disappearing. He couldn't find the strength to form words though. He just looked me in the eyes and continued holding my hand as if wanting me to promise to carry on his charge. As if in his last moments he wanted nothing more than for me to usurp the king and kill him.

But he never got to say those words. He never got to say anything at all, his injuries too great.

I felt my magic building and didn't bother to stop it as I held tightly onto Theodore's hand until his last breath. And when he took that breath, when I heard his lungs rasp and give out under the weight of his wounds, I knew. I was going to kill the king.

Right this very minute.

I heard a slight smacking noise followed by the king's voice. "Good thing your plans don't ruin lives, son."

I snapped my head Keir's direction to see his skin brighter than I had ever seen it before. "That sword wasn't even the real one, you jackass! It was a fake! That we had planted." Keir shook his head and rolled his neck as if he were about to unleash fire and hell upon his father. "You just killed a man for stealing a fake sword. One that he didn't even steal because he was working the stables."

The king stilled, cocked his head, and a faint smile graced his lips. "Not bad. Not bad at all."

I stood, envisioning my magic wrapping around the king to immobilize him, ready to help Keir every step of the way, but before I could even let out a single strand of magic, the king grabbed Nara around the waist. His own magic slid them from the room, using her as a human shield in the process. Black magic trailed up the door as he slammed the doors behind them. In the blink of an eye, they were gone.

CHAPTER 38

Blood was splattered on the lace of my wedding dress, making the pattern in the lace more noticeable. I sat on the couch in the adjoining room of Krew's wing staring at it. I had refused to change, refused to shower, refused to go to bed, and only repeatedly pleaded to Krew for us to find and murder his father. Tonight.

The king had to sleep sometime, didn't he?

Owen held out a cup of steaming tea while sitting down right beside me on the couch.

I shook my head, too angry to even remember how to drink.

Owen put a hand between my shoulder blades. "I know, honey. I know. Please breathe. You are glowing rather vibrantly."

"Good," I snapped. "All the better to kill him with."

Owen rested his head on my shoulder. "We can't kill him tonight and I think you know that. But he did flee from the room once he saw the three of you all about to unleash your magic on him. He might have gotten away tonight, but only just barely. He didn't just leave, he fled."

I inhaled deeply, listening to his words, the conviction behind and within them.

"He may have gotten away tonight, but not for long."

I gasped as more tears filled my eyes. "I don't want another shot at this, I want this tonight. Theo—" I cut off, unable to finish.

"I know," Owen agreed. "I know."

There was a tapping noise from our bedroom and Krew, who had been pacing after trying to console me a variety of different ways, said, "I'll be right back, love."

Seconds or minutes later, I had no idea, he came back in with Keir.

Keir dropped a sword onto the oval table with a clunk.

Seeing it sitting there, knowing that Theodore had to give his life for this sword, this master plan to get the sword away from the king, it was all too much.

"The night was not in vain," Keir said, voice cracking. "Yet I am left with many regrets this night. I'm so sorry, Jorah."

"Me too," I gasped as the tears consumed me, Owen gently placing the teacup on the ground to better hold me.

"I'll have it tested first thing in the morning," Krew said quietly.

Keir shook his head. "I can't believe we didn't assume he might have something planned for tonight too. Of course his schemes and ours had to overlap."

"It actually worked to our advantage for a while in there," Owen said gently.

I didn't bother to wipe at my eyes. There were too many tears. "What about the guard I threw at the wall?" I might have killed a man tonight. And that wasn't even the oddest part of this night. The oddest part of this night was that I might have killed a man and I didn't even care.

Krew moved to crouch next to me, so our eyes were level. "When he fell from the wall, the fall broke his neck."

Not only was I unbothered, but I actually preferred it that way.

"Died a proper piece of trash's death," I offered. But then my brow furrowed as I remembered something Krew told me long ago about magic. "I thought our magic was not supposed to decide life or death? It could cause unconsciousness, but not death itself?"

Krew gave a half shrug. "These were extenuating circumstances. Technically your magic didn't kill him either, the fall did. So it was a bit of a loophole."

I sighed. "I expected to feel bad having taken a life, but I don't. I really don't."

"You might eventually," Owen offered. "You might not. Either way, no one in this room looks at you any differently. You defended an innocent man."

I looked toward the window, the calm and serene forest I knew that laid below it. "How many more innocent men like Theodore have to die?"

"None," Krew promised, voice rough. "We let our magic recoup, and my father is now without his sword. We confirm the sword has our mother's magic and we make our move soon. In a few days."

Keir gave a nod as he moved to unsheathe the sword. It didn't hum or have purple tendrils of magic winding around the blade like I'd always expected, but then again, I knew nothing about objects containing siphoned magic. "I suspect he was just wanting to get a feel for how powerful the two of you are together. Out of sheer luck, your magic never combined so he remains somewhat clueless. But the mind games he played tonight are too far even for him." Keir paused while looking at the sword. "Anyone could have accidentally gotten a glass shard lodged in their body and bled out. He is not stable. And the longer he stays on that throne, the more bloodshed there will be."

Krew's eyes were on mine as he promised, "The only blood which needs shed is his."

* * *

I SLEPT VERY little that night except maybe an hour or two. Krew had helped me into the bath before we finally went to bed, so I was clean, yet all I saw was blood.

Owen and I headed down to the forest in the morning. I couldn't sit around and just relive the night before, asking myself if I should've used my magic sooner. If Krew and I combined our magic in front of the king, would we have saved Theodore and been able to kill the king? Would all this already be over if only we'd been just a few seconds faster, smarter?

"So that's new," Owen offered.

A third wolf was waiting for us at the forest.

I slowed and looked at Rafe. "I am not sure I feel up to running today, boys. Boys and girl, that is," I amended while looking at the timid gray wolf with beautiful blue eyes. "But I do want to try to walk it, if you will all be so kind as to walk with me."

Rafe reached over and pressed his nose under my hand as if he had heard every word. As if he somehow knew what had gone on in the castle last night or at the very least, saw that I was struggling today.

So we took off. As much as I didn't want to admit it, Krew might have been correct about needing to take a few days to recoup our magic. I didn't feel the pull to use my magic like I did most mornings, as I had used a lot of magic the night before between chucking the guard at the wall and killing him, and then trying and failing to put up the dome around Theodore. Owen and I needed to discuss that. He had held onto hope my protective domes could be used to keep us safe from the king just before we killed him. But in that moment in the ballroom, it had taken seconds and the king had just shattered it.

Like it was nothing.

I wasn't sure we were going to be able to use the domes at all.

Rafe walked closer to me than normal, as did Shadow on my other side. Meanwhile the new gray wolf kept her distance but followed along with us, constantly looking through the trees for any threat to burst through at any moment.

We walked toward the lake instead of along the path because I had decided spur of the moment I wished to see the clear lake, if only to be reminded that things were changing.

I didn't wish to scare the new wolf off, but I couldn't take seeing the deadened trees either. I had been healing one tree a day around the lake, but this morning I couldn't bring myself to only do one. I knew I was supposed to be recouping my magic, but I also had a few days to do so.

So I did one. Then another. And another.

I watched the wolves while my magic poured out, hoping that it wouldn't scare them off, and it didn't. They looked as if it was a common, everyday occurrence. And it was. I did this most days, just never this close to them.

I kept pouring my magic into the trees, visualizing them healed and healthy. I hated that whatever this healing entity was in my magic couldn't have helped Theodore. Was I too late? Was he just too far gone by that point?

My magic could heal, but Theodore had also been brutally stabbed in the back too.

Feeling the tears back with a vengeance, I closed my eyes and continued to send my magic.

I stood there, breathing deeply and letting the magic flow from my fingers and send that jolt of energy racing across my blood. I was still not okay about the night before. About being partially responsible for Theodore's death. About the fact that Krew had left early this morning to personally take Theodore's body and deliver it to Nerede today while dropping off the sword along the way.

He'd offered to take me with him, but I just couldn't bring myself to go. I was Nerede's princess. I had vowed to serve my subjects justly. And while some royals might not take that vow seriously, I did. There was nothing just about last night. I had failed my people on my very first night on the job.

So I took the coward's way out. I was avoiding them. I was avoiding seeing the faces and tears of the people who I had let down so thoroughly.

"Jorah," Owen snapped.

I opened my eyes and saw that my silver magic wrapping around those three tree trunks were not only making a growing circle of green grass around them, but they were also . . . oh gods, the trunks looked like they were also *growing*.

I immediately shut down my magic. "I'm so sorry. I had meant to do three, feeling the need to use my magic to at least do some sort of good after last night, but I had no idea I was—" I cut off, shaking my head and looking up at the trees. "Were they actually growing?"

Owen was nodding, eyebrows up. "They definitely grew. A foot or so judging by the rest of the trees in the area."

I hadn't known I could do that.

A tear slipped down my cheek. I tried to sniff the rest away. I tried to push them down like I did to keep my magic contained, but it wasn't working. There were just too many tears there to will them away.

"Jorah?" Owen asked softly.

I shook my head and gestured at a tree. "How is it I can do that? Make three trees grow, but I couldn't use my magic to heal Theodore?"

Owen let out a long sigh. "It was too late."

I gasped, and sat down, tucking my knees in and putting my arms around them as I rocked myself back and forth.

Owen's voice was soft as he added, "I don't doubt had the wound not punctured any vital organs that you could have helped him, saved him even. But the damage was already done at that point."

I looked up at the sunlight through the branches. "Why?"

"I don't know why." Owen shrugged. "But we tried to help him, Jorah. It isn't as if you just stood around and watched him be murdered. You did try to prevent it from happening."

I rested my head on my hands and tried to slow my breathing.

Soft fuzz rubbed against my arms. "Rafe, I—" As I brought my head up, it wasn't grey fuzz I saw, but black.

"Shadow." I let out a huff of breath, the snot and tears angrily taking over my sinus passages. "I'll be okay, buddy. Maybe not today, but eventually."

So there I sat. Rafe on one side, Shadow on the other. In no hurry to leave, they sat there with me until my breathing calmed and the tears slowed. Taking pity on me, Shadow even allowed me to pet him.

When I returned back up to Krew's wing, I showered despite not being sweaty for once. I walked out of the room to find Owen propped up against the headboard.

"This again?" I whispered.

"You didn't sleep much last night." Owen grabbed something off the nightstand before scooting over and patting the bed. "But there is an addition this time around."

I got under the covers next to him and moved my damp hair away from my face. "Okay."

Owen's response was to open my book I had been reading, turn it to the page I had marked when last reading it, and begin reading from the top of that page.

I snorted a laugh. "You are not. That is a romance, Owen."

Owen glared at me. "And you don't think I can handle a little romance?" He cleared his throat dramatically and then began reading. Whenever the female character spoke, he made his voice atrociously high to read her parts.

It had me laughing.

I wasn't sure after the last day that I was still capable of laughing, yet somehow, I was. Theodore was gone, the sword was ours, and we were left to just carry on breathing and living life somehow.

After living through this many nightmares at the castle, I found sometimes it was just easier to sleep with the sun. As I listened to the rhythm of Owen's voice, it wasn't long before I fell into a deep sleep.

* * *

I WOKE WITH A START. It was early evening judging by the light outside, but my own anguish hadn't been the one to wake me.

Krew?

Give me a moment please, love.

Can you at least tell me you're okay?

I am not okay, but I am also not being harmed either. I will return home to you within the hour.

It wasn't like him to be so dismissive with me. Did that mean he was in the middle of something and just couldn't talk to me? Or that he wouldn't? Those were two vastly different scenarios.

I felt down the bond for his location, wanting to know if he was with his father, and instinctively knew he was on the way back but wasn't through the last wall to Kavan Keep yet. Though I had felt less of his emotions the farther from me he went, I had still been able to feel his location even from within Nerede.

Meanwhile Owen was snoring next to me on the bed. I wanted to be amused that the book in his lap was a considerable distance from the spot he'd been reading to me, but I was also worried about whatever I felt coming from Krew.

I gave Owen a slight shove.

He jerked awake, soldier mode immediately. "What is it?"

I shrugged. "I don't really know. I woke feeling anguish from Krew and he told me he isn't okay, but he is also not being harmed. He said he'd be back to the castle within an hour."

Owen cocked his head. "If things got aggressive in Nerede, you'd think you would have felt it long before now."

"Unless he is just finally within range of the emotional part of our bond or something," I added.

"The king sent more than thirty guards with him so it shouldn't have gotten violent." Owen gave his head a shake and moved to stand up. "Well, I guess let's ring for some sandwiches and wait. Since there is nothing more we can do."

I bit down on the inside of my cheek. I didn't like this. I didn't like this at all.

I'm worried. Can you tell me anything more about what is going on? I pleaded.

I will when I get there.

Why can't you now?

Because I want to be next to you to discuss this.

My shoulders slumped in utter defeat. It was bad. Whatever we needed to discuss was bad enough I was feeling Krew's emotional turmoil over it, and he wanted to wait until he could see me until he told me what it was. I tended to think of our bond, the ability to feel Krew's emotions, as a good thing, a way of protecting our relationship and each other. But it also made it nearly impossible to keep things from each other. And in cases like this, when some things are just better said face to face, it could be bothersome.

I quickly filled Owen in.

"Can't be worse than yesterday, can it?"

I groaned. "Please do not tempt fate like that. He's enough of a prick as is."

Owen's chin went back. "How do you know fate is a *he*?"

I squinted at him. "Because all the biggest pains in my ass are."

Owen took a drink of his water as he went to set it on the tray for the staff. "Fair."

The next hour passed slowly. I was barely able to eat at all despite Owen's constant badgering. I wasn't sure I breathed normally until I felt Krew in the castle.

I took a deep breath and moved to sit at the edge of the couch in the adjoining room. I hadn't even consciously known I was doing it, but I had been pacing Krew's normal track in the rug.

The door opened and Krew came in. He walked right over to his bottle of whiskey and poured himself one.

"That good of a day?" Owen asked gently.

"That good of a day." He put the glass down and spun toward me, moving to sit next to me on the couch.

"What?" Tears were already rushing to my eyes because I knew whatever he was about to tell me was going to further crush me. "Did everything go all right in Nerede?"

Krew took a steady breath and looked to Owen before looking to me. "As well as it could." He let out a sigh and I again just felt aguish coming off him. "It's the sword."

I stopped breathing altogether.

"It isn't the object my mother's magic is siphoned into. Just like the ring, there is no magic within it."

I swallowed, trying to focus on those words. Trying not to let the weight of my combined sorrow and defeat take me to the ground.

"Is it possible the king just absorbed your mother's magic or something?" Owen asked. "We've tried the dagger, the ring, and the sword."

Krew clenched his jaw. "But not the crown itself. The thing only he would touch."

"Or it could be the necklace, or a chain or something," Owen added. "Something he wears under his tailcoat that we cannot see."

While they bickered about what object it could be, I questioned whether we were right at all. Had we been right to jump to the conclusion that the king had the queen's magic? We'd never even seen it be used. What if the king was just that strong? And there was no easy way to weaken him?

"So," I offered, interrupting their ongoing debate on the object. "You mean to tell me that we had this grand plan to steal the sword from the king. We somehow pulled it all off and got it, and then we lost Theodore to that plan. And Theodore died for nothing?"

Owen shook his head at me. "No. Don't you go there. Theodore died for nothing either way. He was innocent the entire time. The king is and has always been responsible for his death."

Krew reached over and wiped a tear from my face.

"That may be," I bit out angrily, "but it doesn't change the fact that instead of being a few days from killing the king, we are entirely back to square one."

CHAPTER 39

"Cards, or are we not in a card playing mood?"

Molly and Renna stayed an extra day, all things considered. I had been in too much of a retrospective mood to do much the day before, but knowing they were due to leave this afternoon to go back to their homes in Savaryn after the wedding, if I wanted to see them at all, I had to do it now. We went to our old card playing room as they were staying in that wing of the castle, so it just seemed easier. They, of course, had heard about what had happened in the ballroom. The whispers about what happened had spread throughout the castle and had likely already swept through Savaryn and Rallis too.

"I am not sure." I tucked my legs under me in one of the chairs by the fireplace I had already lit. Jo handed me over a steaming cup of tea. "Thank you."

"No problem, Your Grace."

I groaned. "Not you too, Jo!"

"You do quite literally have a crown on your head," she argued. She looked at my sound barrier at the door before adding, "And are more deserving of it than some who wear them."

I rolled my eyes. "Well when it is just the four of us, you can call me just Jorah."

"So cards then, Just Jorah?" Molly chirped.

I shook my head. "Not yet. I need for someone to tell me some juicy Savaryn gossip or something. Anything."

"Jorah," Renna said gently. "We can definitely distract you with that in a moment, but I feel the need to say this first." She paused. "You can't change what happened no matter how many times you think it over. It happened. It was awful and it happened. And it wasn't your fault."

I closed my eyes. "It feels a little like it was." I opened my eyes and blinked rapidly. "Day one after being officially crowned and I failed the people. And not just any people. Nerede. *My* people."

Molly let out a long sigh. "I can't believe the sword wasn't it."

My shoulders gave a weak shrug. "I really thought it was." I closed my eyes again and took a deep breath, seeing for what had to be the thousandth time the fake sword being rammed into Theodore's body. "And there was just so much blood."

"I think," Molly began gently as she brought her own teacup back down, "that for the deepest hurts of life, time itself is the only ointment. What you had to see? Being forced to carry on living and breathing like nothing happened in its wake?" she paused. "There is no remedy for the horrors of both of those things."

"I'm not sure time will really help either," I admitted.

Molly smirked. "But it will. Because you will remember how to laugh. You will remember the people in your life you have to love. You will remember that there is still good to be found and had. You will let go of the horror and cling to the good if only to fill your lungs completely for a few moments. To remember what it's like to breathe deeply."

A tear rolled down my cheek at her beautiful words. "I killed a man. I threw him at a wall and his neck snapped when he fell. I should feel shame. I should feel guilt. All I feel is terror. Terror at whatever will be the king's next game. My mother is going home for a few months just to get her away from the king." I paused, my chin quivering with what I needed to admit next. "And I am absolutely horrified the king will take Krew with him when he finally rids us of his presence."

"Oh honey," Renna whispered.

"I watched Theodore die. Brutally. I need to be there to help Krew because we are stronger together." I gasped a breath. "And I don't want to watch Krew die too. I—"

Love? Krew asked down the bond.

Just chatting with the girls, I told him. *Discussing Theodore and the other night.*

Just let me know if you need me.

"I cannot see another innocent person killed because of the king's actions," I finished. "And as much as I feel through our bond, Krew's emotions and even pain, I won't just have to see him go . . ."

"Oh gods, you'll feel it too," Jo gasped, eyes wide as she looked at Renna.

"I never thought of that," Molly added.

"Or worse than feeling his pain," I paused to fight off a shiver, "feeling his void."

"But that is all based off the assumption that Krew will have to die in order to accomplish this," Renna reminded me. "He has you strengthening him. His brother's help as well. Owen's. The Six. If he fought him one-on-one, sure. But he is no longer alone in this endeavor. And hasn't been for quite some time."

"I know, but it was just something he had resigned himself to when we first started having real feelings for one another. And knowing that, knowing his resolve and how determined he is to see his father off the throne, it's become my greatest fear." I paused. "I guess my fear of his father's reign never ending and my fear of losing Krew battle one another daily for my greatest fear, but you get the idea."

Molly shook her head vehemently. "No. I am not buying it. Krew is just too stubborn to die."

My eyes went wide. After her rather eloquent speech earlier, she followed that up with a rather blunt statement.

She tilted her head unapologetically. "That is not to say I think it is fair you have to carry this responsibility upon your shoulders. The princes should not have to conspire how to kill their own father. Though I am still rather mad at one such prince, Wylan could not have a better future in each of them."

I looked in the direction of the window where I knew the forest was. "But every day that horrible man stays on that throne, Wylan grows weaker." He might not have poisoned Wylan, but he hadn't needed to. He was the poison.

Renna propped her feet up on Jo's leg as she sat down on the couch next to her. "Do we have a plan for when this will happen? I suppose conveniently harboring The Six and myself in the castle just before it goes down would be too obvious?"

I sighed. "Nothing has been decided. Owen and Emric wanted to become bonded to Krew so that all of our magic could combine, but the sage who married us urged them against it. He said that more than two bondings per person has been believed to weaken the potency of the bonded magic as more of them are added. So we are back to square one, trying to decide if it is better to seek out the object again, whatever it may be, and give Keir more time to figure out his Assemblage responsibilities, or if we just disregard the object entirely and make a move before the king knows the extent of our bonded magic."

Molly wrinkled her nose. "Well I like neither of those plans."

"I concur," I laughed.

"Why can't he just die of natural causes already?" Molly snapped. "He's had a long and selfish life."

Renna snorted. "As if it would be that easy. But if the object is not retrieved, we just need more hands on deck for when it happens."

And it was that thought which had me thinking. I had killed a man. I hadn't *meant* to, but I had *wanted* to. And as I grappled with the ramifications of all that, there was one person who kept popping into my thoughts and had all morning.

I stayed for another hour, drinking tea and chatting with the other women. We spoke about Nara for a while and then just talked about the wedding and what it was like returning to the castle. I was not in the best of moods and I knew it. I had wanted to see them, but also didn't want to ruin their day, so I excused myself after a while.

In the hallway with Owen, I stilled before we left to the darker hallway and put up a sound barrier.

"I'd like you to take me to see someone, please," I said quietly.

He looked over his shoulder. "Your mother?"

I shook my head. "No. Not my mother."

Owen glared at me. "I am not delivering you to the king for a murder attempt without at least some more backup. Though we are pretty impressive, if I do say so myself, it's going to take more than just you and me."

My lips tugged into a smile. "Also not it."

"Well, are you going to tell me?"

"Are you going to let me?"

"Fine."

"Easton," I said, hating the cadence of his name on my lips. "I would like to see Easton."

* * *

AFTER OWEN PICKED up his jaw off the floor, he crossed his arms and glared at me. "Why?"

"I'd just like to see him. I know he was supposed to remain

locked away until the end of the Assemblages, but Krew's is officially over. And now that I can defend myself and also have a better handle on my magic, I'd just like some closure."

"Fine. But tell Krew. Tell Krew first and then I will fetch him for you."

"Okay. But I don't want him there for it," I stated.

"What? Why?" Owen's brow was furrowed.

I let out a deep breath. "Because I know how I feel about Easton. And I know how Krew feels about Easton. And if I have to feel the weight of all that dislike, his and mine both, it is going to make it even harder."

"Actually, that makes quite a bit of sense." Owen made a brushing motion with his hand in my direction. "Go on now. Do your super odd thing where you are talking to nothing."

Krew?

Yes, love?

I would like to speak to Easton today. Owen wanted me to let you know beforehand. So this is me letting you know beforehand.

There was a pause long enough I wondered if he walked away from someone. *Why?*

Because I need a bit of closure. That's all.

If this is about what you did to that guard, it's not the same, he responded strongly.

It is and it isn't. It's just something I want to do.

Okay. I'll find you in twenty.

Alone, I added.

What?

I can't feel the hatred and disappointment rolling off you matching my own. I feel it often enough when around your father to know that it makes my magic harder to contain.

I do not like the fact that you have a point.

I will let you know as soon as I am done.

I trust you. I trust Owen. Just please be careful, Jorah.

I turned back to Owen with as much of a smile as I could muster. "We're good."

"So can I trust you to stay put in Krew's wing while I fetch him?" Owen asked.

"Let's just go there," I offered. "Wherever he is. I don't want him in Krew's wing ever again. It's my safe space within the castle."

Owen cocked his head. "Okay, fine."

My step forward faltered. "He's not *in* the mountain, right?"

"No. He's close to it in some run-down servant quarters."

I gestured with my arm out. "Well let's go get this over with then, shall we?"

Owen sighed. "I guess."

It took a twenty-minute walk to get there. The farther in the direction of the mountain we walked, the cooler the temperature got. Though I was walking, I was still cold by the time we arrived outside a door. The walls were cracked, and we were on what I assumed was the second level.

I didn't want to know where exactly the entrance was to the castle dungeon. It was creepy in this part of the castle. While the rest of the castle was gleaming marble floors and extravagance, this part of the castle looked like something you'd find in Nerede. It was old. And not only was it old, but it was unkept. The lanterns casting what little light there was along the way had been covered in a thick layer of dust. Twice I had seen massive spider webs in the corners of hallways. Though we hadn't stepped foot outside the castle, it felt like we had. It felt like we were in a ramshackle cottage of sorts.

Owen nodded to the two guards at the door. "We are here to see Grant."

The guard looked to me and to Owen, then back to me. "I'm not sure that's a good idea. We were told no visitors."

"Yes, me neither," Owen snapped. "But Her Highness had it approved with Prince Krewan."

The guards looked at each other and then the one who seemed to be in charge banged on the door. "Company."

The other turned the doorknob for me, and I walked into an old room.

There was one small square of a window with bars over it which overlooked half of a boulder and half the forest. And on a single bed scooted close to the fireplace sat Easton. His beard was grown out, and his hair longer. So much so that I hadn't realized how dark his hair was until it was this length. He didn't look starved though. He just looked . . . isolated. Like a man who was bored out of his mind.

His mouth fell open as he moved to put down the book he was reading. It was a history book, best I could read the worn cover.

"Is this my execution day?" Easton asked as he crossed his arms tightly over his chest. His voice was so quiet, I wondered when the last time it was that he had spoken to anyone.

My eyes widened. "You think we are here to kill you?"

"You are wearing a crown," he pointed out. "So that leads me to believe the rumors are true and you are more than likely Enchanted now."

"She is," Owen snapped. "And she is also a princess so you will refer to her as Your Grace or Her Highness."

Easton put a hand in the air. "My apologies, Your Grace."

I shot Owen a look. He was still mad at Easton apparently, despite the fact that within The Six they had been a variation of friends. I crossed my arms and moved a few steps closer to Easton, second guessing this entire adventure. "Look, I'll make this short and sweet." I paused. "I killed a man the other day."

Easton's head snapped back as if that was the last thing he ever expected me to say.

"I killed a man and thus far it has not bothered me much. Because the man deserved it. But there is still a . . . *weight* to having been the person responsible for the perishing of a life. A weight that comes with the power of delivering death. But I don't feel bad for doing what I did. I don't know if I ever will." I paused. "And having done it, I thought of you. Of how over the course of that summer those weights must have added up. How though I do not feel guilty or bad for what I did, there was something within you, that though you were following orders, gave you a sense of wrongness. Guilt."

Easton just sat there, quiet, while I kept talking.

My voice went cold. "I will never forget what you took from me. I will never forget how it felt to try to sleep after I found out it was you. How I was afraid to sleep after that, knowing my father's murderer had been right outside my door the entire time."

Easton's eyes fell to the floor.

"But I am glad that you do feel that guilt. Though I am angry," I paused as a ripple of magic trailed up my arms. And I let it because I was just that cold. "Though I am angry, I can still see that just as easily as you could have felt the guilt of what you've done, you could have just become numb to it. Like the king." I paused. "You removed yourself from the situation so that you wouldn't have to take any more innocent lives."

"Jorah, I'm so sorry," Easton said, voice shaky.

"It is *Your Grace*," Owen barked.

Easton nodded. "Sorry. I am so sorry, Your Grace."

I remembered what my mother said about showing others mercy and forgiveness. We didn't do it for their sake, but rather to rid ourselves of the emotional shackles that tied us to them.

"I am done hating you," I added. "I have hated the man who killed my father since the moment he was ripped out of my life. Far before I even knew it was *you*." I took a shaky breath. "And no amount of hatred or anger will bring back the man who taught me how to dance in my mother's kitchen." A tear slipped out and Owen moved in closer as if to help me, but I shook my head. "The man who would get off wall duty and rush to the bakery just to help us with dishes. So that we could all spend time together as a family. The man who I watched love my mother fiercely. The man who no matter how exhausted he was, read me bedtime stories in different voices and made me fall in love with books." I closed my eyes and breathed. "He's gone. And I realize the king is as much to blame as you are. But I am done hating you."

Easton swallowed and when his voice came out, it was a mere whisper. "How can you not?"

I shrugged. "Because I don't want my emotions tied to you for a moment longer. I understand the horrible position you were put in. I understand you didn't have much of a choice in it at all. But I want to be free of you." I paused. "I don't need to hate you a moment longer. Because that's your job. To hate yourself for it. To let your own guilt gnaw at you. To have to come to grips with what a kind and good man you took from the realm. Orders or not."

I noticed the tears on Easton's face, but I had to finish this.

"I can't honestly say that I wish to see you again. Being in your presence is painful for me. But I do not wish for you to permanently waste away here either."

His eyes shot to mine, as he seemed to hold his very breath.

"I will speak with Krew about where you can go. What you can do."

"Anything," Easton pleaded. "I will do anything. Please let me help you all. I may have let you all down, but I am still disloyal." I noted his word choice. He had used the term disloyal but nothing about The Six. Krew must have trusted the guards standing outside the door only so far.

He added, "I am still motivated to try to right my wrongs. I don't think that guilt will ever leave me."

"You can never fully right the wrong that took my father," I snapped. "He is gone and can never come back."

Easton closed his eyes. "You are right, Your Grace. But I can help you take down the king. I can help the disloyal in the different townships. I know the princes don't trust me and likely won't again but let me try to atone for this somehow." He paused. "I know that may not be possible and either way I will live with the hurt I have caused, but please let me do something."

"Even if that is not something in Kavan Keep?" I asked.

He nodded. "Even if. I will work with the tensions in Nerede. Or work with the disloyal in Rallis. Whatever you'd like, Your Grace."

He couldn't go to Nerede. Not as long as my mother was there. I would never allow her to cross paths with him. She would never even know what he looked like. I sighed. "I will speak with Krew. That is all I can promise." I paused. "This watered-down forgiveness is the only form I can offer right now. Though I hate that my father is gone, I do not hate *you* any longer. I do understand the impossible circumstances. And no matter how hard I try, I also cannot forget what happened either. I just don't wish for you to rot away in here. I refuse to start my reign as a princess with more cruelty."

I turned to leave, giving Owen a wince of a smile.

"Jor—Your Grace?" Easton asked from behind me.

I turned to look back at him.

"Thank you."

I gave him a tight smile. "Don't thank me yet."

He bowed his head. "No matter if you get me out of here or not, thank you for being the type of person who shows mercy. Even when it is not deserved."

"If you weren't remorseful, you'd already be dead," I admitted. "It's almost harder that you are. It makes the question of what to do with you more difficult."

He shook his head. "I still breathe because of you."

My eyes went back to the fire and how close the bed was moved to it. I couldn't get over how cold it was in this part of the castle. But I also shouldn't care that my father's murderer was cold. "Is it always this cold in here?"

He didn't hesitate. "Yes."

My eyes went to Owen as I spun back to leave. "Remind me to never end up in the mountain."

Owen's voice was thick with emotion as he gestured for me to go first, "You will *never* go near those cells, Jorah."

Easton added from behind us as I stepped out of the room, "Long may she reign." He'd said it at a whisper so soft I wasn't sure we were meant to hear it.

Outside of Easton's room, I felt like my lungs were working easier than they had in weeks. Rather than continue to avoid it and shove it aside, I needed to work through my grief with my father and come to terms with Easton's role in it. So that I could let go of it. While most days I didn't think of Easton, I had every day since having killed that guard.

I could hate what happened when my father died while still giving his murderer a modicum of credit in feeling remorse for what happened.

I could hate the circumstances and not the person. Because at the moment, I had the capacity to violently hate only one person. I was saving and storing it all up for him. The king.

I immediately told Krew down the bond we were on the way back up to his wing, feeling that he was already there. I had skipped lunch to get seeing Easton over with. So I asked Owen to ring for lunch for me as I headed in to find Krew.

He was seated at his usual place around the oval table, a whiskey in front of him.

"Krew?" I asked softly.

He looked up at me, and I saw it looked like he had been crying or close to it.

"What's wrong?"

He gave his head a shake. "Nothing. Absolutely nothing."

I heard the door shut as Owen joined us.

"What happened?" he asked, obviously picking up on the same feeling I had gotten.

"Nothing," Krew repeated as he finished the last of his whiskey.

"Krew," I begged. "What is it?"

"You can feel my emotions, read them," he offered.

My forehead creased. There was a tinge of anger and something like helplessness. But he was also proud. Also . . . adoration. But none of that should have made him like I was seeing before me. I cocked my head. "You feel angry about something. Yet also adore me?"

Krew put the glass down, gripping it loosely. "I was worried about you, so I read your emotions the entire time you were there." He paused. "I felt your dislike. I felt your anger. I felt your grief." Another pause. "And then I felt your compassion. Compassion for a man who was responsible for taking your father from you."

I looked to Owen who looked just as confused as me.

"I have never been more proud to call you my wife. That you felt that much grief, yet still somehow found it in you to worry about him. If it was me, I likely would have already killed him. Or left him." Krew shook his head, his eyes piercing into mine as I felt down the bond exactly how strongly he felt about me. "You are the best of us, Jorah. You. And I am struggling right now not to go rip my father off that throne and place you on it."

My breath caught. "Oh."

"So, I think I am going to disappear," Owen offered as he spun and gave me a knowing look.

As soon as the door clicked shut, I held my hands out in an exaggerated shrug. "It's not as if I offered him total forgiveness. I only offered him what I could."

Krew was shaking his head and then he was there before me. He used his magic to move himself faster, and it was a bit jarring how quickly he could cross a room like that.

"You," he said, wrapping a hand around my neck underneath my hair. "*You* are a queen. And when I fell for you, I was too busy selfishly thinking of my own wants to really see it. It was remiss of me to not see from the very beginning. I think I refused to even consider it for such a long time. And now that I have, I am . . . *hungry* for the throne in a way I haven't ever been. I want it. For you."

I knew exactly how he felt because I felt that way too, but about him. I shook my head. "No. We cannot go there. This is the one dream we don't get to dream, Krew, because it isn't even up to us or our own efforts. And even if it is Keir, we cannot be mad. He will do Wylan well."

"Yes, but you will do Wylan better," Krew argued as he moved in closer.

"We cannot get our hopes stuck on this," I whispered. "It'll be too hard when we watch Keir and Gwen or Keir and Delaney take the throne."

He bowed his head down to brush a kiss on my neck. "Doesn't change the fact that you are a queen." He trailed kisses across my collarbone. "If not of all of Wylan, *mine.*"

It was the middle of the day and I was half starved. There were a thousand things we needed to figure out and do as we made a new plan for taking down his father. But with the odds mounting against us and the clock continuing to tick, I couldn't think of anything I would rather do than steal away these few moments with my dark prince.

CHAPTER 40

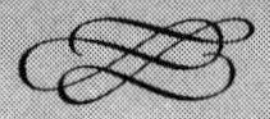

This day would be pure agony.

We were going to Nerede, personally returning Flora and my mother back for a while. Hopefully, it would be the last time she'd have to leave Kavan Keep before making it her permanent home. Not that she was complaining about life in Nerede, I just selfishly wanted her with me.

Theodore had been gone for a week. They would have already held his funeral pyre. I felt guilt for not being there, just as I felt guilt over the need for a funeral to begin with.

But it was time I faced my people. Even if doing so meant I was staring at my failures.

Krew kissed my head as he walked by where I was sliding on my shoes. "Stop fretting, love. They know it was not your fault."

I gave him a defeated shrug. Now if only I could convince myself.

"Do you know what they whisper about most with Theodore's unfortunate passing?" Krew said as he threw on his tailcoat.

"What?"

"They do not mention the fact that all of us tried to prevent it from happening, though that part is in the story that has been whispered around Wylan."

My eyebrows creased as I continued to listen.

"Possibly the only part of the story that is not exaggerated is that you were the one who brought his killer to justice right in front of the king."

"Because I failed!"

"That may be," Krew argued, "but they know more of the story than you'd think. And just because you couldn't save Theodore, doesn't mean you aren't still one of them."

I hadn't realized how much I needed to hear those words until I felt the tears prick my eyes.

He offered me his hand and I took it. We were meeting my mother, Flora, and Owen downstairs where we would walk through the forest together before leaving for Nerede.

It was going to be a tough day, but I was not alone.

We had just taken the first step out into the sunshine and blue skies when I heard a voice from behind me.

"Jorah of Nerede."

What could he possibly want? Krew sent me through the bond.

I spun slowly and bowed as much as was deemed necessary. "Your Grace."

"You are returning your mother to Nerede today?"

My heart thundered in my chest, not because of the question itself but because of what the sunlight at the doorway reflected off of.

A sword.

A sword identical to the one we stole. The one which didn't hold the queen's magic. But that exact sword, the one we'd stolen, was still with Hatcher in Savaryn along with the ring. There was no way this was the same sword, but it looked just like it down to the gem in the center of the royal blue hilt.

Was this our replica, the one which had killed Theodore? Or

did the king have a replacement already made? Our replica had a slightly smaller gem, but I couldn't tell by just glancing at this sword if it was our fake or not.

I swallowed hard and tried to focus. I angled my body between the king and my mother. "Yes. She is returning to check on the bakery and a few things."

The king gave her a nod. "You honor your country with how well you feed them."

My mother gave a little bow but wisely didn't say anything.

I turned toward Krew to take our leave, but the king grabbed my hand and stopped me.

"Do not allow them to let you feel guilt over that thief. It was his own actions, not yours." He brought my hand up gently to brush a kiss upon it. I wanted to rip my hand away, knowing that Krew was going to lose his mind with his father's lips on even just my hand. But it wasn't the kiss that was the reason my breath stilled in my lungs.

As he still held onto my hand, he tapped on my palm from underneath.

Twice.

Just like the disloyal did.

I felt my magic surging to the surface, but I pushed it down and forced my face to look confused. The king just held my hand there after kissing it and looked at me, scanning my face as if trying to see what I would do. Though feeling horror creeping down my spine and into every pore in my body, I continued to force my face into confusion instead. I absolutely could not acknowledge what just happened with anything but confusion.

Krew must have felt a jolt of panic or terror from me because he took a step in and placed his hand at the small of my back.

"Your Majesty?" I feigned the kind of stupidity he preferred, looking at my hand and then to the king's eyes. "Are you quite all right?"

A flicker of surprise crossed his face and then he released my hand. "Be sure to report back to me on the improvements of the contractors."

I gave him a winced smile. "As you wish, Your Grace."

His eyes flicked over to Krew's and then back to mine. "And if you'd like to bring back a disloyal or two, that'd be nice."

"I'll do my best," I promised. Krew and I returning counted as two, right?

We fled down the steps and away from the king's presence as quickly as possible.

He tapped my hand, I sent Krew as I tried to keep walking and standing upright like I wasn't about to lose my mind. *Just like the disloyal.*

Krew's eyes snapped to mine as we headed for the pathway through the forest. *What?*

He knows that's what the disloyal do. He knows.

Krew let out a sigh. *We can't stop at Hatcher's to let them know because with all the extra guards he demanded we take he'd know we made an unplanned stop.*

You're right, but we need to figure out a way to warn everyone. No one is safe. Not a single disloyal.

I believe our timetable just got moved up. We make our move on the throne. Soon.

"WHAT HAS the two of you so skittish?" My mother asked almost halfway through Savaryn.

I sighed. I wasn't sure why we had tried to keep it from her. "The king knows the disloyal secret greeting, it seems. He just did it to me back there."

My mother and Flora's eyes went wide.

"At least he did it before a trip to Nerede. We need to let the disloyal know right away to cease doing it," Krew added. "And Jorah was hoping to visit Beau Jones so that is a great place to start."

For the rest of the trip we chatted. I wanted to focus on the king and how we were going to make our move. I wanted to talk about the new sword he wore on his person.

But today was not about all of that. Today was about getting my mother back to Nerede for her own safety. And apologizing to Beau Jones for the loss of his son. Plans for the king would have to wait until our return trip.

Today was about facing the nightmares the king forced us to live through. Tomorrow we'd figure out a way to deliver one of our own.

As soon as the final wall creaked open, I took a deep breath and closed my eyes.

My mother reached across the carriage and gripped my hand. "You have nothing to be ashamed of. You did not kill Theodore."

Krew had the carriage drive to the stop before the merchant street so that we could go together to see the progress of the new bakery.

We walked the streets, arm in arm as we headed in the direction of the bakery. I knew Krew wanted to see Warrick today too. So I wanted to see the bakery, but also be mindful of our time.

I turned the corner to see the bright gold lettering on the bakery window. "Demir Family Bakery" it told all of Wylan. It had always said that, just now the lettering was larger and seemed a bit louder also.

It wasn't just the Demir bakery, it somehow now had a Valanova touch to it.

I rather preferred the old one, the worn spots in the counters and the stools that were barely more comfortable than standing.

As we walked in, I noted the door didn't yet have a bell. Merchants in Nerede always had bells on their doors. So that if they were busy working, they'd hear they had a customer. But the king's contractors couldn't have known that.

It was beautiful though. The first thing I noticed was my mother had not one large oven, but now two. The white counters were spotless. The glass around the showcase where my mother liked to sell her pastries was shining in the sunlight without a single print on it. It would make my mother's life easier having a new kitchen. I had to keep reminding myself of that as I mourned the kitchen that had such an integral role in raising me. For some reason it felt like this new bakery had removed some of the memories with my father. It was in the same exact space, but entirely different. And I wasn't sure I would have ever been ready to lose even more memories of him. Fancier kitchen or not.

"It's lovely," Flora admitted as she looked around.

"It is," I agreed.

"But also not quite the same?" Krew asked me quietly as he brushed a kiss to my temple.

"Not quite the same," my mother agreed, "but nothing likely will be again. And that's okay." She turned to me and smiled. "More than okay. Particularly if I were to become a grandmother in the near future."

I gasped. "Mother!"

Owen snorted a laugh from behind us.

Krew chuckled. "I think we need to make sure Wylan is safe for a child first, then I am all for it." He stole me a glance that promised all sorts of things.

My mother decided the best way to break in the new bakery was with tea. After fetching the proper supplies, we were laughing at the table before long. It wasn't the same table, and the new one was slightly taller than the old one. Even that felt stuffier. Like we were farther away from each other.

"I mean, I only had the other designers look down their noses at me for three-quarters of the time I was at the castle," Flora laughed.

My mother snickered. "I lost count of the times I heard the phrase, *'Just a baker.'* "

I winced. "I still get rude comments made to me or about me, so it is safe to say, particularly should either or both of you live in the castle someday, you have that to look forward to."

"I rather enjoy being underestimated," Flora commented as she tucked a stray strand of her red hair into her bun. "It is fun to watch people eat their words."

For a seamstress, Flora could be quite brutal sometimes. She took her artform seriously. And I couldn't blame her. They were magnificent.

There was a knock on the backdoor that interrupted our light-hearted chatter.

My mother got to her feet, but Krew put a hand up to stop her. Owen instead walked from his post at the window over to the backdoor.

"It is Mr. Jones," Owen offered as I heard the door creak back open.

"Please let him in," I said, rising to my feet. We had planned on seeing him after our trip to the orphanage anyway.

Owen came around the corner and there he was. Beau Jones. A successful man in Nerede for all intents and purposes. He had always been well put together. But today? Today he looked . . . exhausted. Dark circles looked at home beneath his eyes, and he looked as if he had been pulling at his hair frequently.

He stalled in the doorway. "I just saw the carriage and wanted to stop by to say something." He paused, swallowing, and then his eyes went to mine. "Thank you for trying to help my son." He swallowed hard. "Thank you for taking care of his murderer so that I never even have to consider my revenge."

"I am so sorry," I gasped out. "I—" I shook my head. "It isn't fair. Theodore should still be with us."

"I know. That is also why I have come to ask that you send the other two Nerede men home. Just in case they are considered accomplices by default," Beau pleaded.

"Of course. Of course I will give them that option," Krew nodded. "I am not sure if they will listen after recent events, but I will offer it. And do my best to be persuasive."

Beau gave him a nod of appreciation and turned back to me. "They—" he cut off, his voice cracking. "They say you stayed with him. It was your wedding banquet, yet you stayed with my son." A tear trekked down the old man's cheek. "So that my son wouldn't die alone." He looked to me, his green eyes full of the torment of grief I knew well. "Is that true?"

I nodded, my own tears joining his. "Of course it is true. He was from Nerede. He's family."

Beau gave me a nod as his chin crumpled. "Thank you for that, too. Thank you for staying with him." And then he lowered himself to a knee. "Long may you reign, Our Princess."

I rushed over to him, and went to my own knees, throwing my arms around his neck. He must have been in shock, but then in a moment he put an arm across my back and hugged me back.

"I am so sorry I couldn't save him," I whispered.

His voice whispered back, "Me too, but I am glad that you stayed."

A full minute passed and then my mother's voice asked kindly, "Beau, would you like some tea?"

I removed myself from him and stood, offering a hand up for him. As he stood, Beau's eyes went to each of us in the room. "I do not mean to intrude or dampen the mood. I just wanted to see Jor—Her Highness before they returned back to the castle."

Krew let out a sigh. "Please sit and have some tea, Beau. There is something I need to tell you in regard to the disloyal if you feel up to it."

Beau's brow furrowed. "More bad news?"

Krew gave a nod. "Afraid so." He very quickly explained what had occurred that morning, Beau's eyes going wide with the information.

"I had considered," he began, "giving it all up. The day that Theodore returned home to us, I wanted nothing more to do with the disloyal." He paused. "But I must warn Nerede of this."

I gave him a nod. "None of us are safe anymore."

"My father needs off that throne," Krew said, his voice lathered in determination and promise. "Soon."

* * *

ON THE WALK back to the carriage from the orphanage, I felt lighter. Seeing Warrick, Hattie, and the others had been exactly what I needed. While I understood that some people would see me differently as an Enchanted now, those children immediately understood I was still me, still Jorah.

Flora had gone back to her shop after tea. My mother went with us to the orphanage, and we would drop her off at our cottage before heading back for the castle. It had been a long day for all of us, but one well spent. I hoped it was the last of such trips before my mother became a permanent, but safe, resident of Kavan Keep.

When we reached the carriage, Krew gave the driver some instructions. He wanted to drop off my mother and then drive by the ongoing construction.

Just as he was walking back toward us to help us into the carriage, I felt my magic slither. Having ignored that feeling one too many times, I immediately began scanning the area.

And then I saw it. Ivy Westhaver Arquise. The now widow. She had a tomato in hand from one of the farmer's open-front shops and brought it back like she would chuck it at Krew. She kept watching Krew, her jaw set and her eyes filled with fury.

I watched her, willing her to put it down. I knew she had to be thinking of her husband. How little time they'd had together. And likely blaming Krew, though she knew her husband had been the one to attack first.

I watched for two moments more, and when the tomato finally took to the air, I was ready and immediately stopped it with my magic.

Her eyes went wide in horror as my magic froze the tomato midair.

I was rather protective over my husband, but I knew in this case she was just hurting. It wasn't a murder attempt. She was just mad. So rather than unleash my magic on her like I somewhat felt inclined to do, I instead walked toward her, grabbing the tomato right out the air and handing it to her.

"I believe this is yours?" I held it out for her.

She didn't take it. "I—" For a moment I thought she might find me naïve enough to try to lie her way out of this. Instead, she offered, "My husband is dead because of yours!"

I gave her a pained smile. "I could see how that version of the story is easier for you in your grief, Ivy. But your husband is dead because of a massive misunderstanding. Of which Prince Krewan tried to avoid at all costs."

Other people had stopped what they were doing and froze to watch us.

"And now Theodore too!" she continued while angrily shaking her head.

I sighed. "Yes. Theodore was innocent. Entirely. A horrible situation that I do feel an enormous amount of guilt over. Don't assume I do not."

"And you killed his murderer!"

I cocked my head. "Yes. I don't even remotely regret it. He deserved it."

"Don't you see?!" she said more loudly, almost yelling at me.

"See what?"

"Death follows the two of you." She gestured at the royal carriage. "People wind up dead wherever the two of you go."

All the air left my lungs.

Krew, who had been patiently waiting for me, now ate up the space to be at my side. He grabbed the tomato out of my hand and placed it back in hers. "Ivy, death does not follow us. My father is a cruel man. There is a haze of evil around the crown, so I'll give you that. But I will not allow you, even in your grief, to place blame upon my wife for things she did not do. She did not even have magic for half of the things you speak of. She is not responsible for any of it."

Ivy whispered to him, "You're truly disloyal?"

He gave her a tight smile. "The original founder, yes."

She brought her free hand up to her mouth, the basket around her arm raising. "But that means—"

It meant her husband tried to kill one of his own, another disloyal, and died in the process.

"It means," Krew offered, "your husband was severely misinformed. His actions were brave, the information behind them wrong." He paused. "You may hate me for what happened. I can understand that. But raise your voice to your princess again, and we will have a problem." He spun me back toward the carriage. "Good day, Mrs. Arquise."

We loaded the carriage in a tense silence. I tried not to be too bothered by what Ivy had said. But this was Ivy. We had become better friends the first night at the castle. And then were friendly when I saw her and Jeremy at the Harvest Festival. And now? Now she had just told me that death followed me.

It was hard to ignore that. Worse yet, it was hard to admit she had a point.

"She is just upset, dear," my mother offered as the carriage slowed outside our cottage.

I looked out the window of the carriage, checking to see that her guards from the castle were staying with her. One would be her shadow during the day, another standing guard at night.

"She can be upset at me," Krew snapped, "but I can't stomach her turning it on Jorah."

I sighed. "Well, more death is on the agenda, so she does have a point." My eyes went to Krew's. "But hopefully just one." I looked back to my mother. "I know she is just grieving. Finding herself disappointed and grieving not only the man she had just married, but also her dreams of the life they'd live together."

Krew grabbed my hand and squeezed. "That will not be you, Jorah."

I tried to smile back at him. I knew he couldn't make me any promises. "I hope not."

My mother's eyes were watery. "Please be careful. I know you both feel like you have to take a leading role in the demise of our king, but I wish you didn't have to. I also believe there are forces at work here that none of us understand. I have to believe that those forces will ensure you both see the other side of this. Plus, as we all know, I selfishly want grandchildren."

I had no idea what to say to that.

My mother's lips twitched. "Next trip may I reserve some time to inquire about the grandchild I may possibly already have?"

My jaw fell open. She'd figured out Warrick was Krew's child. I guess I had figured it out too, and she'd seen us at the orphanage on multiple occasions, so of course she'd eventually connect those dots.

Krew put up a sound barrier immediately. "My father killed his mother," he explained. "He is here for his own protection."

She reached a hand across to squeeze our joined hands. "I figured it was something like that. And he may have another grandmother out there somewhere, but knowing your mother is also gone, I promise to love him as my own anyway."

I felt down the bond Krew's shock at her words. He hadn't at all expected that. He took a shaky breath. "Thank you, Eleanor. I—" he shook his head. "Thank you."

She patted our hands. "Now. I don't foresee I'll be sleeping at all until the moment I see the both of you next, alive and well. Hopefully fetching more than just me for life at the castle."

I managed the most ugly and un-princess-like sniff.

That last hug and goodbye nearly killed me. I had no idea what the coming days or weeks would bring, but I hoped it was the last goodbye wrapped up in dangerous implications.

Then again, I had thought the king's reign had been running out for a while now. More than once, I had thought things would come to a head. First the morning I charged into the throne room and again at our wedding banquet.

Some days it just felt like his reign would never run out.

CHAPTER 41

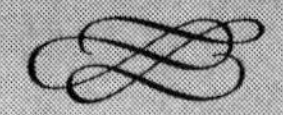

Another parliament session was the last thing I wanted to be doing right now. The Six had a late night meeting the night before to bicker and argue some more about when to make a move on the king. And how. I'd eventually given up and just gone to bed while they continued to theorize.

"Ready, love?" Krew asked as he adjusted his cuff.

I sighed and grabbed for my wrap Silvia had laid out for me if I got too cold. I was not going to forget it this time. The throne room was always cold, in more ways than one.

"No, but yes."

As I reached him, he just stood there smirking.

"What?"

"You're forgetting something," he said gently.

I looked myself over. I had the wrap. I was dressed in a light pink gown somehow fancier than a day dress but not as fancy as a ballgown, the adequate amount of pomp to be the queen's proxy for this parliament session. "What?"

"Your crown." He didn't delay to head to my nightstand where my crown sat in a silver case with royal blue velvet lining.

It wasn't heavy, and often times I forgot it was even on my head, but I also wasn't used to wearing it. I knew I was royalty now, but I wasn't sure I would ever be able to wear a crown as naturally or stoically as Krew did.

He gently placed my crown on my head and then rested his head on mine, crown to crown. "I know these joint parliament sessions in the throne room are not your favorite, but I also want to remind you how powerful it is that you are even posing as the proxy right now. Were it not for you, my father likely would've already caved and given into Savaryn's demand for a tax increase." He inhaled deeply before brushing a quick kiss to my lips. "You are making a difference, love, even now. And you are showing parliament where you stand. That you are not to be shoved around."

I inhaled deeply. "Thank you for reminding me of that. It all just feels so . . . insignificant with everything else going on. I don't want to sit through three hours of this. I want to spend time in the forest healing trees. I want to spend time with you. Arguing about things that will never get passed and do not matter is worthless to Wylan right now."

"I agree, but even just your presence there matters."

I pulled back and smiled. "Okay, My Prince. You have adeptly inspired me for another boring day. Shall we?"

"In a moment." Without warning he pulled me back into him and kissed me.

As he deepened the kiss and trailed his fingers down my back, I conveniently forgot we needed to go anywhere at all. I wasn't sure I even knew my own name I was so focused on his touch and the trail of his fingertips. Dangerous fingertips that could immobilize a man in mere moments with the power of his magic yet were so gentle and potent in the way in which they touched and held me.

The door opened. I heard footsteps clomp in. "Hey," Owen greeted us, amusement on his tone.

Neither of us moved, but we did at least stop kissing.

"We have to leave for parliament. Or were you two planning on skipping today?"

Krew just closed his eyes and rested his head on my forehead.

"Hey," Owen repeated, snapping his fingers twice. "We need to go."

"Can I just use my princess powers and demand he get out?" I asked Krew.

"We are already late enough as is," Owen said exasperatedly.

Krew moved but took my hand in his. "Why didn't you say so?"

I smirked, knowing he hated being late to things.

Owen rolled his eyes. "You two are annoying."

With a giggle from me, we finally left.

Sure enough, we entered in through a side door. I wanted to be embarrassed or feel bad considering we were late only because Krew got a little carried away, but I really wasn't.

As soon as I took my proper proxy throne, the king leaned over, resting his elbow on the arm of his seat closest to me. "You're late."

I smiled at him in faux sweetness. "A man has needs you know."

Krew choked on a laugh, having heard me.

The king rolled his eyes.

It was one of my absolute favorite new things to do in making him uncomfortable. I didn't care how much of a harlot it made me appear. If he was uncomfortable, I was there for it.

Just when I was beginning to feel the exhaustion of the late night before settle in, choosing to speak with Krew through our bond so that I didn't fall asleep in my chair, I heard the name "Brakken" and snapped my attention back to parliament.

Keir cleared his throat. "After Jorah's ability to bring the lake back to life after all this time, I thought it best we reach out to Brakken and see if they have had any change in their Enchantment being stuck. If the disease which decimated their magic was finally weakening there as well."

The king listened but didn't seem unnerved. Likely because he knew it wasn't. And I knew he was to blame for this so-called disease. I didn't have proof. But I knew it. Then again, I had thought I knew in my gut the sword was the object holding the queen's magic, and I had been wrong about that. Was it possible I was wrong about this too?

"And?" Mr. Winston asked.

Keir gave his head a shake. "My correspondent I sent to Brakken has reported back that there has been no change in their magic. But word of our lake finally being healed has spread there. Though a large population of Brakken's Enchanted believe their powers are dead and gone forever, those who had never quite given up are renewed in their hopes."

"Need I remind you," the man I only knew as Martese began, the same elderly parliament member who had stood up to the king, "if Dra Skor comes back into the full power of their own magic, the tension between their country and ours might also be renewed."

The king swatted a hand, the ruby ring on his thumb reflecting the light with the movement. "I understand your concern, Martese, but while the rest of the countries have been struggling to retain their powers, Wylan has been strengthening ours. Because of our efforts to keep the disease from our shores, we have been stronger over the last ten years, and they know that. Not to mention the blow their economy had when the disease hit. They are still recovering from that alone. It would take an act of sheer idiocy on their part to attack us the moment their magic came back. And even if they did, we could handle it."

The next thirty minutes were extremely interesting to me as the parliament members brought up each country in the realm, and the previous tensions within those countries. Brakken and Wylan had the best relationship, which was no surprise to me as Keir had told me as much a while ago. Dra Skor was bigger than

Wylan and by default always the country with which tensions were harshest. Agria kept to themselves and always had. Corsha was a series of volcanic islands to the far east of us and had an ally in Dra Skor for most matters, it seemed. I was intrigued to learn their Enchantment had been visions, specific to their lands so they knew which island was going to erupt and were able to evacuate the people safely.

As someone who had thought magic inherently evil for most of my life, it was yet another example of magic being used to protect and not harm.

I also remembered back when the king had first tried to knock me out to get my blood, how the princes had gotten me out of that card game with the king by some sort of forged letter between Dra Skor and Agria.

It seemed while Krew had taken control of the disloyal hunting within Wylan, Keir had busied himself with foreign affairs.

But there was still so much I didn't know.

What is Dra Skor's Enchantment? I asked Krew.

It has always been kept somewhat hushed yet surrounded by rumors, but it has to do with the unique creatures that roam their land. My father doesn't even like to speak of it.

Was it odd that only made me want to visit?

Do the other countries have bonds? I asked. I assumed Dra Skor wouldn't if their magic was in their creatures and not their people, unless a creature and human could bond, kind of like the connection I had with Rafe.

Yes. Though the ceremonies themselves differ from country to country, the sentiment is the same. Blood to blood exchange of power which must be consensual.

So what happens if someone from two different countries bond?

It is very rare, Krew explained. *People rarely marry or have a friendship strong enough to consider bonding with someone else when they live in different countries. But in some rare cases, the pair takes on a weaker version of each other's Enchantments, in others the stronger magic is rooted in both.*

Why isn't more of this common knowledge? I feel like I barely even knew of the other countries names before now.

Because my father likes to believe Wylan's magic is superior to the rest of the forms of Enchantments. So why even take the time to learn about the other cultures?

Oh how I loathe him.

"Dra Skor has done a better job of keeping the lines of communication open recently," a parliament member argued. "Perhaps it is in our best interest to begin to repair our relationships with the other countries."

The king gave an indifferent shrug. "Dra Skor has always manipulated the other countries to bend to their will. I will not barter with those bullies or their pets."

"What about Agria?" Someone else asked. "Or Corsha?"

The king cocked his head. "Fine."

"And Her Highness's vote?" Mr. Winston asked.

The king turned his head to me and gave me a nod.

All of this enraged me. Absolutely enraged me. I thought of the pain Krew felt when the gauntlets were on him, how it felt to have his magic suffocated. And some countries still didn't have their powers back? How many lives had the king ruined when he poisoned the other countries? "Of course we should reach out and begin mending our relationships with the others."

"I will send my correspondents with letters," Keir said with a nod. "Often times the letters are not received well and are rarely responded to, but maybe news of our lake being healed will be cause enough for them to listen."

"They are just jealous we were able to keep the disease out of Wylan and they were not," the king declared.

"Or perhaps they are suspicious," I offered quietly to the king.

Be careful, Krew snapped.

"Of what?" the king asked me from around a hand resting on his chin.

Content with the decision to send correspondence to Agria and Corsha, parliament switched topics to the construction of the rather ostentatious Savaryn mansions. My absolute favorite topic of these sessions.

"Jorah," the king whispered.

I looked to him and then back to the discussion like I was paying attention. I made sure my voice stayed quiet. "Perhaps they are suspicious of the fact that all the other countries, who were once powerful in their own right, have been severely crippled by this so-called disease while Wylan has not suffered much. A lake and forest turned black, but no power was lost."

The king's eyebrows went up as he now fully turned toward me. "Are you trying to imply that it was not a disease?"

My eyes went to his. "Aren't diseases a *poison* to the body after all?"

His eyes widened quickly. "So you think that *I* would have had the wherewithal to create this poison? Effectively weakening the other countries and avoiding a war? While strengthening the magic within our own borders and causing Wylan to thrive? That would be quite the scheme. Quite the scheme indeed."

My eyes were on his as I said, "There is nothing I don't think you are capable of, Your Majesty."

We both knew I didn't mean it as a compliment.

His lips twitched for only a moment. "Your theory flatters me."

I rolled my eyes. "As if your ego needed it."

The king chuckled.

Of course he hadn't denied nor confirmed my suspicions. But the way he had smirked when I explained it told me everything I needed to know. He was responsible. I didn't know how deep his efforts ran, but I knew he was partly to blame for the disease.

The doors creaked open and in came George, the busboy, with two guards.

I feared he was in trouble, and we were in for Theodore round two, so I allowed my magic to run along my skin's surface as soon as I saw him.

"What is the meaning of this?" the king snapped. "These sessions are long enough without interruptions."

The guard bowed low. "We apologize, Your Majesty, but we thought you'd want to hear this. He was trying to sneak into the balcony to get Her Highness's attention."

The king nodded and gestured for them to continue as my magic immediately increased. If George was brave enough to try to get to me, something was wrong. Though no bruises or marks graced his body, I noticed how out of breath he looked. Like he had ran here.

The guard shoved George ahead. But he wasn't looking at the king, he was only looking at me. "The forest. She burns."

CHAPTER 42

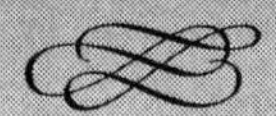

If looks could kill, I'd have his still beating heart in my palm. My eyes had gone directly from George to the king. A fire in the forest? There was only one Enchanted in the realm who loved to terrorize with fire. The king.

Though I didn't remember standing, everyone was, Krew's hand at the small of my back. A few parliament members moved toward the large windows. A guard moved to open one of the huge windows, and that was when I realized it was more of a door than a window. A door which opened, but with no balcony. An elaborately designed waist-high metal barrier was there to prevent anyone from just walking off the door to their death.

"He's right," someone gasped.

"Looks to be in the direction of the lake."

I couldn't seem to take my eyes off the king. He looked back at me with a cruel tilt to his lips. "Do you blame this on me as well?"

"Yes."

He took a step forward and lowered his voice to a whisper. "Imagine, my dear Princess, if I really were to blame for all that you presume." He was watching me intensely, as if waiting to feed off my fear.

My entire skin was now slithering with silver, and I was certain I was glowing brighter than the rather ostentatious chandelier thirty feet above me. I felt no fear, only the weight of my rage. "Yes. *Imagine.*"

I felt Krew's magic burning through the bond. He was going to tear his father limb from limb. And I wasn't about to stop him, but first we had a fire to put out.

A wolf howling in the distance was the only thing that snapped my attention from the king.

People were crowding around the open window, all trying to watch the fire.

"Everyone stay put," the king barked. "No parliament member leaves."

I wasn't a parliament member though.

"Move," I commanded with a voice I had never used in this room before. A voice that demanded response. The voice of a royal.

With only a glance at Owen to let him know what I was doing, I took off, sprinting for the open window. As soon as I hit the window, I gripped the metal of the barrier and launched myself over it.

I used my magic to slide me to the courtyard ground, the silver beneath me sending a tingling sensation through the fancy heels at my feet.

Once I hit the ground, I was running. I could have used my magic to get me there faster but judging by the smell in the air and the amount of smoke I saw billowing out of my beloved forest, I was going to need to save my magic. The forest was not just on fire, the entire forest was burning. Also I didn't want to fall on my arse in front of parliament and the king.

I heard a loud thump and felt Krew catch up to me in seconds.

A second thump. Owen was on my left side.

And then a third. I turned to look over my shoulder to find Keir had also joined us.

The four of us sprinted across the meadow and into the forest. We did not need to say words, we all knew from that night in Nerede exactly what needed to be done.

A few parliament members followed, Krew sent me. *Knowing it is going against my father's direct orders.*

Good. We might need them, I sent back.

"Make sure you keep using your magic to keep the smoke away from you," Owen yelled at me.

The last time around, I hadn't any magic of my own to help. But I was not just a helpless little Nerede girl anymore. Krew had made sure of that.

"Jorah, where are you heading first?" Keir yelled as the smoke thickened.

I gave the only answer there was. "The wolves."

"You and Krew get the wolves." He gestured toward Owen. "We've got the lake."

And just like that we split, two branches of Enchanted barreling into the forest, hoping against all odds, we'd be able to save it. I knew this was another test or game from the king. I knew it in my soul, but now was not the time to consider what. Now was the time to channel all of my focus into wielding my magic.

Krew began sending small bursts of magic out to push the smoke back at the fire. In one such case, the smoke was so thick, the fire couldn't breathe and immediately went out.

There was no magic barrier protecting the fire to contain it, but the king wouldn't have needed to use one with how dry the mostly dead forest was. The thicker the trees became, the more disorienting it became. Thick black smoke was billowing everywhere as the fire appeared to be in multiple directions.

With smoke coming in at all sides, I felt like the entire mountain was on fire. And I was hot. My magic was humming beneath my skin, yes, but it was more than that. My feet getting air out from under my gown were the coolest part of me while my chest and arms were sweltering hot.

The forest was so dry even the smallest of fires had made an inferno.

I would have loved to have changed or grabbed even a different pair of shoes for running through the forest, but there hadn't been time. And going barefoot with how hot it was, not to mention all the leaves and rocks, was a bad idea. So I was going to have to tough it out in my heels. But thankfully they were the short heels and not the tall ones.

Through the haze, I thought I was hallucinating when I saw a shape take form. It was black, but running along the ground, not billowing upward. I altered my course to run for the wolf.

We were now in towards the middle of the forest, and there were no trails, but we continued to run and use our magic to clear a way. My silver magic looked wavy in the heat coming from the flames. I could see the flames in the distance, but barely through the smoke. While I knew the smoke came from the flames themselves, it felt like smoke was consuming the forest, not the flames.

"Shadow," I coughed as I finally found him.

Krew was beside me, coughing as well.

My eyes and lungs were burning. The good thing about the forest being abandoned from most animals was that all we had to worry about was the wolves, keeping it away from the stables, and then putting out the forest. But it was so dry, if we weren't careful it'd take the forest and the castle right along with it.

Come to think of it, I wasn't entirely opposed to that idea were there not innocent people in the castle.

Shadow looked toward me and then back behind him.

"Take me to them, buddy," I said as I grabbed my knees. "We will help."

Like he understood entirely, he led the way. It took only a few minutes before the smoke was so thick, I really began to worry. The wolves would have tried to run for safety from the flames, but with smoke this thick and coming in from every direction, I had no idea how they kept breathing.

Soon we entered a portion of the forest that didn't feel as hot but was impossible to see. I suspected we were in the direction of their den, but I had no idea because I could barely see Shadow before me.

Finally, I resorted to putting one hand on Shadow's back as he guided us and then used my other hand to clear the way with my magic so we could see farther than a foot in front of us. While I did that, Krew was actively blowing as much smoke away from us as he could.

Just when I thought we were going to get trapped weaving through the trees and rocks forever, I saw some other forms within the smoke. It was the rest of the pack. Rafe was standing there among them on high alert as he circled around his pack. What I could only hope was all of them.

"They tried to run from the fire," Krew said as he looked both directions. "Then met another fire."

"How many fires did that prick light?" I asked as I fought off the urge to cough again. I didn't want to cough because it felt like then I got even more of the smoke into my lungs.

"I think multiple, but with how dry it is, it wouldn't have taken much," Krew said, his voice strained.

We needed to get them out of here. Now. And then we could use our joined magic to take out as much of the fires as we could. "I'm putting a moving dome around them," I offered. "I'll make sure the fire and smoke can't touch us, but it'll take a lot of focus."

Knowing how much magic it would take for that, Krew gave me a nod and I understood he would use his magic to combine with mine.

I let the magic out of my fingertips as it reached for all the wolves. Then I imagined a breeze taking all the smoke away from my protective barrier. It took so much magic and effort just to clear the air of the dome that Krew's navy magic had to wrap around mine to accomplish it. But once it did, and we all started to feel the effect of it, the wolves seemed to jerk to life. It was an odd sensation standing in a dome free of smoke but being able to smell it and see it all around you. Even if the smoke wasn't still actively burning my lungs, it was burning my nostrils and had already invaded my lungs.

"Let's move," I said to Krew and the wolves both.

It was slow work; I had to keep a constant stream of magic coming out of my fingertips and keep my focus on the dome at all times or whisps of smoke blew in. I also added my magic beneath us, imagining walking on frost bitten grass. I didn't want the wolves' paws to get burnt where we had to walk. While Krew and I at least had shoes on, they did not.

Once we entered what I assumed was the middle of the forest, it got worse. I had to move one foot at a time and felt sweat run from the back of my neck down my spine. I wasn't sure if it was from the heat of the fire or the exertion of using that much magic. Either way, we were crawling through a burning forest.

At one point the bright orange and white flames nipped at the edges of my dome, but I sent another surge of energy into my magic and the fire just hissed at us.

Rafe and Shadow moved to walk on either side of me, just as they did every morning when we ran our trail. Every so often Rafe would press his nose into the backs of my legs. I wasn't sure if it was his form of encouragement or if he wanted me to hurry. Either way, I appreciated his concern.

What felt like hours later, we made it into view of the meadow.

Refusing to let the dome fall, I waited until all of us were on the brown meadow grass before I released my barrier. The parliament members who had come to our aid stood at the edges of the meadow and were sending blasts of magic into the fire that had now made it to the northern most meadow border. On one half of the meadow stood Enchanted using their magic to put out the flames and push away the smoke, and on the other, the kitchen staff had used some of the garden hoses and were spraying everything down.

As the barrier fell and the parliament members saw that I had just brought an entire pack of wolves to safety, many took a step back, scared at the sight of the wolves.

Rafe and the others walked toward the castle, right up to the back hedge. Rafe and Shadow stood guard, while the rest laid down to wait in safety.

"Now what, love?" Krew asked me gently, brushing a kiss to my forehead.

"Now we breathe," I said, taking in pulls of air that seemed to singe my lungs. The air was so acrid I felt like my lungs were burning from the inside out. "And then we attack the fires."

Krew called over a few parliament members who were there, one being Hatcher. We formed a line of five of us and we started at the side closest to the castle itself and started walking north, a human wall as we pushed the fire and smoke away from the far edges of the meadow.

Much later, we finally made it to the lake, where Owen and Keir had saved the trees I had healed and were frantically working in multiple directions to keep the lake from burning to a crisp. The lake that was still fortunately clear.

For some reason with the odd happenings in this forest, I had wondered if I wouldn't return to find it blackened again.

"Where," a parliament member panted, "is the king?"

No one answered because we all knew where he was. Where he

always was. Basking upon his throne. Creating messes for the rest of us to clean up.

On and on it went. Just when we got one portion of the forest under control, another would flare up and tear through an entire section of trees before we could get to it.

Some of the guards from the barracks on the other side of the forest, over by the stables, were helping from that side. Working together, we finally got the smoke all flowing in one direction, which helped things immensely.

"How are you feeling?" Krew called to me as I threw out my magic on some flames and then tugged on the strands of magic, effectively suffocating the flames on the spot.

Honesty was always best. "Pissed off."

"I meant your magic," Krew called. "We have most of the fires out. The guards can finish pushing it the rest of the way. Why don't you take a break?"

The parliament members had long since switched, most pushing themselves to the brink of exhaustion and only stopping when the trickle of blood started running down their noses. But when one Enchanted left, another would step in, working together to continue pushing the fire away. I wasn't sure how many Enchanted had seen the smoke and came running from Savaryn, but there were dozens of Enchanted working to help us.

I threw my magic on a row of trees, blanketing them in silver as I put out the fire. "Why don't *you* take a break?"

"Ready when you are, love," Krew grinned, throwing a blast of his magic over where I had been working, our magic combining midair, his powerful added breeze pushing the smoke away.

As I took another step forward onto crispy ground, I decided I had never been more in love with his man.

Finally, we met up with the crew working the opposite side of the fire. We pushed and pushed, and just when I felt that dull pounding in my head which was a tell of burnout settling in, Krew sent out a large blast of magic, and the last of the flames flickered out.

There was a moment of eerie silence as we all took in the fact that we finally had the fires out. And then came the cheers. It started with the Enchanted next to us, as we all hugged and clapped each other on the back.

"The horses?" I asked one, imagining the horror of the stalls on fire.

"Are fine, never got the barns, Your Highness," the man said with a tired smile. "We made sure of it."

"Thank goodness," I sighed. I wrapped my arms around Krew's waist and clung to his side while he continued thanking people by name.

And then once we finally settled down, we heard the cheers coming from the direction of the meadow.

Bone tired, Krew, Owen, Keir, and I headed back toward the meadow. The forest had always been black, but now it was burnt to a crisp. It was going to take me weeks, if not months to begin to repair this damage.

Just before we reached the meadow, I felt my first tear fall. I was too tired to bother with a sound barrier. "Why?" I gasped out. "Why would he do this?"

Keir shook his head. "Some sort of test, but a horrible one. The entire castle could have gone up in flames."

I looked down at myself. There was soot and ash everywhere. My light pink dress was torn in places, and even had small holes in it here and there. My heels were covered in ash, and the tops of my feet were black where they had not been covered with my shoes. I was a wreck. Remembering the crown still on my head, I reached up to feel it, and found as my hand came back black, it also had ash and soot clinging to it. It would likely take the royal jeweler a week to get it cleaned.

After the longest trip back to the meadow, we finally saw the people all waiting there. As soon as they saw us, they started clapping again despite all being tired in their own rights.

I smiled. We were all tired. It'd taken all of us, and we hadn't saved all of the forest, but we had done what we could. And it wasn't even dinner time, but the haze leftover from the fires made it feel like it was later than it truly was.

"Thank you," I said as loudly as my hoarse voice would carry. "Thank you."

"Long may she reign," one of the staff called as he continued clapping.

My shoulders tensed as I spun in his direction. Everyone seemed to go silent, waiting for what I would do.

And I was just too exhausted to mince words. "This night was not about your sovereigns," I began, "it was simply about doing the right thing. It was my honor to fight alongside you all. Thank you." My voice cracked. "Thank you for doing what you could to save the forest I have worked—" I had to stop to swallow. Krew's hand at my back felt like it was the only thing holding me upright. "I have worked so hard to heal," I finished.

As I made it back to where we'd left the wolves, Rafe and Shadow still standing to protect the others, the baby wolves started yipping as if feeling restless.

"I know, guys," I offered. "But I'm so glad you made it out of there."

They'd been so entirely close to getting suffocated with smoke. I would never forget this day, the image of those wolves trapped in smoke likely staying with me forever.

Rafe let out a single, loud howl that made every hair on my arms stand up. And then he laid down before me.

Like the night of our wedding, the others followed suit.

Was this their way of thanking me?

Krew leaned into whisper in my ear, "I suppose you can be their queen too."

By the time we made it up to Krew's wing, we tried to eat something, changed out of our destroyed clothes, quickly showered the stench off of us, and fell into bed. Tomorrow we would process this evil. For now, the wolves and as much of the forest as we could save were saved. For now, our magic and our souls needed rest.

* * *

I WOKE from a deep sleep to my magic blinding me in the darkness. It was too soon. I was shot after fighting the fires. My magic needed to recoup, not wake me in the middle of the night. But I had been dreaming about the fire, being trapped within so much smoke, never able to blow enough of it away.

I took a deep breath to remind me my lungs were finally free of the smoke and rolled over. I looked out the windows, realizing the curtains were drawn but from what I could see around them, it was still night. Or very early morning.

I put my hand on Krew's back and snuggled back into the covers. One of the scars on his back was thicker than the rest, and that was always the one I tended to reach for to trail my fingers along. I was just about back asleep when I heard a weird clank of a noise.

I listened, trying to figure out what I was hearing. Worried about flare ups, some of the Enchanted had agreed to keep watch over the forest for the night. I must have been hearing the commotion of all the people still in the meadow below us.

I snuggled into Krew, wrapping the sheets tighter around my nightgown. I was so exhausted I couldn't even think straight.

Minutes later, I jolted awake to a louder clanking noise followed by another shortly after. My left arm was glowing brightly. While my right was cold. I tried to move it away from the cold, but the cold moved with it. Barely. I couldn't move my arm.

I sat upright and saw the dark outlines of multiple men in the darkness.

And my arm wasn't just cold, there was a gauntlet on it.

CHAPTER 43

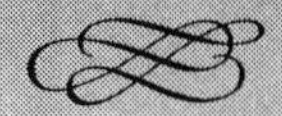

I immediately sent magic out of my free hand at the men I saw, two grunting as they smashed into one another and the wall. I turned my attention back to the gauntlet, and that was when out of nowhere, another man slammed into me, pinning my shoulders to the bed. I thought my left shoulder was going to tear off entirely, and my other shoulder was already bearing a heavy weight, making it extremely hard to move at all. Another gauntlet was slammed around my free hand, effectively cutting off my magic.

I thought or foolishly hoped for the briefest of moments that since I was immune to another Enchanted's magic, maybe I would be immune to the gauntlets too. But as my magic was flaring with no outlet, no way out to help me, I realized I was not. The gauntlets worked on my magic just like any other Enchanted. The gauntlets themselves weren't magic, they just restricted it.

I looked to my left to see around numerous dark shapes that Krew had also woken, and already had one arm in a gauntlet as well. I felt his panic mirroring my own, as he noticed I was already wearing two gauntlets. It was still so dark the only light in the entire room was the navy magic sprawling across Krew's left side, my legs glowing a bright silver, and flashes of the Enchanted's magic before us as they struggled to contain us. While only a few men were needed to get the gauntlets on me, even more were needed for Krew. It felt like there was an entire army of men in the room with us.

I tried to move my fingertips, trying to send my magic out to help his by habit before realizing I couldn't do a thing. Tearing my eyes away from Krew to look down at myself, I saw the skin at my shoulders and chest was glowing brightly, and my legs were glowing, but just after my shoulders, my magic faded, and my skin was clear. Even just pulling myself up to sit under the weight of the gauntlets was excruciating.

Seeing me wrestle under the weight of the gauntlets, I felt Krew's immediate rage.

Krew tossed three men at a wall before I had time to blink. As I tried to move my legs under me to get off the bed, I felt a prick of cold steel at my neck. Another Enchanted snapped his fingers and an orange hue lightened the room like a torch hovering at the man's finger.

"Move, and I cut her," the voice threatened.

I begged through our bond, *Don't listen to him. You're stronger than he is even in one gauntlet.*

Krew pulled his magic to the surface of his skin, his shirtless chest glowing more on the side without the gauntlet than the one with it, but then the man pressed the dagger into my skin. A small bead of blood ran down the length of my neck and onto my chest.

Krew hesitated as he saw it, and in that brief moment another two men attacked out of the darkness. Grunts and groans filled the space and I couldn't see what was happening on the other side of the bed, but I knew when I felt Krew's wince of pain they were successful in getting the second gauntlet on him.

"Let's go, Your Highnesses," the man with the dagger at my throat said.

I'm sure Father is just wanting to scold us and teach us a lesson, Krew sent me. *Try to stay calm, love. Stay calm and we will talk ourselves out of whatever this is. Keir or Owen will save us.* He paused. *But I will kill the man who made you bleed.*

Through the bond I felt the intensity behind his words. They were not mere words, or even a promise, they were a resolute truth.

My magic was there, my anger only increasing it. And yet there was no outlet. No way I could use it to get us out of this. It was one thing to be helpless and not understand the level of helplessness you found yourself in. It was another entirely to have a powerful well of magic within you, a way to save yourself, and no possible way to use it.

The king's guards attached a chain to my gauntlets, another to Krew's, and without delay, started walking us toward the door. I felt a flicker of hope. Krew always had two-night guards outside his door. They would come to our defense.

But as the door swung open, there were two bodies slumped in pools of blood. One was Romero. Krew and I had both really liked Romero.

I closed my eyes. They were dead. These men had killed them first. When I had first woken and heard a noise I presumed to have come from the meadow, it was actually these men being murdered. I had been right there in Krew's wing and hadn't trusted my magic. I could've helped. I should have woken Krew and then we both could have done something rather than just sleep while they were murdered right outside our door. But I had just gone right back to sleep and not bothered to do a thing.

No part of this is your fault, Krew reminded me.

I should have known.

We were both on the brink of burnout last night. Krew and I exchanged a glance in the hallway light. *And now we know what the fire was for.*

To wear us out?

Exactly, love. Be ready for anything.

This day. I knew in my gut *this* was the day we had all been dreading and striving for. This was the day we would take down the king or die trying. And starting it off in gauntlets didn't exactly bode well for us.

I love you, I sent him.

And I love you. Just try to stay calm, okay?

How can I when these things are so damn heavy?

I was not at all surprised to find we were being delivered to the throne room. To keep calm, I listened to the chain clanking against my gauntlets as I counted the guards. There were eleven guards delivering the two of us to the king. The bald one to my left was the one with the key to the gauntlets, as I saw the same type of large key I had taken off the king.

As we continued downward, of course having to take the stairs under the weight of the gauntlets, I searched around every corner and turn, looking for the staff. I didn't know what they could do, other than warn the others. By the time we made it down the stairs, my legs were burning, and my shoulders ached. Were it not for the man with the chain pulling on the gauntlets before me, I was sure I would have fallen down the stairs.

Not finding people as we continued for the throne room, I also looked out the windows for light. Owen hadn't been on duty yet, so it was still night. But when morning came, he'd find us gone, the guards murdered, and he'd grab The Six and Keir to come to our rescue. Keir might even sense something was wrong with Krew's magic again, just like he did the night of our bonding. All the help we needed was right here within the castle walls.

We had to stall. We only had to distract the king long enough for the sun to come up.

The tall throne doors opened slowly.

My fear multiplied when I saw Keir already in the throne room with four more guards. As I glanced again at the faces of all these guards charged with putting the gauntlets on us and bringing us before the king, I knew that none of them had helped us with the fire the night before. They likely hadn't been allowed to. Because of this.

Keir looked at us and I could see his rage in both his magic burning along his bare chest and torso, and also in the look he gave us. He likely thought the king's guards wouldn't have been able to overpower the both of us.

But he'd been wrong.

The men holding our chains brought us forward so we were all standing in a line twenty feet from the dais. Krew on my left, Keir on my right. I was in my favorite light pink nightgown, both of them were barefoot and shirtless, wearing only the pants they had slept in.

I kept my eyes on the guard who held the keys as he moved forward to the left of the dais.

"Good morning," the king sneered from where he lazily sat on his throne.

"Coward," Keir spat.

The king just switched his attention from Krew and me to his other son. "Mmm?"

Keir was furious, his neck muscles tensing as he spoke. "You slapped gauntlets on us and pulled us from our beds in the middle of the night."

The king gave a noncommittal shrug. "Got the job done, did it not?"

Keir's eyes stayed on his father. "You are a *coward*."

The king stood slowly and took a deep breath. "I have ruled for far longer than you've been alive, son."

"We cleaned up another one of your messes and now we are

being punished for it," Keir seethed.

"*You,*" the king snapped. "The two of *you* have been creating far more messes than I."

My stomach dropped. He knew the princes were disloyal. My magic was burning and pulsing. There was no way out of this. None other than to stall, but my magic felt like it would burn me from the inside out if I didn't use it soon. And yet, I couldn't.

The king continued, "And as a ruler I can appreciate the initiative of creating a plan to get the throne out from under me, hell I even half expected it." He paused, his face going red with his anger. The guards were all silent. "But I did not expect to learn the leaders of the disloyal movement were my own gods damned sons!"

Neither Krew nor Keir bothered to try to deny it.

"You could have lit the entire castle on fire," Keir argued, his magic also fighting to be freed.

"He knew we'd save it, Keir," I offered, trying to get him to calm down. If the goal here was to stall, Keir needed to pace himself. "He just needed us weak."

The king nodded toward me. "She gets it. She figured out far more than most too."

"So you admit you poisoned the other countries?" Krew asked, his voice ragged. "*You* were the disease?"

"Wylan is now the strongest country in the realm," the king explained slowly. "I don't think you realize the sacrifices that have had to occur to ensure that. At one point, war was imminent."

"Sacrifices like our mother's magic? *Our mother's life?*" Keir snapped. "You took her magic. And it killed her bit by bit."

The king didn't deny it. "Your mother had to willingly siphon the magic."

"So you forced her into it," Krew bit out.

The king pulled out the new sword on his belt from its sheath.

I gasped. It wasn't a new sword at all. With his hand on the hilt, there was purple magic wrapping along the blade and into his hand. His own magic was surging along the surface of his skin, begging to be used.

The king stayed on the dais and walked to be in front of Keir before turning to walk in front of Krew. "You were so close. So close. Yet you forgot that you were not the only one who could create a fake."

I inhaled sharply. "So it was the sword."

He gave me a nod. "You weren't wrong. You just didn't steal the correct sword."

"So let me get this right," Keir began, "we stole the wrong sword. You used the fire to weaken us enough to put these damned gauntlets on us, and now you are just going to kill all three of us, thus leaving the superior Wylan you've worked so hard to build without an heir?"

The king now strode down the dais to our level.

My eyes frantically went to the tall windows. This was all happening too fast. We needed to stall. We needed more time.

"My sons have been consorting with the disloyal. Helping the disloyal. That sort of treachery will not be allowed."

Realization dawned on me. He wasn't going to kill the heirs. He was going to kill me. To punish them.

"You will only make me a martyr," I offered at a whisper as Krew's magic went into overdrive next to me. "The disloyal movement will not end with my death, in fact it will strengthen it."

The king stopped to look at me. "I do not intend to kill you, Jorah of Nerede." His eyes flicked to Krew and then to Keir. I stilled as the king strode directly for me. "But in all your scheming and planning, half of which even made me proud at times, the two of you forgot one very simple detail."

My magic was now pounding with every beat of my heart. We weren't going to be able to stall our way out of this. My eyes went to those damned keys on the guard that remained to the left of us. If only we could get ourselves free, we'd have a chance.

Despite my recoil backwards, the king grabbed me from around the neck. He still had the sword in his left hand, but it was just out of reach. Not to mention with the gauntlets on my hands, it was not as if I could make a grab for it. But I could possibly kick it out of his hand if I waited for the right moment.

The king kept his hand at my neck as he leaned over me. He looked directly into my eyes as he said, "I can always make more heirs."

I snorted a laugh of disgust. I couldn't help it.

"You laugh?" the king asked.

I grinned. "Nara is not Enchanted. At your core, you are all about your need for power. So yeah, make more heirs with Nara. They will not be as strong as Keir and Krew and you know it. You'll leave Wylan vulnerable yet again."

The evil grin that slowly crossed the king's face made my magic pulse. "Why would I need Nara when I have one of the most powerful Enchanted in Wylan within reach?"

Krew had to be restrained by multiple guards.

I felt his anger and mine multiplying together.

"It's the bond. He's threatened by your bond," Keir said to me. "He wants your bond gone."

It all slid into place in my head. The threat about making more heirs. His promise not to kill *me*. Krew and I being a threat to the world the king had worked so hard to create, in which he was the most powerful Enchanted in the realm.

The king wasn't going to kill me, but he *was* going to kill Krew.

I cocked my head and stayed still as hatred flowed through every inch of me, vibrating with my rage and my magic I couldn't use. "You are going to kill Krew." I clenched my jaw tightly. "Say it. *Say it.* You are going to kill your own son. Your own flesh and blood."

The king moved in even closer, so our eyes were inches apart. "I am."

"I will never become bonded to you. I will never willingly give you even a drop of my magic," I told him.

The king moved his hand to trail a finger down my neck to my collarbone. "Your being a willing participant is not a requirement, darling."

I had never hated him more. And I couldn't use my magic despite my skin glowing and pulsing with every beat of my heart, but I sure as hell was not about to just stand there and watch him murder my husband either. I couldn't fight like the powerful Enchanted I was, the gauntlets had made sure of that. But that didn't mean I couldn't fight at all. I wasn't just an Enchanted princess, I was a Nerede princess.

So I leaned in, just to be sure I was close enough. The king stalled, likely in confusion over why I was leaning in. His eyes dipped to my nightgown at my cleavage just as I had hoped, and that was when I spit, right into his face.

The king jerked back, stunned, but then started groaning in pain. He brought his hand not holding the sword to his cheek and eye, and then backhanded me across the face with it.

With the weight of the gauntlets and weight of the blow, I fell to the ground, but the guard holding the chains to my gauntlets jerked me back to my feet. The pain of the iron slicing into my skin at my forearms made me gasp.

But I noticed the silver magic on the king's face, in the process of apparently scalding him. I hadn't just used my spit, I'd used magic. And though my tears had been known to carry magic, they'd really only healed things.

I'd just used my magic. Where else could I use my magic from? I was under the impression the Enchanted had to use and wield their magic with their hands. But there was plenty of magic glowing and at my disposal. I just had to figure out how to send it out of my body without my hands. It was easier to use my tears or spit as those were closely tied to my emotions. But if I focused hard enough, was it even possible to send it out of my body a different way?

The king gestured to the guards to bring Krew forward to the dais.

Instinct moved me forward also, but the guards moved in to stop me. Keir was also struggling but getting nowhere.

The king stood sideways next to his throne, facing Krew, who was brought forward and shoved to his knees before the king as he faced the windows.

As I spun, trying to jerk free of the guards, I noticed how my bare feet were entirely lit up with my magic, ready and willing to help. I slammed my eyes shut.

Please work. Please work. Please work.

I stomped down hard, willing my magic to get the guards away from me, willing it to find a way to leave my body somewhere other than my hands. To find a way out and help us out of this situation which was becoming more dire by the moment.

Though it took far more energy than using my hands, so much so I already felt slightly dizzy, my silver magic rippled across the ground. Keir and I both, along with our guards, were knocked to the ground.

I quickly got up and saw the king raising his sword toward Krew. "Don't worry, my son. I will be sure to take care of your wife."

Krew was glowing as brightly as I was, and I saw him close his eyes.

I love you, Jorah.

I didn't respond because I couldn't do this. I couldn't watch this. I couldn't lose him like this.

I wouldn't.

I sprinted forward.

I was going to be too late. The gauntlets were slowing me down. And though if I focused hard enough, I could apparently release magic from my feet, I couldn't take the time or risk the chance that I'd knock myself to the ground again. Not when my whole world was tearing at the seams.

So I ran.

CHAPTER 44

I threw up my gauntlets just as the king brought the sword down diagonally on Krew. The side of the sword slammed into my gauntlets, and I was thrown backwards, hitting the ground hard. Purple magic shook the ground and raced up the sides of the wall, followed by a trail of silver.

The queen's magic. And my own?

My ears were ringing, my shoulder blades sharp with pain, but I slowly brought myself up to sitting. The blast had knocked everyone to the ground. The king had been thrown backwards into one of the windows as shattered glass now sprinkled the ground. And all over him. His crown was rolling along the ground away from his body. In the power of the blast, the silver throne itself had even toppled over backward, laying crooked and on its side.

I reached for Krew next to me and that was when I realized my hand was free. My fingers were reaching for Krew, not the gauntlets.

My gauntlets had shattered in the blast and lay before me open at my feet. I was free.

I was free.

Before the king got back to his feet, I quickly moved, my eyes immediately going to the bald guard on the ground who had the keys.

Ears still ringing, I reached out with a hand, sending my magic to retrieve those keys and bring them to me.

The guard, who was just starting to come to, was pulled along with the keys before the ring holding the keys snapped, and then in a blink of a moment they were in my hands.

Krew was sitting up next to me, his eyes on mine as I jammed the key into the gauntlet on his wrist and freed the first one.

The king groaned and rolled to his side. I still felt dizzy and out of sorts from the blast, but I had to hurry. I had to get Krew free so we could combine our magic and take down the king.

Get Keir free, Krew told me. *I'll deal with my father. We'll need Keir for all the guards in the room.*

The second gauntlet opened with a click.

One of the guards next to Krew made a move for him as we both stood up. Krew used his magic to fetch the man's own dagger from its sheath and as soon as it reached his hand, slammed the dagger into the guard's chest.

It'd been the man who made me bleed. And I knew through the bond that Krew had absolutely no regret about it.

The resolute truth of a promise made into fact.

Krew's entire body was pulsing with navy magic now, ready to use at his disposal. I'd never seen him that lit up with his magic before, and that was saying something.

Krew was not just furious, his rage was absolutely unre-strainable.

My own body was no longer glowing, as I had apparently used a large blast of magic in getting the gauntlets off. But I was already moving, heading for Keir as fast as I could before all the extra

Enchanted in the room got their bearings. I didn't run straight or as quickly as I wanted, but I got there.

The guards near him were trying to stand, but I sent a blast of my magic at those three guards, focused on their hands and pinning them to their sides, wrapping my magic around them and forming a gauntlet of my own. It took a constant stream of magic from one hand, while I jammed the keys into one of Keir's gauntlets.

My eyes were on Keir's as the first one slid open.

He grabbed my hand and stopped me. "The sword," he whispered. "Where is the sword? It amplifies his magic."

One hand free, I left the key with Keir as I stood and began looking around for the sword.

"Afraid of a fair fight, Father?" Krew asked as he stood between Keir and me and the king.

I saw both Krew's magic and the king's were covering their skin. The first blast of black magic rattled the floor and sent me backward into Keir, who was now free and caught me.

The other guards in the room were coming around, closing in on Keir and me. I was still immobilizing the three guards I'd needed to get past to get to Keir, but we were vastly outnumbered. Keeping focused enough to find the sword, immobilize the guards, and also know when Krew needed me to send my magic to help his was going to be difficult.

It was chaos. Utter chaos. But the good news was that in this exact moment, the king did not have the sword on his person. The playing field was level. For the first time in years.

When a guard advanced on me, Keir and I both reacted, our magic combining as Keir's magic wrapped around the guard like rope.

I paused. Though I had often combined magic with Keir, Krew's magic had always been present too. But our magic had just combined without Krew's. Likely because of both our bonds with Krew?

Keir gestured with his head toward the throne, snapping me out of my thoughts. "I'll handle them. Go."

Magic of a variety of colors began being tossed about the room. Only a few steps away, I heard a wolf's howl just before the throne room doors burst open. In ran Maurice, Jakob, George, and Tilly. They had armed themselves with the largest kitchen knives they could find and had brought help. In the form of two wolves. Rafe and Shadow.

And just behind them was Owen. His shoulders were at an awkward angle as if he'd already had a skirmish of his own, and he couldn't move as quickly as they were, but he'd still found us.

Of course they'd come.

They immediately moved in to attack the guards while Krew and the king continued to fight, strong bursts of black and navy magic coming from everywhere.

Knowing that Krew, Keir, and I hadn't even had a full night for our magic to recoup, we needed to find the queen's sword and end this. As quickly as possible.

"What do you need, Tiny?" Maurice called as he headed in my direction.

"The queen's sword," I admitted quietly as I poured more magic out of my hands and toward a guard who was now moving toward us, blasting him toward the wall and wrapping him in what looked like silver vines.

Keir's magic combined with mine. He must have wanted to make sure that guard stayed down a while.

Shadow charged into motion, heading for another guard aiming for the kitchen staff. It was safe to say that one would be staying put.

The remaining guards were now using their magic, fighting Keir and trying to get to me.

Up past the toppled throne, I saw a glint of silver. The sword was up there. I didn't want to use my magic to bring it to me in case the king still didn't know where it was. So I used my magic to slide me to it faster.

But then I was forced backward to avoid a throne flying at my head. The king had used the same chair I sat in for parliament sessions and chucked it at me. I jumped aside and froze the chair. I was caught by Keir again, though he had only one free hand to catch me with this time, the other busy wreaking havoc on the guards.

Sensing that Krew was going to need my help, I willed my magic out of my fingertips and started to combine my magic with his. I also put a small silver dome around Krew as he faced his father. Just an extra level of protection. I knew the king could shatter it, but it still made me feel better all the same. If I had to go after the sword and not physically touch Krew right now, I had to do something.

Krew and the king were sending a constant stream of magic into the air, but everywhere black magic was thrown, navy magic wrapped in silver met and stopped it.

I was still slowly making my way toward the sword, trying to help Keir attack the guards with one hand, while sending a steady stream towards Krew with the other.

I was finally in view and was about to step up onto the dais when my magic pulsed. I turned, only to find the shattered glass from the window wrapped in black and barreling toward me. Not only was the king's power strong, but it was so quick there was barely time to think of how to protect myself.

With only a split second to spare, I put up a shield of my magic to stop it, dropping to the ground to duck under it. But the distraction had cost us, I lost my hold on a few guards.

With pure chaos continuing to rain down around us, Rafe and

Maurice had inched around the perimeter of the room and beat me to the sword.

Maurice didn't hesitate to pick it up and head in my direction.

Keir and Krew now had their backs to each other. While Krew focused on the king, Keir, Owen, and the kitchen staff fought off the king's guards. Or the ones still alive anyway, as there were at least two bodies on the ground not moving.

The guard I'd knocked away from Maurice had stood and Shadow was growling and closing in on him. I had no idea what happened to the first guard Shadow had cornered.

As I noticed my dome around Krew had shattered, I also saw the king had been slowly moving in the direction of the sword also. But it was too late. Maurice already had it. He reached out to hand it to me, but then suddenly Maurice was jerked away, encased in black magic.

Like he was a mere object and not a huge man, the king started moving Maurice in the direction of the wall.

I threw my magic out to try to get him back, but the king's magic pressed against mine, and then mine shattered as if it were nothing. A simple firework in the air.

Maurice was suspended in the air, arm still extended to give me the sword, but out of reach to do so.

I sent more of my magic out to help, but it was met with black magic and stopped in its tracks.

In one swift move, the king threw Maurice at the wall, dropping him headfirst onto the ground. I willed more magic to the wall, trying to catch him. Trying to get Maurice turned so he wouldn't land headfirst.

It was too late. The king's magic was just too fast. My breath caught as I heard an awful crunching noise. Maurice's neck laid at an awkward angle facing the wall.

"Learned that little trick from you, Jorah," the king called out to me.

I screamed. I ran for Maurice but was stopped when random objects wrapped in black began attacking me.

We were weak enough from the fires the night before that the king was still stronger than we were, even without the queen's sword in hand. Even with a level playing field.

Though I had lost my focus when the king had thrown Maurice at the wall, I inhaled deeply and sent more magic toward Krew, strengthening his. Our combined magic was going to be the only way it seemed. And I was torn between wanting to be able to touch Krew to protect him from the king's power and wanting to get to the sword before the king did.

The king was fighting both of us and began walking sideways to where Maurice laid, moving for the sword.

If he got to the sword first, we were all as good as dead.

We were finally free of the gauntlets, and we still weren't strong enough to keep the king from that damned sword. I felt burnout creeping in, but I ignored it and poured my magic into Krew's as it lashed and attacked the black magic swarming from the king.

Just when the king bent down to pick up the sword, a gray blur charged out of nowhere.

Rafe.

The king's magic dropped entirely for a moment as he cried out in pain. Rafe latched onto his arm.

I need one more big push of magic, love, Krew sent me. *Now.*

The pause was enough of a distraction to the king for Krew's magic to reach him and waste no time in beginning to encase him in navy and silver, starting with the hand Rafe hadn't attacked. I directed both hands and everything I had at Krew's magic, strengthening it. Imagining cement as strong as the castle walls immobilizing the king. Immobilizing his cruelty.

The king winced as Krew's magic hit his skin and shook Rafe

off his arm. Black magic delivered Rafe to the same wall he'd thrown Maurice at.

There was a crunch as Rafe hit the wall, followed by a yelp when a dagger wrapped in black magic sunk deep into his fur. I knew that sound would haunt me for the rest of my days. Green magic immediately sent the dagger flying back at the now restrained king, and he grunted when it stuck into his leg.

Meanwhile, I had already sent magic out to catch Rafe as he fell, a thin streak of blood smearing the wall as he slowly and softly landed into my cushion of silver.

Tears fell down my face as I felt a trickle of blood flow from my nose, but I refused to shut my magic down. While the king still breathed, I would keep sending it until I was either unconscious or it was gone. I needed to get to Rafe to see if I could heal him, but I couldn't move while I concentrated on sending more magic at the king with Krew. Not when we finally had the chance to end this.

Our magic wrapped around and around, tightening our hold on the king. His second hand now covered, he couldn't move, so he couldn't get toward the sword either.

I heard an odd rattle of a noise and then Keir was there. His magic added to our own, surrounding it as he walked over to his father and slammed a gauntlet down onto one of the king's arms.

I staggered a step, burnout now crawling throughout my skin, but refused to stop sending magic to help the princes. Even just the king having only the use of one hand helped the pressure we felt working against our magic.

The second gauntlet slammed shut. The king's hands were immobile. And though he could try to use magic elsewhere like I had, he was currently encased up to the neck in our joined magic. Short of spitting his magic out like I had, he was stuck.

"Love," Krew said gently. "That's enough."

I dropped my hands, wiping at my nose, and staggered toward the sword which now lay next to the knocked over throne.

My eyes went to Maurice's eerily still body and Rafe. The king's guards now all contained, Owen had made it over to Maurice and was checking for a pulse.

He looked at me and gave a slow shake to his head.

I tipped my head back to the ceiling and let out a scream of fury.

Looking back to Rafe, I saw him put his front paw toward me but whined, the pain too great. I feared he was paralyzed from the impact his body had made with the wall. His back legs were oddly angled and still behind him.

I leaned over and lifted the sword. As soon as I grabbed the royal blue handle, I felt the buzz and burn of the queen's magic. And when I brought my thumb over the gem setting centered in the hilt, I felt it pulse. As I stood back up, I took in our surroundings. The kitchen staff, Owen, and Keir had taken care of the guards. The ones still breathing were being held in blue or green magic. Meanwhile the king himself was currently encased in navy, blue, and silver magic, wearing gauntlets, and on his knees.

I slowly turned toward Krew. We had the sword. We had the king on his knees. This was as good as over.

Blood still trailing out of my nose and down my face, I looked to the king, never feeling more hatred toward a person than I did at that moment.

"Love?" Krew asked.

I could do it. I could drive the queen's sword right into the king's chest this very moment. Owen had taught me a chest blow was too difficult to be efficient. But I could drive it right down his neck at his collar bone. I could do it now and end this.

But I couldn't.

Not yet.

I held up a finger with my free hand. "One moment."

I staggered over to Rafe where he laid and put the sword on the ground next to me. The queen's magic was in that sword, but I didn't know how to use it to amplify my own. Did it only work with the king's magic because they were bonded? I had no idea how to tap into the queen's power and I was desperately running out of time.

"Really? The wolf?" the king bit out.

Krew's magic still pouring out of his hands tightened further, a tendril of navy magic wrapping around and squeezing the king's neck. The king stopped talking.

I put my hands on Rafe and thought of all the healing I had done in the forest. How I wanted Rafe running through the forest, healthy and alive. That I wanted every bone in his body healed, I wanted him to not just survive, but truly *live.* I called my magic forward, but I had only whisps of magic left. And though the magic I could send immediately wrapped around his body, I knew it wasn't going to be enough.

I didn't have enough magic left. And the queen's power was right there beside me at my knees, yet I didn't know *how* to use it. All I could feel while holding the sword was the buzz of power. I didn't even need the queen's power in this moment, I just needed more of my own.

I cried out in agony and tried again. I slammed my eyes shut and thought of healing Rafe. How I only needed enough magic to heal him.

Rafe took a shuddered breath beneath me. He was bleeding and dying before me, and I had nothing left to help him with. I could only sit here and watch it all happen.

I willed more magic into Rafe, but only one small strand left my fingertips.

"No!" I sobbed, running my fingers through his fur. This could not be happening. Not again. Rafe had sacrificed himself, and that distraction had been the thing to throw the king's focus enough to help us stop him. I had the ability to heal Rafe, but I was out of magic.

I heard footsteps next to me. Owen did something with his hands and then he was there, offering his bloodied palm out to me.

I kept my hands on Rafe's shuddering body. "What?"

"Take my magic," Owen offered. "It'll strengthen your own. It's worth a shot. We don't have the time to figure out the sword."

I took my eyes off Rafe to look at Owen. He had wanted to become kin bonded to Krew, not me. "I—"

"Jorah, there isn't time. He's dying." Owen moved, reaching over to take and slice my hand. He pushed his into mine. He didn't hesitate to say the words. "I willingly give you this magic, Jorah Collette Demir Valanova. To protect, to empower, to honor. A thousand lifetimes may pass, yet I will stand steady, bound with you."

Tears poured out of my eyes as I choked out, "I willingly receive this magic, Owen Raikes. To protect, to empower, to honor. A thousand lifetimes may pass, yet I will stand steady, bound with you."

I felt the tingle where our blood met, and then a sizzle of sting as magic poured into my body. Since I was already Enchanted, there was no settling in time, it was immediate.

Rafe's breath made a gurgling noise.

Owen didn't move his hand from mine. "Try again. Hurry."

With a shaking breath, I called my magic up and into Rafe without delay.

I winced, worried nothing would be there, but there was. Silver magic poured out of my fingertips and into Rafe. It was working. Owen had given me some of his magic, but in doing so, he'd made my own stronger.

With my right palm still in Owen's, I sunk the fingertips of my left hand into Rafe's fur and along his skin. I took a deep breath and willed more magic into him, willed him to be healed. Willed him to somehow be okay. I pictured him running through the forest at my side, healthy and alive.

My tears were falling onto his fur too, but now they had a silver tint to them, when just a moment before they hadn't.

As my tears and magic wrapped around the wolf, Krew's magic joined mine, trying to further strengthen it. I didn't even know if that would work for healing, but I was grateful he tried.

Owen sent some of his too. And then Keir also.

There in the middle of taking down the king, we fought like hell together to save a wolf. A wolf who'd sacrificed everything to help us do the impossible.

At first nothing happened. I thought maybe we were too late yet again. Rafe was gone. But he took one breath, the wet rattling absent. Then another clear breath. And another.

I gasped and kept pouring magic into him. I didn't stop until he opened his eyes to look at me and then I threw my arms around him.

We'd done it. We'd saved Rafe.

I moved to hug Owen just as hard.

He slowly helped me to my feet, handing me the queen's sword and giving me a nod.

I spun back toward the king, knowing that although Krew still had magic left, he and Keir also couldn't keep their hold on their father forever. The gauntlets weren't enough. It was time to end this.

I slowly walked toward Krew. Owen's magic had given me the energy to get through this, though I still felt the blood on my face and now also coming out of my ears.

I pulled up to a stop before the king. This man who had promised just this morning to kill his own son.

Wylan deserved so much better.

Krew deserved so much better.

I deserved so much better.

I looked to Krew and held the sword out at arm's level. My shoulders still hurt from the weight of the gauntlets.

Krew took the sword from me and brushed a kiss against my temple.

"Would you do the honors?" I asked quietly.

"I am your father!" the king boomed from under the weight of two different hues of blue magic. "I am your king!"

I wiped at my nose. "If you have to remind others of either of those, it means you are adept at neither."

Krew turned toward his father, his magic still pouring from one hand to keep the king on his knees, even as he held his mother's magic in the sword. "My son will never know you," Krew promised as he strode forward. "And the entire realm is better off without you."

"You have no son," the king bit out.

Of course he'd argue up until the very end.

"Don't I?" Krew asked.

The king's brow furrowed.

Krew brought the sword above his head, both hands on the hilt. "Your reign has run out." And he drove the sword down, the exact spot Owen had trained me to hit, between the collar bone and the neck. He sliced through the king's body, then brought his mother's sword back out.

Blood spilled from the king's body as he fell to the side with the blow.

Krew's magic fell, and I noticed he too had blood at his nose.

Unable to take my eyes from the king, I saw he was dead immediately. It'd been a far swifter death than he deserved. I was somehow expecting all his dark magic to fly out of his body, but it didn't. One moment he was alive, the next he was simply gone.

Silence blanketed the throne room as we all stayed put. Shadow broke it a few beats later when he sent up a howl which made me shiver. Rafe responded with one of his own. Out the broken glass of the window, I heard another howl in the distance.

Keir's boots crunched on the broken glass as he walked over to where the king's crown still sat on the ground and picked it up, loosely holding it in his fingers as he made his way back over to Krew.

And there on the dais in front of a toppled throne stood two princes. One with a bloodied sword in his hand. One with their father's crown in his. They stood side by side, victorious.

They'd saved Wylan. For all of us.

Owen was the first one to take a knee, and one by one everyone else in the room, including the guards, did too. Wylan had a new king.

King Theon Valanova was no more.

CHAPTER 45

As the sun painted the sky with the first rays of golden morning light, I stood before the pyre and felt nothing other than relief. The king was dead. Finally.

It had been two days since that fateful morning. I'd collapsed shortly after the king died, exhaustion taking over as soon as the adrenaline wore off. I'd slept for an entire day.

The princes had asked for the papers from the king's safe to be brought forth immediately. The ones where they would finally, after twenty-six years, learn who was born first and would be taking over the throne.

But getting into the safe had turned out to be quite the chore. Even in his death, Theon Valanova couldn't make things easy for his sons.

Nara, meanwhile, was removed from the king's wing, and taken to a much smaller room, much like the ones we had when we first arrived at the castle. She was being given time to mourn before she would eventually be going back to Rallis. Though it wouldn't be as grand as castle life, the princes would make sure she lived comfortably there.

Yesterday, we had taken Maurice's body back to Rallis and stayed for the lighting of his pyre. It was a sad affair, and I wasn't sure how to wrap my head around the fact that such a vibrantly loud man could really be gone.

He'd given his life to make sure we took down the king. We'd all risked everything that morning. And Maurice was gone because of it. I'd shed hundreds of tears before Maurice's pyre yet found not a single one left for the former king.

"Let this stand as a fresh start in Wylan," Keir began as he stood in front of the pyre. His voice didn't waver or shake. Krew was to the right of him, and I was to the right of Krew, tucked under his arm. Numerous Savaryn families and parliament members were present, so this wasn't a speech to remember the king, but rather a message the princes were ready to send. As if word of their killing their own father hadn't already sent message enough. "There is no mourning. This is simply the end of tyranny in Wylan. The beginning of a new era."

Krew added, "The greatest thing my father ever did for Wylan was freeing it with his death. Though we still do not know which of us will become king, neither my brother nor I wish to rule in the same manner. My father wasn't always as cruel in his early reign, but toward the end of it he let his thirst for power turn him into a traitor of his own country. Let this lighted pyre serve as a reminder. That we will not tolerate tyranny, in any form."

Keir took back over. "And that we will always work to right the wrongs of our father. There is no honor in this death. Only the comfort in the dawn of a new reign." He paused. "For Wylan. Justice served, may we now restore her to a healthy, thriving country. Greater than any of her kings, long may Wylan prosper."

Someone handed Keir the lit torch, and he wasted no time leaning down to light the pyre.

As the flames soon danced, my only thoughts were of good riddance. This man who had failed so spectacularly at being king was finally gone. He'd likely poisoned the entire realm in his pursuit to make Wylan strongest. In his pursuit to make *himself* strongest. His greed and poison had ruined the lives of so many people. And his cruelty had been the root cause of many deaths.

And though there was immense relief I felt in his absence, it was exhausting to think of the mess Theon had left behind that Keir, Krew, and I would have to work to correct.

There were ongoing trials being held for the guards present when the king had tried to kill Krew. Most were finding that Krew and Keir had no empathy for their having just followed orders. Furthermore, the Savaryn families who had been chummy with the king were about to find themselves enemies of the princes, for no other reason than their closeness to the former king. We still didn't even know who the new king was, and things were already different.

And yet, the princes found themselves grieving their father. This man who was the only father they'd known and had repeatedly failed them on that front. Though the king's death was a cause for celebration throughout Wylan, they would still grieve. For the man that could have been, but never was.

I knew both princes were angry. Angry their father couldn't have been a better man. Angry that death had been the only way for them to reach their father and save their country. Save themselves.

I knew their father's demise had also brought up memories of their mother, reviving the grief they felt for her death too, knowing that the king was responsible for taking away the parent who had loved them well. The parent who had ruled well.

There was a long road ahead of us in healing both the land and each other. Theon Valanova was gone, but his legacy of fear and manipulation couldn't be erased in a few days.

Then there was Warrick. Krew was waiting to see if he was the king or not, as that would set the tone for how Warrick would be introduced to the kingdom. He was already working on choosing the guards for Warrick's security and having discussions with The Six on when the announcement should be made. Warrick was still a rightful heir to Wylan after all, if his father was king or not.

A lot was happening, but we would charge ahead into the light together. And no matter which brother would reign, I knew Wylan was in better hands.

A new reign was coming.

* * *

THE NEXT MORNING was the first time I felt my magic was finally recouped. I wasn't ready to go running through the forest yet, but I was getting there. I'd barely used it the previous day, other than to make sure it was still there.

"I hope you know," Owen began, "that even if you become queen, our training sessions are not yet complete."

I rolled my eyes as we walked for the trees. It seemed odd that a man with his arm in a sling would be talking about training.

And I hadn't seen Shadow or Rafe since the morning they'd ran into the throne room to help us. Rafe had saved the entire country when he attacked the king and prevented him from getting that sword.

"I'm not sure you'll have time to do that," I laughed. If Krew and I took the throne, we were absolutely making Owen and the rest of The Six our advisors. If not, I knew Owen would likely go back to working with Krew. "Besides your at least six weeks of recovery with your collarbone, your days of having to babysit me are numbered."

Owen leaned over to put the food scraps in the dish with his free arm. "Like Krew trusts anyone other than me. Finding my replacement will take a while."

"Good point."

We just turned back in the direction of the meadow when I felt the wolves.

Owen must have too, because he turned back to look, his magic slightly aglow as if he'd called it forward just in case it was something else.

But in seeing that flash of green, I realized I had also felt it. Like I felt when Krew used his magic. I closed my eyes and focused. A tether, much like I had with Krew but different, was there. And though using my bond with Krew was normal and natural, I hadn't thought much of my bond with Owen. I knew I was soul bound with Krew and kin bound with Owen, but I hadn't thought much about the strength of those bonds because I had simply assumed my bond with Krew would be more powerful.

In my mind, I felt for the bond with Krew. Krew was in our wing, about to have a meeting with The Six. But then I felt the other. Not as strongly, but it was there. I likely hadn't noticed it until now because Owen was always so close in proximity to me. Or maybe it was because my magic had been all but depleted just a few days ago.

While my tether to Krew felt warm and exciting, almost a buzz of anticipation, this new one felt entirely different. It felt only protective instead. In place of the excitement of my bond with Krew, I found there was a push and pull, an almost stinging feel to my bond with Owen. I had no siblings, but I imagined if I did, how I felt about them would feel just like this.

I grabbed ahold of that new tether. *Owen?*

"What?" he asked out loud.

Smiling I added, *I wasn't talking to you out loud.*

"What?"

I opened my eyes to find him standing there with his mouth ajar.

Apparently, I can talk to you like this too.

"What?!" Owen's eyes tried to leave his head entirely and I had

to bite down a laugh. "How?" He shook his head. "But why? We aren't soul bound?"

"No. Our bond doesn't feel the same as my bond to Krew. But that doesn't mean it isn't strong. It's definitely there."

"I—"

"I didn't think to even try it until now." I paused. "And what is your middle name anyway? I didn't even know it to say during the bonding."

Owen snorted. "It's Gerald. My dad's name. Well, except he has always gone by Gerry."

I couldn't help but smile. "Owen Gerald. It fits you."

A crunch of a twig close to us drew our attention away. It was Shadow, standing there, looking at us.

"Hey, Shadow," I smiled as he came close enough to sniff my hand. "Don't worry, buddy, we will be back to running the forest soon. I have lots of trees to heal. We'll be back."

Rafe came from around a tree and marched right over to me, not hesitating at all.

I ran my hand along the fur on his back. His back that was healed, carried by his legs that were moving perfectly with every step he took. "I am so happy you're okay, Rafe."

He pressed his head into my palm.

"I told myself I wouldn't say this, but," Owen began.

I smiled at Rafe before looking at Owen. "This ought to be good."

"I know I'm biased, but I really hope the queen of the forest becomes the queen of us all."

Tears stung my eyes, but I refused to let them fall. "Dammit, I'm trying not to get my hopes up, Owen."

He threw his free arm around my shoulders. "I know, but we're both doing a poor job of it."

The wolves went for the food, so we turned back to walk the meadow. "I want it to be us," I whispered. "And I know that's selfish, all things considered. The king is finally gone. That's all that really matters."

"It's okay to want it," Owen stated. "It's not like you'll kill Keir if he takes the throne. You guys aren't Theon."

I sighed. "No, we are not. But Krew would make an excellent king."

"He would," Owen agreed. "And soon enough you'll know one way or the other so you can stop torturing yourself with knowing what you want and not knowing what will become of it. Once you know, you can move forward, disappointed in your wants or realized in them."

It's too early in the morning for your inspirational speeches.

He squinted at me. "All right, you have to teach me how to do that."

I tipped my head back to laugh. "I'd rather not yet. Once you and Krew are both in my head, it might get a little crowded."

"At least I can't hear him flirt with you. I see that enough in real time."

Laughing, we headed back to the castle. The castle that for the first time felt safe. Like *home.*

* * *

IT HAD TAKEN days to get the king's safe open. The royal sages and Enchanted had to work together in figuring out how to get into the damn thing.

In the end, it hadn't been any amount of magic which had opened it. It'd been a disloyal from Rallis who had a penchant for lock picking. It was a twisted sort of satisfaction I gained watching a Rallis ruffian opening the king's safe.

But we now had the papers in hand to find out who the next king of Wylan would be. Both princes had agreed to wait to open the papers until the next morning. We had all agreed that all walls would be opened and everyone in the kingdom free to come to Kavan Keep for the announcement of the next king of Wylan.

So tomorrow morning, the new king would finally be announced. To us and to the country at the same time.

"You do not have to decide tonight, brother, who your queen will be," Krew said as he took a drink of his favored whiskey as we finished planning the announcement the next morning.

Keir's eyebrows went up as he looked to me and then to Krew.

"You can continue your Assemblage for as long as you'd like," Krew explained. "There is no need to rush it. You control your Assemblage. Our deceased father can no longer interfere. Take your time. Wylan can wait."

The same sage who had married us was also in this meeting and piped in, "By law, you can extend your Assemblage as long as you want, king or not. Your father was already king when his Assemblage began."

Keir rubbed a hand across his forehead. "I've barely even spoken with either woman in the past few days. There's been . . . a lot going on."

"There always is in an exchange of power, even a peaceful one," the other sage in our meeting, River Galloway, added. This man with a white beard and glasses was one of the few royal sages the princes trusted.

We had a long road ahead of us of weeding out who we could and couldn't trust in this castle.

"I think I know what is best anyway," Keir said with a sigh.

I pitied Keir and this decision while at the same time wishing selfishly Molly could still be at his side. "The best for you or the best for Wylan?"

His eyes were on mine as he said, "Both."

"Well think on it," Krew offered. "There is no reason to rush into a decision tonight just because of what the morning might bring."

Keir gave him a smirk. "Can we get back to our mother's sword and what we are going to do with it?"

"There's also another . . . *complication* we need to discuss," I offered, my eyes going to John, the sage who'd married us.

He gave me a look. "Which is?"

I looked to Krew and smiled. "I recently found out Owen and I can speak telepathically. We are only kin bonded. Yet I can speak to him like I speak to Krew."

John's eyes went wide. "Oh."

I'm still a little disappointed we can't all talk though, Krew sent me down our bond.

I'm not. The two of you would drive me to madness. You two can find someone else's brain to torment with your schemes.

My eyes flew to Owen as I added, *Don't you start with me, Owen Gerald.*

Owen just grinned.

Krew snorted a laugh next to me as I turned to John. "Have any of you ever heard of this before? Do we chalk this up to my Iron Will or what?"

The other sage shook his head. "No. The bonding has always been about the strength of the relationships. I have heard of other kin bondings being that strong, though none recently. Then again, it hasn't always been safe to broadcast a strong bond pairing."

"It is incredibly rare to have one such bonding, two is . . . ." John shook his head, unable to find a word to describe it.

"You had a strong relationship with Officer Raikes before bonding though, yes?" River asked.

I nodded as I looked to where Owen stood leaning against the wall. "Of course. He is the closest thing I have to a brother."

"Which she means in only an abundance of adoration," Owen added. "And for the record, though I specifically willed her enough magic to save both herself and the wolf, I'm not sure any of my magic is gone. I seemed to have retained most of it just like with Krew."

John put up a hand and turned to me. "Odd though. In both, the extenuating circumstances of your soul bonding and your kin bonding, we know more than a drop of magic was willed to you. And more than that, in both instances, done so with the purest of motives. That combined with the strength of these relationships makes this more believable." He paused. "It is still my belief that the pure motives of Prince Krewan are the reason why he retained all but a few drops of his magic to begin with. There has to be something in the motives behind these bondings. And I suspect neither of you will ever fully recoup these last drops of magic either. Think of it like a small payment over time rather than a large sum."

River nodded his agreement. "Though please do not go randomly bonding yourself to others just to check us on these theories."

John cocked his head. "We have found numerous texts previously thought to be gone in the safe of the king's. As if I wasn't already itching to get my hands on those texts, I will be sure to take a look through there and see if anything is to be found about either Iron Will or multiple bonds."

"So does that bring us back to the sword?" Krew asked.

We were both exhausted. Between recouping our magic and all the seven hundred thousand things that needed to be done since removing his father from power, we'd barely had a moment to ourselves that wasn't spent sleeping to help our magic recoup faster.

"Is there a way to free the magic from the sword?" Keir asked them. "A reversal of however he managed to get her magic into it in the first place?"

The head sage shook his head. "Not that I know of. And the king killed everyone who helped him in that endeavor, so we unfortunately cannot ask them. Again, maybe there is something within those books that have been locked away for decades, but we do not know at this time." He paused. "And there is the very real possibility that we will never know what exactly your father did to get your mother to siphon that magic over, how it was done. How it was successful." Another pause. "It might even be best for the realm for us to never know. I still firmly suspect when the queen willed her magic into that sword, she also willed that it would never be used to harm either of her sons."

Which helped explain why the queen's magic had seemed to explode from the sword and shatter my gauntlets. But again, there were parts to this story that we would never have all the answers to. Forces at play greater than any of us.

As for keeping the information we had learned from others, I didn't know about withholding information at all anymore. Theon had remained in power as long as he had by changing information and selecting what knowledge he shared. I wasn't about to wish to siphon another's magic, but maybe if we knew how it was done, we could learn how to undo it. Or make sure others never did.

Keir leaned back in his seat. "So we just lock the sword up, then? There have been whispers about the sword and half of Wylan already believes the theory that it was the queen's magic who helped free Jorah from the gauntlets."

"Someone will eventually try to steal it," Krew added. "It is a miracle a greedy Savaryn loyal to my father hasn't already."

Just like it had occurred any time the sword was brought up the past few days, my eyes darted to the window and the forest.

I had the odd feeling the sword should go to the forest. Not to be destroyed necessarily, but to keep it . . . *safe*. And I was absolutely certain that made me deranged. I thought highly of the forest, of course, but with the queen's sword? How did that even make sense?

"Locking it up while we research what to do with it seems the only solution," River explained. "That doesn't mean it will be locked up forever, but it is likely the best temporary option."

A shiver raced down my back as I looked out the window.

"Love?" Krew asked. "What is it?"

"It's nothing," I muttered to him.

"I disagree," he said as his eyes met mine. "What's on your mind?"

I took a deep breath. "I know this makes me sound absolutely mad, but I keep having this thought that it should go in the forest."

"Well, that's one way to hide it," Keir offered.

"But it's less of me thinking that the forest is a safe place, and more of . . ."

Krew squeezed my hand underneath the table. "Go on."

I pinched my nose, not believing I was truly saying this out loud. "More of me thinking that the forest wants it?"

The sages exchanged a look.

"Again, I know how that sounds."

John shook his head. "No. The rules of that forest have always been . . . *odd*. There is a deep magic there. A magic that doesn't abide by the rules of our realm. But rather the rules of . . ."

"Of what?" I asked, holding my breath as I waited for his answer.

John's eyes were directly looking into mine as he said. "Justice."

I felt another shiver.

River rubbed a hand across his beard, like I was learning he did when deep in thought. "The forest went black around the same time we believe, with your recent input, the king poisoned the other countries. It worked in his favor to say the disease affected Wylan too, so the other countries believed our innocence. It helped the king in that endeavor, but it always irked him to no end that it was dead."

My mouth fell open. "So the forest was punishing him?"

"Or letting him know it knew what he'd done," River finished. "The greedier Theon got, the darker the forest became."

My breath caught. "Wow." I didn't know how I felt about the forest being that . . . *sentient.* Here I'd just wanted to see it alive and healthy. I didn't consider how alive it could really be if healthy.

"I'm curious now," John offered. "If we take it into the forest, what would happen?"

Krew looked at me as he said, "There's only one way to find out."

CHAPTER 46

Naturally, we had to do this in the dead of night. But Keir and Krew insisted this was the best time as no one else would be in the forest, so we'd all taken the secret stairwell down.

"Think it'll heal the forest?" Owen whispered to me as we neared the meadow, making me jump.

I smacked his good arm for scaring me. "No. I don't think it'll be that easy. Nothing with this forest ever is." I paused. "Though maybe I should stop talking about it like that out loud. It seems to know far more than I ever gave it credit for."

As if it had heard me, a cool breeze slowly trailed across our faces.

I stilled, my eyes going to Owen's.

He gave me an exaggerated nod. "That was . . . normal. Entirely normal."

Krew laughed. "I told Jorah from the beginning that her healing this forest had more to do with her will and less to do with her blood."

"Hmm," John said from behind us. "Pure motives yet again."

He had a point. I'd never wanted anything from the forest other than to help it. To see it healthy. Much like I'd wanted for Wylan, really. Until recently, I hadn't cared who ruled Wylan as long as it wasn't Theon.

I naturally led us to the lake. I didn't know why. I just felt like it was the center of the forest, though it really wasn't. It was just the center of my experiences with the forest.

"Now what? We chuck it in the lake?" Keir asked as he held the sheathed sword out.

"No!" River exclaimed. "That would be careless. Anyone could just happen across it. Particularly now that the lake is clear."

"We could bury it in some sort of locked box," Krew offered. "It would keep it safe and hidden both."

While listening to them debate and taking in the moon reflecting off the lake, I caught out of the corner of my eye some leaves blowing in the breeze. But instead of just blowing one direction, the leaves blew in a circular motion right along the ground.

A cold shiver traveled down my back and arms. I looked up at the moon and back again, the full moon casting just enough light for me to see it. "I have to be losing my mind."

"I think in all actuality, you lost it a long time ago, honey," Owen provided.

Without another word, I walked over to the spot, standing there.

Owen was by my side. "I'll be damned."

"Tell me I'm seeing things?"

A hand found the small of my back at the same time Krew answered, "No, you are not." To Keir he added, "Can you hand that to Jorah for a moment? The forest seems to be communicating to her what we should do." He gave his head a shake. "Which feels odd, I know, but it also feels right to listen. Just go with it."

Keir gave me a smile as he passed it over. "You and this forest."

I again tipped my head back to the moon. "This is absolute madness."

River reached over to touch my shoulder. "You have always had a connection with this forest, dear. You have worked countless hours to heal it. To put the fires out. The forest trusts you. It is your turn to trust it back."

With a deep breath, I dropped to my knees, feeling the cool dirt under my dress. I laid the sword, still sheathed, onto the dirt where the leaves continued to swirl.

I almost laughed at the absurdity of it all. The odd sensation I had of somehow knowing that the sword should be out here. Even though the idea hadn't been from me at all.

But as soon as the sword was on the dirt, it sunk quickly under, the forest seeming to swallow the sword whole.

I gasped, my eyes wide as I watched the last bit of the blue handle sink into the dirt as if in mere sand and not dirt at all.

And then there was a groaning and creaking noise which drew all of our attention to the same spot, the spot which had swallowed the sword.

Krew grabbed me by the waist and hauled me to my feet and back.

"So that happened," Owen deadpanned as the forest went quiet again.

And then the ground was moving, branches shooting upward, causing all of us to step back in horror.

It was moving so quickly, there wasn't time to think. I wondered if I should put a protective barrier around us all, but then I realized it was a tree. The forest was birthing a massive tree. At the exact spot where we had buried the sword.

In minutes, it was towering over us all, branches swaying.

"I have never—" River shook his head, taking off his glasses and putting them back on.

As the final roots sprawled across the ground and burried themselves in the soil, somehow avoiding where we were standing, a single purple bloom formed on the tree.

Purple. The same color as the queen's magic.

Owen approached cautiously, looking around on the ground. "It's gone. Or under the tree."

"Hydrangeas," Keir whispered. "Her favorite."

It was the largest hydrangea tree I'd ever seen. And a circle of about ten feet all around the tree was also healed back to green grass.

Krew brushed a kiss to my temple. "Mark this off the list. We've found the resting place for the sword."

"It's beautiful," I gasped.

"I will not be able to sleep for a week," River said to no one in particular as he rubbed at his eyes. "I will be out here multiple times just to remember this really happened. That I was witness to this."

"I am with you," John agreed.

We stood there for countless minutes, all in varying degrees of shock. The forest had wanted the sword. And had given us the most beautiful space to keep it safe. I didn't know why. I didn't need to know why. But I understood that the sword was safe. It might be gone, it might not be. But the forest would keep it safe. It just felt . . . *right.* I knew the forest which had punished the king for his actions would keep it from falling into the wrong hands.

"Let's go, love," Krew said, as everyone was leaving to head back to the castle.

"One moment," I said with a smile.

I walked over to the tree and placed my hand on the bark. The tree was so large I wondered if I could wrap my arms around the trunk of it. And when this thing bloomed in the spring, it was sure to be a sight to behold.

I felt a slight warmth and buzz beneath my fingers, the power of the queen's magic. It wasn't gone, it was just living in this tree. An extension of an amazing woman.

"Thank you," I whispered. "Thank you for saving us in the throne room." I inhaled a shaky breath. "Thank you for the messages in the journals." I loathed the fact that I would never get to know this woman. "And thank you for raising kind men who will serve Wylan well."

Just as I turned to walk back to Krew, I felt something fall and instinctively reached out my hand. The lone hydrangea blossom fell into it.

My eyes went to Krew's.

This had to be a dream. There was no way the forest had just swallowed the sword and then grown this tree. And given me a flower. Yet we lived in a world where the impossible was possible right beneath our very fingertips.

"Unbelievable," John gasped. "It—" he shook his head. "It heard you."

"I think she likes you too," Krew said softly, his eyes never leaving mine. "Or her magic does. Whichever."

I turned the flower in my hand. "I feel like someone is going to wake me up at any moment now."

"Me as well. Also, we need to discuss the protection of this tree," River said as he and John launched into a discussion on the way back to the castle.

We were almost to the back hedge when I heard the wolves. Multiple wolves all joining in some sort of low howl. It sounded . . . *reverent.*

What was it about the wolves howling that always got to me? It was a music and cadence only they understood, but I found it beautiful all the same. "This is the first time I've ever felt certain the forest is going to be okay," I admitted to Krew quietly. "The sword. The wolves. The forest." I shook my head. "We have the announcement in the morning, and then no matter what, I get back to work. Healing this forest."

"Not without me you don't," Owen said with a wry grin.

I smirked. "Of course not. If I'm not mistaken, the forest and wolves have grown on you too."

Owen snorted. "Fine. Maybe a little."

I laughed. "Fine."

Keir threw an arm around Krew's shoulders. "I think we all get to work tomorrow, no matter what. Healing ourselves, Wylan, and then eventually, maybe even the whole damn realm."

"Lofty yet honorable goals," Krew laughed. "And quite the list."

"Together," Keir added. "No matter what?"

Krew moved to hug his brother. "Of course."

We were going to be okay. Krew and I. Owen. Keir. Gwen or Delaney or whoever Keir married. Wylan. All of us.

As soon as we were back in Krew's wing, Krew placed the bloom gently into my half empty water glass on my nightstand and wasted no time kissing me senseless. I was soon clawing at his clothes and gasping for air. It was late, so late we should just sleep given the seriousness of the announcement in the morning. We could be becoming king and queen. Or we could be tasting the disappointment of Keir becoming king instead of Krew. Either way, we needed sleep for what was sure to be an emotional day.

"Krew," I panted.

He leaned down to trail kisses up my neck before whispering in my ear, "If you thought I was insatiable before, when I thought I was living off borrowed time, you are about to find out that now forever is ours, there is only one thing I really want."

"The throne?" I joked.

His body crashed into mine. "*You.*"

Feeling his love and *want* down the bond, there were no other words that needed to be said. Tomorrow we would find out if Krew would become king. If I would become queen.

But tonight? Tonight, this was enough. And no matter what the morning brought; it would always be enough. I had never chosen the crown, but I would always choose Krew.

CHAPTER 47

The sound of the people below was surprisingly loud. The doors were shut for now, but the chatter and excited energy was still heard through the walls and windows, making the castle feel more alive than I had ever felt it.

I had peeked out a window minutes before to find the crowd of people who had decided to come up the mountain to Kavan Keep reaching as far as I could see. Instinctively, the people knew to stay away from the forest. Likely because they were still afraid of it. But the streets and the gardens were filled to the brim with people everywhere. From around a lady fanning herself with a small book, I saw a child on his father's shoulders among the crowd. Children were even being included in this day.

We all were.

Keir was there with us, but with neither Gwen nor Delaney. Krew and I had a discussion telepathically and decided to leave it alone. Maybe he was finally taking Krew's advice and decided not to rush his decision. Or maybe with taking the sword out to the forest the night before, there just hadn't been time for him to make his decision. Either way, Keir was there alone in his black-on-black tailcoat.

I was wearing a mauve gown with vines and flowers sewn into the top portion in jewels, Krew was in a black tailcoat and gray textured vest next to me. All three of us wore crowns on our heads, but those of princes and princess. The larger crowns belonging to the king and queen sat on a table in open boxes, nestled on royal blue satin and waiting for the new king and queen.

If Krew really was crowned king, I was demanding a new crown to be made and that one to be burned or melted down and destroyed. Or maybe I'd take it to the forest to see if it wanted the honors.

Ready, love?

No, I answered honestly.

He leaned over and brushed a kiss to my temple. *Either way, Wylan will thrive now that my father is gone.*

I gave him a nod. He was right. We both wanted this. We wanted to be a part of leading Wylan out of Theon's era, but we also didn't have to be king and queen to do so. We'd maybe even have more freedom to help if we weren't the ones in charge.

No matter what, it was all going to be okay. Wylan was going to be okay.

"We will let the two of you open the letter, and the announcement will commence in a few minutes," Winston, the parliament leader, stated. "The longer we let them wait, I fear someone may get trampled down there, so take your time, but also hurry."

I snorted a laugh, having not expected that.

We stood in the empty ballroom, the one we had spent so many nights in when I had first arrived at the castle. The announcement would be made from the balcony, overlooking the people.

This wasn't just information *we'd* been dying to know, this was information all of Wylan had been wanting to know for years. Yet another piece of knowledge the king had kept locked away that never should've been.

"Ready, brother?" Krew asked as he moved to stand closer to Keir. "Let's get it over with."

The royal blue waxed seal brought over on a silver tray by River made my heart start hammering in my chest. This was it. The moment we had waited for. One paper.

"I feel like someone should say something wise," Keir offered as his shaky hand picked up the parchment.

Owen laughed from where he was leaning against the wall by the doors. "How about don't mess it up?"

"Oddly inspirational, Raikes," Krew deadpanned before giving Keir a nod. "Do it."

Keir closed his eyes and slipped his finger under the seal, popping it open. Hands still shaking, he unfolded one half of the parchment, then the other, moving it between he and Krew as both began reading.

I felt a pang of jealousy down the bond from Krew and that was when I knew.

Keir was king. Krew and I were out.

Keir let out a shaky breath, as Krew slapped him on the back with a hug. "Wylan is in good hands, brother."

Keir grabbed his forehead and took another shaky breath as Winston walked over to take out the king's crown and bring it forward for Keir.

I wanted to cry. Or scream. It should be Krew getting crowned. He was the king Wylan needed. Keir would be a good and kind king, but Krew? Krew would've been a great king.

It's alright, Jorah love, Krew sent down the bond.

The gentle tone and adoration sent with the words took my breath away. But then my eyebrows slammed together. *You are disappointed but not surprised right now. Why is that?*

His eyes were on mine as he admitted, *Since he tried to kill me to sever our bond, it confirmed for me what I had always suspected, Keir was the rightful heir. I was merely the reserve should anything go awry.*

Tears sprang to my eyes. I knew Krew had to be thinking of all the times Theon had treated him poorly and understood now that it was because Krew would never be king, and though Krew didn't know that, Theon did. He'd used Krew's own hope as a weapon against him.

I also suspected it back when my father didn't care much about your switching to my Assemblage. He didn't care if you were princess, but he didn't want you as queen.

My breath caught. He was right. He was so right. The king had been far less hostile as soon as I switched Assemblages. I had falsely assumed it was because of my blood healing things.

Keir was still taking deep breaths while reading and rereading the parchment in his hands.

I reached over and slipped it out of his hands, since Winston was standing there waiting for him to get his emotions together before placing the Wylan crown upon his head. "Go," I said gently. "Go be the best damn king Wylan has ever seen."

Keir's eyes were on mine. "I—" he shook his head. "I can't believe it."

"I can," Krew argued. He moved to grab Keir by the shoulders. "You are a man who is always thinking four steps ahead. You are also a pain in the ass to anyone who dares to get in your way. Both will serve you well in this."

Keir took a deep breath and closed his eyes, some emotion I couldn't recognize crossing his face. "Thank you." He turned toward Winston as he opened his eyes, "Let's get this over with, shall we?"

I guessed Keir wasn't looking forward to his speech in front of what looked to be half of Wylan crammed into the courtyard and streets.

Winston went out first, making the announcement to the

people. A few Enchanted placed both on the balcony and among the people in the crowd used their magic to amplify the sound so everyone could hear what was being said without too much straining. It was a short introductory speech, though I was so focused on reading Krew's emotions I heard only a few words of it.

The doors slowly opened, Keir standing there with Theon's crown now on his head. He gave us one last look over his shoulder, and then he walked forward, into his reign.

The cheers from the people were deafening.

Krew wrapped an arm around me. "I love you."

This wasn't the ending we'd wanted. It wasn't how I had dared to dream it, but I was standing here next to Krew, free to build a life with him.

So could I really be disappointed after all?

We could be disappointed and let it go, not allowing it to fester into resentment. So we did the right thing and we walked out onto the balcony and off to the side, a show of support as we listened to Keir's speech.

It took minutes for the crowd to settle enough to let him say a word. The blue Wylan flags were rippling in the breeze off the top of the balcony. The sun was in and out among fluffy white clouds. It was a beautiful day for a king to be crowned. Even if it wasn't my king. I looked up at Krew and smiled.

You'll always be my king, I told him.

He placed a kiss on my forehead. *Always my queen.*

We were going to be okay. More than okay. Just because this wasn't the ending we'd wanted or imagined, didn't mean it was a bad one.

Keir rested his hands on the balcony, his attention forward. His shoulders and neck were tight, but he looked every bit a king. The excitement around who he would choose as queen was also sure to drive Wylan mad with rumors.

“I come before you humbled and proud,” Keir began, the crowd hushing to a silence.

With the Enchanted amplifying the sound of his voice, carrying it on their magic, soon no noise other than the flags flapping in the breeze was heard. That so many people could be so quiet was eerie. But they were all waiting with bated breath to hear from their new king.

“It is no secret my father’s reign left a trail of destruction behind him in his selfish efforts for more power.” Keir paused, his shoulders rising with his deep inhale. “I know this next one will be different. Long overdue, it will be a reign that Wylan doesn’t need, but rather the one that she deserves.”

The crowd roared with agreement, whistles and screams being heard over the sound of clapping.

I smiled knowing Keir was right.

“Wylan,” Keir continued, the crowd going quiet again. “I will always protect you, fight for you, and work to better you. I will always be your heir.” He paused. “But I am not your king.”

My breath got lodged in my throat as my eyes went to Krew’s. He was looking at Keir with a crease in his brow.

The entire crowd had seemed to take a collective gasp.

“I was the true heir, yes. Born seven minutes before my brother, it seems.” He paused and looked over his shoulder at Krew. “But in less than seven minutes, I will give you the king you deserve. Give you the king *and* queen Wylan deserves. My first and only act as king is to abdicate. To my brother.”

Whispers rippled across the crowd in waves as my brain and breath stopped entirely. What was Keir doing? Could he even do this? Was this allowed?

“Seven minutes should not determine which of us should lead Wylan. Not a mere matter of minutes, but rather our character should, who we are. I know in my soul that Krew and Jorah are that for all of us. In the wake of my father, Wylan shouldn’t settle for a mediocre king. It should have the best. And we have that in King Krewan and Queen Jorah. Their reign will be one of kindness and justice bringing an era of healing to Wylan."

Someone from the crowd shouted the question we were all wondering. "What about you?"

Keir answered with amusement in his tone. "I will continue to be a prince of Wylan, continue to fight for and help Wylan, but I will do so under the guidance of our king and queen." He paused. "Wylan deserves the best and I am man enough to know that isn't me." Another pause. "I do not care who the rightful heir is, I care who the *right* heir is. That is my brother, Krew."

With another deep breath, he turned, taking the crown off his head.

I still wasn't sure I was breathing, but I was evidently crying as I felt the moisture on my cheeks. Krew was also stunned, a statue beside me. His disbelief down the bond mirrored my own.

I wondered how long Keir had known he was doing this. When I had asked him if what he needed to do was best for Wylan or himself, he'd told me both.

He was giving it all up? For us? Something he had hoped and wished for his entire life, and just handing it over?

Keir walked over to Krew and placed the crown on his head as the crowd went absolutely insane. When he was done, he gave him a hug, squeezing him hard.

"What are you doing?" I gasped through my tears as Keir moved to hug me.

Keir had to yell over the crowd noise so I could hear him. "Finishing saving Wylan." He pulled back and looked me in the eyes. "You've always been the queen Wylan needed. Whether you believed it or not."

My mouth fell open. He was just handing it over to us? To me?

"Now go be the best damn queen Wylan has ever seen," Keir added with a smirk.

Someone brought the queen's crown to Winston. With as wide and shocked eyes as the rest of us, he was ready to place it upon my head.

Keir moved to get out of the way, but I stepped forward to hug him once more, tugging Krew with me.

Krew and I were king and queen. Not because Krew had been born first, but because Keir believed we were ready and capable. He believed in us. So he'd simply given it to us.

And in that act, I knew that both sons of Theon Valanova could not be more different than their father.

My crown was swapped out for the queen's while I stood there suspended in shock. I had just been nursing the wounds of disappointment a minute before. Now I was . . . I was *queen*?

Winston stepped forward to speak saying, "I am just as rattled as the rest of you, but please allow me the honor of introducing our new king and queen."

The crowd hushed as Krew reached a hand out for me.

"King Krewan Everett Aiken Valanova and Queen Jorah Collette Demir Valanova. Justly may they serve, long may they reign!"

Minutes or hours later, I wasn't sure, we were back in the empty ballroom. Only guards present, otherwise to ourselves. Crowns on our heads, the coronation to be held the following day.

Krew pulled me by the hand and brought me in close. "Which item from our never-ending list would you like to do first, My Queen?"

As if it were even a question. "Let's go get our little boy."

EPILOGUE

"Race ya!"

Krew and Warrick took off for the meadow, sprinting through the knee-length grass.

I laughed, a basket and blanket in one hand while reaching down to feel the tips of the green grass with my other.

"I can take that for you, My Queen," my new guard offered.

I batted him away. "No thank you, Alejandro. I have it." I wasn't yet used to a guard being so kind and . . . less bossy.

It had taken time for Krew to convince Owen to train others to guard us. The only reason it had actually worked was that Krew had convinced Owen he knew us too well and was too close to us, therefore compromised as a guard. So Owen was now a general and working in training, but also as an advisor to the king and queen of Wylan. He'd personally chosen and trained the three guards who followed me everywhere I went. And he'd breathed down their necks for weeks before trusting them enough to leave my side.

We still saw Owen every single day though. Often times he'd linger and play with Warrick at night. It went without saying that

Owen was a part of our family, blood or not. He was always welcome wherever we were.

It had been months since we arrived in Nerede to retrieve Warrick, my mother, and even Flora. The announcement of Warrick being Krew's son came the following day, a special announcement sent out to all levels of Wylan.

Celebrations of our coronation and also Warrick's princedom had happened for weeks afterward, Nerede's being larger and longer than the rest. Nerede had raised a queen *and* the next prince, after all.

I took a deep breath and stretched my neck, feeling the tension lingering in-between my shoulder blades. We'd only reigned a few months, and there was still so much to be done. Parliament sessions were painful, as the parliament members were finding out just how opposite from Theon we truly were. We only had to forcibly remove two parliament members who had been loyal to the former king thus far, but we knew more unrest in Savaryn was brewing. Not everyone was happy to have a queen from the lower levels of the kingdom. They called me "Queen of Rags" thinking they would insult me. I rather chose to take it as a compliment instead.

The walls had been opened the day of the announcement of the new king and then stayed open, much to the Enchanted's dismay. It would be an uncomfortable few years while we all adjusted to a new normal. Any requests to move up levels in the kingdom were being taken on by an advisory board we'd set up. We couldn't just have the entire country up and moving into Savaryn. It was a painstakingly slow process, but it was progress.

We were even trying to reach out to the other countries about the disease, detailing that we feared the dead king was responsible. I didn't know what we could do to help the other countries, but if Theon was responsible for their struggles, we had to do something. We had to try.

And that was how Theon was always referred to by the people now. Never "may he rest" or "the former king" or any other reverent sayings. He was always just "the dead king."

Since he'd killed the forest with his greed, I felt it was only fair.

I took a deep breath. The evening air felt crisp. Fall was coming whether we liked it or not.

I looked toward the setting sun across the meadow, green with growth. I had healed over half of the forest. It was a long and tedious process, but I was still running with the wolves and healing the forest day by day. I'd seen a bee just last week, giving me hope that the birds and other small animals would return soon too.

I finally caught up to the other two, as they were directing me to the spot with the best view for our picnic.

A picnic.

This moment was what I had clung to even when it felt impossible, even when it was the smallest glimmer of light in the shadows. A picnic with Warrick and Krew.

It was our first, but it wouldn't be our last. We had many, many more picnics on the never-ending to-do list.

Warrick didn't delay grabbing his sandwich and begin devouring it. How one little body could eat so much food was beyond me.

"I am going to Nerede tomorrow," Krew reminded me.

I gave him a nod, as I hadn't forgotten.

"Can I go?!" Warrick asked.

We'd only let him go back and visit the orphanage a few times. Krew still struggled with his need to protect both Warrick and me, and now that we were king and queen, Warrick not only an heir, but the heir in line to be the next king of Wylan, it was a constant battle. So Warrick's trips among the people were few and far between for now.

It wasn't that we didn't trust the people of Nerede. We were most concerned with the Savaryn Enchanted who had lost their coveted positions when Theon died.

"Not this time," Krew said as he fluffed Warrick's dark hair. "But we'll talk and figure out a time you can go. I need to see your Uncle Keir this trip."

"Is Uncle Keir still wallowing in Nerede?" Warrick asked without skipping a beat.

I snorted a laugh. This child was honest. Sometimes too honest.

Krew's eyes hit mine and I felt his amusement too. "He isn't wallowing, just working through a few things," he explained to Warrick. "Trying to figure out what he wants to do next."

Keir had evidently dismissed both Gwen and Delaney before abdicating the throne that morning. While he knew Krew and I were the right couple to rule Wylan, he was also struggling with what he should do. With the new base being built in Nerede, he'd gladly volunteered to go, working with the guards and training as the facility was nearing completion. We were also building a row of tourist homes on the shore, not for foreign visitors, but trying to draw the Savaryn and Rallis people to at least visit Nerede and begin to see it as more than the lesser level of the kingdom.

Though he'd never admit it to us, Keir was a little lost. And I knew Krew was worried about his brother. We wanted and needed him by our sides, so we didn't need him disappearing to Nerede. Keir thought it was best for us to begin our reign without anyone reminding us that we shouldn't have been king and queen at all to begin with. We disagreed.

Likely worse than the disappointment of handing off his dream of becoming king to Krew, he was disappointed that his Assemblage had failed. I had seen Gwen only twice since, but she was still not over it either. I had no idea what had happened, other than Keir said he had no desire to ever marry either of them.

The statues honoring Maurice, Theodore, and Rafe were being completed in a few weeks, so he was going to be back to the castle for that. I hoped he stayed. Not because he had to, but because we were family. And Owen had taught me that family didn't let family struggle alone. Though I hoped we were only half as pushy as Owen was.

"When I have magic someday," Warrick began as he often did. "I am going to climb trees and then imagine my magic making me fly!" He used his hand as if showing us how he would glide over the trees.

I rolled my eyes. Thank goodness this child wouldn't have magic for a while. *He is his father's son.*

Krew sent me a guilty grin.

I heard footsteps in the grass and turned to see Rafe and Shadow. I smiled.

"The wolves!" Warrick exclaimed as he sat up straight to better see.

"Don't jerk so quickly," Krew provided gently as he put his arm around Warrick. "Sudden moves scare them."

I was oftentimes taken away at how calm and gentle Krew was with Warrick. I felt the guilt Krew still had over missing so much of Warrick's life. Which was why on those afternoons that Krew wanted to skip parliament sessions or meetings to take Warrick out to the forest to explore, I gladly stayed behind and did my queenly duties, allowing them to make up for lost time.

"How come Mum is the only one who gets to touch them?" Warrick asked with frustration. "I wanna pet a wolf."

Mum. I wasn't sure I was ever going to get used to the word. I'd never asked him to call me that, he had just asked me one day if since his real mother was dead, if he could call me mum instead of mother. It was what Krew and Keir had called Katarina.

I didn't care what he called me, that boy would always and forever be my son too. So of course, I agreed.

Krew's eyes hit mine before going back to the matching blueish gray eyes of his son. "Because she is the one who has earned their trust. You will have to also."

Warrick was far more logical than any other child I knew, so he immediately nodded as if he understood, and then sat still as he watched with Krew.

"Rafe," I greeted as I slowly made my way to him.

He pressed his head into my hand as his usual way of greeting.

"How's the forest tonight, boys?"

Shadow sniffed the ground unfazed, then he too, let me pet his nose.

I let out a little laugh without trying to move too abruptly. Shadow was still new to letting me touch him. "I know, Shadow. You want rabbits back. And maybe even a turkey."

He perked his ears at the word turkey.

I grinned. "Turkeys, huh? We'll work on it."

There was much to be done. Tensions to fix. Walls to tear down. And a healthy, thriving Wylan to build. The forest to finish healing. Maybe a few more heirs once everything calmed down. Last but certainly not least, turkeys.

"Cinnamon oat!" Warrick whispered forcefully as I made my way back over to the two of them, obviously having some sort of quiet disagreement.

"The chocolate ones," Krew argued. "You are just siding with your Uncle Owen because you know he will take you riding."

Warrick nodded, eyes wide. "Fact!" Seeing I was back, he pinned his gorgeous blue-gray eyes on me. "Hey, Mum? Do you think we could make some cookies tomorrow?"

I grinned. With Krew gone the following day that would be tricky to squeeze in, but I'd make it happen anyway. "Of course. Shall we ask grandmum to join us?"

"Yes!" Warrick said with a fist pump. "Best day ever."

The tears pricked my eyes. All these days were the best days ever. More than it was the crown on my head, it was the man I had chosen to marry and spend this life next to. And the little boy we got to call ours.

"She's going to cry again, isn't she?" Warrick asked Krew.

Krew didn't even hesitate. "Yep."

I laughed. "They are happy tears, you both know that."

Warrick put down his food and scrambled over to me, throwing his arms around me.

I closed my eyes and hugged him back. "I just love our life. That's all."

"It's better," Warrick agreed quietly. "Not because of the castle, though it's nice. Just because we are . . . together."

I repeated the phrase he'd said to me dozens of times. "Better now that you're here."

His little hands hugged me harder.

My eyes met Krew's and I didn't think I was imagining the sheen of water in them as well.

Later that night, Krew took me by the hand and led me in the direction of our bed.

"I *feel* as if you're having *feelings*," I teased.

"Numerous feelings," Krew murmured as he yanked me into him. "Not quite sure which one to pinpoint, love."

"You should probably just go to bed," I laughed. "You have a lot to do tomorrow."

"We have a lot to do every tomorrow," Krew argued.

"Good point."

He picked me up and my legs instinctively moved to wrap around him as he carried me the rest of the way to bed.

As he gently laid me down, he took his time traveling his way up my body, stopping to take my hand from where it had rested on his shoulder and turning it to kiss my palm before moving to brush another kiss to my fingertips. His voice was but a whisper as he said, "That something so small is carrying such power."

I thought back to the day I had gotten the letter in Nerede and how I had thought something similar. I had resented that letter. Resented fate.

Whether it was fate or our stubborn wills to blame, I was nothing but grateful that it brought me to him. This man who had lost everything. Yet in his darkest hour he had somehow found the will to begin piecing himself back together brick by brick. That act alone was magic in and of itself. Until one day he was strong enough to free us all.

My dark prince. My king.

My everything.

The End

(For now. Keir will be back with us for Book 4.)

ACKNOWLEDGMENTS

To God. Getting this series off the ground has absolutely felt like a battle. I am forever grateful it is one I haven't had to do alone. Many, many tears have been shed in creating these three books, and I am grateful my God cares about every single one of them. Jesus took the nails for me, so I'll keep writing these stories in which the darkness never stood a chance. I'll keep writing these flawed characters until we all realize how purely and recklessly loved we are. Nine years ago, I almost lost my life when my son was born. It was that brush with death that caused me to stop ignoring that little "what if" I had about writing a book. Some people may say I am lucky to still be here. I choose to say that I am blessed. That a higher power thought I still had a story to tell. So as long as there's a plot brewing in my head and breath in my lungs, that's what I'll do.

Thank you to my husband, my sons, and our English bulldog Bubs. Me being a writer is just a part of our lives now. Your belief in me, even when I don't see it, maybe particularly on the days when I don't see it, means the world to me. Boys, work hard and smart and go chase down those dreams. You won't find a person cheering harder for you than me. Babe, you never laughed at my dream or did anything other than support me. And Bubs, you could be a little less gassy and that would be helpful, but I don't even know how to write without your constant snoring. I may have thirteen books out into this world, but our family will *always* be my favorite work.

To my writer nerds: Melissa, Sam, Liz, Dirk, and Jackie. The final throne room showdown of this book was created in the company of you all at one of our retreats. Dirk was helping me mastermind. Sam was taking notes and instigating in that way which only Sam can. We had spices on the table, and we worked for hours together trying to get it right. Dirk eventually ate the throne. (The throne has toppled!!) And then when Rafe went down and I was sobbing at my computer, Sam brought me a hug and some butterbeer. The ending of this book would simply not be the same without you all. I am blown away by friends who take time out of their schedules to help me. You all are incredibly rare. I love you all.

Schmidty. God plopped you in my life at exactly the right time. You are kind and rational in a way that stuns this world. I am honored to call myself your best friend. And also, you are stuck with me for life.

To my editor Tanya. You have been both an answered prayer and worth your weight in gold. Working with you has been the best! Not only do you know all the rules, but you somehow also help me clean things up without making me feel like a blubbering fool. It's such a delicate balance and you handle it flawlessly. I don't know how to launch a book without you anymore. And I promise I'll try to stop spelling evidently wrong.

Donna Dear, my head proofer. Again, I don't know how to put a book out into the world without you. Every author needs a Donna. Add in that you encourage me to take breaks and enjoy my boys being little, or just randomly check in, and I'm convinced we all need a Donna. Your proofing skills are out of this world, but your friendship is above and beyond. Thank you.

Tatiana. Thank you for swiftly taking care of my issues and helping me get these beautiful covers done. You are fabulous!

Miranda. I am so proud of you and all your success. You freaking did it!

To my spoiler squad/reader group on Facebook. When I was kicked off social media, forced to get a new Instagram, and couldn't even market the first book in the series, you all took up the torch and did it for me. Without asking. I won't forget it any time soon. One of my worst days as an author, and you all showed me a kindness that defied the darkness. I'm grateful for you all!

To my agent Shannon, who originally tried to shop this series. Thank you for your constant support and holding my hand through the intimidating time of submitting books. Don't worry, I'll keep writing!

To my ARC team: Sam, Jackie, Ashley, Schmidty, Andrea, Mary, Shaina, Christy, Chaside, Kaylee, and Michelle. I appreciate you guys! You always seem to hype me up at exactly the right time. Thank you!

To my Bible study ladies. Without you guys dusting me off and keeping me going, this book launch would have definitely been delayed. When it felt like no one was there, you all were. I'm thankful for you all. You might be some of my biggest fans, but I'm your biggest fan right back.

To my readers. Thank you so much for reading this story. Making the jump from dystopian to fantasy was quite the leap, but a lot of you never even batted an eyelash. I am stunned by your kind words and reviews constantly. Every book I hand over to you, I give you a little chunk of my soul to keep safe, and you all have been found the most trustworthy recipients I could have ever asked for. Whether you've been with me since my very first book or only for this series, the sentiment remains. *Thank you.*

And last but definitely not least, to my Keirs out there. When your dreams are shattering and you feel like you've hit rock bottom, don't you dare give up. Get up again. Even if you have to crawl. Do whatever you have to, just claw your way out. You might not realize it right now, but a beautiful adventure is out there calling your name. Your story? It isn't done. Not even close.

ABOUT THE AUTHOR

Tricia Wentworth is the award-winning author of *The Culling* series. Though she began writing at a young age, she didn't realize her love of writing would take over until after she graduated college with her teaching degree. She currently resides in Nebraska with her husband, three sons, and English bulldog. She hoards notebooks, pretty pens, books, and tea. When not reading, writing, or momming, she can be found squeezing in a run or feeding her sugar addiction by baking something ridiculously delicious.

The next book in the Enchanted Kingdom series is underway!

Be sure to follow the author for release updates and teasers for this series. She is most active on Facebook/Instagram but dabbles in Tiktok too.

ALSO BY TRICIA WENTWORTH

The Enchanted Kingdom series:

Enchanted Kingdom

Enchanted Heir

The Culling series:

The Culling

The Fracturing

The Reckoning

The Legacy series (Culling spinoff):

The Legacy: James

The Legacy: Kennedy

The Legacy: Elijah

The Legacy: A New Era

The Snowed In series:

Snowed In

Locked In

All In

Made in the USA
Columbia, SC
17 December 2024